ABDUCTION

BY
CASSIE MILES

AND

IN BED WITH
THE BADGE

BY
MARIE FERRARELLA

"I want to know your plans."

"Here's the deal, Carolyn. I don't have time to hold your hand and make sure you're happy with our investigation."

"Understood. But you need my help. Things are different on the ranch than in the city. People are different."

"I'm in charge. Get used to it," said Burke. Carolyn's eyes narrowed. "Then we have a problem. I don't take orders. I will, however, respond to requests made with respect."

"You want me to say *please* and *thank you*?"

"That's a start."

COLORADO ABDUCTION

BY
CASSIE MILES

First published in Great Britain 2010
Harlequin Mills & Boon Limited,
Eton House, 18-24 Paradise Road, Richmond, Surrey TW9 1SR

© Kay Bergstrom 2009

ISBN: 978 0 263 88263 6

46-1010

Harlequin Mills & Boon policy is to use papers that are natural, renewable and recyclable products and made from wood grown in sustainable forests. The logging and manufacturing processes conform to the legal environmental regulations of the country of origin.

Printed and bound in Spain
by Litografia Rosés S.A., Barcelona

Though born in Chicago and raised in L.A., **Cassie Miles** has lived in Colorado long enough to be considered a semi-native. The first home she owned was a log cabin in the mountains overlooking Elk Creek with a thirty-mile commute to her work at the *Denver Post*.

After raising two daughters and cooking tons of macaroni and cheese for her family, Cassie is trying to be more adventurous in her culinary efforts. Ceviche, anyone? She's discovered that almost anything tastes better with wine. A lot of wine. When she's not plotting Intrigue books, Cassie likes to hang out at the Denver Botanical Gardens near her high-rise home.

To the ever-encouraging Tess Foltz.
And, as always, to Rick.

Chapter One

Too impatient to wait until the rotors of the helicopter came to a stop, Carolyn Carlisle disembarked, ducked and ran with her laptop in one hand and briefcase in the other. Dirt and dead leaves kicked up around her feet. Her long black hair whipped across her face. When she was in the clear, she gave the charter pilot a thumbs-up signal and the chopper took off, swooping through the Rocky Mountain sunset like a giant white dragonfly.

Silence returned to the wide valley, which sat in the shadow of snowcapped peaks. The surge of joy Carolyn usually felt when she returned to the cattle ranch where she'd grown up was absent. Her home, Carlisle Ranch, was under threat.

Last night, there was a fire at the north stable. Across the pasture, she could see the place where the barn once stood. The blackened ruin stood out in stark relief against the khaki-colored early December fields. The stench of burnt wood tainted the air. All the livestock had been rescued, thank God. But expensive equipment had been destroyed, and the sheriff suspected arson.

She marched up the walk toward a sprawling, two-story, whitewashed ranch house, originally built by her great-grandfather and added to by subsequent generations. Her first order of business was to kick her brother's butt for not calling her last night when the fire broke out.

Dylan had waited until today to inform her, probably because he didn't want her interfering. The family ranch, running about two thousand head of Angus, was his responsibility and he preferred that Carolyn stay in the Denver office of Carlisle Certified Organic Beef. Usually, their arrangement worked out well. She liked the city and loved the daily challenge of running a multimillion-dollar corporation.

But she was still a rancher at heart. As soon as she had heard about the stable fire, she'd had to be here. Hadn't even taken the time to change her business attire—teal silk blouse, black wool suit with a pencil skirt and high-heeled boots.

As she climbed the three stairs to the veranda that stretched across the front of the house, she was confronted by a cowboy with a rifle.

"Who are you?" she demanded.

"I work for Longbridge Security, ma'am." He pointed to a trefoil patch on the arm of his denim jacket.

"Did my brother Dylan hire you?"

"Yes, ma'am." He held open the front door for her.

She considered the presence of a bodyguard to be a good sign. At least Dylan was taking action. They couldn't really expect the Delta County sheriff's office to patrol the thousands of acres they leased for grazing.

Leaving her laptop and briefcase by the coatrack, she went down the hallway toward her brother's office. The door was ajar and she heard voices from inside—angry voices.

Her brother's wife of five years, Nicole, stormed from the room. Her blue eyes were furious. Her jaw clenched. "I'm sorry you had to hear that, Carolyn."

"I just got here." She liked and respected Nicole. Considered her more like a sister than a sister-in-law. "I was just getting ready to yell at Dylan myself."

"Be my guest."

"First, we could go out to the kitchen and have a cup of tea. Or something stronger if you like."

"Right now I just want to be alone." Nicole went to the front door. "I'm going to take a ride down by the creek."

The door slammed behind her.

Carolyn's first impulse was to follow her, but Dylan stepped into the hall. "How the hell did you get here so fast?"

"I chartered a chopper. After you finally got around to telling me about the fire, I wanted to see for myself that Elvis was all right."

"Your horse is fine. He's in the corral by the barn."

She'd intended to read him the riot act, but he already looked miserable. His shoulders slumped. His pale green eyes—identical to hers—were red-rimmed. "We need to talk."

"You missed Thanksgiving. Again."

"I had to work." And she wasn't going to let him guilt her out for shirking family responsibilities. Her every waking thought was devoted to running the family business. "What happened, Dylan? Was it arson?"

"There's nothing you can do." He stepped back into his office and shut the door.

Good old Western stoicism. Closed doors all around. *Never show emotion. Never share what's really wrong. Never ever cry.* That cowboy ethic might have worked in the Old West, but this was the twenty-first century with psychologists on every corner.

In search of a sympathetic ear, Carolyn left the house and headed toward the outdoor corral attached to the big barn with stables in the back. If she hurried, she could catch Nicole who was probably still getting saddled up. Instead, Carolyn looked for her version of a shrink. Elvis.

Reaching over the top rail of the corral, she stroked the white blaze on her horse's forehead. His upper lip curled in the trademark sneer of his namesake. He batted his long lashes, shamelessly flirting though he was over sixteen years old and had expanded his girth since she last saw him.

"No more sweets for you, Elvis."

He whinnied in protest.

She tugged a forelock of his black mane. "If you get any fatter, you won't fit into your white jumpsuit."

As she watched Nicole head out, Carolyn shivered. She should have grabbed a jacket before she came out, but the weather was pleasant enough—probably in the mid-fifties—and her blood still boiled with anger. She had a bad feeling about Nicole riding alone. It didn't seem safe. Not if there was an arsonist on the loose. A few minutes later, a man wearing a jacket with the Longbridge Security patch rode from the barn to follow her.

She turned her attention to Elvis. The horse listened while she talked about her worries about the ranch, about Dylan and Nicole. They'd always seemed like the perfect couple. If they couldn't make it, what hope did Carolyn have of finding a mate? She was thirty-three with no special man to warm her bed. Her last date had been a disaster and…

A noise distracted her. A snap that ricocheted across the valley. A rifle shot?

Carolyn peered across the field. The bodyguard and Nicole were nowhere in sight.

The grizzled ranch foreman, Lucas Mann, came around the corner of the barn, moving faster than his usual bow-legged saunter. "Carolyn, did you hear that?"

"Hush." She listened hard. A volley of shots echoed from far away, like pebbles being dropped in a metal bucket. Sound traveled great distances in the thin mountain air and she couldn't tell where the gunfire was coming from. "Lucas, give me your gun."

"What?"

"You heard me."

Lucas handed over his sidearm. Though he looked like an old-time cowboy, the weapon he carried in his belt holster was a brand-new Glock nine millimeter.

Carolyn tucked the gun into the waistband of her skirt. "We need to find Nicole and make sure she's okay. She was headed southwest toward the creek. I want you to saddle up. Bring one of those security guards."

"What the hell are you fixing to do?"

"Take care of business." If someone had fired on Nicole, she needed backup. And she needed it now.

In her high-heeled boots, Carolyn climbed the corral fence, tore the slit on her wool skirt and slung her leg over Elvis's bare back. As soon as Lucas unlatched the corral gate, she rode through. Digging her heels into Elvis's flanks, she took off across the field.

Riding without a saddle wasn't easy, especially not with the horse's bristly coat snagging her panty hose and an automatic pistol digging into her side. She wouldn't have attempted this ride with any other mount, but Elvis's gait was as familiar as her own jogging style. Her body adjusted instinctively to the rhythm of his gait. In her teens, she and Elvis had won dozens of trophies and blue ribbons for calf roping and barrel racing in local rodeos.

She clung to his mane and directed him with pressure from her knees and verbal commands. The chilly December wind sharpened her tension as she rode toward the area where the valley merged into rocky hillsides covered with forests of ponderosa pine.

She hadn't heard any other shots. If there had been a gunfight, it was over. The damage was done.

What if Nicole and the bodyguard were shot and bleeding? *Can't think about that now.* She needed to stay focused. *That's what I do best—hard-driving, straightforward action.*

Through the dusky gloom, she spotted a horseman coming out of the trees at a slow walk. The bodyguard. He slumped over his horse's neck. As his horse came to a stop, he slipped from the saddle to the ground.

She dismounted and ran toward the injured man. His shirt and denim jacket were covered in blood, his face twisted in pain. She sank to her knees beside him and pushed his jacket aside. If she could figure out where he'd been shot, she could apply pressure and slow the bleeding.

"Nicole." His voice was faint. "Couldn't save her."

Talking was too much of an effort. He needed to calm down and slow the pumping of his heart. But Carolyn had to ask, "Was she shot?"

"No." His eyelids closed. "They took her."

She tore open the buttons on his shirt, exposing a raw, gaping hole in his upper chest. Carolyn took off her suit jacket, wadded the fabric in a ball and pressed against the wound. Blood also stained the sleeve of his jacket and his leg. She had to get him to a hospital.

His hand gripped hers. He forced his eyes open and stared with fierce intensity. "Nicole tried to fight. Two men. One of them hit her. She fell. Didn't move."

Carolyn choked back a helpless sob. *Oh, God. How could this happen?*

"The other guy…" The bodyguard coughed. His fingers tightened. "He stood guard. He got off a shot. Before I could get close enough to…"

"You did the best you could."

"I fell off my horse. Couldn't move. Just lay there." It must have taken a fierce effort for him to mount up. Even now, he struggled to sit. "Saw their faces. I can ID them."

"Settle down." Though she respected his courage, this man wasn't going anywhere. "Help is on the way."

She glanced over her shoulder. What was taking so long? Lucas should have been here by now.

The bodyguard lay back. His chest heaved. Yet he forced himself to speak. "They said Dylan would pay. He'd pay a lot. To get his wife back."

"Are you telling me Nicole was kidnapped?"

"That's right. Kidnapped."

His eyes closed and his body went limp. He was still breathing. But just barely.

Her arms ached from putting pressure on his wound. The jacket she pressed against his chest was already soaked in blood. His chances for survival decreased with every minute.

"Don't die." Tears slid down her cheeks. "Please. Please, don't die."

She heard the sound of hoofbeats approaching and dashed away her tears. If the men found her crying, they wouldn't listen to a word she said. And Carolyn needed to take charge, needed to be strong. Her brother was going to be crazy and illogical—dangerously irrational.

The bodyguard she'd met on the veranda joined her on the ground beside the injured man. "I'll take it from here, ma'am. I'm a medic."

"He's unconscious."

"You did the right thing," he said, "putting pressure on the wound. Don't worry. We'll get him to the hospital."

She stood and stepped out of the way, relieved that the wounded bodyguard would be cared for by someone who knew what he was doing. Turning on the heel of her boot, she faced four other men on horseback. All of them had rifles. They looked like a posse from the Old West.

Lucas swung down from his horse and came toward her. "You've got blood all over. Are you hurt?"

"I'm okay."

"Where's Nicole?"

Her lips pinched together. If she told them Nicole had been kidnapped, they'd take off to rescue her. They were cowboys, experienced hunters who were capable of following the track of a jackrabbit across miles of mountain terrain. If they located the kidnappers, there'd be a shoot-out.

The paramedic called out. "I need the first-aid kit in my saddlebag. Somebody call an ambulance."

"You heard him," Carolyn said. "The first thing is to get this man to a hospital. He's lost a lot of blood."

While the other cowboys followed instructions from the paramedic, she saw her brother racing toward them, leaning low over the mane of his horse, riding like the demons of hell were on his tail. He pulled up and dismounted in a single move, hit the ground running and yanked her into a hug. "Thank God, you're all right."

"I'm fine." She could feel the tension in his body. Every muscle was clenched. Dylan wasn't going to like what she had to say, but there was no way to get around it.

His eyes were wild. "Where's Nicole?"

"Listen to me, Dylan." She grabbed his arm and held on tight, hoping she could save him from his own temper. "Before the bodyguard was shot, he saw two men with Nicole. He heard them say that you'd pay a lot to get your wife back. They kidnapped her."

He tore free from her grasp. "I'll kill the bastards."

Exactly what she was afraid of. "Think about what you're saying. If there's a gunfight, Nicole could be hurt."

He strode a few paces away from her, yanked off his hat and slapped it against his thigh. "What the hell am I supposed to do? Twiddle my thumbs while some son of a bitch holds my wife hostage? Wait for the sheriff to figure this out?"

"Let me handle this. The bodyguard who tried to protect Nicole is already standing at death's door. I don't want anybody else to get shot."

"She's my wife. I've got to find her."

Her brother was the most hardheaded man she'd ever known. There was no point in trying to talk sense into him. "I can see that I'm not going to change your mind."

"Hell no."

"Then give me your gun. I want all of your posse's guns. It can't hurt for you to track the kidnappers, but if you're not armed, you can't start a shoot-out."

"This isn't your call."

"Before Dad died, he told me to take care of my little brother. And that's what I intend to do."

He threw up his hands. "It's not fair to bring Dad's ghost into this situation."

She didn't play fair, she played to win. "Dad wouldn't want you to risk your life. Or anybody else's."

"Fine. We'll leave the guns. What are you going to do?"

"Go back to the house and wait to hear from the kidnappers." That wasn't enough and she knew it. "And I'm calling in the FBI."

TWO AND A HALF HOURS LATER, Carolyn stood on the veranda outside the house. The porch lights shone on a black van that had just parked next to the Delta County sheriff's SUV. This had to be the FBI.

A tall man emerged from the passenger seat. Instead of the typical FBI black suit, he wore jeans and a worn leather jacket. As he strode toward her, he seemed to get even taller. He was probably six foot four. His sandy brown hair was less well-groomed than she'd expect from a federal agent, but he had an unmistakable air of authority—an attitude that immediately put her on edge.

"Special Agent J. D. Burke." He identified himself as he held up his badge. "I need to talk to the sheriff."

"Sheriff Trainer isn't here." At her urging, the sheriff had borrowed a horse and went to keep an eye on Dylan and his posse. She hoped the presence of a lawman might deter any attempt at vigilante justice.

"Who's in charge?"

Carolyn had changed from her bloodstained business clothes into jeans, a pink T-shirt and zippered hoodie. With her black hair pulled up in a ponytail, she probably didn't look like the top executive of a multimillion-dollar company. Still, she resented the way he looked right past her, trying to find a man in charge.

"I'm Carolyn Carlisle." She held out her hand. "I'm the boss."

When he shook her hand and made direct eye contact, she felt a jolt of electricity—a warning. His dark eyes were hard, implacable. She and this fed were going to butt heads.

"Have you heard from the kidnappers?" he asked.

"Not yet."

Three other men left the van and came toward the house. All were carrying equipment in black cases.

"We need to set up," Agent Burke said.

She held open the front door as they trooped through. "You can use the office. It's down the hall to the left."

Ignoring her words, he went past the staircase to the dining room with the long oak table. "This will do."

She hated the way he disregarded her suggestion, not even

acknowledging her. Biting her lower lip, she held back her protest when his men pulled the chairs away from the table. Without a word to her, they opened their cases and began spreading out equipment—all kinds of electronics and computers.

He glanced over his shoulder at her. "We could use some coffee."

His arrogance astounded her. "I'll bet you could."

"I take mine black."

The last straw. No way would she be relegated to the position of fetching coffee.

"Listen to me, Agent Burke." She struggled to keep from snarling. "I called in the FBI. As far as I'm concerned, you owe me an explanation of what you're doing."

"Yeah, sure."

"You," she snapped, "work for me."

Chapter Two

The razor edge in her voice caused Burke to turn and face this slim-hipped woman in cowboy boots. Anger blew off her like a hurricane.

"This is my ranch. My house." Her tone was sharp but controlled. "I insist upon being treated with respect. I'm not your errand girl. I don't bring you coffee. I don't tidy up after you. And I demand to know what's going on."

She looked like a teenager, but there was nothing girlish about her temper. Carolyn Carlisle was a mature and formidable woman.

He peered into her eyes. They were fascinating, with green irises so pale they were almost transparent. She stared back at him, hard and determined, as she waited for his answer.

"What do you want to know, Carolyn?" He purposefully used her first name to establish that he was the professional and she was a civilian.

"Well, J.D…" When she countered immediately with his first name, he almost grinned. This woman didn't miss a beat.

"Actually," he said, "I go by Burke."

"Okay, Burke. I want an explanation of all this equipment you've scattered across my dining room table. But first, I want to know your plans."

"Here's the deal, Carolyn. I don't have time to hold your hand and make sure you're happy with our investigation. I didn't come here to make friends."

"Understood. But you need my help. Things are different on the ranch than in the city. People are different."

As far as he was concerned, a criminal was a criminal. Their motivations and methods might change from place to place, but the underlying stupidity and cruelty were a constant. "This is a crisis situation and I'm in charge. That's the way it rolls. Get used to it."

Her fascinating eyes narrowed. "Get used to what?"

"I give the orders."

"Then we have a problem. I don't take orders. I will, however, respond to requests made with respect."

"You want me to say please and thank you?"

"That's a start."

Her smile was infuriating and at the same time attractive. Even sexy. If they had met under different circumstances, he might have pursued her. But not here. Not now. As a hostage negotiator, he knew better than to become emotionally invested. The survival rate for kidnap victims held for ransom within the United States was less than forty percent. Nicole's abduction probably wasn't going to end well.

The phone on the table rang. "This could be the kidnappers."

Carolyn's bravado vanished. "What do I do?"

"It's on speakerphone," Burke said. "If it's the kidnappers, you need to keep them talking and demand to speak to Nicole."

He pressed a button and gave her a nod.

"Hello," she said. "Carolyn Carlisle speaking."

"Yes, ma'am. This is Wentworth. I wanted to give you an update."

Her tension relaxed. "I have you on speakerphone, Wentworth. I'm here with the FBI. We're waiting to hear from the kidnappers."

"Who is he?" Burke asked.

"One of the security guards my brother hired. Wentworth is at the hospital with the wounded man, Jesse Longbridge, the owner of the security company." She turned back toward the speaker. "How is he?"

"In critical condition," said the voice on the phone. "His heart stopped during surgery. He hasn't regained consciousness, but he's breathing on his own."

"Is he going to be okay?" Carolyn asked.

"It's touch and go, ma'am."

She wrapped her arms around her midsection as if literally holding herself together. To Burke she said, "Jesse saw the kidnappers. He can identify them as soon as he wakes up."

If he wakes up. He leaned toward the phone. "We appreciate the update, Wentworth. This is Special Agent J. D. Burke of the FBI. Can you call in another man from your security company?"

"Yes, sir."

"Good. I want two of you at the hospital, keeping an eye on Jesse Longbridge. He's a threat to the kidnappers and they might come after him."

"We'll keep him safe, sir."

Burke recognized the crisp attitude. "Are you former military, Wentworth?"

"Marine Corps. Two tours of duty in Iraq as a medic."

There was no need for further conversation. Burke had complete confidence in Wentworth's ability to keep the witness safe. The first lesson for a Marine was never leave a man behind. "Carry on, Wentworth."

"And thank you," Carolyn added before he hung up.

He figured that the veneer of politeness she insisted upon

was a way to maintain control. It was a small price to pay for her cooperation. "Carolyn, would you please tell us the events leading up to the kidnapping."

She gave a brief nod. "It was dusk. Nicole went for a ride. She wanted to be alone, but the bodyguard, Jesse, left a few minutes later. I heard shots and went after them."

"How long between when they left and when you heard gunshots?"

"Maybe ten minutes."

"Did you pursue on foot?"

"On horse. Bareback. I happened to be near the corral." She frowned. "I wasn't dressed for riding, and I ruined a perfectly good skirt. Tore the slit all the way up the side."

His mind formed an image of her long legs pressed against the flanks of her horse as she raced across the field. It must have been something to see. "Then what happened?"

"I saw Jesse coming out of the trees. Even though he was badly wounded, he managed to tell me that he saw two men grab Nicole. She struggled, but they knocked her unconscious. They said that my brother would pay a lot to get his wife back."

Apparently, this wasn't a planned abduction. There was no way the kidnappers could have known Nicole would be out riding at that particular moment. Not unless she was part of their plan. If that were so, she wouldn't have struggled, wouldn't have needed to be rendered unconscious. More likely, this was a crime of opportunity. Nicole happened to be in the wrong place at the wrong time.

Bad news. Burke preferred to deal with professional criminals. Amateurs were unpredictable. "What happened next?"

"The men from the ranch rode up. Wentworth took care of Jesse. And he was nothing short of amazing. He got Jesse loaded into the bed of a truck and took him to the hospital before the ambulance arrived."

Jesse Longbridge had been lucky to have the battle-trained expertise of a Marine medic. Wentworth's fast action and triage skills had probably saved his life.

"After that," Carolyn said, "I had to deal with my brother, Dylan. He wanted to track down the kidnappers and kill them. But I insisted that all the men leave their guns behind. The sheriff is with them now. They're still looking, talking to people at nearby ranches."

Burke needed to put an end to this chase as soon as possible. He strode from the room.

"Where are you going?" she asked.

"To get us some coffee. It's going to be a long night."

NEAR ELEVEN O'CLOCK, Carolyn paced back and forth on the veranda, waiting anxiously for her brother to return. After half a dozen calls on her cell phone, she'd finally convinced him to allow the FBI to handle the kidnapping. Even if Burke was a pain in the rear, he was an expert.

The equipment he'd finally deigned to show her was impressive: GPS surveillance, heat-sensing infrared imaging, audio scanners, computer linkups to monitor e-mail activity. These high-tech tools made her brother's posse on horseback seem positively archaic.

She knew Dylan would be impressed by the technology. The problem was Burke. If he tried to order her brother around, there'd be hell to pay.

Her first impression of Burke as a brusque, authoritative jerk had changed. He'd shown patience when he'd explained how to handle the ransom call. He'd told her not to confront but to stand firm. And to keep the caller talking. There were two reasons for that strategy. First, so they could get a clear trace. Second, the more the kidnapper talked, the more information they could gather. Little sounds in the background were clues to the kidnapper's whereabouts.

Burke and his men had practiced with her so she'd know what to say. They'd told her to use her feminine wiles to stall—a useless bit of advice. If she'd ever had wiles, they were buried under years of dealing with ranch hands and businessmen who didn't respect a woman who cried or pouted or giggled.

According to the FBI experts, her number one goal when talking to the kidnappers was to get proof of life.

She shuddered when she thought of the alternative. Nicole could already be dead. Her fingers tightened on the porch banister, anchoring her to something solid and tangible.

Burke came onto the porch and stood beside her. The sheer size of the man was impressive. He stood well over six feet tall with long legs and wide shoulders. She couldn't really guess at his age, but assumed that a senior FBI agent would be in his late thirties. A little older than she was.

"Are you chilly?" he asked.

"Not a bit." She stuck her hands into the fur-lined pockets of the hip-length shearling jacket that protected her from the December cold.

"It's beautiful out here," he said. "Peaceful."

"When I was growing up, I couldn't wait to get off the ranch. After I left, I kept wanting to come back."

"But you live in Denver now. Tell me about your job." He paused for a moment. "Please."

"You've asked so nicely, I can't refuse."

She glanced up, catching a twinkle in his dark brown eyes. Though he was willing to play along with her insistence for respect, he made it clear that the decision was his choice. He was still in charge.

His attitude was familiar. All her life she'd been dealing

with taciturn, stubborn men. Cowboys weren't known for wearing their hearts on their sleeves unless you put a guitar in their hands. A mournful tune could bring sentimental tears to the eyes of the most calloused ranch hand.

She strolled to the end of the veranda, climbed onto the porch swing and tucked her legs under her.

"My job," she said. "I'm the CEO at Carlisle Certified Organic Beef. I handle oversight of the product, sales and distribution for this ranch and more than sixty others throughout the west. Anybody who contracts with us agrees to follow sustainable ranching procedures that my father pioneered in the 1980s. All Carlisle Certified cattle are grass fed. We don't use antibiotics or growth hormones."

"With the craze for organic food, you must be doing well."

"The business keeps me hopping, and we're also doing something good for the planet. Our system of shifting cattle from field to field prevents overgrazing. I like to think that we have a contented herd."

"But they still get slaughtered."

She leaned forward, setting the swing into motion. The chain that attached to hooks in the porch ceiling creaked. "I hate to think about that part. For a long time I was a vegetarian."

"On a ranch?"

"Don't even think about giving me a hard time. I've heard it all." She swung a little harder. "Currently, we have plans to build a state-of-the-art, humane slaughterhouse a couple of miles from here."

"I can't get a handle on you." He regarded her with curiosity. "Are you a hard-driving businesswoman? Or a tree-hugging environmentalist?"

"A little bit of both. I try to avoid politics."

He sauntered toward her and sank into a sturdy, carved

rocking chair beside the swing. "I'd find that statement easier to believe if the FBI hadn't been alerted to Nicole's kidnapping by the governor's office."

She hadn't wanted to waste time going through regular law enforcement channels. "The governor is a friend. I called in a favor."

"But you're not political."

She didn't need to justify her position to him. What an *irritating man!* "Why do you want to know about my job?"

"Motivation," he said. "I'm trying to figure out who has a grudge against you or your brother. For the past couple of weeks, somebody has been causing a lot of trouble at the ranch."

"Trouble?" Dylan hadn't mentioned anything until today when he told her about the stable fire. "Please explain."

"I read the police reports your brother filed. Uprooted fence posts. Damage to the irrigation system in the hay field. A couple of pieces of stolen equipment." He leaned forward, elbows resting on his knees, and peered at her through the dim light. "You didn't know."

"These incidents sound like minor mischief. Dylan probably didn't want to worry me." Still, he should have kept her informed. It seemed like he didn't trust her anymore. What was wrong with him? He'd never been secretive. Before today, she'd never heard him fight with Nicole.

"It was more than mischief," Burke said. "Sounds like deliberate sabotage at the ranch. Have there been any threats on the corporate side?"

"Not that I'm aware of. Of course, we have competitors. And disgruntled former employees. But that kind of hostility usually shows up in the form of a lawsuit."

She heard the sounds of horsemen approaching and saw the posse riding toward the barn. Slowly, she uncurled her legs and stood, watching. Dylan handed his reins to one of the other ranch hands and strode toward them. With his head down and his face shadowed by the brim of his Stetson, she couldn't see his expression. But she knew he was troubled. His gait was stiff-legged, not surprising for someone who'd been on horseback for several hours.

He had to be devastated about the kidnapping. No matter how much she wanted to ask him why he hadn't told her about the sabotage, now wasn't the right time.

Dylan stepped onto the veranda. He pulled off his leather gloves and his hat, dropping them on a rocking chair. His matted black hair stuck to the sides of his head. His complexion was red and raw from exposure to the cold night air.

"Dylan, I want you to meet Special Agent J. D. Burke."

The two men faced off as they shook hands. Burke was taller and broader, but Dylan was clearly the aggressor.

"You find my wife," he said. "I want a search helicopter. First thing in the morning. And bloodhounds. Hell, I want you to call out the National Guard. And I—"

"Dylan," Carolyn interrupted. "What did you find when you were tracking?"

"They went across the back ridge to a paved road. We lost their track. We've been going door-to-door at the nearby ranches. Nobody's seen anything. Not a damn thing."

One of Burke's men pushed open the door. "Carolyn, it's the phone."

"The kidnappers," Dylan said. "I'll take that call."

"No," she said. "You won't. I've been practicing. I know what to say."

When he started toward the door, Burke stepped in front of him. "Let Carolyn handle this."

"Like hell I will."

She slipped inside and ran to answer the phone before Dylan could do anything to stop her.

Chapter Three

Burke would have preferred being inside, listening while Carolyn talked to the kidnappers. But he knew his men would record the conversation. During the next few hours, they'd replay it a hundred times, doing voice analysis and isolating every miniscule background noise.

Right now, it was more important to hold Dylan back. Burke wouldn't hesitate to kick this cowboy's ass to keep him from barging in and botching their procedures. He stood in front of Dylan like a brick wall.

"Let me pass." Dylan seemed dazed, in shock. His pale green eyes—the same color as Carolyn's—flickered nervously. "I need to be in there."

Burke didn't waste time on logical explanations. He doubted Dylan Carlisle could hear anything other than the roar of outrage inside his head. It must be an all-consuming noise, louder than an avalanche.

"We're staying out here," Burke said.

"She's my wife."

"I understand." If Burke had allowed himself to become emotionally involved with the people on a case, he would have felt sorry for this guy.

"My wife…" His voice cracked. "I love her."

Though Burke hadn't touched him, Dylan staggered backward a few paces. The air deflated from his lungs in a gush of cold vapor. He turned, facing the night sky. His fingers gripped the banister. "We had a fight. Right before she rode off by herself, we argued. I said things. Hurtful things."

Burke stepped up beside him but didn't look at him. He stood silently, listening like a priest in a confessional.

"Nicole wants a baby." The words spilled from Dylan as if he'd been holding everything inside for too long. "We've been trying for eight or nine months. But no luck. From the start, we knew she might have to be implanted because she had internal injuries from when she got kicked by a horse a couple of years ago. Kind of an occupational hazard, I guess. She's a large animal veterinarian."

Burke heard the pride in his voice. Dylan truly loved his wife.

He continued, "She's a tiny little thing. But tough. First time I saw her, she stuck her arm into a cow's birthing canal and pulled a slick, wet, newborn calf into the world." He shook his head. Something like a sob came through his lips. "You've got to love a woman like that."

That wasn't Burke's number one criteria, but he understood. "She was right for you."

"We were supposed to go to the fertility doctor today. He'd scheduled the implant procedure. But I couldn't go. Not with the stable fire. I had to be here."

Actually, he could have called Carolyn. She was more than able to manage the ranch while Dylan was at the doctor with his wife. Burke guessed that something else was going on. Maybe Dylan wasn't ready for kids.

He continued, "I told her we could do it tomorrow or the next day. Why did it have to happen today? What difference could one day make?"

A big difference. It took less than a day to change someone's life. Sometimes, less than a minute.

Carolyn pushed open the door and stepped onto the veranda. She trembled. "A million-dollar ransom. He wants it by tomorrow afternoon."

THE SOUND OF THE KIDNAPPER'S voice set fire to a fuse inside Carolyn. She was furious. And terrified. They had to rescue Nicole. *Now, damn it. Right now.*

But there were procedures to follow, and she trusted Burke's expertise. He moved around the dining room, checking the various instruments and conferring with his men in technical jargon that sounded like a foreign language.

Needing something to do, she picked up Burke's leather jacket from the dining room chair where he'd dropped it. The lining was still warm from his body heat. He glanced in her direction. Was he smirking? In spite of her earlier insistence that she wasn't an errand girl, she'd been reduced to tidying up. Immediately, Carolyn dropped the jacket and stood tall, arms folded below her breasts.

Sheriff Trainer had joined them. The only other person in the room was her brother. Dylan leaned against the wall by the door, near collapse.

"We're going to play back the ransom call," Burke said. "I want you all to listen for any sound that might give us a clue to the kidnapper's identity or his whereabouts."

"Wait a minute," Sheriff Trainer said. "Didn't you get a trace to tell us where he is?"

One of Burke's associates, Special Agent Corelli, stepped forward. He was the technical expert, the only man in the room wearing a suit and tie. He pointed to a rectangular black box with several dials. On the screen was a map of the area. A red dot blinked on a secluded road, too small to be given a name.

Corelli pointed to the dot. "When he made the call, he was here. I'd guess that he's on horseback or in an all-terrain vehicle."

Dylan staggered forward and squinted at the screen. "Does he have Nicole with him?"

"Sorry," Corelli said. "There's no way of knowing."

Carolyn went to her brother's side. "Sit down, Dylan."

"Can't." He stumbled back to his position against the wall. "If I sit, I'll fall asleep."

"That sounds like a good idea."

"I won't sleep until Nicole is in the bed beside me."

A noble sentiment. But it wouldn't do Nicole any good if he pushed himself beyond his limits and had a total breakdown.

The sheriff tilted his hat back on his head and stared at the blinking dot. Though he wasn't holding a cigarette, Carolyn smelled the residual smoke that clung to his uniform. "Seems to me that we ought to head out in that direction."

"He'll be long gone," Burke said. "He was smart enough to know that the phone call would be traced. He's in a remote area with no witnesses. There's no way we could have gotten there in time. He used a disposable cell phone so we can't ID the number."

"There are still records of those things," the sheriff said. "We can find out where he bought it."

"We're running those records," Corelli said.

Carolyn was surprised that the Delta County sheriff was so attuned to complex investigation techniques. She'd always thought the skinny, gray-haired man was a nice guy, but not particularly competent.

"The good news," Burke said, "is that our kidnapper is still in the area. More than likely, he's a local. Somebody you might know. That's why I want you to listen to his voice. And the way he puts his words together."

He pressed the playback button and Carolyn heard her own voice. She was surprised that she didn't sound as terrified as she'd felt at the time.

"Hello, this is Carolyn Carlisle."

"I want a million dollars." The kidnapper spoke in a rasping, ominous, barely audible whisper. "I want it in cash."

"You'll have to repeat that. I can't hear you." She'd been stalling, doing as Burke had suggested. "Please speak up."

"Listen hard. A million dollars. Cash. Nothing bigger than a hundred."

"Do you have Nicole with you? I need to talk to her."

"Pay me. Or she dies."

On the playback Carolyn sounded confident. "Don't you worry. You'll get everything you want. If it's a million dollars, you'll get a million." She'd been rambling, keeping him on the line. "Please let me talk to Nicole."

"I want the money tomorrow afternoon at five."

"It's going to be hard to scrape that much cash together in one day." More stalling. "Tomorrow is Saturday. And the local banks probably don't have a million dollars on hand. We'll have to go all the way into Denver."

"Not my problem."

She remembered Corelli giving her the thumbs-up signal. They had successfully made the trace.

She heard herself say, "I need proof of life."

There was a pause. "What's that?"

"Proof that Nicole is still alive. Let me talk to her."

"You'll get your proof."

That was when he disconnected the call.

She looked into Dylan's face. Tears streaked down his cheeks. Carolyn couldn't remember the last time she'd seen her brother cry. When she touched his arm, he collapsed against her.

"This is all going to work out," she assured him. "I'll take care of putting the money together."

Burke cleared his throat. "Anybody recognize the voice?"

"Not really." The sheriff patted the pocket in his shirt where Carolyn could see the outline of a cigarette pack. "That whisper could have been anybody. I didn't hear an accent. He didn't use any slang."

"Proper language," Burke said. "Instead of saying 'Ain't my problem' he said 'Not my problem.' And he didn't know what proof of life meant."

"What does that indicate?" Carolyn asked.

"He's not a professional kidnapper. He might not even have a criminal record."

"Which means," Corelli said, "that his fingerprints might not be in the system."

Burke nodded toward the other two men, both of whom were wearing black windbreakers with *FBI* stenciled across the back. "Special Agent Smith and Special Agent Silverman are both trained profilers. Sheriff, they're going to need to talk to everybody on the ranch. Starting now."

"It's the middle of the night," the sheriff protested.

"The first twenty-four hours are crucial." Burke turned to the Smith–Silverman team. "Start your interviews with the sheriff. Keep me informed."

Carolyn could feel Dylan's knees beginning to buckle. His body was literally giving out. Before he went limp and dragged them both to the floor, Burke came up beside her and slipped his arm around Dylan's torso. "Let's go, buddy. You need a rest."

He tried to rally. "Can't go to bed."

"Just a catnap," Carolyn said. "On the sofa in your office. You'll be close."

With Burke supporting her brother, she went down the hall, through the entryway, and took a right. The second door was Dylan's office—a large, masculine room with a wall of books and windows that opened onto the veranda. Opposite the huge oak desk that had belonged to her father were two brown leather chairs and a matching sofa.

Burke sat Dylan on the sofa, and Carolyn peeled off his jacket. Getting his boots off was an effort but she managed. Her brother stretched out, immediately asleep. She covered him with a crocheted afghan, striped in green and brown.

Closing the door, she stepped into the hallway with Burke. "Thanks. I couldn't have carried him by myself. Whoever said 'He ain't heavy, he's my brother,' didn't know Dylan."

"The Hollies," Burke said. "They sang it."

She leaned against the wall outside the office, allowing this moment of quiet to soothe her frazzled nerves. It was nice to be here with Burke—someone who didn't depend on her. "I'm worried about him."

"Dylan blames himself for what happened." His voice was low, intimate. "He and Nicole argued before she took off."

"I heard them." That was less than six hours ago but it felt like an eternity. "I didn't catch what they were saying."

"They were trying to get pregnant. Your brother didn't want to take time out of his schedule to see the fertility doctor. That's why Nicole was angry."

"Dylan told you all that?" She gazed up into his stern, craggy face. In the soft light, his features seemed warmer, more appealing. "If I can't get him to open up to me, why would he talk to you?"

"Sometimes, it's easier to tell your secrets to a stranger."

Unexpectedly, he reached toward her and brushed a loose

strand of hair behind her ear. The stroke of his fingertips on her cheek set off an electric reaction that sizzled down her throat and into her chest. "You don't seem all that strange. Actually, you're kind of all right."

"High praise," he said wryly. "Don't make me more than I am, Carolyn. I'm just doing my job."

She didn't quite believe him. Burke tried to stay detached, but the hard-nosed attitude didn't come naturally. "You're not as tough as you pretend to be. You care about what happens to Nicole. And to Dylan."

"Caring is human. But I don't let empathy get in the way of my work."

"I don't mean to put you on the spot. It's just—"

"And I care about you," he said.

Her heart thumped against her rib cage. Her gaze dropped from his face to his broad chest. Just for a moment, she wished she could rest her head against him. "Thank you."

"You're trying to carry your brother, run the corporate business and manage the ranch." He rested one hand on her shoulder. With the other, he lifted her chin so she was looking into his dark eyes. "Who takes care of you, Carolyn?"

No one. She had no one to share her burdens. No one who really cared for her. "I talk to Elvis."

His lips parted in a grin. "First the Hollies. Now Elvis. Are we on a tour of the golden oldies?"

"Elvis is my horse. I tell him my secrets and he listens."

Burke leaned down and kissed her forehead. He stepped back so quickly that she wasn't sure what happened. But her forehead tingled. She felt suddenly warm. Hot even.

One of the other agents—either Silverman or Smith— came into the hallway. "Burke, you need to hear this."

"What is it?"

"The sheriff says the most likely suspects live on a ranch near here. The Circle M."

Burke turned to Carolyn. "What do you know about the Circle M?"

"The ranch belongs to Nate Miller, but he's renting the entire property and all the outbuildings to Sam Logan and a group of his followers."

"Followers?"

"They call themselves the sons of something or other. They're survivalists."

Burke looked back toward the other agent. He said just one word. "Waco."

In a flash she remembered television images of burning buildings and reporters talking about the women and children who had died in the confrontation between the FBI and the Waco cult.

"It's not the same thing," she said quickly. "Sam Logan isn't that kind of guy."

"How do you know?" Burke asked.

She swallowed hard. "He used to be my boyfriend."

Chapter Four

Sam Logan hadn't been the love of Carolyn's life. He'd been two years ahead of her in high school, and they went out on exactly three dates before he told her that she wasn't "sophisticated" enough for him. In his dictionary, "sophisticated" meant having sex, which wasn't something she wanted to try at age sixteen.

Several years later, after she'd graduated from college, she and Logan hooked up again. Their relationship had been far more complicated the second time around.

"Well?" Burke glared at her as if she were a suspect. "Are you going to tell us about your survivalist boyfriend?"

"I need coffee for this."

She pivoted and went down the hall toward the kitchen where the family's housekeeper, Polly Sanchez, was taking a batch of her famous raisin rolls out of the oven. The heat from her baking steamed up the north-facing windows. A mouthwatering aroma filled the huge kitchen.

"Can I help?" Carolyn asked.

"Good heavens, no. I'm in a hurry, and I don't have time to clean up after you." With an expert flourish, Polly spread gooey icing on top of the rolls. "Soon as I'm done here, I'm heading home to catch a couple of winks before morning."

As Carolyn watched the icing melt into rich swirls she realized that she hadn't eaten for over ten hours, not since noon when she had sushi from the new Japanese fusion restaurant down the street from her Denver office. Lunchtime seemed like decades ago.

She rested her hand on Polly's round shoulder. "Thanks for coming over to help out."

Beneath her curly gray hair, Polly's forehead crinkled with worry wrinkles. "You know I'd do anything for your family."

For the past twelve years, Polly had worked at the ranch as housekeeper and chief cook. Her husband, Juan, had been a full-time ranch hand—and an expert at repairing machinery—until three years ago when he was stricken with MS. Now, his hands were too weak and unsure to hold a wrench. As soon as she'd learned of his illness, Carolyn authorized payment for a full pension and upped Juan's medical coverage to pay for treatment. She'd offered to do the same for Polly so she could stay home with Juan, but the buxom little woman insisted that she needed to keep busy.

During the spring calving and fall roundup when they had a full crew, Polly had two employees working under her. At this time of year, her schedule was less demanding.

"You need me here," Polly said in a brisk tone. "Tomorrow morning, Juan and I will move over here to the ranch house, and we'll stay until Nicole comes home."

"That's really not necessary," Carolyn said.

"Honey, you've got a houseful of FBI agents and bodyguards. And you can't hardly boil water without setting the house afire. How did you plan to feed all these hungry men?"

"I can call for pizza."

"Pizza for breakfast?" Polly clucked her tongue on the roof of her mouth. "Y'all sit right here at the kitchen table. I'll bring your coffee and raisin rolls."

Taking the seat opposite Burke, Carolyn knew that the time had come to answer his question. "Okay, here's what happened between me and Sam Logan."

"Logan?" Polly set mugs of coffee on the table. "He's turned into a regular nutcase. He runs that Sons of Freedom bunch over at the Circle M. It's not all Sons. There are families. The women all wear housedresses and tie their hair back. Same with the kids."

Burke turned toward her. "Is it a religious group?"

"Lord, no." Polly bustled back to the counter. "Logan doesn't have a religious bone in his body. Does he, Carolyn?"

"Not when we were going out." She remembered Sam Logan as a tall, lean guy with a blond ponytail and a charming smile—handsome enough to cruise by on his looks. She wasn't surprised that he'd gathered followers.

"His group," Polly said, "wants to go back to the pioneer days. They're against big business, government interference, taxation without representation and all that."

Burke shrugged. "Doesn't sound so bad to me."

His comment surprised Carolyn. What kind of fed was opposed to government interference? She'd thought FBI agents couldn't wait to bust down doors and take everybody into custody.

Polly placed a plate full of raisin rolls on the table. "People around here call them SOF for Sons of Freedom. Or Silly Old Fools. If the only thing they wanted was to go back to the good old days, I wouldn't have a problem with them. Live and let live, I always say."

"But you have a problem," Burke said. "What is it?"

She reached behind her back to untie the strings of the gingham apron she wore over her jeans and cotton shirt. "Their back-to-nature ideas don't extend to alcohol. A couple of the SOF boys drove into Riverdale, drunk as skunks, and raised hell. A local teenager got hurt. The sheriff could tell you more."

Carolyn bit into her raisin roll and let the gooey sweetness melt in her mouth.

"How do they support themselves?"

"Lord knows where they get their money. But they seem to have plenty. Nate Miller didn't rent out his land for cheap, that's for dang sure."

Carolyn glanced over at Burke who seemed totally focused on devouring his raisin roll. His dark eyes took on a glaze of contentment. His jaw relaxed as he chewed. The other FBI agent was likewise transported.

"These are great," Burke said. "Ma'am, you've got to come back tomorrow."

Polly pinched his cheek. *Actually pinched Burke's cheek!* Carolyn couldn't believe that Special Agent I'm-In-Charge would stand for such familiarity. Then she remembered his kiss on her forehead. Underneath the tough exterior, he was kind of a marshmallow.

"I'll be back in time to throw together some breakfast." Polly turned to Carolyn. "The guest bedrooms are made up with fresh sheets and towels. Call me if you need anything else tonight. G'night, y'all."

She headed out of the kitchen toward the front door.

"Nice woman," Burke said. "Must have been good for you to have Polly around while you were growing up. She's real motherly."

"I have a mother," Carolyn said quickly. "Her name is Andrea. She and my father divorced when I was seven."

"Does she live around here?"

Thinking of her stylish mother choosing to stay in rural Colorado amused Carolyn. "Not hardly. She runs an art gallery in Manhattan where she lives with her second husband and my twelve-year-old half sister."

"Big change in lifestyle."

"Yeah, she traded in her cowgirl boots for designer stilettos."

Carolyn regretted that she hadn't spent more time with her mom when she was growing up. Andrea had wanted to take her and Dylan with her when she left, but they both chose the ranch. It was their home, their heritage. "I should call Mom and tell her what's going on."

"Tomorrow is soon enough," Burke said.

He was probably right. There was nothing her mother could do from New York, and Carolyn had more pressing concerns for tonight. "I need to get on the phone with my financial officers. And my bankers. I've got to start putting together the money for the kidnappers. Maybe I should—"

"Later," Burke said. "First, I want to know more about Sam Logan."

"Like what?" The sugar rush from Polly's raisin rolls had energized her. The inside of her head churned with dozens of things she needed to handle ASAP. "There's not much to tell."

"When you broke up with him were there hard feelings?"

"Some," she admitted. "It was a long time ago, right after grad school. I'd come back to the ranch and I was trying to figure out what I wanted to do with my pretty new MBA."

For lack of any other plan, she'd started dating Logan, who was a great guy to party with—handsome, charming and sexy. When their relationship started to get serious, she was uncomfortable. Her father, who had been ailing, sided with Logan, telling Carolyn it was high time she settled down.

But she'd just returned from school in New York where she had a chance to watch her career-focused mother. The corporate lifestyle appealed to Carolyn, and she figured she had the rest of her life to make babies. Now, almost ten years later, she wondered if she'd waited too long.

"Logan wasn't the right guy for me." She exhaled a sigh. "And I wasn't the barefoot-and-pregnant type of woman he was looking for."

"Do you think he holds a grudge?"

Taken aback, she grasped what he was suggesting. "If you think Logan kidnapped Nicole to get back at me, you're wrong. His ego is too big to realize that I was dumping him as much as he was dumping me."

"He could be nursing bad feelings toward you."

True, her former boyfriend had a petty streak. "He wouldn't sabotage the ranch. Our cattle-raising process is natural and organic. We're not his enemy."

"Are you sure about that?" Burke raised an eyebrow. "Carlisle Ranch is an international corporation. Big business. That's what he hates."

Burke's logic made a certain amount of sense. The success of her family's business might be a slap in the face to a loser like Sam Logan.

IT WAS AFTER MIDNIGHT when Burke and his men completed their interrogations of the employees of Carlisle Ranch. Once these cowboys got talking, they were as gossipy as a bunch of hens with ruffled feathers.

Burke still didn't have much to go on. Only a basic assumption: the kidnapping had been unpremeditated and was related to the recent vandalism at the ranch.

On a wide-screen computer in the dining room, Agent Corelli had pinpointed those acts of sabotage on a map of the area. Most of them bunched along the border between the Carlisles and a neighboring ranch.

Corelli, whose black suit still looked crisp, pointed to the red dots. "That pattern can't be a coincidence. Who lives on that ranch?"

"A young widow and her four-year-old child." Not likely suspects for a brutal kidnapping. "It's not a working ranch. Less than a hundred acres."

"Who's next to her?"

"National Forest," Burke said. "There are a couple of oil rigs in that area but nobody lives there."

Logan's compound was across the road and further to the east. Burke considered the survivalists his most likely suspects. They were the only ranch who had refused to talk to Dylan's posse when they had made their search.

Burke needed to get inside the SOF compound. His gut told him Logan had something to hide.

He stepped away from the table and stretched, trying to ease the tension that knotted the muscles in his neck and shoulders. "We need continuous monitoring tonight. In case the kidnappers call again," he said. "We'll sleep in shifts. You three go first. Silverman, I'll see you at three-thirty to relieve me."

Stretching again, he watched his men troop out of the command central/dining room. Upstairs, Polly had prepared two guest rooms for them with two beds in each. Twin-sized beds were always too short for Burke, but it would have felt good to lie flat, even with his feet dangling off the end of the bed.

In the living room that adjoined the dining room, he'd spotted a big, beige, corduroy easy chair with a matching ottoman. He hauled the chair around to face the battery of equipment on the table and settled in.

The house was quiet but not peaceful. The anxiety of waiting—not knowing what had happened to a loved one— permeated the old walls. The creaking of floorboards reminded him of the crackle of a long fuse, burning slowly toward an explosion. More trouble was coming; he could feel it.

Years ago, when he had started in law enforcement as a street cop in Chicago, he'd learned to trust his gut feelings. Subsequent training with the FBI gave him the tools to analyze.

Eyes half-closed, he did a risk assessment. Two violent crimes—arson and kidnapping—had occurred within two days. If he assumed that the same perpetrators were responsible for both, it was unlikely there would be another attack tonight. Typically, there was a lull after kidnappers made their ransom demands.

He heard a rustling from the hallway and turned his head with his eyelids still drooping. Carolyn entered the dining room, cell phone in hand. When she saw him, she stared for a moment as if deciding whether to wake him. Wispy strands of black hair had come undone from her ponytail. Though she fidgeted, she still looked capable. *And damned attractive.*

Her hidden vulnerability appealed to him. Behind her facade, he caught glimpses of a touching innocence that made him want to gather her into his arms and promise her the world. Which still didn't excuse him for kissing her forehead. He wasn't usually so unprofessional, but he didn't regret that kiss. Her skin tasted spicy—warm and soft.

"What do you need?" he asked.

She started. "I thought you were asleep."

"Just resting."

"I have a question."

"Shoot."

She placed her cell phone down on the table and approached him. "What if I can't put together the ransom by the deadline?"

He'd prefer that she not pay ransom at all. "Problems?"

"We don't have a million dollars in liquid assets, so the ransom requires a loan against our collateral, which, in turn, requires a ton of paperwork. Also, my financial adviser tells me that the local banks, even in Delta, can't pull that much cash from their reserves. We'll have to use a Denver bank and fly the money over here."

"I'm impressed that you found out that much tonight."

"I get things done, Burke."

She wasn't bragging, just stating a fact. He had no doubt that Carolyn wouldn't hesitate to wake up the entire Colorado banking community to get what she wanted.

"If you can't get the money, explain it to the kidnapper. Ask for more time."

"And if he refuses?"

"He won't."

She turned away from him and wandered around the table, checking out the equipment. When she came to the screen with the map and the red dots, she pointed. "What's this?"

"A map."

"I can tell it's a map," she said with some exasperation. "And not a very good one. If you want more detailed maps of the area, we've got plenty. Dylan uses them to keep track of the different fields, pastures and grazing rotation."

He hauled himself out of the comfortable chair and went to stand beside her. The top of her head came up to his chin. In her boots, she was close to six feet. A tall woman. He liked that.

He pointed to the red markings. "These dots represent incidents of sabotage."

She counted. "Seven incidents. Since my brother hasn't seen fit to keep me informed, can you tell me about them?"

Burke had plenty of details. During the interrogations, he'd listened to dozens of complaints from ticked-off cowboys. "Like you said before, it was just petty mischief until the barn burned down."

Her soft pink lips frowned. "I still don't understand why. We're good neighbors. We provide employment to the people in this area. Why would anybody do this to us?"

"You want motives?" He flipped open the notepad where Silverman had recorded their notes. "There are over twenty names listed. People who bear grudges against the Carlisles."

She leaned over the table. Her manicured fingernail—a feminine contrast to her ranch clothes—skimmed down the list. "I don't even know half these people. How did you come up with this list?"

"Your employees told us about them. By the way, all the ranch hands were quick to say that they like their jobs and your brother is a good, fair-minded boss."

She pointed to a name on the list. "Who's this?"

When he bent down to see where she was pointing, her ponytail brushed against his cheek. The scent of lilacs from her hair distracted him and it took a moment for him to read the name. "He works for an oil company. Your brother wouldn't allow his equipment access through Carlisle property."

"That hardly seems like an incitement to vandalism. Or kidnapping."

Though Burke agreed, he knew better than to overlook any motive, no matter how slight. Some people could work themselves into a homicidal frenzy over a stubbed toe.

She read another name. "Nate Miller. That's no surprise. He's hated us forever, blames us for his father's failure on the Circle M."

"There are a couple of other ranchers on the list who don't like the competition from Carlisle Ranch."

"It's business," she said. "Why make it personal?"

"Your success hurts their bottom line. People tend to take bankruptcy personally."

"But we're always fair. Always." She tapped the name with her finger. "Dutch Crenshaw runs the meatpacking plant in Delta. We've given him millions of dollars in business over the years."

Burke considered Crenshaw's motive to be one of the best. "But you're thinking about building your own slaughterhouse."

"I gave him a chance," she said. "I told him that we wanted to use state-of-the-art humane technology, but he refused to modify his plant."

"So you're going to put him out of business."

She frowned. "Okay, maybe you've got a point."

His focus on the list was interrupted by a loud crash, followed by the sound of gunfire. The shots came from the front of the house.

Chapter Five

Burke's risk assessment had been dead wrong. They were under attack. He caught hold of Carolyn's upper arm and turned her toward him. "Go upstairs. Don't turn on any lights and—"

"The hell I will." She wrenched free. "Those were gunshots. Somebody's firing at my house—the house that's been in my family for three generations, the house my grandpa built. Don't ask me to hide behind the lace curtains in my bedroom."

Stubborn woman. "I go first. Stay behind me."

"Of course. I'm not going to put myself or anyone else in danger."

He grabbed his handgun from the shoulder holster slung across the back of a chair, aware of seconds ticking away. Whoever fired that shot would be making his escape. Moving quickly through the house, Burke turned off lights as he went. Carolyn followed in his footsteps.

Her brother staggered into the moonlit hallway, rubbing his eyes. "Carolyn? What's going on?"

"Stay with him," Burke ordered as he flipped the latch on the front door. "I'll be right back."

Leaving Carolyn behind—thank God—he slipped outside

onto the veranda. Aware that he might be the next target for a man with a rifle and a nightscope, Burke stayed low. He dodged around the rocking chair and porch swing. At the end of the veranda, he jumped over the railing and ducked into the shadows.

Wind rustled the bare branches of a cottonwood. Nothing else appeared to be moving.

"Over here, Burke."

Burke followed the sound of the voice and saw a security guard crouched behind a truck that was parked on the wide gravel space beyond a hitching rail. Burke hustled toward him. "Where's the shooter?"

"Didn't see him. I was behind the house when I heard the shots."

His heavy jaw was thrust forward. His name, Burke remembered, was Neville. He'd been in the Secret Service for five years before joining Longbridge Security. "What about a vehicle?"

Neville shook his head. "I didn't hear a car."

Cautiously, they peered around the truck. The driveway leading to the house was a long gravel lane. The yard was about an acre of winter-brown grass, separated from the road by a whitewashed fence. On the other side of the road, the land turned rugged with lots of trees and rocks—plenty of hiding places for a sniper.

"He could be dug in behind those rocks," Burke said.

He nodded. "A decent rifle would be accurate from four, maybe even five hundred yards away."

After that first burst of gunfire, no other shots had been fired. Likely, the shooter had already hightailed it out of there. "Do you think he's gone?"

"I don't want to test that theory by taking a bullet," Neville said.

"Let's find him," Burke said. "You go right. I'll go left. We'll meet at the fence by the road."

As Burke moved across the yard, he scanned the cold, moonlit landscape. There was virtually no cover. Burke longed for the city streets, crowded with parked cars and doorways to duck into. This sniper was probably an expert hunter. Not like the city punks who held their guns sideways, more concerned with looking cool than taking careful aim.

When he reached the fence and no other shots had been fired, he was fairly sure that their sniper was gone. He heard the door to the house open. A mob spilled onto the veranda. Carolyn and her brother were both carrying rifles. The other three FBI agents accompanied them.

Lucas and two other cowboys—also armed—charged toward the veranda from the two-story bunkhouse.

"There are way too many guns on this ranch," Burke said. This was the land of the Second Amendment where the right to bear arms would not be infringed upon. He turned and looked across the road. From where he stood, he spotted four good positions for a sniper to hide, if he'd even bothered to take cover. With Neville behind the house and no one else keeping watch, the sniper could have stopped in the road, dropped to one knee, taken aim and fired. But why? What did he hope to gain by rousing the household?

"Sorry I missed him," Neville said.

"Not your fault. One man can't patrol an area this size."

As he and Neville walked up the drive toward the house, Burke shivered in the December cold. He wasn't wearing a jacket or hat, and hadn't bothered to put on gloves. Responding to the threat had been his sole focus.

The gunfire bothered him because it didn't make sense. As a rule, kidnappers kept close tabs on their hostages.

But two men had abducted Nicole. One could be with her while the other came here. Why? By now the kidnappers had to know that the FBI had been called in. Why take the risk of coming close?

He stopped behind the black rental van he and his men had driven from the Delta airfield. The back window was shot out, and there was a neat bullet hole in the rear license plate. None of the other vehicles showed signs of damage. The FBI van had been the target.

Carolyn stepped up beside him. Her rifle rested on her shoulder. "Looks like a pretty clear message, Burke. Somebody doesn't like you."

For a moment he grinned. He liked a challenge.

AFTER SHE'D HERDED EVERYONE back into the house, Carolyn took Burke and her brother into the office to talk strategy.

Somehow Carolyn had to turn the situation around and make it work. *But what can I do?* She couldn't put in extra hours to get the job done. It didn't matter that she was smart and strong. She couldn't change fate.

Pacing on the carpet, she snapped at her brother, "Don't drink that coffee. Caffeine keeps you awake."

"Somebody needs to be alert." He leaned against the desk and faced the sofa where Burke sat. "Looks like we made a mistake."

"What's that?" she asked.

"The kidnappers don't want the FBI involved."

"Of course they don't." Her temper flared. "That's exactly why Burke and his men are staying here. We need their expertise."

"Why? We're paying the ransom. I'm not taking any chances with my wife's safety."

"You want reasons?" In spite of her brother's distress, she

had to be brutally honest. "I don't think I can get my hands on a million dollars in cash by the deadline."

"Why not? I'm sure there's a way."

"Even if we pay, there's no guarantee that the kidnappers will bring Nicole back."

A muscle in his jaw twitched. "I know."

"We're ranchers, Dylan. We don't know squat about crime. The best way to deal with these kidnappers is to follow the advice of experts. Right, Burke?"

He didn't bother to nod. Instead, he sat in self-contained silence. She couldn't tell what he was thinking, but hoped he had some kind of plan that involved more than sitting here waiting for the next call from the kidnappers.

Lucas Mann poked his head into the office. "I got a question for you, Carolyn. The men are asking if maybe you could see fit to give their guns back."

"Seems to me that you've got plenty of other guns."

"Well, sure." He raked his fingers through his thinning salt-and-pepper hair. "Most everybody has backup weapons. But we want all the firepower we can get. Especially since some polecat is shooting at us."

"And I suppose you're missing your pretty new Glock nine millimeter?"

"Ain't she a beaut?" A proud smile stretched his face, and she noticed the wad of chewing tobacco that made a pouch in his cheek. "I bought it when all this sabotage started up. Gave my old piece to MacKenzie, that new kid."

"I'm assuming," Burke said from the sofa, "that you legally transferred ownership."

"Speaking of sabotage," Carolyn said, quickly changing the subject. If Burke got official about the paperwork for all the firearms on this ranch, there would be trouble. "What's your opinion, Lucas? Who do you think is behind it?"

"Don't know who," he said, "and I don't know why. But it all started when we moved a couple hundred head onto the south grazing pasture, near the Widow Grant's property."

Dylan grumbled, "Don't start."

"Carolyn asked a legitimate question," Lucas said. "And she deserves an answer."

Apparently, there had been a dispute between these two. "Please, Lucas, continue."

"The first time I found a fence post torn down, I told Dylan that we should herd them cattle to a different area. He wouldn't hear a word of it. Then we had another incident. And another. Dylan still wouldn't change his mind. He sure can be pigheaded. Not meaning any disrespect."

"I didn't move the cattle," Dylan explained, "because I'm trying a new system of rotating the herd."

On the sofa, Burke leaned forward. His heels hit the floor with a loud thump—a subtle but effective way to get their attention. "Lucas, can you tell me why having cattle in that pasture might provoke vandalism?"

"Don't know why. I just wanted to keep the herd safe."

"They weren't in danger," Dylan said.

"We were damn lucky we didn't lose any cattle when they broke through the fence."

"Stop bickering." Carolyn felt her temperature rising. "I don't give a damn about what happened yesterday or last week. We need to concentrate on now. Right now. This very minute."

Lucas took a backward step, hoping to escape. She caught him with a glare. "How do you explain this, Lucas? When you put those cattle in a pasture that's usually empty, our men would be paying more attention to that area. Right?"

He thought for a moment. "Yep."

"So, these vandals would be more likely to get caught when the cattle were there."

"Guess so," Lucas said.

She spread her hands, palms up, presenting them with her conclusion. "It's counterintuitive to attack there. Why would they take the extra risk?"

"Because they're not very smart," Dylan said.

Clever enough to burn down the stable without being caught. She turned away from her brother before she snapped his head off. "Lucas, tell me about the fire."

"It was late." He shifted the tobacco wad to his other cheek. "And damned cold. Everybody was in bed, but I couldn't sleep and I remembered Polly had left some peach pies. So I came back here to the house for a midnight snack. That's when I saw the flames."

"You raised the alarm?"

"Yep."

"I'm sure the sheriff investigated. Did he say how the fire was started?"

"Nothing fancy. That stable was dried-out wood. All it took was gasoline and a match."

Burke unfolded himself from the sofa and stood. His height made him an impressive presence. "I have a plan."

Her automatic reaction was to object, but Carolyn was desperate to make some kind of forward progress, even if it meant stepping back and letting Burke take charge. "I'm listening."

"If we were in the city right now, I'd call in every free cop and state patrolman to provide surveillance and protection on the ranch."

"We ain't in the city," Lucas pointed out.

"But we have resources. A lot of men and a lot of guns."

She watched as her brother turned his attention toward Burke. Their gazes locked. They seemed to be communicating at a level she couldn't comprehend. Man to man.

Dylan gave a slow nod. "I think I know what you're planning."

"We need to set up a perimeter around the ranch," Burke said. "Deploy men at every place the security could be breached."

"All around the ranch?" She hated this idea.

"The house, the barn, the bunkhouse, all the nearby structures. The center of activity."

"You make it sound like we're under siege."

"Maybe we are."

"I like it," Dylan said. He set down his coffee, pushed away from the desk and took a step toward Burke. For the first time since Nicole's kidnapping, he grinned. "The next time these guys get close, we'll catch them."

Though the two men didn't bump chests and exchange high fives, she felt the testosterone level in the room raise by several degrees. Deploying armed cowboys sounded like a shortcut on the road to disaster.

Chapter Six

The next morning after she showered and dressed, Carolyn went downstairs to the kitchen where Polly had four burners and a grill fired up. With the efficiency of a short-order cook, she assembled breakfast burritos and wrapped them in foil. "Good morning, Carolyn. Hungry?"

"All I want is coffee."

Though she was trying hard not to show her agitation, her insides churned like a washing machine. She couldn't stop thinking about the sabotage, the list of enemies and the million things she needed to do today. Most of all, she was concerned about Nicole.

"How are you holding up?" Polly asked.

"I'm worried." Carolyn filled a mug from the coffee urn. "I've been meaning to tell you that I'm sorry I missed Thanksgiving."

"It was quite a feast," Polly said. "I even made that oyster dressing that Nicole likes so much. I don't think anybody else took a bite of it."

"Cowboys don't eat sushi. Or anything that resembles it." She sipped her mug, amazed that Polly could make gallons of coffee in an urn taste like custom brew. "How's Juan doing?"

"My husband is full of energy this morning. He walked

down to the bunkhouse. Using his cane, of course." She paused her whirlwind of activity to pat Carolyn on the cheek. "We've all got to keep up our strength. Now, what can I get you to eat?"

Her stomach was far too tense to consider food. "Just coffee for now. But I'll be back."

Taking her mug, she went down the hall to the office, looking for Dylan or Burke. Instead, she found Lucas, Neville and the new kid, MacKenzie. They'd set up a whiteboard with some kind of schedule. One of Dylan's detailed topographical maps was spread on the coffee table with chess pieces scattered across it.

MacKenzie jabbered into a walkie-talkie. His language was vaguely military, using terms like "Roger that" and "Bravo team" and "Boots on the ground."

"What's this?" she asked as she pointed to the whiteboard.

"A surveillance schedule," Lucas explained. "We set up a perimeter. All these chess pieces on the map are different guys. Neville used to be in the Secret Service. He showed us how to maximize our security."

Neville, the Longbridge security guard, gave a sheepish shrug. "As you can see on the hour-by-hour schedule, I've worked in downtime so the men can rest, but nobody wants to take a break."

"Cowboys aren't always good at following orders," Carolyn said. "Too damned independent."

"So I've learned," Neville said.

Lucas chuckled. "I'll tell you what, there ain't going to be nobody taking potshots at this ranch house."

Which still didn't put them any closer to finding Nicole. She turned to MacKenzie. With his brown hair flopping over his forehead and freckles across his nose, he looked about twelve years old. "Where did you get the walkie-talkie?"

"I found them," Lucas said. "Remember a few years back, before everybody got cell phones, we tried using these things. Didn't work too good."

She remembered. Several of the walkie-talkies got lost or thrown away, mostly because the men didn't like having somebody check up on them. Consensus among the ranch hands had been that the old ways of communication were the best. Everybody had cell phones now, which were mostly kept turned off unless a cowboy on the range wanted to make a date with his honey in Riverdale.

MacKenzie obviously enjoyed this opportunity to play G.I. Joe. He turned away from her and spoke into his walkie-talkie. "Listen up, y'all. HQ is awake and on the move."

Amused, Carolyn asked, "What does that mean? HQ?"

"We gave everybody nicknames," MacKenzie said. "You know, like the real Secret Service. When they talk about the President, they call him POTUS. It stands for President Of The United States."

"I thought HQ would mean headquarters. Is it a person?"

"Yes, ma'am. It's you."

She glanced over at Lucas and Neville who appeared to be doing their best not to laugh. "What does that stand for? HQ?"

"That's not important." MacKenzie looked a bit scared. "We had to come up with a whole lot of code names really fast. Like your brother. He's BB for Big Boss. And Burke is TF for Tall Fed."

"And HQ?"

"Ma'am, it stands for Heifer Queen. And that's not saying you're a cow or a heifer, which is a cow that hasn't had a calf. It means you're the queen of the whole ranch, cattle and all. And that's accurate because you're—"

"Stop." She held up a hand to forestall further excuses. "My code name from now on is…Carolyn."

"Yes, ma'am."

She pivoted and left the office. Heifer Queen. It wasn't the worst thing she'd been called.

BURKE CHECKED HIS WRISTWATCH. Approximately one hour and ten minutes ago, the first gray light of dawn had crept across the windowsills in the dining room. He'd pulled up the shades and given tasks to his three agents. Dylan had joined them.

After they had coffee and something to eat, Corelli, dressed in his suit and tie, had cleared away the plates. Agent Corelli was a bit obsessive-compulsive—an appropriate character disorder for someone who worked with complex and often frustrating electronics.

Now, they had settled into a routine of monitoring phone calls, studying maps and pacing. Waiting.

Burke looked toward the door to the dining room, anticipating the moment when Carolyn would appear. In addition to the pleasure of seeing her, he needed her help to execute a plan that might bring her sister-in-law home safely. Only Carolyn could help him; she held the key.

When she finally came through the door with coffee mug in hand and her smooth black hair falling loose to her shoulders, her gaze went straight to him. Without speaking, she seemed to be asking a question. Without threatening, she threw down a challenge.

How the hell would he convince her to do something she most likely wouldn't want to do? Sweet talk wouldn't work; she'd see right through him. Nor could he scare her into going along with his plan because this woman was fearless. Burke figured his best tactic was honesty.

Dylan slung his arm around her shoulder. "About time you got up, sis. It's almost half past eight."

She hugged him back. With their long lean bodies, matching black hair and green eyes, they looked like a male and female reflection of each other. The yin and yang of the Carlisles.

"Anything happening?" she asked. "Other than a bunch of crazy cowpokes yakking on walkie-talkies and pretending to be surveillance experts?"

"Don't be snippy," Dylan said. "Setting up the perimeter gave the men something to do. It's not like anybody can concentrate on work while this is going on."

Burke noticed that neither brother nor sister had mentioned Nicole's name. They held the anguish he knew they must be feeling at a distance, and he appreciated their tough, taciturn attitude. In other kidnapping cases he'd worked, the families had been devastated to the point of breakdown. This was better.

"Good morning, Carolyn," he said, remembering to be polite. "Deploying the ranch hands might look crazy, but you've got to admit that we're well protected. Nobody's going to get close enough to take another shot at this ranch."

"I'm sorry about your van," she said.

"It was a rental."

Dylan directed her to a computer monitor where Agent Corelli sat with headphones. "Let me show you the setup. All of the landlines for the phones are routed through this monitoring station. The ringers are turned off, which is real good. Everybody we know has been trying to get in touch with us. Those calls are going straight to voice mail."

"How will the kidnapper get through?"

"If the number he used last night comes up, Corelli will let it ring. He does the same with any call that isn't from a familiar number."

Burke circled the dining room table and stood beside her. "Dylan and I practiced how to handle a call from the kidnappers. The same way I showed you last night. I think your brother should take the next call."

"I want to hear his damn voice," Dylan said.

She lifted her chin and studied her brother for a long moment. She approved of what she saw, and nodded. "Fine with me. In about a half hour, I need to get busy talking to the bankers about that million-dollar ransom."

Burke stood close enough to smell the lilac fragrance of her shampoo. He needed to get her alone to make his pitch. "Before you get started with the finances," he said, "I want you to take me to the field where all the sabotage started."

"Shouldn't you be here at the house? If the kidnappers call, Dylan might need your expertise."

"Agent Silverman is a trained negotiator. And Dylan knows how to handle himself." Burke checked his wristwatch again. Managing time gave him the illusion that he was in control, even though he knew that the only agenda that really mattered was dictated by the kidnappers. "If we leave now, we can get back by the time the banks open."

"I suppose I could take you over to the south pasture. Actually, I wouldn't mind getting outside."

Dylan dug into his pocket, took out a set of keys and held them out. "Use my truck. It's parked in front."

"Burke, you can drive," Carolyn said as she pulled her cell phone from her pocket. "That way I'll have my hands free to get started with my phone calls."

They made their way past the two cowboy bodyguards with their walkie-talkies and rifles on the porch, and then drove to the front gate where they encountered two more cowboy guards. Both of them tipped their hats to Carolyn.

"Take a right, Burke." She cast a rueful gaze at the guards. "With all these guns and the surveillance, it feels like we're conducting some kind of military operation. Baghdad in Colorado."

He appreciated the protection, even if it was excessive. But that wasn't what he wanted to discuss with her.

Burke needed to get inside the SOF compound and take a look around. Using force was out of the question. Survivalist groups were notoriously volatile, and he didn't want to provide an armed standoff. Carolyn had a natural inroad. She could use her influence with Sam Logan to set up a meeting. Unfortunately, from what she'd said yesterday, he didn't think she'd be too keen on talking to her former boyfriend.

The two-lane road curved around a thick stand of pines. When they came around the trees, the view took his breath away. Snowcapped peaks reached into a cloudless sky of pure blue. Forested foothills bordered a terrain of brownish grass and shrubs. The leveled, cultivated earth beside the barbed wire fence was surprisingly verdant with long rows of two to three inch shoots. "Green? In December?"

"Winter wheat," Carolyn said.

When Burke was growing up with his single mother in Chicago, he'd spent several summers in Wisconsin dairy-farming country with his grandparents. They were school-teachers and lived in town, but he'd spent enough time with local kids to learn the basics of riding horses and life on a farm. "I've never seen the winter wheat."

"Soon enough this crop will go dormant when we get more snow, but I love the way it looks right now. The green promises new life. And hope."

They were approaching the herd. Across an open space, he saw the boxy black silhouettes of Angus cattle. He'd been told there were only a couple of hundred head on this pasture. *Only?* It looked like a lot of cattle to him. The magnitude of this sprawling ranch operation impressed the hell out of him. "How far does your property extend?"

"Far enough," she said. "Slow down. Here's where we turn."

He made a right onto an unpaved gravel road. The truck tires bounced over a cattle guard. At the metal fence, Carolyn hopped out to unlatch the gate for the truck to drive through and closed it behind them. Though she was bundled up in a black shearling coat and wearing a flat-brimmed hat, he'd never confuse her with a cowboy. Her gait was purely female.

She climbed back into the truck. Her eyes were bright. "Thanks for bringing me out here, Burke. I needed to smell the land, to hear the cattle lowing. Music to my ears."

"Another golden oldie?"

"How about 'Moo-oo-oon River?'"

"Very funny," he said. "There's another reason I wanted to get you alone. I need your help, Carolyn."

"Hold that thought," she said. "We've got another gate to go through."

As she repeated the opening and closing procedure on the second gate, he reconsidered his plan. He had no right to ask her to get involved with Logan and the SOF. She wasn't a trained investigator, and he might be leading her into danger.

Instead of getting back into the truck, she motioned for him to drive forward and get out. "Come with me, Burke."

She strolled through the field toward the herd.

In Wisconsin, he'd seen plenty of cows, but those were friendly black-and-white-spotted Holsteins. These heavy-shouldered Black Angus looked rugged and undomesticated. Beef cattle. Western cattle.

Her cell phone rang, and while she answered, he stroked the solid flank of a steer that turned, glared and ambled toward a water trough. The south pasture wasn't open range. A barbed wire fence ran from the road to the rugged cliffs of the foothills. He noticed a trail outside the fence.

Carolyn finished her call and joined him. "That was my attorney. He's not happy about paying a ransom."

"Neither am I," he admitted.

"There might not be a choice."

Her tone was crisp and matter-of-fact, as if she were discussing a business transaction instead of a kidnapping. He wondered how long her strict self-control would last. How much pressure could she take?

As she casually smoothed the hide of another massive steer, she asked, "Why are we here?"

"I wanted to see the field where the sabotage took place so I could figure out why it happened here."

"Easy access," she suggested. "It's close to the road."

"But still hidden from direct sight of the ranch house." He pointed to the trail at the edge of the fence. "Where does that lead?"

"They call it the Indian Trail. It connects with a pass through the mountains." She tipped back the brim of her hat and looked up at him. "You said you needed my help."

He nodded. "You know who I consider my number one suspect."

"Sam Logan and the SOF." The moment she spoke his name her expression darkened. "You could be right. From what Polly said, it sounds like those guys like to cause trouble."

"I want to get inside the SOF compound and take a look around."

"Go for it, Burke. Do you need a search warrant?"

"It's going to take more than a piece of paper. A militia group that's opposed to government interference isn't likely to open their gates to a fed. This could end in a standoff."

"Like Waco," she said.

"It occurred to me that Logan might be convinced to show off for his old girlfriend. He might even offer to take you on a tour."

Her eyes narrowed. "You want me to call Logan and ask him if I can come inside?"

"We need to get in there."

"I can't do that." She lowered her head and stalked back toward the truck. Halfway there, she turned. "Logan hates me. What makes you think he'd respond to me?"

"Ego," he said. "Logan is the head of the SOF. He'll want to brag, to show you how important he is."

"Damn it, you could be right." She circled the truck and climbed into the passenger seat.

As soon as Burke slid behind the wheel, she started talking again. "Even if I could convince him to let me into his little kingdom, I don't see what good it will do. Logan might be a jerk, but he isn't stupid. If he's involved in the kidnapping, he won't lead us to Nicole. Not unless I have a million bucks in my back pocket."

"You can try."

Her cell phone rang again. She answered in a brisk tone, then inhaled a gasp. "How did you get this number?"

She looked at him with terror in her eyes.

"What is it?" he asked.

"Please hold on," she said into the phone. "I can't hear you. Let me put you on speakerphone."

Pressing a button, she held the phone so he could hear.

"Go ahead," Carolyn said.

"This is the kidnapper," said a scratchy falsetto voice. "I bet you're glad to hear from me."

What the hell? In his years of negotiating, Burke had never encountered a second introduction call. Last night, they'd heard his demands. Was this a second kidnapper?

The voice continued, "Do what I say and Nicole won't get hurt."

Chapter Seven

The last thing Carolyn expected was a call from the kidnapper. Corelli had all the equipment for this call set up at the house, and this squeaky voice was nothing like the whisper from last night. "Who is this?"

"Nicole is wearing a plaid shirt, red and blue. Wrangler jeans. The inside of her wedding ring says *My horizon*."

Carolyn felt the blood drain from her face. Very few people knew about the inscription on the wedding rings. "Is Nicole there? Let me talk to her."

"I want five hundred thousand in cash. By Monday night."

"Half a million?" Why had the amount dropped? Why was the deadline changed?

"You'll pay."

"Yes," she said quickly. "Don't hurt her. Please don't hurt her."

"I'll call again, Carolyn."

The phone went dead.

What just happened? Staring through the windshield, her vision blurred. It felt like she was going to pass out.

Gently, Burke took the phone from her hand. Her arm fell limp to the seat. All the strength left her body as she collapsed against the seat on the passenger side of the truck.

"Carolyn." Burke sounded like he was a million miles away instead of sitting beside her. "Carolyn, look at me."

She was too devastated to move, couldn't even summon the will to turn her head. She mumbled, "I did all the wrong things. Didn't ask for proof of life. Didn't keep him on the phone. I messed up."

Burke flipped back the center partition and pulled her across the seat toward him. Weak as a rag doll, she rested against him. The warmth of his body did little to melt the chill she felt inside. As if her heart had frozen. *Why is this happening to my family? Why?*

A sob tore from her lips. She fought desperately for control. *I'm not the kind of woman who cries*. She forced herself to hold back the storm of emotion that had been building inside her. Her hands clenched into fists and she held them against her mouth, pressing hard.

"It's okay." Burke stroked her trembling shoulders. "Let it out."

Still she fought. If she turned all weepy, nobody would respect her. Hell, she wouldn't respect herself.

"Go ahead and cry," he whispered. "I won't tell a soul."

Another sob wrenched through her. Another agonizing gasp. Her body convulsed. The floodgates burst. Tears poured down her cheeks. She completely lost control. For a long moment, she clung to him, weeping and trembling.

"It wasn't the same guy," she said between sobs. "Not the same as last night."

"Probably not." He caressed her hair. "It wasn't the same voice or phone number."

"But he knew about the wedding ring." Her tears streamed. "How could he know?"

"There were two men who abducted Nicole." His calm,

rational voice soothed her. "Maybe they had a falling out. Maybe they went their separate ways."

"Why?"

"That's what we need to find out."

"You're right." And her outburst was wasting precious minutes. Ashamed and scared and angry, she pushed against his chest, separating herself from him. "What should we do?"

He held up his cell phone. "I'm calling Corelli. If that phone number from the call is listed, he can give us a name."

Still shuddering from the outpouring of emotion, she sank back against the seat and listened to Burke's end of the conversation. While he talked, he linked his hand with hers.

From the moment they met, he'd told her that he didn't come to Carlisle Ranch to make friends. He'd warned her that some of his advice would seem cold and hard. But she'd felt his compassion. With her free hand, she pulled her shirt collar out of her jacket and dabbed the moisture from her cheeks. It had been years since anyone saw her weep. Even when her father died, she'd kept her tears to herself.

Ending his call, he squeezed her hand. "Are you okay?"

"I blubbered all over you, and I don't even know your first name. What does the J.D. stand for?"

"Jeremiah Davenport."

She could understand why he went by initials. "You're definitely not a Jerry."

"Or a Davenport," he said. "Let's get back to business. Who would call you on that phone? Who has that number?"

"This is my personal phone," she said. "It's not the PDA I use for business. Some people in Denver have this number, but very few. That's why I used this phone to contact my financial people. I wanted to keep the line clear."

"Here at the ranch," he said, "who knows the number?"

"Only Dylan." *But somehow the kidnapper knew.*

"Last night when we heard the gunshots, where was your phone?"

She cast back into recent memory. "I was in the dining room, talking to you. The phone was in my hand. I set it down on the table."

"And when we responded to the gunfire?"

"I left my phone on the table. Didn't pick it up until much later."

"After half the people on the ranch had come into the house. Any of them could have picked it up and gotten your private number."

She didn't like the direction this conversation was taking, but she couldn't deny his logic. "Are you saying that someone on the ranch is working with the kidnappers?"

Burke's cell phone jingled and he answered.

Dark thoughts of betrayal flooded her mind. When she'd learned of the many people who held grudges against the Carlisles, she'd been surprised and hurt. This was worse. Someone who worked for them—a trusted employee—was involved in Nicole's kidnapping. Anger sparked inside her, burning away the last vestige of her tears. When she got her hands on that traitor, they would pay dearly.

"We're in luck," Burke said. "The kidnapper's call came from a public telephone in Riverton."

FIFTEEN MINUTES LATER, Burke parked the truck at the only gas station in Riverton—a small town that was about ten miles from Delta and an equal distance from the Carlisle Ranch. He'd considered taking Carolyn back to the safety of the ranch house but decided it was more important to follow this lead as quickly as possible.

The public phone hung on a dingy brick wall beside the

closed doors of the auto repair bays. The windows of the gas station were dark. "What time do they open?"

"Whenever Silas O'Toole gets around to it. Usually, that's from about ten in the morning until six at night."

When the kidnapper called Carolyn at a few minutes after nine, he had a reasonable expectation of privacy. Using the public phone was actually a clever move because their trace resulted in a dead end.

It seemed unlikely they'd find any witnesses in this dusty little western town. Main Street's sidewalk stretched one block with storefronts and offices on either side. Limp red bows hung from the streetlights in a feeble attempt at Christmas decorating. At the other end of the block was a bar with a Closed sign hung on the door. The only activity appeared to be at Winnie's Café where two vehicles were parked outside at the curb.

Burke had already put in a call to Sheriff Trainer in Delta, requesting a forensic team to take fingerprints from the phone. Not that he expected to find much in the way of evidence. Even amateur criminals knew enough to wear gloves.

"I don't see many pedestrians," he said.

"Most of the people who live here work in Delta. Even the kids are bussed to school." She cracked her door open. "Shouldn't we be poking around and asking questions? Someone might have seen the kidnapper using the phone."

"I hate to have you involved in this." Any kind of investigation carried a certain element of danger. And he was concerned about her emotional state.

"You need me," she said. "People around here don't like to talk to strangers, especially not to a big city guy in a leather jacket who's carrying an FBI badge."

"But they'll talk to you."

"They'd better."

Her smile showed a cool determination that he hardly

believed was possible after her torrential breakdown. In the space of fifteen minutes, Carolyn had not only recovered her poise, but actually seemed stronger.

Though there was something to be said for Western stoicism, he'd seen the passion that burned inside her. Reaching toward her, he wiped away a smudge the tears had left on her cheek. "You're okay?"

"A hundred and ten percent." Her long black lashes fluttered as she blinked. "I won't fall apart again. My dad always used to say, 'When you get thrown from your horse, the best thing is to get right back on.'"

He didn't see how that advice applied. "What's that mean?"

"Don't waste time sitting on your butt and crying."

She climbed out of the truck and he followed. He unzipped his leather jacket, allowing easy access to his shoulder holster.

They talked to two women on the street, an insurance agent and the owner of the feed store that was directly across the street from the gas station. Everybody was friendly to Carolyn, but none of them had seen anyone using the phone.

Their next stop was Winnie's Café. The front window was painted with a Santa Claus and a snowman. As soon as they stepped through the door, he heard Carolyn curse under her breath. She nodded toward a wiry man in a beat-up Stetson. Like the hat, his face was weathered. Leathery brown skin stretched tight across high cheekbones and a sharp chin. Burke guessed that he was probably near forty.

Quietly, Carolyn said, "That's Nate Miller."

He remembered the name from the list of potential kidnappers. Miller blamed the Carlisles for the loss of his cattle ranching business. He had leased his property to the Sons of Freedom. "Introduce me."

He could see her jaw tighten as she approached the square wood table where Nate sat reading the sports page of the Denver newspaper and sipping coffee.

Keeping her voice level, Carolyn greeted him. "Mind if we join you?"

"Suit yourself." He squinted at Burke through hostile eyes. "I haven't seen you around here before. Has this got something to do with what happened to Nicole?"

Though he obviously knew about the kidnapping, Nate hadn't offered condolences or any expression of concern to Carolyn. That was cold. "What time did you get to the café this morning?"

"Same as every damn morning. Nine o'clock."

That gave him enough time to stop at the gas station and make the ransom call. "Did you drive?"

"Must have." He sneered. "That's my truck sitting outside at the curb."

Carolyn's cell phone rang. She carefully checked the number before she said, "Excuse me, gentlemen. I need to take this call."

As she politely stepped away from the table, Burke watched for a reaction from the man who sat opposite him. Nate Miller didn't move a muscle, didn't betray any sign of his grudge. When he lifted his coffee mug to his lips, his hand was steady.

If Miller was one of the kidnappers, he had to be the coolest criminal Burke had ever encountered, and that list included professional hit men, bank robbers and terrorists.

"Do you live in town?" Burke asked.

"I've got a little place up the road near Delta. It belonged to my ma before she died."

Nicole could be there. "Address?"

"I don't have to tell you."

Burke slid his FBI shield from his pocket and placed it on the table. "Yeah, you do."

"FBI." He sneered. "Of course, the high-and-mighty Carlisles would call in the feds. They know people. They've got more money than is right."

"You know what happened to Nicole."

"I heard about it. Everybody's buzzing." He set his mug down on the table. "It's a shame. Nicole's a nice woman. Can't say the same for her husband."

"Somebody might have kidnapped her to get back at him."

Anger flared in his squinty eyes. "It's no secret that I hate the Carlisles. Because of them, I lost my livestock and my livelihood. My wife left me. Took my son. If it wasn't for Sam Logan paying me big bucks to rent my land, I'd have lost my ranch, as well."

When he stood, Burke growled, "Sit down, Miller. I have more questions."

"Here's your answer." Miller remained standing. "I didn't kidnap Nicole."

Burke had no intention of letting this guy walk away. He glanced around the café. There were only four other customers. Burke saw no reason to bust up this pleasant little establishment if this confrontation turned physical.

He took out his wallet, peeled off a twenty, dropped it on the table and stood. "Let's take this outside."

Miller made a beeline for the door and Burke followed.

Still on the phone, Carolyn watched with concern in her eyes. He gave her a wink. If it came down to a fight, he could take Miller without breaking a sweat. Not only was Burke six inches taller and probably forty pounds heavier, but he knew how to fight. He'd been taught by the best at Quantico. Before the FBI, he'd had five years on the street as a Chicago cop.

Truth be told, he almost wanted Miller to resist. Carolyn had eased her tension with tears. Burke would find a similar release in kicking butt.

On the sidewalk, Miller turned to face him. His thumbs hitched in his pockets. Not a fighting stance.

"Here's my address." He rattled off a street number. "Is that all you want from me?"

"Where were you last night?"

"Home in bed. Alone."

"Before that?"

"I work as a handyman now that I don't have a ranch to take care of. And I had a light day. I was done by two."

"Can anyone verify your whereabouts?"

His thin mouth curved in a smirk. "I own a horse. You could talk to him."

Burke had faced men like Miller before. Men who believed they'd been wronged and the world was against them. They expected the worst. And they lived their mean little lives for the sake of their grudges. Even if Miller had nothing to do with Nicole's kidnapping, he was taking great pleasure from the pain this caused Dylan and Carolyn.

"This morning," Burke said, "when you drove into town on your way to the café, did you pass the gas station?"

He gave a nod. "I did."

"Did you see anyone?"

"Matter of fact, I did. I noticed because I needed a fill-up, and I thought O'Toole might have opened early. But it was just a guy using the phone."

"Did you recognize him?"

"Sure. It was Sam Logan."

Chapter Eight

Burke and Carolyn, who continued talking into her cell phone, returned to the gas station—which still wasn't open for business. Sheriff Trainer had parked beside the Carlisle truck, and Trainer himself leaned against the wall beside the phone. When he saw them coming, he stubbed out his cigarette and tossed the butt in a trash can.

"Is this the phone?" the sheriff asked.

Burke nodded. "Be sure to check the coins inside for prints."

"You got it. Anything else?"

"Do you know Nate Miller?"

"He's a mean son of a gun. When his wife separated from him, she had to take out a restraining order. I guess they patched things up since then because she withdrew the order and, from what I understand, she lets him visit with his kid."

"I want you to search his house."

The sheriff showed very little surprise. "You think he kidnapped Nicole?"

"He's a suspect." And a man without an alibi. "He claims he was alone all day yesterday. Difficult to verify, but see if you can find anyone who saw him. After that, I'd appreciate if you could come out to the ranch house."

"I'll be there." He reached inside his jacket pocket and

took out a toothpick wrapped in cellophane, which he peeled. He stuck the pick in the corner of his mouth. "I sure wish I'd done things different. The first time Dylan called me about the sabotage, I should have undertaken a serious investigation, maybe even called in the state cops."

"Do you think the kidnappers are the same guys?"

"Don't you?"

"The obvious conclusion isn't always correct." As an investigator, Burke kept an open mind to all the possibilities. "This investigation is going to be a whole lot easier when our eyewitness can make an ID."

"The security guard," Trainer said. "How's he doing?"

"Still unconscious. The doctors expect him to wake up, but they won't say when." He returned to more positive action. "I want a detailed, thorough search at Miller's house. Copy the hard drive of his computer. Search his files. Check for footprints and fingerprints. If there's a single hair from Nicole's head, I want you to find it."

Trainer bit down hard on his toothpick. "We've got the forensic equipment and the training. But I can't guarantee that we won't miss something. We're not as experienced as the Colorado Bureau of Investigation."

Burke didn't want to involve another law enforcement agency. Last night he'd arranged for other FBI investigation teams—a chopper and tracker dogs. All of whom would answer directly to him. "I'll send Agent Smith over to Miller's place to give you a hand. See you back at the ranch."

In the truck, Burke held off on telling Carolyn about Miller's supposed sighting of Logan at the public phone. Nate Miller was an unreliable witness. And she appeared to have her hands full with bank negotiations. Since the moment she'd answered that call in Winnie's Café, her cell had been glued to her ear.

His suspicions turned toward the inside man at the ranch. Someone—one of those supposedly loyal cowboys—had taken her phone and passed the number to the kidnappers. Burke considered gathering up all the cell phones and running a check on recent numbers called. But that still wasn't proof. The inside man could have used somebody else's phone. It was better not to alert the traitor that they were looking for him.

Carolyn disconnected her call, sank back against the seat and exhaled in a long whoosh. "I've got the ransom."

"How's it going to work?"

"With reams of paperwork, transfers of funds and a friendly contact at the Federal Reserve Bank. One million in cash."

"I'm impressed." Truly he was. Not many people could summon up a million in cash on a few hours' notice.

"In our business, we regularly handle large transactions," she said. "In addition to our own herd, we work with sixty other cattle ranches of various sizes."

He remembered her earlier explanation of their international business. "Other producers of certified organic beef. They're contracted with you for distribution."

"We pay them on delivery of their stock, even when we don't have payment from the end purchaser."

She took off her hat and smoothed her black hair into a ponytail. Though she looked like a cowgirl, she'd gone into high-power executive mode. She was an impressive CEO, no doubt about it.

And yet, she'd wept in his arms. Normally, he didn't respond well to tears, but he'd been relieved when Carolyn had her outburst. Even when vulnerable, she was strong. The only woman he had ever loved had been formidable—a law professor—tough, independent and intelligent. Sexy as hell.

Much like Carolyn.

"My attorney," she said, "is working through our Denver

bank to get the cash. He'll charter a helicopter and deliver the ransom after lunch."

"A million dollars is going to make a heavy package."

"I've thought of that," she said. "The money will be placed in one of those giant mountain-climber backpacks."

"Sounds like you've handled every detail." Though she didn't look like the strain had affected her, he purposely lightened the mood. "Here's what I think. We should take that backpack and hike to the top of a fourteener. We unzip the pack and we throw all that cash into the wind."

She gave him a puzzled look. "Why?"

"Greed is a prime motivator in crime. From kids stealing hundred-dollar sneakers to million-dollar ransoms, it's all about greed. Get rid of the money and you'll cut down on crime."

"For a fed, you have some strange ideas."

"Haven't you ever thought of what it would be like to live on a deserted island without a penny to your name? Surviving on coconuts and berries."

"My fantasies run more toward riding off into the sunset and never looking back." Finally, she grinned. "Just ride forever. No more spreadsheets, stock quotes, negotiations and conferences. A simple life."

He'd like to give her that peace of mind. He wanted to see how she acted when she wasn't under life-and-death stress. Would she laugh when he made jokes? What was her favorite food? More importantly…what was she like in bed? Though he had no right to think about her that way, his imagination formed an immediate picture of Carolyn stretched out naked on satin sheets, her black hair fanned out on the pillows, her arms reaching for him and her toes pointed.

He shook his head to erase that vision. After this ordeal, she'd never want to see him again. His mere presence would be a reminder of this terrible chapter in her family history.

"We need a plan," he said.

"For what?"

Her full lips parted. Her eyes were warm and expectant, as if waiting for a kiss. Instinctively, he leaned closer to her. His voice lowered. "A plan for when we get back to the ranch. If the kidnapper has an inside man, we need to be sure he doesn't overhear any of our strategy. For example, we don't want him to know you've arranged for the ransom."

"I get it."

"Good." He was pleased with himself for reining in his fantasies and sounding rational.

"But I need to tell Dylan. He needs to know about the inside man. And the ransom." Her fleeting grin was replaced with renewed tension. "You're right about throwing the money away. If we weren't rich, Nicole would never have been kidnapped."

"True." Kidnapping was a crime that affected the privileged. "But if you were poor, you'd have a whole different set of problems."

Her lips were pinched. "As soon as we get to the ranch house, I'll tell Dylan we have to talk in private. I'll take him upstairs to my bedroom. You meet us there."

As THEY ENTERED THE RANCH house, they put their plan into effect. While Burke briefed his men and dispatched Agent Smith to assist the sheriff with his forensic investigation at Miller's house, Carolyn pulled her brother aside.

Grabbing a mug of black coffee, Burke headed upstairs to join Carolyn and her brother. He climbed halfway up the polished wood staircase and looked down. A husky cowboy whose name he didn't recall sauntered through the front door. The newly hired MacKenzie bounded past him, talking nonstop into his walkie-talkie. From the kitchen, he heard

Polly giving instructions to her cooking crew who grumbled back at her. Too many people had access to the ranch house; finding the traitor wouldn't be easy.

He continued up the staircase. The dark green carpet runner muffled the thud of his boot heels. On the landing he hesitated. He and his men were housed in guest rooms at the north end of the upstairs hallway. Carolyn had told him that her bedroom was the second door on the south. Without knocking, he stepped inside.

A tall glass cabinet beside the window housed a display of riding trophies and blue ribbons, but that was the only hint of cowgirl. Her furniture was modern with clean lines. Blond wood and burgundy. Her bed was neatly made.

In different circumstances, entering her bedroom might have been akin to entering the Promised Land. Not now. The tension in this room was thick.

Carolyn stood by the window, scowling fiercely.

Dylan's hands were clenched into fists. He looked like he was ready to punch a hole in the smooth, cream-colored wall. Apparently, Carolyn had already given him the bad news.

"I can't believe it." His jaw was so tight that his lips barely moved. "A traitor. One of my own men."

"I'm sorry," Burke said. And he meant it.

"There is good news," Carolyn said. "I've made all the arrangements for the money. It'll be delivered by three o'clock."

"Dylan," Burke snapped his name, compelling his attention. "The information about the ransom is the kind of thing we need to keep secret. When the kidnapper calls again and you talk to him, don't tell him you have the cash. Ask for more time."

"Why?"

The truth was brutal, but it was better to face reality. "As long as he doesn't have the ransom, he needs to keep Nicole alive. She's his bargaining chip. And we need proof that she's all right. Do you hear me?"

Dark circles surrounded Dylan's eyes. In their depths, Burke saw a terrible pain. He'd experienced that agony. He knew the hell of losing someone you loved, and he knew there was nothing he could say or do to alleviate the suffering.

Dylan squared his shoulders. "Until the kidnapper calls, what do we do?"

"We investigate. As we speak, the sheriff is executing a search warrant on Nate Miller's house."

A commotion from downstairs interrupted him. It sounded like twenty cowboys on horseback had stormed through the front door.

The three of them hustled from the bedroom to the staircase. A redheaded cowboy waved from the bottom of the staircase and held up a manila envelope. "I found it. Here it is. I found it."

Burke reached down and plucked the sealed envelope from his hand. In square block letters, it read: "Dylan Carlisle. Proof."

"Where did you find this?" Burke asked.

"Tied to a fence post in the south pasture." A huge grin split his face. "I went to feed the herd and there it was. I didn't open it. On account of it was addressed to Dylan."

Dylan patted his shoulder. "You did the right thing."

Actually, Burke would have preferred having the envelope left in place. There might have been clues, like footprints or the way the knots were tied. "Agent Silverman is going to open the envelope. He'll need to handle it carefully in case there are fingerprints or DNA."

In the dining room, they stood waiting while Silverman— wearing latex gloves—slit the edge of the envelope and removed a photograph.

"A Polaroid," Silverman said. "You don't see many of these anymore. Not with digital cameras."

The picture showed Nicole with a determined smile on her face. She held the front section of today's newspaper.

"Proof of life," Carolyn whispered.

Silverman placed the photo on the table. "Don't touch it. I doubt we'll find fingerprints, but we might get lucky."

As the others crowded around to take a closer look at the photo, Burke moved to the end of the table where Corelli was still monitoring phone calls. In a low voice, he issued instructions. "That's a Denver newspaper. Find the delivery time in this area, the locations for delivery and a list of local subscribers. Get the sheriff to canvass stores where the paper is sold."

"Got it." Corelli gave a nod.

"Is there any way to set up continual surveillance on that south pasture? It's about thirty acres."

"I could do it with satellite," he said. "I don't have that kind of equipment here, but I could interface with Denver. Don't get your hopes up, Burke. The mountains are hard to search. It depends on sight lines and location."

Burke grabbed the red-haired cowboy who was still beaming proudly. "I need for you to think carefully."

"Sure thing."

"Describe the terrain in the area where you found the envelope."

"It was up by the trees. I wouldn't have noticed at all except for this." He reached into his pocket and pulled out a long yellow scarf. "I saw it flapping in the wind."

"It's Nicole's." Dylan took the scarf from him and gently caressed the material. "I bought it for her myself."

Technically, the scarf was evidence and needed to be treated as such. But Burke doubted there would be any viable prints or DNA after being stuffed in the cowboy's pocket. There was no harm in allowing Dylan to cling to this scrap.

Turning away, he glanced at Corelli. "How about surveillance in the south pasture?"

"The best surveillance for this much land is probably a helicopter."

"I've already arranged for a chopper." He'd made that call last night. His superior had objected to the expense, but he reminded them that the FBI was investigating this kidnapping at the request of the governor.

He checked his wristwatch. "They should be here by noon. They're also bringing tracking dogs."

Corelli raised an eyebrow. "Things are about to get real exciting around here."

"Is there anything else you can do with computers? What about thermal imaging?"

"I brought a heat-sensing camera with me. It's long range. I can scan from about fifty yards away."

"That might come in handy."

Carolyn appeared at his side. "Come with me."

She led him through the front door and into the yard. When they were out of earshot of the cowboy guard posted on the porch, she whispered, "Nicole was giving us a clue."

"Enlighten me."

"Her hands. The way she was holding the newspaper." She illustrated. "On one side, she held it with her thumb and forefinger. On the other, she had three fingers outstretched."

He studied her hands for a moment. "A circle on one side. And the letter *M* on the other."

The Circle M Ranch, headquarters for the Sons of Freedom, was the clue.

"It's time," Carolyn said tersely. "We need to pay Sam Logan a visit."

Chapter Nine

Carolyn knew how to control her emotions. Since childhood, she'd been trained to keep her outbursts to herself. *Never cry. Never shout. Don't even laugh too loud.*

But the rage she felt as she took the turnoff leading to the Circle M surged too close to the surface. Her pulse raced like a stampede. If Sam Logan had done this terrible thing, if he'd snatched Nicole, she'd kill that bastard with her bare hands.

She pulled onto the shoulder and parked.

"What's wrong?" Burke asked.

"I need to get a grip." Fiery embers exploded behind her eyelids. She could barely see straight. "I'm fighting mad."

He removed his sunglasses. "Look at me, Carolyn."

As if that would do any good. Burke wasn't the most calming presence in the world. "Leave me alone. I'll manage."

But he cupped her chin and turned her face toward him. She had no choice but to stare into his dark eyes. His gaze held her. In the morning sunlight, his irises were a rich, chestnut brown. His features seemed set in granite.

"How do you do it?" she asked. "In your job, you deal with bad guys all the time. How do you keep from lashing out?"

"Do you hunt?"

"Only with a camera."

A smile twitched his lips. "You grew up on a ranch and you don't hunt?"

"I don't like killing animals. What's your point?"

"My hunting analogy was supposed to make you think of focus. Emotion comes from your right brain. The left brain is logical. If you start thinking with logic, planning what move you're going to make next, you'll pull some of the focus away from your anger."

"Planning," she said. "I'm good at planning."

"Think about what you're going to say to Logan." His voice was calm. "Concentrate on what steps we need to take. Once we're inside the SOF compound, we need to assess the area. Make a mental map of the buildings. If they're holding Nicole, where is she? Who would know where she is? Somebody must be bringing her food and water. Which person is most likely to help us?"

"Think of the end goal."

"We need names," he said. "Usually, I can count on Corelli to pull up this kind of information, but the SOF is too insignificant to be on the FBI radar. If we have individual names, we can run them through our database."

"I'm good at remembering names."

"Me, too." He caressed her chin. "You're trembling."

"Holding back my anger." She needed an immediate release—a way to express the raging emotion that rushed through her veins.

"How can I help?"

Without thinking of the consequences, she slid out from behind the steering wheel and across the bench seat of the truck. She moved into his arms, pressing against him.

They kissed, hard and fierce. She willingly surrendered to her passion. Her body arched toward him. The pressure of his mouth against hers sparked a fire within her. It felt good.

A controlled burn. Like the kind the forest rangers set to stop a wider conflagration.

Her lips parted. She drew his tongue into her mouth. Her senses went wild. Every cell in her body responded to him.

When he separated from her, she was breathing in gasps. She hadn't cooled down. In fact, the opposite. But this fire made her stronger, braver, better. She felt like she could take on the world. One creepy ex-boyfriend like Sam Logan was no problem.

She turned the key in the ignition and drove to the gate outside the Circle M. Between sturdy gateposts, a double-wide gate—about five feet tall with horizontal white slats—was latched and locked with a chain. A dusty-looking cowboy ambled toward them, rifle in hand.

Carolyn parked at the side of the road, hopped down from the truck and strode toward him. "Tell Sam Logan that Carolyn Carlisle has come calling."

"Don't care," he said defiantly. "Nobody gets in. No trespassing."

"Use your cell phone." She wasn't about to let some half-baked guard stand in her way. "Tell Logan I'm here."

Burke had gotten out of the truck and stood behind her. The cowboy glanced toward him, then back to her. "I'll call."

She and Burke stepped back. His kiss still burned on her lips, and she was incredibly attuned to his presence. If they'd been alone, she would have been all over this tall, handsome fed, but that wasn't an option. She was here to gather information from the SOF, to find Nicole.

She leaned against the hood of the truck and watched as the cowboy returned to his guard position and took out his cell phone. Burke stood beside her.

"Logan will be out here in a minute," she said. "You were right about his ego. He won't be able to resist bragging about how he's the big shot leader of a gang of crazies."

"After he shows, what's your plan?"

"I'll get him to invite us in."

Though she kept her focus on logic, she couldn't think of a single rational reason why Logan should open his doors to her. Her method of persuasion had to be based on emotion. She'd mention their past relationship. "Have you ever been in love, Burke?"

"Have you?"

"You're doing that negotiator thing," she said. "Answering my question with a question of your own."

"Yes, I've been in love. It changed my life." Through his sunglasses, he looked at her. "And you?"

"Not with Logan. When we were together, it seemed like the right time to get married and settle down on the ranch. But I didn't love him."

"How did he feel about you?"

"It might have been love." She'd had years to analyze this failed relationship. "Or he might have been in love with the idea of getting a piece of Carlisle Ranch. My father liked him. If we'd married, Logan would be a rich man today."

"Maybe," Burke said, "he was using you."

A rueful awareness seeped into her thoughts. Years ago, when she broke up with Logan, he'd seemed shattered. He'd tried everything to win her back. "You think he was only after my money?"

"It fits the profile for a cult leader—someone who's manipulative, egotistical and uncaring about the needs of others. With SOF as his power base, Logan has found a way to use these people and, apparently, to provide himself with an income."

"All these years," she said. "I've felt guilty for rejecting him."

"Which is how he wanted you to feel."

The road on the opposite side of the gate led to a barn. A stand of trees blocked the view of the house and the other outbuildings. Logan rode toward them on that road. A majestic sight on his pure white horse. His dark brown leather vest looked like a doublet. He was bareheaded, and his long blond hair flowed past his shoulders and glistened in the sunlight.

At the gate, he reined his horse and looked down at her. In the six years since she'd seen him, she'd forgotten how truly good-looking he was. Not as tall as Burke, but broad-shouldered and lean. His features were as picture-perfect as a movie star's. No wonder she'd fallen for him.

Carolyn ambled toward the gate. She climbed the slats to the top rung, making her nearly as tall as Logan on horse-back. She looked directly into his baby blue eyes. "Well? Aren't you going to invite me inside?"

"You look good, Carolyn. City life agrees with you."

Instead of giving him the satisfaction of telling him that he was still as gorgeous as ever, she patted his horse's neck. "This is a fine-looking stallion."

"I'm keeping him for stud."

"Is that what you do here?" She bit the inside of her cheek to keep from smirking. "Stud service?"

"We train horses. One of my men is Butch Thurgood, a rodeo champion bronc rider."

She'd never heard of Thurgood, but Carolyn didn't keep up with the latest rodeo news. "I'd like to meet him."

"I remember when you used to be the queen of the barrel race." He glanced toward the guard with the rifle. "Back in the day, me and Carolyn were a couple. I considered marrying this young woman, joining with her to become part of the all-powerful Carlisle family. Imagine that. Me, being a corporate, capitalist stooge?" He gave a completely phony laugh. "I came to my senses and saw the error in my ways."

Spare me the sermon. "Last night, when my brother and the sheriff came by, your men wouldn't allow them to enter."

"We don't recognize the law represented by Sheriff Trainer." He looked past her to Burke. "Or by your friend over there. FBI?"

"Special Agent J. D. Burke." He took a step forward. "I haven't come here to accuse you, Logan."

"I don't believe you."

"I don't have a search warrant or a judge's order," Burke said. "Carolyn and I are merely looking for information. We want to talk to your people. To find out if anyone saw anything suspicious last night when Nicole Carlisle was kidnapped."

Logan sneered. "The government and the agents of the government are liars."

"I'm not armed." Burke held his coat open, showing his empty shoulder holster. Apparently, he'd left his handgun in the truck. "I just want to ask questions."

"We're neighbors," Carolyn said. "Aren't neighbors supposed to help each other in times of need?"

"Carlisle Ranch represents the establishment. You and your brother are the nemesis of freedom."

She tamped down her anger. It wouldn't do any good to insult him. "You knew my father, Logan. He liked you, believed in you."

"Sterling Carlisle was a good man."

"I'm not your enemy." *Not yet, anyway.* "Please let me come inside. I'm worried about Nicole. Maybe one of your people saw something. Maybe they can help me find her."

He dismounted, passed the reins to the guard and unlocked the gate. With a sweeping gesture, he announced, "I have nothing to hide."

Entering the Circle M, she strode down the road, flanked by Logan and Burke.

In her younger days, she'd been satisfied in a relationship

with a handsome cowboy like Logan. Now, she needed more complexity, more depth and a hundred times more honesty— qualities Burke had in abundance.

In a conversational tone, Burke asked, "How many people live here at the Circle M?"

"Gathering information for your FBI database?"

"We keep track of groups like yours," Burke admitted. "But I'll tell you the truth, Logan. We don't have a listing for Sons of Freedom. You're not dangerous enough to be on the radar."

"Just because you haven't heard of me," Logan said, "doesn't mean I'm not important."

"The FBI has bigger fish to fry. Terrorists. Hijackers. The Russian Mafia. Those are the real enemies of the state."

Logan puffed out his chest, possibly hoping to inflate his bruised ego. "You have no idea who you're talking to."

"How many people have you got here? Ten or fifteen?"

"Twice that. Twelve men and fifteen women and children."

"Husbands and wives?" Burke asked.

"We don't believe in the overregulated institution of marriage."

"How does that work?" Carolyn asked.

"If a couple chooses to be monogamous, their decision is respected. If not, that's accepted."

"Are you monogamous?"

"Not at present." His blue-eyed gaze slid over her body. "Sorry, Carolyn. You already missed your chance to be with me."

Silently, she thanked her lucky stars.

Burke asked, "How much acreage do you have?"

"Enough to live on. Nate Miller is trying to sell the rest of his land. Hasn't had much luck."

"And how do you pay the bills?"

"The Sons of Freedom are establishing a new way of life, based on the real foundations of America. Self-sufficiency, simplicity and old-fashioned hard work." He glanced toward Carolyn. "I'm writing a book."

The World According to Peabrain? "I didn't know you could write."

"A man can do anything he sets his mind to."

They were within sight of the main buildings. Compared to the Carlisle ranch house, the Circle M was plain and shabby. The house was a simple, one-story structure with beat-up siding the color of soured milk and a shingled roof in need of repair. The other outbuildings were equally ugly. A shiny, new double-wide mobile home was parked near the ramshackle barn.

She saw two women walking together. Each of the women's hair was pulled back in a bun. Beneath their jackets, shapeless dresses hung to their ankles.

"Interesting fashion statement," she said. "You say that a man can do anything. What about a woman?"

"Our women are respected and revered," he said. "They're the glue that holds civilization together. They raise our children, provide sustenance and create a healthful environment."

To Carolyn's ears, his language was code for cooking, cleaning and popping out babies. "That doesn't sound like much of a life."

"Not to someone like you." His upper lip curled in a sneer. "A career woman."

What did I ever see in this jerk? His golden hair, broad shoulders and perfect features didn't make up for his ridiculous, misogynistic ideas. "You haven't changed a bit."

"Because I've always been right." His sneer turned into a dazzling white smile. "Our women are happy here. You'll have plenty of opportunity to talk to them and hear for yourself."

"Wonderful." The way she figured, some of these respected, revered ladies had to be dissatisfied. They were probably the best lead to finding Nicole.

Two cowboys stalked toward them. Unlike their leader, they weren't smiling.

Logan motioned to the taller of the two and issued an order. "Escort Carolyn to the kitchen. She can help the ladies prepare lunch."

She hadn't come here to peel potatoes. "If you don't mind, I'd rather—"

"I do mind," Logan said. "We have a division of labor. The men discuss business. And the ladies…"

"Prepare lunch?"

"I'm glad you understand. Run along now."

Nobody, but nobody, told her to run along. She was the CEO of an international corporation. She negotiated with heads of state. She knew the governor.

But this wasn't about her. She was here to get information about Nicole. And the women would probably be more sympathetic than the men.

Baring her teeth in a false smile, she said, "You boys have a good time. Don't tire yourself out with too much heavy thinking."

She pivoted and strode toward the ranch house.

Chapter Ten

Burke watched as Carolyn stormed toward the house. The cowboy who accompanied her tried to take her arm and she yanked away so fast that he stepped back, giving her plenty of space. *Smart move.* After Logan's women-belong-in-the-kitchen comments, Carolyn was volatile.

Though she could probably take care of herself, Burke still didn't like the idea of being separated from her. When entering a dangerous situation, partners should stick together.

"I see the way you're looking at her," Logan said.

"I'm concerned," Burke said. "She's a victim. A kidnapping hurts the family almost as much as it hurts the person who has been abducted."

"Carolyn's a fine looking woman."

Burke lied, "She's not my type. She'd just as soon kick my ass as kiss me."

The short cowboy who stood with them chuckled. Burke introduced himself and got the other man's name—Wesley Tindall. If he got enough names for Corelli to investigate through criminal databases, they might have a clue about what actually went on at the Circle M.

He looked toward the bunkhouse where two guys were working on a huge piece of machinery. "Installing a generator?"

"I told you. We want to be self-sufficient. Except for the house, all our heat comes from propane."

"But you still have to buy the propane tanks."

"We have a big stockpile."

Burke cringed inside. If it came to a showdown with the SOF, a stray bullet could penetrate the stockpile of propane tanks and cause an explosion that would rock the mountains. "Let's get down to business, Logan. I'd like to interview your men. Someone might have noticed something unusual last night."

"Like what?"

Logan's voice sounded suspicious. The best way to get information from this guy was to constantly feed his giant ego. "Damned if I know. This case has me baffled. You might have some ideas."

The handsome blond cowboy shrugged. "Ask your questions."

"First, I'd like to get my bearings." Burke took a couple of steps and looked beyond the bunkhouse to the west. "I'm a city guy. Pretty much lost in all this wide-open space."

"I've lived here all my life," Logan said smugly. "I know every rock and tree."

Burke deliberately pointed in the wrong direction. "Is the Carlisle Ranch that way?"

"Not even close." Logan aimed his forefinger like a gun. "The house is over there—only about four miles away as the crow flies. Following roads, it's more than that."

"And where's the Widow Grant's place?"

"Do you see that break in the hills? It's an old Indian trail. Widow Grant lives just south of there."

Carolyn had mentioned the Indian Trail at the edge of the south pasture where all the sabotage had taken place. Burke wondered if it was significant.

Logan asked, "Why are you interested?"

"Nicole was kidnapped by two men on horseback somewhere between the Widow Grant's place and the Carlisle ranch house. Do you think the kidnappers came this way? Toward the Circle M?"

"Our land is fenced with barbed wire. Nobody came through here on horseback."

"Why is it fenced? You're not running cattle."

"Horses," Logan said. "We keep them in the barn at night and let them run free during the day."

Looking toward the barn, Burke noticed a surveillance camera attached above the door. Another lens was visible on the mobile home. No attempt had been made to hide the cameras. "You have electronic surveillance."

"State-of-the-art, equipped with night vision," Logan drawled. "Some people don't like us. We need to keep ourselves protected."

Were the fences and the surveillance used to keep people out? Or to keep the Sons of Freedom in? "Any chance that I could take a look at the footage from last night? The cameras might have picked up something that would help me find Nicole."

Logan showed no sign of being worried. "What time was she kidnapped?"

"Before dark. Somewhere between five and six o'clock."

"You're out of luck," Logan said. "During the day, we have enough people around to make sure nobody breaks in. We generally don't turn on the surveillance until after dinner. That's around seven or eight. Too late to show anything that would be useful to you."

He'd answered quickly, almost as if he knew the time of Nicole's kidnapping before Burke had told him. Was she here? In addition to the mobile home, the house, two bunkhouses and the barn, there were several smaller buildings.

Storage sheds. A smokehouse. Other motor homes and trailers. There was probably a root cellar under the house.

Altogether, there were too many damn places for Logan to hide a kidnap victim…if she was still alive.

IN THE RANCH HOUSE KITCHEN, Carolyn was the only woman wearing jeans and boots. Her clothing wasn't the only thing that made her different. She stood taller. She had energy, fire and ambition.

These three women—dressed in shapeless frocks, limp sweaters and leggings—seemed like the life had been drained from them. After they politely introduced themselves using only their first names, they returned to their chores, quietly performing their tasks with dedication and zero enthusiasm. Like prisoners, they seemed robbed of their will, caught in an endless cycle of boredom. What could possibly cause these young women to come to this place? Why did they stay?

"I hear you raise horses," Carolyn said. "This would be a wonderful afternoon for a ride."

"The men handle the horses," said the tall blonde who appeared to be in charge of the kitchen. Her name was Sharon, and Carolyn guessed they were the same age—mid-thirties. The other women were at least a decade younger.

"We get to brush and curry the horses," peeped a very pregnant woman who had identified herself as Sunny. She waddled across the kitchen floor with all the grace of a Mack Truck. Her formerly blond hair had grown out several inches at the roots.

"Do the men let you muck out the stables?" Carolyn asked.

"Sometimes."

"Lucky you." Carolyn laughed into a pall of silence.

There was about as much vitality in this group as a gathering of tree slugs. Somehow, she needed to get them talking, to find out if they'd seen or heard anything that might lead to Nicole.

Sauntering across the gray tiled kitchen floor, she zeroed in on Lisa—a scrawny brunette with tattoos of thorns around both wrists. "You seem familiar," Carolyn said. "Are you from around here?"

"No, ma'am." She concentrated on chopping a zucchini into one-inch cubes. "I grew up in Denver."

"That's where I live most of the time. Maybe we met there," Carolyn said. Remembering Burke's suggestion that they get names that could be run through the FBI database, she asked, "What's your last name?"

Sharon cleared her throat. "When we joined the SOF, we gave up our last names. This is a new life. A fresh start."

Sunny teased, "Lisa wants her last name to be Richter. She wants to be Mrs. Pete Richter."

"No, I don't." The paring knife in Lisa's hand trembled. "I don't like Pete. Not that way."

"You don't have to pretend anymore. Not since your sister took off." Sunny explained to Carolyn, "Both Lisa and her sister had a thing for Pete."

"But your sister left?" Carolyn questioned.

"Yes." Lisa centered another zucchini on the chopping block.

"Do you know where she went?"

A single tear slid down Lisa's cheek. "She's gone."

"Forget about her," Sharon said harshly. "Your sister was a fool. She wasn't suited to our lifestyle."

Carolyn rested her elbows on the counter beside Lisa and spoke quietly. "I've lost someone, too. My sister-in-law, Nicole. Yesterday, she was knocked unconscious and kidnapped. I'm trying to—"

"I know who you are," Sharon said. "Carolyn Carlisle of

the fancy-pants Carlisle Ranch. You own half the county. Why should we help you?"

"Because it's the decent thing to do. Like it or not, we're your neighbors. We need your help."

In her business, Carolyn was accustomed to tense negotiations with international distributors and local ranchers. These three women were the most hostile group she'd ever encountered.

"Let me tell you about Nicole," Carolyn said. "She's a good and decent person. She's worked all her life as a large-animal veterinarian. The first time I met her, she'd spent the night in the stall with a horse that had colic. She was exhausted, barely able to walk. But she was grinning because the horse recovered. A good person."

"We don't care," Sharon said.

Carolyn continued, "Nicole married my brother five years ago. They're deeply in love, trying to have a baby." She went to stand beside Sunny. "It's hard for Nicole to get pregnant. She's had internal injuries."

Sunny frowned. "That's too bad."

"When are you due?"

"In a couple of weeks, I think."

"You're seeing a doctor, aren't you? Or a midwife?"

Sharon stepped between them, positioning herself as a shield and precluding any further conversation. This tall blonde, who would have been stunning with makeup, looked Carolyn in the eye. "You should leave. Now."

Her pupils were dilated, and she licked the corner of her mouth. Was she on drugs? Carolyn said, "Logan wanted me to help you with lunch preparations."

"Fine," Sharon said. "Then you need an apron."

"Right." *I need an apron like I need a toe growing out of my forehead.*

THE INTERIOR of Logan's double-wide mobile home was an office with fairly high-end equipment. Apparently, the SOF goal to live like pioneers didn't preclude the use of computers, scanners and GPS mapping instruments.

Burke operated under the assumption that Logan's survivalist philosophy was a convenient cover story for some other endeavor. Probably criminal and lucrative. If Corelli could hack into these computers, they could decipher the real basis for the SOF in about five minutes.

Under Logan's supervision, he'd spoken to ten different men, most of whom were typical taciturn cowboys. The notable exception was a guy with a thick Brooklyn accent who admitted that the only cowboys he'd seen before moving to Colorado were in the movies.

"That's everybody," Logan said. He sat behind his big oak desk with his chair tilted back and his boots propped up on top. "Like I told you, nobody saw anything out of the ordinary."

"You said there were twelve men." Though Burke hadn't taken notes, he'd memorized every name. "I counted only ten. And I didn't meet that rodeo star you mentioned. Butch Thurgood?"

Logan's gaze sharpened. He didn't like being caught in a lie. "Butch and Pete are in Denver for a couple of days."

"And what about the ladies? I'd like to talk to them, too."

"The women keep busy. They didn't see anything."

"Never can tell," Burke said. "Sometimes, women notice more details than men."

Logan stuck out his lower lip. Petulant, like a child. "I don't encourage gossiping and nosiness."

Or independent thinking? For the life of him, Burke couldn't figure out what Carolyn had ever seen in this petty tyrant. Sure, Logan was handsome, but so was a tiger before it ripped your arm out of the socket.

Logan continued, "The women who live here are grateful to have a roof over their heads. Some of them came from the streets. SOF is a fresh start for them, and they're happy to be obedient and hardworking."

Burke sensed an undercurrent to this speech. Was there dissatisfaction among the ladies? A rebellion brewing? If he wanted to find out what was really going on inside the SOF, he needed to listen to the women. Maybe Carolyn was having some luck in talking to them.

He rose from the straight-back chair beside the desk. He'd already affixed one bug under the lip of Logan's desk, but he had another listening device that he wanted to get inside the house. "Let's pick up Carolyn at the house, and you can show us around."

"Nothing special to see."

"Looks like you've added a lot of improvements."

"Nothing special," Logan repeated.

"What about a meeting place?" He was hoping for a big room with slogans on the wall or other traceable clues. "It's like you're running a little town here."

"That's right," he drawled. "And I'm the mayor."

"Where do the kids go to school? Where do you all sit down to eat?" *Where's your stash of propane tanks? Where would you hide a kidnapping victim?*

"We meet where we eat in the men's bunkhouse. It's nothing fancy, just a big plain room with tables. There's a wall that separates the meeting area from the sleeping area."

"And a television?"

"Why would you think that? We're trying to lead a simple life here. Like the noble American pioneers who settled the West."

And wiped out the native population? Burke wasn't impressed with the phony rhetoric. "I assumed you had television because I saw a dish on top of the house."

"We're connected to the outside world. At times, it's necessary to know what's happening." He shrugged. "Maybe, we watch the occasional football game."

Finally, Burke found common ground. "I have a friend with a skybox at Invesco Field. If you come into Denver, I'd like to take you to a Bronco game."

"Yeah?" Logan grinned. "A big guy like you probably played football."

"I did."

"Me, too. Quarterback. If I'd been on a halfway decent team, I would have made all state."

From outside the office, he heard the whir of helicopter blades. The FBI search team must be arriving at the Carlisle Ranch.

The moment of friendly bonding over football vanished as Logan glanced up. "One of yours?"

"Probably. I requested assistance. Choppers and dogs."

"Don't expect to enter this property again."

"Come on, Logan. We were getting along so well."

"We shoot trespassers." He pulled his long legs down from the desktop and stood in one smooth move. "We're done here."

WEARING A PLAIN MUSLIN APRON with old stains across the midsection, Carolyn looked up at the sound of the approaching helicopter. She felt like running into the yard and waving her arms, screaming to be rescued from the doldrums of the Circle M kitchen. This had been the most frustrating half hour of her life—peeling potatoes and trying to get these women to talk.

Hoping to engage their sympathies, she'd told several

stories about Nicole. The only one who responded was the pregnant woman, Sunny.

The other two women, Sharon and Lisa, became even more sullen. At one point, Lisa sat at the table with her hands folded neatly and stared, unmoving, for a solid thirty seconds. When Carolyn asked if she was okay, Sharon informed her that Lisa was praying. Drugged was more like it.

Carolyn set down her potato peeler on the countertop and wiped her hands on the hem of the apron, being careful not to touch the prior stains. "I'm finished."

"Me, too," Sunny said. "Gather up your peelings in that rubber tub and we'll take it all out to the compost heap. Is that okay, Sharon?"

The blond woman nodded. Slowly.

Outside the back door, Carolyn walked beside Sunny toward a fenced-off area that would be a vegetable garden in the springtime.

"You have to help me." Sunny paused for a moment and scribbled on a scrap of paper with a pencil stub. "Please."

"Yes, whatever you need."

"Don't let them see you talking to me. Keep smiling."

Carolyn tossed her head and smiled, trying her best to look utterly mindless. "What's up?"

"I've got to get out of here before my baby is born."

"They won't let you leave?" Carolyn asked.

"I know too much. Can't explain now." She dumped her peelings onto a stinking compost pile, stood up straight and rested her hand on her huge belly. "Lisa's sister didn't disappear. She didn't leave. They killed her."

Dear God, this place is a nightmare. "What about Nicole?"

"Sorry, I don't know anything about her." She glanced over her shoulder. "Here comes Logan. Pretend like you're shaking my hand."

Carolyn did as she asked. With a huge smile, Sunny whispered, "Meet me at midnight tonight."

Carolyn pocketed the scrap of paper Sunny had passed to her. "Always glad to help."

Chapter Eleven

The most dangerous aspect of any incursion into hostile territory was the exit strategy. As Burke watched Carolyn saunter toward him and Logan, he hoped she wouldn't do anything to provoke retaliation. They needed to get the hell away from the Circle M.

Through his sunglasses, he noted the positions taken by three of the men he'd met. All were scanning the skies for the chopper. All were armed, and these weren't the type of rifles used by casual sportsmen. The Sons of Freedom had broken out the automatic assault weapons and sniper rifles. Evidence of this brand of firepower combined with the stockpile of propane tanks made the SOF an extremely volatile enemy—a fact that didn't seem to concern Carolyn in the least.

Without breaking stride, she unfastened the strings of her apron and peeled it off. She slapped the fabric against Logan's chest. "Thanks for your hospitality."

"It's good for you to work in a kitchen for once." He signaled to one of his men, who responded quickly. "Escort our guests to the front gate."

Burke made an attempt to keep the tenuous line of communication open. "I appreciate your cooperation." He held out his hand for a friendly shake. "This is an impressive operation."

Logan turned his back and walked away. Over his shoulder, he said, "Get the hell out."

Carolyn called after him, "Hey, Sam."

It was the first time she'd used his given name, which Burke thought was an effective use of a negotiating tool. Carolyn was sharp. In one word, she'd reminded him of their prior relationship.

He faced them. "What is it, Carolyn?"

"There's no call to be rude. The pioneers had a tradition of Western hospitality. When someone offers the hand of friendship, it's not right to turn away."

With his men watching, he couldn't be churlish. He grasped Burke's hand. In a low voice, he said, "We're not friends."

Logan turned to Carolyn with hand extended. When she placed her hand in his, he pulled her close. "You hurt me once, honey. This time, it's my turn."

"Is that a threat?"

"Not if you stay out of my way."

As he and Carolyn walked up the road to the gate, Burke held his silence. Earlier he'd counseled Carolyn about containing her outrage. Now he had to apply those same restrictions to himself. *It won't do any good to explode.* He was smarter than that, better than that.

But Logan's smarmy attitude ticked him off. That blond son of a bitch with the perfect features was nothing more than a cowboy con man, hiding behind phony rhetoric about the noble American pioneers.

When Burke slid into the passenger seat of the truck, he immediately opened the glove compartment and retrieved his gun. The weight of it felt good in his hand.

"Your ex-boyfriend is one of the coldest, most calculating liars I've ever met, and that's saying a lot. I've dealt with terrorists and serial killers. Sam Logan disgusts me more."

"More than a serial killer?" Carolyn started the truck.

"Logan isn't crazy. He knows the difference between right and wrong. And he consciously chooses wrong."

She wheeled around in a U-turn and drove away from the Circle M. "What happens next?"

"When we get back to the ranch house, all hell is going to be breaking loose." Burke holstered his gun. "I'll need to coordinate choppers and dogs and a half-baked patrol of cowboys with rifles. Not to mention keeping everything quiet so the traitor can't report our every move to Logan."

"You're sure that Logan is the kidnapper?"

"Not a hundred percent." Logan's alibi was the SOF. They could all stand in a circle and swear that they were all together at the time of the kidnapping. Which didn't necessarily mean they were lying. "I'm certain he's engaged in some kind of criminal activity. Maybe he's got a meth lab hidden in one of the outbuildings. Maybe he's doing some kind of smuggling."

"His men were carrying some pretty fancy weapons. He could be trafficking in guns."

"Could be." As Burke started his left brain thinking, his anger faded. "In any case, he's using the SOF as a cover for himself and his sorry gang of outlaws."

"And the women?"

"He never lets them get involved in business, right?"

"Right," she said.

"I doubt they know what's going on. The women and children are, basically, hostages. Logan is using them as a human shield. The FBI can't come after him with guns blazing while there's a danger to innocent women and children."

Though they were still a mile away from the Carlisle

Ranch, she pulled over to the side of the road and parked. "I need to talk to you about the women. I got the impression that some of them might be on drugs."

"Logan told me that some of the women came from the street, which I assume means they were either hookers or runaways." The thought of Logan approaching some poor soul down on her luck and luring her to his ranch revved up Burke's temper again. "He said they were lucky to have a roof over their heads."

"Not lucky at all," Carolyn said. "One of them was murdered."

He hadn't expected this bombshell. "Murdered?"

"One of them talked to me. Her name is Sunny. Can't be more than twenty years old, and she's pregnant. She wants to get away from the Circle M." She dug into her jeans pocket and took out a scrap of paper. "She wants me to meet her at this location. Tonight. At midnight."

He read the scribbled words on the scrap. "West field. By the pines."

"She mentioned a name, Pete Richter. Maybe she was trying to tell me he's the killer."

He recognized the name. "Logan said that Richter and Thurgood weren't at the ranch. They could have taken Nicole somewhere else. Or they could be guarding her in one of those outbuildings."

"We need to get back in there," she said. "We need to search."

Easier said than done. Following the legal parameters for a search with a warrant was out of the question. And Logan would never give up without a fight.

The only way Burke could search for Nicole was to send in an assault team. And risk the lives of the women and children at the Circle M? Even if it meant rescuing Nicole, he couldn't put others in danger.

As BURKE HAD EXPECTED, the pastoral setting of the Carlisle ranch house had erupted into chaos. Polly was trying to serve lunch. The ranch hands with their walkie-talkies were still patrolling. An FBI team with bloodhounds and cadaver dogs had arrived. And the chopper pilot stood waiting for instruction.

Burke's first order of business was to delegate. He put Agent Silverman in charge of coordinating these various operations.

Neville and the cowboy protection patrol would keep up their surveillance with one major difference: they had to move out of Dylan's office and into the bunkhouse. As soon as they left, grumbling with every step, the noise level in the house returned to something near normal.

While Silverman prepared to deploy the chopper and the dogs with grid maps of the area, Burke took Carolyn and her brother back to her bedroom sanctuary. In the relative quiet, he filled Dylan in on what they'd discovered at Logan's compound.

Dylan turned to his sister. "What did you ever see in that jerk?"

"You liked him," she reminded. "Both you and dad were ready to march me down the aisle to marry him."

"Because I didn't want to see you move to New York and turn into a corporate witch."

"Like Mom?"

He exhaled in a whoosh. "Let's not paw through that old garbage, okay?"

"Have you called her? Told her about Nicole?"

Burke stepped in before their conversation deteriorated into what appeared to be an old family argument. "Dylan, I want you to work with Silverman to coordinate the search efforts. The FBI teams need backup from your men who know the territory. You should make those assignments."

"Got it," he said.

"Keep in mind that we've got a traitor in our midst. Don't tell any of your men about obtaining the ransom or our suspicions about the Circle M."

"What about the ransom?" he asked. "That money is going to get here any minute. How are we going to pick it up and still keep it a secret?"

"I've got it covered," Burke said. "It's better that you don't know the details."

Identical pairs of green eyes stared at him in disbelief.

"A million dollars in cash," Carolyn said. "*Our cash*. We need to know."

Clearly, she had a point. Burke quickly explained, "The ransom is being flown to Delta. We already have two Longbridge Security guards at the hospital watching over the man who was shot, and I figured—"

"How is he doing?" Carolyn interrupted. "Jesse Longbridge? Is he conscious?"

"Not yet. Technically, he's not in a coma because he's responsive to external stimuli. But he's still not awake." Which was unfortunate on many levels. If Jesse woke up and could give them an identification, they'd at least know who they were looking for. He continued, "Those two guards are picking up the ransom and keeping an eye on it."

Carolyn and Dylan exchanged a glance. Both nodded.

"I trust Longbridge Security," Dylan said. He headed toward the bedroom door. With his hand on the knob, he paused. "I didn't mean to snap at you, Carolyn."

"Same here."

When the door closed behind him a hush descended.

The atmosphere in her bedroom, though quiet, was charged with suppressed emotion. She'd perched on the edge of the bed. Her hair was out of the ponytail, tumbling loose to her shoulders. She tilted her head back and stretched, arching her throat. "Dylan never forgave Mom for leaving the ranch. He couldn't see how stifled she was. The ranching life isn't for everybody."

"Is it for you?"

"I have the best of both worlds. In Denver, I'm Corporate Sally. Out here? Annie Oakley."

He sat beside her on the bed—a move he might regret. Developing a relationship with the victim's family in a hostage situation was nearly inevitable, but empathy didn't include the kind of passionate kiss they'd shared in the truck. He'd already gone too far with her.

When she looked up at him with those intriguing green eyes, his discipline and training ebbed. He wanted to make love to this woman. When she reached up to stroke his cheek, he caught her hand.

"We can't do this," he said. Yet he didn't release her hand.

"Which part of me scares you the most?" she asked. "The businesswoman or the rancher?"

"Well, let's see. The CEO might drive me to ruin. But Annie Oakley might fire a blast of buckshot into my ass." He raised her hand to his lips and kissed her fingertips. "I'm not scared, Carolyn. Are you?"

"Not a bit."

In any other situation, making love would be the next natural step. He was drawn to her. The magnetism was palpable, so strong that he began to sweat. He forced himself to stand, still holding her hand. "We have a lot to do."

He pulled her to her feet and into his embrace. Just one kiss, he told himself. One more kiss wouldn't hurt.

But she stepped back. "I don't like unfinished business, Burke. Once I start on a project, I close the deal."

"Meaning?"

"I want more from you than just one kiss."

And he'd be happy to deliver. *The whole enchilada, baby.*
"I suggest we continue this negotiation at a later time."

"Suits me."

When she left the bedroom, he followed. He had about a
hundred things to do, but his focus at that moment was
simple. He couldn't take his eyes off her long legs and round
bottom in her snug jeans. Denim had never looked so good.

AFTER CAROLYN REALIZED there was nothing useful she could
do in the house, she stepped outside to take a breather. Her
path led, predictably, to the corral outside the barn where she
climbed onto the fence railing and gave a low whistle.

Elvis approached, swinging his hips. At the fence, he
leaned his neck toward her, welcoming a hug.

Mindful that someone might be listening, she kept her
voice low. "Here's my problem, Elvis. Burke is just about the
sexiest man I've ever seen in my whole life. He makes me
want to drag him into the hayloft and make love."

Elvis nodded.

"It's totally inappropriate."

Not to mention heartless. How could she be fantasizing
about lovemaking while Nicole was being held captive and her
brother was going through hell? A chill took root in her
heart—a dark cold that had nothing to do with the December
weather.

In the proof-of-life photo, Nicole appeared to be unin-
jured. Was she tied up? Chained? Were they holding her in
a dark cell? "Oh God, Elvis. What am I going to do?"

He shook his head, and his black mane flopped over the
white blaze on his forehead. Just like a real shrink, Elvis
always turned the question back to her. Rightly so. The
answers were usually within her.

But this time there was very little Carolyn could do. She'd

arranged for the ransom to be delivered, and she'd made contact with Sunny, who might be the key to getting inside Logan's compound. Other than that, she was helpless.

And what am I going to do about Burke? Clearly, her attraction to him was a way of distracting her from terrible thoughts about the kidnapping. If fear was cold, the way she felt about Burke was a bonfire.

"It's not like I want a relationship," she confided to Elvis. Though she and Burke both worked in Denver and could certainly see each other again, she didn't expect anything long term. They were both too demanding, too competitive.

All she really needed from Burke was an uncomplicated moment of passion. After that, they'd go their separate ways.

Lucas came toward her. "Hey, Carolyn. Talking to that fat, old horse again?"

"Don't listen to him, Elvis. You're still a hunka hunka burning love."

He leaned against the fence beside her. When his jacket brushed aside, she saw that he was carrying his new Glock in a hip holster. He was holding an evergreen wreath in his gloved hand.

"What are you doing with the wreath?" she asked.

"I thought I might tie a red ribbon around it and hang it over the gatepost out front."

Celebrating Christmas was the last thing on her mind. Still, she said, "Good idea. Nicole loves Christmas decorations. When she comes home, she'll be happy to see that wreath."

When she comes home. Carolyn repeated those words to herself. *Nicole will be home for Christmas.*

"Ain't this something?" he said. "With the feds and the choppers and bloodhounds and all."

"Dylan said he'd call out the National Guard if that's what it takes."

They went quiet. She never felt a need to make conversation with Lucas. In the many years she'd known this old cowboy, he'd always been prone to taciturn silence. According to gossip from Polly, Lucas Mann had a reputation as a ladies' man when he went into town, but Carolyn found that characterization hard to imagine.

He shifted his weight from one boot to the other. "You and Burke went over to the Circle M. How'd that turn out?"

Unable to adequately describe her disgust with the Sons of Freedom, she shrugged. "Okay, I guess."

"Logan's not a bad kid, you know."

When she was dating that scumbag, Lucas had been one of the guys who thought she should marry him. "He's changed."

"Betcha he was downright happy to see you."

Why would Lucas make that assumption? "How much do you know about the Sons of Freedom?"

"Not much. They're against the government getting in the way of everyday people. Going back to the good old days."

"When women had fewer rights than cattle?"

"Don't get your panties in a bunch, Carolyn. Ain't nobody fixing to send you back to the kitchen." He lifted the wreath onto his shoulder. "It don't seem like the SOF means any harm."

Not unless you count murder. And whatever other criminal activities they were engaged in. She'd seen the sophisticated weaponry. Old-time pioneers didn't need automatic assault rifles. "If I ever see Sam Logan again, it'll be too soon."

The front door of the ranch house slammed and she looked toward the sound. Her brother stepped onto the veranda and gripped the railing. Even at this distance, she could see tension weighing down upon him, bending his shoulders.

Giving Elvis a final pat, she hurried back to the house. The closer she got, the more distress she saw in Dylan. When she touched his arm, he was trembling.

His voice was so low she could barely hear him.

"We got another call from the kidnapper."

Chapter Twelve

When Dylan was a toddler, two years younger than Carolyn, she hated to see him cry. At the first sign of tears, she'd cuddle him, tell him stories and sing songs until he smiled. If only she could do the same thing now—sweep her brother up in her loving arms and ease the aching in his heart.

She wrapped an arm around his middle and leaned her head on his shoulder. Memories of long-ago lullabies whispered in her mind, but she couldn't bring herself to offer false promises that everything would be all right.

"I told the kidnapper," Dylan said, "that we were having a hard time getting the ransom in time because of the banks. He changed his deadline. We have until Monday at five o'clock."

"That's good news," she said.

"Not for Nicole. She has to be with those bastards for two more days. God only knows what they're doing to her."

Burke joined them on the porch. His manner was subdued but assertive, striking exactly the right tone of calm control. She wondered if that attitude was something they taught at Quantico or if it came naturally.

He said, "You did a good job on the phone, Dylan."

"That's not what I'm thinking," he said darkly. "I'd rather give them the money and get my wife back."

In an ideal world, that was how a negotiation should work. But not with a kidnapper. If Nicole was being held at the Circle M, Logan would never free her—she could identify him. If the pregnant woman, Sunny, was to be believed, Logan had already presided over one murder. Nicole might be the next.

"We have two more days to find her," Carolyn said. "You did good, Dylan. You bought us more time."

"And Dylan got the kidnapper to promise one proof of life a day. More photos of Nicole give us more clues," said Burke.

Thinking of evidence, Carolyn asked, "Did you trace the call?"

"Not this time. He was too fast, and there aren't a lot of cell towers in this area to use for tracking. But it was the same cell phone number as the first call."

"Sheriff Trainer was trying to get information on the phone," she remembered. "Figuring out where the disposable cell was purchased."

"Thus far," Burke said, "he's been unsuccessful."

"And what about Nate Miller?" she asked. "Did the sheriff find anything at his house?"

"Smith joined the sheriff and his deputies for that search. He has nothing good to say about Miller."

"Nobody does," Dylan said. "He's as mean and bitter as his old man."

She agreed with her brother. Being around Miller made her skin crawl. "But did they find evidence?"

"Nothing that links him to the kidnapping, but he doesn't have an alibi for yesterday or last night. We'll keep him on our list of suspects."

A list that was ridiculously long. "Are you talking to other people on that list?"

"Silverman will be coordinating those interviews with

Sheriff Trainer." He met her gaze. "As you pointed out when we were in town, a lot of these people won't open up to the FBI. At least they'll talk to Trainer."

The painstaking process of gathering clues frustrated Carolyn. She was a big picture kind of person who made decisions and charged ahead, figuring the details would eventually sort themselves out. "Have you got anything, Burke? Any new leads at all?"

"We're working on it."

In the distance, she saw the helicopter approaching, flying low over the rugged landscape of forest and rock. Dylan gave her a squeeze and separated from her. "There's nothing more I can do here. I'm going up with the chopper while there's still daylight."

She was glad he'd be getting away from the tension-filled house. "I'll be here. If there's nothing I can do to help the investigation, maybe I'll start with some Christmas decorating."

"No," he said firmly. "That's Nicole's job. She loves doing that stuff."

"Should I go in the helicopter with you?" she asked. "Another pair of eyes can't hurt."

"You need to stay here," Burke said. "Corelli is ready to interview you."

She sensed there was something more he wanted to talk to her about. The midnight rendezvous with Sunny? Carolyn needed to be there to reassure Sunny. If that poor girl saw a bunch of FBI guys in bulletproof vests, she'd certainly be spooked.

Waving goodbye to her brother as he ran toward the chopper, she turned to Burke. "Tonight at midnight," she said. "I'm coming with you."

He glanced left and right, looking for spies. The only person she saw was bowlegged Lucas, ambling toward the front gate with the evergreen wreath hanging from his shoulder.

"We'll talk," Burke said. "Inside."

Compared to the chaos of this morning, the dining room had taken on an aura of quiet efficiency.

At one end of the table, Agent Silverman stood before a battery of computers and maps. He wore a phone headset, leaving his hands free to make notes. She'd barely noticed this young man before, probably because he looked like she thought an FBI agent should—totally average. With his brown hair, brown eyes and medium build, Silverman could easily fade into the background. This morning, he'd traded his FBI windbreaker for a faded green Stanford sweatshirt. When she smiled at him, he acknowledged her with a quick grin before he refocused on the task of coordinating the search efforts.

At the opposite end of the table was Corelli, wearing his neat black suit and striped tie. He could have been the junior partner in a law firm.

Burke stood with her behind Corelli's left shoulder. "Take a look at what we've got so far."

Corelli clicked a few keys on his computer, bringing up a rogues' gallery of photographs. "This is what I've found on the names Burke gave me for the SOF."

She scanned the driver's-license photos, recognizing some of the faces from the men she'd seen at the Circle M. The only one who jumped out at her was Butch Thurgood. Even without a Stetson, he looked like a cowboy with a thick, old-fashioned mustache. "Tell me about Butch."

"No criminal record," Corelli said, "but a Web search gave me a lot of info. He's a former rodeo star, a bucking bronc rider. Won the championship title at Cheyenne Frontier Days in 2004 and 2005."

He brought up a full-length photo of Butch Thurgood on the computer screen. A rangy, good-looking man, he wore an embroidered Western shirt and a silver belt buckle the size of a saucer. "He has a reputation as a horse whisperer, somebody who can tame wild mustangs."

Oddly, Carolyn felt reassured. Since Nicole was a veterinarian, she might have something in common with Butch.

Beside her, Burke checked his wristwatch. "Now the bad news. Pete Richter."

Corelli clicked a few keys. The photo that appeared was a police mug shot. His dark eyes had a mean squint. Like Butch, Richter had facial hair but his patchy beard was the result of careless grooming.

"I assume," she said, "that he has a criminal record."

"Starting when he was eighteen," Corelli said. "Shoplifting, vagrancy, DUIs. He served two years in prison for assault."

The reassurance she'd felt when looking at Butch turned into dread. If Nicole was in the clutches of Richter, things couldn't be good. "What about the rest of the SOF men?"

"Minor charges, here and there. One dishonorable discharge from the military. They're low-level, petty criminals," Burke said. "Amazingly, Sam Logan has a clean record, apart from one arrest for fraud that never resulted in trial because the woman he'd stolen from dropped the charges."

She wasn't surprised. "Logan can be charming."

Burke scoffed, "Ready for more information?"

"I suppose."

He waved his hand like a magician going for the big reveal. "Okay, Corelli. Show her the money."

The Sons of Freedom bank statement appeared on the screen.

"Wait a minute." Carolyn averted her gaze. "Can you do this without a warrant? Is this even legal?"

"Corelli knows how to follow protocol and he's a talented hacker."

On the screen, she read the balance in the account. "One thousand two hundred dollars? How can Logan support all those people on that amount? There must be another account."

"Nope," Burke said. "No other account in Sam Logan's name. Nothing else for the SOF."

"Credit cards? Loans?"

"Nothing."

Corelli flipped through a series of other financial documents while he explained, "Here's how it works. Before a bill comes due, Logan deposits just enough money—in cash—to cover the check. *Always in cash.*"

Finances were Carolyn's area of expertise. When taking on a new supplier for Carlisle Certified Organic Beef, she carefully reviewed all their financial documents. "Seems like a clever way to avoid paying taxes. If he only balances out with small amounts, he can claim it all comes from contributions."

"Good insight," Burke said. "Source of income is the important factor. It's hard to know exactly how the SOF makes their money when everything is on a cash basis."

"I'm not a forensic accountant," Corelli said, "but I feel safe in assuming that Logan has a boatload of cash that isn't banked."

"That might explain the security cameras," she said, "and the heavy-duty firepower at the SOF compound. They're afraid of being robbed."

Burke raised a skeptical eyebrow. "Let's not characterize Logan as a little old man who stuffs his mattress with ten-dollar bills. He needs his guards to keep his business secret, to protect his little kingdom."

"From what?"

"Feds like me," Burke said. "Whatever he's buying and selling is illegal. Could be weapons, could be drugs, could be any number of black-market items that would be highly interesting to the DEA or Homeland Security."

Though Carolyn agreed that Logan was probably involved in some kind of illegal activity, she didn't think of her former fiancé as a terrorist. "Logan isn't that clever."

"He's no mastermind," Burke agreed. "But he could be working for one. His compound could be one stop on a distribution chain."

She didn't like the picture he was painting, especially didn't like the thought that Nicole might be in the middle of this spider's web. Not to mention the other innocent women and children.

They needed to get everyone out of there, starting tonight with Sunny.

TWELVE MINUTES BEFORE the midnight meet with Sunny, Burke lay on his belly in the cold, dead grass outside the west field bordering the Circle M. He peered through infrared, heat-sensing binoculars at a stand of pine trees, watching for any sign of movement. From this vantage point, he couldn't see any of the buildings of the SOF compound. Except for the clump of pines, this field was flat and featureless.

Carolyn crouched beside him, hiding behind the bared branches of a shrub. His backup—Neville and Silverman— were both heavily armed. They'd separated and found their own hiding spots, fading into the landscape. The only way Burke could see them was through the heat-sensing binoculars.

He didn't like this setup. With very little cover, they were exposed to the possibility of ambush. If Logan and his men charged toward them on horseback, escape would be difficult. They'd parked a couple of hundred yards away, and he didn't like their chances for a safe retreat if they were out-numbered and attacked with a barrage of bullets from semi-automatic weapons.

He especially hated that Carolyn was here. She'd insisted on being part of this operation, dug in her heels. He'd wanted to pull rank, reminding her that he was in charge. But her argument made too much sense. If, in fact, Sunny truly wanted to escape from the Circle M, she'd be alarmed if she didn't see Carolyn—the person she trusted.

He glanced toward his companion. Dressed all in black, she was as slender as a shadow. "I'd feel a whole lot better if you were wearing full body armor, like Neville and Silverman."

"This bulletproof vest is enough," she said quietly. "The whole reason I'm here is to keep Sunny from being scared. If she sees me dressed like a robot, she'll run."

Again, her logic made sense. For exactly the same reason she'd stated, Burke was only wearing a Kevlar vest. "Let's go over the plan again."

"It's not that complicated," she said. "I stay with you. When you give me the go-ahead, I run to the trees. No time for conversation. I take Sunny by the hand and bring her back here."

"If you hear me call out a warning, what do you do?"

"Seek cover." She turned so she was looking at the flat land between their hiding spot and the pines. "There isn't much to hide behind."

"Hit the dirt," he said. "The main thing is not to stand and run, making yourself a big, fat target."

"Excuse me? You think I'm big and fat?"

"Your body's great."

"Do you really think so?"

"I like the way you're put together." This wasn't the right time for this conversation, but he couldn't control his thoughts. Even now, in the midst of a life-threatening situation, his brain flashed snapshots of Carolyn. The swing of her hips when he followed her up the staircase. Her long legs striding with purpose. Her casual grace when she sat on her bed. "Oh, yeah. You've got a great body."

"You're no slouch yourself," she said. "Do you work out or do you get enough exercise chasing the evildoers of the world?"

He didn't answer, preferring to concentrate on the business at hand. After a moment of silence, he lowered his binoculars and checked his wristwatch. Five minutes until midnight.

"I've been thinking," she said, "about Logan being part of a distribution chain."

He peered through his binoculars again. "And?"

"If somebody is bringing illegal goods into this area, the most logical route would be the pass that follows that old Indian Trail. It comes out of the mountains at the south pasture where all the sabotage was taking place."

After studying topographical maps of the area, he'd been leaning toward the same conclusion. He and Corelli had been listening to the chatter from Logan's office where Burke had hidden a bug. There had been talk about making a pickup, but no one mentioned where or what would be delivered. "You could be right about the route."

"The sabotage started after Dylan moved the herd into that pasture."

"Logan and his men might have been causing trouble so Dylan would move the cattle. If they're using that trail, there's less chance that someone would see them if the pasture was empty."

"We can't tell Dylan about this," she whispered. "He's already blaming himself for Nicole's kidnapping. Lucas kept telling him to move the cattle."

A suspicious note in her voice caused him to lower the binoculars and look toward her. "What else are you thinking?"

"Nothing really." She shook her head. "Forget it."

She'd mentioned the foreman—Lucas Mann. Was there something more sinister behind his warning to move the herd? Was Lucas the traitor? He knew that Carolyn would find it hard to accuse that bowlegged cowboy, a trusted employee who had worked at the ranch for years.

Burke was less sanguine about the foreman's loyalty. Lucas could have been bribed; he had enough extra cash to buy that new Glock, which wasn't a cheap weapon. "Is there something you want to tell me about Lucas?"

"I said forget it."

Lucas had been in the house when somebody took the phone number from her cell. He'd also discovered the fire at the stable and acted quickly to rescue the horses. Could he be responsible for setting that blaze?

Burke looked up at the waning moon and a sky sprinkled with a multitude of stars—thousands of tiny spotlights. That beautiful, clear night sky worked to their disadvantage. He would have preferred cloud cover, even snow.

Aiming his heat-sensing binoculars again, he picked out a figure, moving slowly. "She's coming."

Carolyn peered though the dark. "I don't see her."

"Looks like she's alone. Let's get closer."

He traded his binoculars for night vision goggles. Bent low, they crept across the field. He clearly saw the blond pregnant woman in a long dress and a parka. She walked carefully, pausing every few steps to look back over her shoulder. Her hand rested protectively on her swollen belly. Her apparent fear seemed to indicate that she wasn't part of an ambush, which led Burke to his next worry: Was someone coming after her?

He hoped that Sunny was clever enough to avoid being caught by the surveillance cameras.

"I see her," Carolyn said. "She's almost to the trees."

"It doesn't appear that anybody is following. Go quick."

She darted across the last stretch of open field. For tonight's operation, Carolyn had exchanged her cowboy boots for running shoes. She moved with admirable stealth, standing when she reached the trees.

Through his goggles, he saw the two women meet. Carolyn wrapped her arm around Sunny and pulled her forward. Instead of running, they came toward him slowly.

Still no sign of pursuit.

Burke hurried forward and joined them. Sunny clung to Carolyn's arm. Her face contorted.

"I could use a little help," Carolyn said.

"Is she injured?"

"You need to carry her, Burke."

"What's wrong?"

"She's in labor."

Chapter Thirteen

Burke's jaw dropped. He froze, standing in the middle of the open field between escape and the Circle M. He'd just warned Carolyn not to do what he was doing. *Don't just stand here like a big, fat target.* A successful hostage extraction required stealth and cunning. *Not babies.*

"In labor," he said. "Right now?"

"Yes," Carolyn hissed. Though she was making a valiant effort to hold Sunny upright, the young woman's knees folded. In slow motion, she sank to the ground, dragging Carolyn with her in a tangle of limbs. Through clenched teeth, Sunny emitted a sound that was something between a creaking door hinge and a feral growl.

"Help her." Carolyn bounced to her feet and punched him in the arm. "She's not going to make it to the car by herself."

He handed his night goggles and gun to Carolyn, then squatted beside Sunny. She gasped and her belly heaved. Her face was pale and round and scared.

He needed to reassure her. "Um, congratulations."

"Burke," Carolyn snapped, "pick her up."

"Right." He got down close to Sunny. "I'm going to carry you, okay? Can you put your arm around my neck?"

"Yes," she whispered, "thank you."

Holding her under the arms and at the knees, he lifted her off the ground. Her weight wasn't too much; he could easily bench-press two-fifty. But Sunny's body was awkward—regular-sized arms and legs attached to a ripe watermelon.

From the SOF compound, he heard a shout. A woman's voice. "Sunny? Where are you, Sunny?"

"It's Sharon," Sunny said. "She's supposed to keep an eye on us at night."

They needed to make tracks, but he couldn't exactly break into a sprint with a pregnant woman in his arms. Though this field was flat, the ground was rocky. He didn't want to stumble.

"How close are the contractions?" Carolyn asked as they lurched forward.

"It wasn't bad until just a little while ago."

"There's nothing to worry about." Carolyn's voice was soft and gentle. "Just keep breathing. Try to relax."

Relax? Was she joking? He wasn't sure how Sunny felt, but he was operating under red alert panic.

Other voices joined the woman who had been calling Sunny's name. Other people were looking for her. If the gang at the compound checked their surveillance cameras, they'd know which direction to go. The men would be armed. Burke could already sense the bullet piercing his back.

"Silverman," he snarled into the darkness. "Neville."

The two men in full body armor, goggles and helmets rose from their sniper's nests in the field and jogged silently toward them.

When Sunny saw them, her eyes popped wide. "Oh, my God."

"It's okay," Burke said. "They're with us."

"They're from outer space." She struggled in his arms. "Am I being abducted by aliens?"

Silverman flipped up his goggles. "I'm a person. See?"

"Settle down." Burke gave her a shake, hoping her brain would engage. "You're safe now."

"I don't feel safe."

"Trust me," he ordered. "Can you do that?"

She groaned, "Okay."

"I'm taking her to the car," Burke said to his men as he staggered toward the trees. On the other side, their van was parked. "Stay back and cover our retreat."

"They have flashlights," Carolyn said. "They're coming this way."

He wanted to make sure Neville and Silverman knew they had to hold fire as long as possible. There were still innocent hostages at the Circle M, and he couldn't take a chance on anyone getting hurt.

"Don't shoot unless—"

He couldn't speak. Sunny's arm had clenched around his neck in a stranglehold. Her body had gone into a spasm.

Only twenty more yards and they'd be in the shelter of the forest.

"Keep breathing," Carolyn whispered.

He gasped. "Thanks."

"I wasn't talking to you, Burke."

His forward progress stopped. He kneeled, fearful that he was going to drop her. Sunny's contraction caused her to stiffen. She bit her lower lip to keep from crying out, and he appreciated the effort. If the SOF searchers found them, they might open fire. Definitely not optimum circumstances for delivering a baby.

As soon as she calmed down, he summoned all his strength and ran into the forest. Beneath the sheltering branches, he turned to look behind them. He saw flashlights bobbing on the opposite side of the field.

They were a good distance away. He hoped they wouldn't connect Sunny's disappearance with him or the Carlisle's.

"Almost safe," he said to Sunny.

"Hurry."

They moved in a clump toward the van. Silverman dashed past them and slid open the rear door. Burke set the pregnant woman inside. Before he could go around to the driver's side, she grabbed his jacket.

The strength of her grip astonished him. He wanted to peel her clinging hands off him, wanted to leave her in Carolyn's care. But Sunny's wide eyes pleaded. "Stay with me," she said. "You told me to trust you."

"I did say that." And how the hell could he refuse a woman in labor? He reconfigured the third row of seats into a long bench and climbed in beside her. "Carolyn, you drive."

Neville took the passenger seat. Silverman sat in the middle seats. They took off.

The immediate danger seemed to have passed. They had successfully extracted a hostage from the Sons of Freedom compound. But nobody in the van was breathing a sigh of relief.

Without turning on the headlights, Carolyn drove as fast as she could along a rutted dirt road. Burke sat with his back against the window. Sunny leaned against his chest with her legs stretched out in front of her. She groaned as Carolyn jolted over a deep furrow. "I want my mom."

"Later, you can call her," Burke said as he pulled out his cell phone. "First, we contact your doctor."

"Don't have one. Logan said we don't need doctors. We're like the pioneers, using natural herbs and stuff."

"Are you telling me that the children at the compound don't get vaccinations? No checkups?"

"I know it's not right," Sunny sighed.

It sure as hell wasn't. In his book, the lack of medical care at the SOF compound amounted to child abuse. "Do the others want to leave the Circle M?"

"Most of the women do," Sunny said. "But we don't know where to go. We've got no money. Nothing but these ugly clothes. At least Logan makes sure we all get fed."

"How long have you lived there?"

She stroked her belly. "Nine months. I thought I was in love with Butch Thurgood, but he's as rotten as the rest of them."

In the middle seat, Silverman had taken off his helmet, goggles and much of his body armor. He leaned between the seats. "See? I'm not an alien."

Not an alien. Just an idiot. "She understands, Silverman."

"I didn't mean to insult you," Sunny said. "I was just, you know, confused. You looked really scary in the moonlight."

"My name is Mike." He reached back and touched her leg. "You're going to be fine. Everything's going to be fine."

With a sweet smile, she said, "Thank you, Mike."

Oh, sure. Thank him. He didn't carry you across the field. Burke was pretty sure that he deserved a medal—at least a written commendation—for his actions tonight. At the very least, he wanted to get some useful information from Sunny.

"You told Carolyn about a murder," he prompted.

"Lisa's sister. Her name was Barbara."

"Last name?"

"I think it's Ayers. None of the women use their last names. We're supposed to be part of a new family."

Stripping away identity was a typical technique for handling hostages. "What's your last name, Sunny?"

"Lansky. Sunny Rebecca Lansky."

"That's good." He gave her a little hug. "Tell me about the murder."

"It was awful."

Carolyn drove onto a paved road and turned on the headlights. She hit the accelerator and said loudly, "Burke, this might not be the time to have this talk."

"I want to tell him," Sunny said.

But she went rigid in his arms. She'd suffered quietly in the field, but there was no longer a need to hold back.

"Go ahead," Burke said. "If you want to yell, go ahead."

She grabbed his hand and let out an earsplitting screech. From the middle seat, Silverman coached her. "Hang in there, Sunny. You can do it. Do you know the breathing? Hee-hee. Hoo-hoo."

The screech continued. Nothing hee-hee about it.

"She's not having the baby now," Burke snapped.

"She could," Silverman said.

"Oh. Hell. No. She's waiting until we get to the hospital." In the meantime, she was crushing his fingers into pulp. "Hold it in, Sunny."

"Doesn't work that way," Silverman said. "When it's time, it's time."

"Since when are you a midwife?"

"I helped my sister give birth. I know all about this stuff."

Sunny went quiet, breathing heavily. Her grip on his hand relaxed. "Barbara wanted to leave the SOF. She never really wanted to be there in the first place. She only stayed because of her sister. Lisa has a drug problem."

"What about you? Drug problem?"

"No." She shook her head. "I never got into drugs."

Sunny seemed like a decent kid, even though she was kind of a mess with her blond hair growing out at the roots and her baggy dress with long woolen leggings. "Are there drugs at the Circle M?"

"Some kind of supposedly herbal supplement. I never took it. Because of the baby."

"Good for you," Burke said. "Tell me about Barbara."

"She found out she was pregnant, too. We talked about leaving together. When we told Logan we wanted to go, he got really mad. He reminded us what it's like on the outside for a single mother. No friends. No money."

"There's always someone," Silverman said. He maneuvered around and stretched out his arm to dab her forehead with a red kerchief. "Somebody who will step up and—"

"Do something useful," Burke ordered. "Call the Delta hospital and tell them we're coming."

"Sunny needs to know there's a support system."

Agent Mike Silverman was usually an efficient operative who had no problem with following orders. Something about being around a pregnant woman had messed with his head. "Make the damn call."

Glaring at Burke, he pulled out his cell phone. Since Carolyn was driving at about a thousand miles an hour, they ought to be at the hospital in minutes. "Okay, Sunny. Both you and Barbara wanted to leave. Then what?"

"Her baby's daddy was Pete Richter. A real bastard. She made the mistake of talking to him. I saw him slap her really hard. She was unconscious. I wanted to help her. Really, I did. But I was scared."

"You're safe now," Burke assured her. He wanted to get the whole story before her next contraction. "What happened next? Give me the short version."

"Richter and Logan dragged Barbara off into the barn, and I never saw her again. Logan told us she ran away."

"But you didn't believe him."

"She never would have left without saying goodbye to Lisa. A couple of days later, I was out walking. Not far from the trees where you came and got me, I found a plot of fresh-turned earth. I know that's where they buried her."

It would have been neater if Sunny had actually witnessed

the murder. Finding the body would be useful, but it wouldn't tell them who killed Barbara Ayers.

"New topic," Burke said. "Can you tell me anything about the woman who was kidnapped? Nicole Carlisle?"

"I never saw her."

"Is there a place at the Circle M where they could hide her?"

"Plenty of places. Root cellars. Trailers." She shrugged.

Burke pressed for a more definitive answer. "If Butch and Richter were holding Nicole captive, where would they be?"

"There's a trailer behind the bunkhouse where a lot of couples go to make love. Butch didn't like it. He wanted more privacy. He took me to this place. We had to ride on the Indian Trail to get there." Her voice broke. "It was springtime, just starting to warm up. It felt like he loved me. Everything was so beautiful."

"Where was this place?"

"A shallow cave that looks out over the mountains and valleys. Right above the Cathedral Rocks with all the spikes and spires."

She grabbed his hand. "Here comes another one."

"So soon?"

"Four minutes apart," Silverman announced.

"How far are we from the damn hospital?"

"Not far," Carolyn yelled over her shoulder. "We're almost in Delta."

Sunny let out a long wail. Her knees drew up and separated as if she was ready to shoot out the baby.

Silverman held out his hand, and she latched on to him, too.

"Don't push," he said. "We're almost to the hospital."

"Did you hear that?" Burke whispered in her ear. "No pushing."

Sunny ended the contraction with short, huffing gasps. "I need my mom."

"Absolutely. No problem." Burke waved his cell phone. "You can call her. Where does she live?"

"Mom," She sobbed, "doesn't even know I'm pregnant."

Burke held the phone in front of her. "Tell me the number."

"No time. I want this baby out of me."

Carolyn whipped into the emergency entrance for the hospital and leaped from the car. In seconds, two guys in scrubs had loaded Sunny onto a gurney. Silverman went with them into the hospital.

Burke leaned against the van and exhaled a long breath.

Carolyn stood beside him. In the harsh light outside the E.R. entrance, he saw her smirk. "That went well."

In spite of her sarcasm, he was pleased with the way his team had extracted Sunny—a witness who had given them useful information against Logan.

While they were at the hospital, they'd checked on Jesse Longbridge. Burke hoped for a lucky break. If the body-guard was out of his coma, he could identify the men who kidnapped Nicole.

Chapter Fourteen

Hospital visiting hours had, of course, ended much earlier. And the nurses didn't seem pleased about the after-midnight exception they made for Carolyn and Burke after he showed his FBI credentials.

Walking beside him down a clean corridor, she tried to keep her sneakers from squeaking on the tile floor. Her hands were washed, but the black clothes she'd worn for the meeting with Sunny were filthy and sweaty. She felt like a germ invading sterile territory.

Hospitals made her uncomfortable, especially this one—it was where her father had passed away. She shouldn't be here, shouldn't really be involved in anything like a hostage extraction. She was a CEO, not part of the CIA. But the alternative was doing nothing, and she had to admit that rescuing Sunny had been a rush. Escaping from pursuit and racing to the hospital made her feel like she was accomplishing something. And it looked like there would be a happy ending to that story. Sunny was already in the delivery room with Silverman. If only they could rescue Nicole so easily, Carolyn could get back to her regular life—a life that didn't include Special Agent J. D. Burke.

She wasn't exactly sure how she felt about never seeing

him again. Like her, he was dressed in black—a color that should have made him appear smaller. But he looked huge and dangerous. His jaw was tight. His dark eyes burned with a purposeful intensity that fascinated her.

Perhaps she'd miss him.

At the end of the hall, they entered Jesse Longbridge's private room. Wentworth and another guard from Longbridge Security greeted them with a handshake and stepped aside.

Dim night-lights gave the room an ethereal quality. Jesse lay motionless and unconscious under a white sheet. IV lines ran into the veins in his right arm. The left was bandaged. A large dressing covered his left shoulder. A nasal cannula delivered oxygen to his lungs, but he was breathing on his own. His chest rose and fell steadily. The heart monitor made a regular beep.

As Carolyn approached his bed, she felt a strong connection to this man who was, in fact, a stranger. They'd never been introduced, but his blood had flowed through her fingers and stained her clothing.

She gently brushed his thick black hair off his forehead. He was rather handsome. She'd heard that Jesse was half Navajo and could see his heritage in his strong features. His eyelashes flickered, and she thought for a moment that he would waken. But the slight movement faded into stillness.

Concentrating, she sent positive thoughts from her brain to his. *You're going to get better, Jesse. You will be well again*. He'd risked his life trying to protect Nicole. Frankly, he was the answer to all their questions. When he woke, he'd be able to identify the kidnappers.

Seeing him lying there—so still and quiet—saddened her. He didn't deserve these injuries. He was one of the good guys, someone who tried to do the right thing. And how was he repaid for his efforts? *Damn it, this wasn't fair*.

Burke stood close behind her. "He's expected to make a full recovery."

That knowledge didn't assuage her anger. "What if he doesn't?"

"He will."

She turned her head. In Burke's expression she saw strength and determination, but he couldn't affect Jesse's medical condition. Some things were simply out of his control. And hers, too.

Quietly, she stepped away from Jesse's bed. Wentworth accompanied her and Burke, leaving the other guard in the room to keep watch. He led them past the nurse's station into a private office with file cabinets, a computer and a couple of chairs. Wentworth closed the door.

Burke asked, "What's the update on Jesse's condition?"

"Same as before. No broken bones. No organ damage. All his systems are functioning and he's got brain activity. A couple of times, he's opened his eyes, looked around and then zonked out again. The docs say he'll be okay."

"I'm sure he will be." Burke took his cell phone from his pocket, checked the caller ID and excused himself. "Sorry, I have to take this call."

"Thank you, Wentworth," Carolyn said, "for all you've done."

"It's my job, ma'am."

"Can you explain to me why Jesse isn't awake?"

"There's no medical explanation, ma'am. But I'll tell you this. Jesse's no slacker. When he decides to wake up, I guarantee he'll be raring to go."

Though Wentworth was obviously concerned, he kept his fears to himself. His stoicism reminded Carolyn of the cowboy ethic. Never show emotion.

She wanted to scream, to jump up and down and rail

against the bastards who had put this good man in the hospital.

"Is there anything I can do?" she asked. "Should we call in a specialist?"

"Jesse's getting first-rate care," Wentworth said. "It helps to have two of us here, 24/7. We're also keeping tabs on your ransom money."

Swept up in concern for Jesse, she'd almost forgotten that the ransom had been delivered here to the hospital so the traitor at the ranch wouldn't know the money had arrived. A million dollars in cash! How could she forget? "It's in a backpack?"

"Yes, ma'am. A real big backpack."

Burke completed his call and rejoined them. Without missing a beat, he said. "We'll be taking the ransom with us."

"Yes, sir."

Burke slipped easily into the leadership role. Though he wasn't Wentworth's boss or his client, he still commanded respect. The only time she'd seen that fierce composure slip was with Sunny. Handling a woman in labor had dumbfounded Special Agent Burke.

He turned to her. "That was Corelli on the phone. Logan has called the ranch twice, looking for you. It's worth finding out what he wants."

"It's probably about Sunny."

"Most likely," Burke said. "If he tries to contact you again, Corelli will patch the call through to my phone."

"Okay." She didn't want to talk to Logan, but Burke was right. She might learn something useful.

"Wentworth," Burke said, "I've got another assignment for you. We have another witness at the hospital who needs a full-time guard. She'll be in the maternity wing."

Though Wentworth nodded, he said, "Could be a problem,

sir. There are only two of us, and we need to take turns sleeping and watching Jesse."

"I'm leaving an FBI agent here with you."

"Silverman?" she asked.

"He might as well stay here," Burke said. "You saw how he was fawning all over Sunny."

"I thought he was sweet," she said.

Burke turned to Wentworth. "Can you manage with three guards?"

"I'll work it out, sir."

"Actually," Carolyn said, "you'll be watching three people. Jesse, Sunny and a newborn baby."

Burke's cell phone rang. He checked the ID and handed it to her. "It's Logan. Don't tell him anything about Sunny."

She took the phone from him and answered, "What do you want?"

"I knew you'd be awake," he said. "There are probably a half dozen feds monitoring the phones. Did they get you out of bed? Are you wearing one of those skimpy little night-shirts? I remember a blue one with butterflies."

A shudder of revulsion went through her. She hated that he knew what she wore to bed. "Why did you call?"

"Where's Sunny?"

"Who? What are you talking about?"

"Sunny," he repeated. "She was one of the women you were talking to today. She ran off, and I'm pretty damn sure she came to you for help."

From the way he was talking, she didn't think he'd actually seen them rescuing Sunny. It would be useful to know if any of those people with flashlights had spotted them. "Why would you think she came to me?"

"Because you put ideas in her head. I know how you are."

He knew nothing about her. And, apparently, nothing about

their hostage extraction. She gave a short laugh and said, "You think I poisoned her mind? Convinced her to leave you?"

"That's right."

"In case you hadn't noticed," she said, "I kind of have my hands full. Why would I care about some woman who was dumb enough to join up with you in the first place?"

"Like you," he reminded her. "You used to be with me."

"Thank God I came to my senses."

"Where else would Sunny run to? She came to your ranch," he said. "You should know that she's a liar. A runaway that I picked up off the streets. You can't believe a word she says."

"She's not at the ranch, Logan."

"Don't mess with me."

"Or else?" She laughed again, harshly. "What are you going to do?"

"You think you're untouchable. You're the high-and-mighty Carolyn Carlisle. But I know how to bring you down."

Was he talking about Nicole? Would he hurt Nicole to get back at her? "Are you threatening me? Again?"

"Take it any way you want."

The phone went dead.

AN HOUR LATER, sitting in the passenger seat of the van, Carolyn had pushed aside her sadness about Jesse and her frustrated anger at Logan. Her mind filled with happier images as she thought about Sunny's beautiful baby girl. After their wild ride to get her to the hospital, the actual delivery—assisted by Silverman—had been uncomplicated and fast. And the result?

Carolyn grinned. Sunny had given birth to a perfect little being with wise, curious eyes and rosebud lips.

She sighed. "Babies are so miraculous."

"Yeah," Burke said. "Bundles of joy."

"Come on, tough guy. I saw your face when you were holding the baby. You liked it."

"Don't confuse me with Silverman." He frowned at the road ahead. "I don't know what the hell's gotten into him. He's single, never married. What does he know about babies?"

"More than you," she teased.

The atmosphere between them was different tonight—more intimate. In the dark, when she couldn't see clearly, her other senses were heightened, as if she could hear him breathing and feel the warmth emanating from his body. His voice seemed more resonant; the tones vibrated inside her.

They'd experienced so much in one day. The emotional high of rescuing Sunny. And the low point this morning when she broke down in tears. In some ways, Burke knew her more thoroughly than men she'd dated for years. But she still didn't have much of an inkling of his background. Now—when they were finally alone—was her time to find out about him.

"Did you have siblings?" she asked.

"I was an only child, raised in Chicago by a single mom."

She was surprised that he'd offered so much biographical information—a whole sentence. Usually, he answered her questions with a question of his own. She pressed for more. "You grew up in the city?"

"Mostly."

Pulling answers from him was like sucking on a bent straw. "Does that mean you also lived somewhere else?"

"I spent a lot of summers in rural Wisconsin with my grandparents. That's where I learned how to ride."

He yawned. She knew that his defenses were down. "After high school, what did you do?"

"Is there a point to your questions?"

"I'm trying to get to know you," she said.

"Why?"

"Because I like you, Burke."

As the words left her lips, her heart took a little jump. She wasn't usually so direct; Carolyn knew how to play the dating game. But there wasn't time for them to do the traditional get-to-know-you dance. For them, there would be no candlelit dinners or long walks in the park. They didn't even have time for a first date.

If anything was going to happen between them, it had to be as fast and furious as a tornado. *Is that what I want? To be swept up in a wild vortex?* She reminded herself that tornadoes were generally looked upon as disasters.

"You like me," he said.

Lights from the dashboard showed a grin that was a bit too arrogant for her taste. She backtracked, not wanting to give him an edge. "Maybe I do."

"Maybe?" He turned his head and gave her a cocky look— a challenge that made her want to raise the stakes.

"When I first met you," she said, "I thought you were an insensitive, domineering jerk."

"And now?"

"You're sensitive enough." And sexier than she wanted to admit. "The problem is that I don't know you well enough to form much of an opinion."

"Fine," he said. "Ask your questions."

"You said you were once in love. Tell me about that."

"I was a first-year law student," he said. "She was my professor. Beautiful and tough, she was the smartest person I've ever known. I couldn't stay away from her." He sighed. "I wanted to be with her, even after she told me about her illness."

His voice had deepened, lending weight to his words.

"What did she have?" Carolyn asked.

"An inoperable brain aneurysm. For most of her life, she faced the knowledge that she could die at any moment. We lived together for six months. Then she was gone."

The tragedy was still with him. She could feel his sorrow. "I'm sorry, Burke."

"I dropped out of law school and joined the Chicago P.D. Stayed there for five years. My mom was killed in a car accident, and I moved to the FBI." He shrugged. "That's it. My life story."

A story of love and loss. No wonder he was so guarded. "How did you become a hostage negotiator?"

"The FBI decided that's where I fit. You'll have to ask profilers, like Smith and Silverman, for the psychological details."

She didn't need more explanation. He'd trusted her. He'd shared his past. And that was enough.

Through the windshield, she saw the lights of the ranch house. Though it was after two o'clock in the morning, someone was still awake. Not Dylan, she hoped. Her brother needed more sleep. "Is Corelli still monitoring the equipment?"

"That's his job," Burke said. "He's listening to the bug I left in Logan's office. It'll be interesting to hear what they have to say about Sunny's disappearance, especially after your conversation with him."

And Logan's threat. "I could have handled that better."

"You did fine."

She looked toward the house. After this brief reprieve, they were returning to the crucible. Tension tied a knot in her gut. She wanted more respite, wanted to be with Burke, wanted their intimacy to increase. She wanted to spend the rest of the night in the safety of his arms. *Am I ready to make love to him? Is he ready?*

Carolyn pushed the thought away. "Why did you want to bring the ransom with us?"

"It doesn't do much good to have the money if we can't deliver."

"I'm surprised," she said. He'd been consistently opposed to handing over the ransom. "You're thinking of paying the kidnappers?"

"Only if there's no other way."

She wouldn't miss the money. All she wanted was for Nicole to be back home. Safe.

Chapter Fifteen

After they parked, Carolyn followed Burke into the house. He carried the massive backpack over his shoulder. Not exactly a subtle way of transporting the ransom, but it couldn't be helped. They went immediately to her brother's office and closed the door. Carolyn knew exactly where to stash the money.

"My father had this safe installed ten years ago," she said. "We'd had a couple of robberies and he was worried about the amount of cash we keep on hand."

"Is the safe big enough for this backpack?"

"Oh, yeah."

She pulled the window curtains tight, remembering the day when her father brought her and Dylan into his office and told them that no one—absolutely no one—was to know the combination to his safe. No one except for Dylan and herself.

Thinking back, she realized that he was probably over-reacting. "Dad wanted a safe that was large enough to hold our cash on hand and the most valuable pieces of art that my mother had picked up."

"You said that she runs an art gallery in Manhattan, right?"

"Mom has amazing taste. Very expensive taste. For a while, Dad locked up the Gorman sculptures and the paintings by Georgia O'Keefe." She gestured to a priceless Charles Russell painting of a cowboy roping a steer above the leather couch. "I convinced him that art was supposed to be seen. If he wasn't going to put those paintings on the wall, he might as well send them to my mom."

She unfastened two hidden latches on a bookcase. It swung open like a door on well-oiled hinges. The wall safe behind it was five feet tall.

"Excellent," Burke said. "The money should be safe in there."

She twirled the combination lock and opened the safe. There was plenty of room inside. As soon as Burke deposited the backpack, she closed the steel door and returned the bookcase to its original position. For now, the million-dollar ransom was secure.

She turned and faced Burke. He leaned against her brother's desk with his arms folded across his broad chest.

"About those questions you asked in the car," he said.

"Yes?"

"Did I pass your test?"

"I wasn't—"

"Sure you were. You're checking me out, trying to decide what to do about this attraction we're both feeling. Don't deny it, Carolyn."

"It's what I do," she said without apology. "I gather information, make decisions and take action."

"You're an effective businesswoman. No doubt about that."

But was she so skillful when it came to more personal decisions? She tried to make an assessment. From the way he conducted his life and the way he coped with his past, she assumed that he was a good man. Decent. Strong. A leader. But not someone she'd look to for a long-term relationship.

He definitely wasn't a man who wanted to settle down and have babies. "You've been honest with me."

"I have."

His smile drew her closer. There was no logical way to analyze the magnetism between them. She couldn't explain the sensual shivers that prickled the hairs on her arms. Nor could she deny them. "You're a man I can trust."

She approached him, deliberately unfolded his arms and stepped into his embrace. Then, she kissed him.

Without hesitation, he responded. His mouth was hot and demanding. He closed his arms around her, enveloped her, dominated her, held her so tightly that he took her breath away.

Carolyn reeled in his arms, unaccustomed to such fierce passion. Her leg wrapped around his thigh, squeezing hard, rubbing against him. Arousal spread through her like wildfire. She wanted more from him. Demanded it.

He tore off her jacket, discarded it on the floor of the office and peeled off his own. Her hands dove under his black turtleneck and climbed his chest, reveling in the touch of crisp hair and hard muscle. Kissing him again, her arms encircled him. Her fingers clutched at his back.

A deep growl emanated from his throat, and she met that primitive sound with a moan of her own. No more time for thought. Only action.

He swung her around so she was pressed against the desk, and she was glad for the support. He yanked her shirt over her head. In a deft move, he unhooked her bra. He tugged at her barrette and her hair cascaded out of the ponytail.

For a moment he paused. His dark eyes slid over her body, naked from the waist up. "Beautiful," he murmured.

Slowly and purposefully, he cupped her breasts and lowered his head to suckle at her rose-colored nipples.

Her back arched. She bared her throat as a burst of pleasure exploded inside her.

He went lower, trailing his clever tongue along the center line of her torso. Her belt was open. He unfastened the top button of her jeans.

Breathing hard, she slithered through his grasp and sank to the floor in front of the desk. No way would she be the only person naked in this equation.

"Your shirt," she growled. "Take it off."

"You like to give orders."

"I like to be obeyed."

When he took off his shirt, she stared, unabashed. Oh yes, he was something else. Big. Strong. Gorgeous.

She lay back on the woven Navajo rug. "Now your jeans."

"You're going first."

Teasing, he tugged at her jeans while she made a half-hearted effort to keep them on. This was a battle of wills that she had no intention of winning.

Finally, their clothes were gone. He lowered himself on top of her. The sensation of flesh meeting flesh created a friction unlike anything she'd ever experienced. Burke matched her passion and overwhelmed her.

He drew away from her and reached for his jeans. "I need a condom."

"It's okay. I'm on the pill." In his eyes, she saw a hint of hesitation. "Damn it, Burke. I'm clean. This is the safest sex you'll ever have."

"There's nothing safe about you, lady."

He was right about that. Nothing safe about either one of them.

Burke hadn't come to the Carlisle Ranch to make friends, and he never expected to find a lover. Her long, sexy legs wrapped around him. Her arms held him tight. Before he realized what she was doing, she'd rolled over so she was on top, straddling him. In control.

Oh hell, no. He wanted more from her before he reached climax.

He pulled her back down and rolled again. He looked down into her fascinating green eyes. Her lips parted. He covered her mouth with his own, stealing her breath.

She turned her head away. Her body writhed beneath him. "Now," she demanded.

"Not yet."

His need had grown to an almost unbearable level, but he intended to make this moment into something she'd remember for the rest of her life. Paying careful, sensual attention to every part of her body, he brought her to the shivering edge of climax.

"Please," she gasped. "Please, Burke."

"Since you ask so politely…"

He entered her with a hard thrust. She drew him tighter, tighter. The time for game playing was over. He couldn't hold back for one more second. Driven by a primal need, the fierce rhythm of their lovemaking raced, fast and furious, until they exploded together.

He collapsed onto the rug beside her, holding her trembling body against him.

There was no need for words.

Finally, he and Carolyn were in total agreement.

Gradually he became aware of the reality of their surroundings. They were lying on a woven rug on a hard floor. The air was chilly. He kissed the top of her head. Her black hair was soft and smelled like spring flowers. "Carolyn?"

She responded with a muffled sound and snuggled closer.

"Carolyn, are you asleep?"

He separated from her and looked down. Her eyes were

closed. A contented smile curved her lips. He studied her face in a way she'd never allow if she'd been awake and scrappy. In the smooth curve of her forehead he saw innocence and sweetness. The stubborn jut of her chin relaxed as she slept. She was a pretty woman, extremely pretty. But he preferred Carolyn when she was awake and full of fire.

He stood and gently lifted her from the floor. Though she shifted in his arms, she gave no sign of waking up. He placed her on the leather sofa and covered her with an afghan. Later he'd figure out a way to get her up to her own bed.

In moments he was dressed. He wished he had more time to stay with Carolyn. Spending the night in her arms would be sheer luxury.

But he had work to do.

In the dining room, he found Corelli hunched over his bank of computers. In spite of the hour, the only sign that Corelli was frazzled was the loosening of the knot on his necktie.

"Have you gotten any sleep?" Burke asked.

"Catnaps," Corelli replied. "I only require four hours a night."

Burke understood. He was much the same way. During the course of a job like this, he stayed pumped on adrenaline and coffee. Afterwards, he'd keel over and sleep for twenty-four hours. "What have you heard on the bug in Logan's office?"

"A lot," Corelli said. "If you want, I can play back every conversation."

"Give me a summary."

"The SOF mounted a search for Sunny. They have no clue that you were involved in her rescue, but Logan was quick to blame Carolyn. He said she was a bad influence who probably put the thought of running away in Sunny's mind. Then he called off the search. Their assumption is that she's here at the ranch."

Which validated what Carolyn had told him after her

phone conversation with Logan. Burke hadn't planned on taking Sunny to the hospital. But that move might have turned out to be a stroke of good fortune. "Tell me more."

"Apparently, there's discontent among the other women. Several of them—especially those with children—want out."

Burke would do his best to accommodate their wishes. If he could get the innocents away from Logan, there might be a chance to get inside the SOF and search for Nicole. "Any talk of the kidnapping?"

"Not a word," Corelli said. "The major topic of conversation is a big delivery. They're real careful not to say what it is. Even among themselves, they call it the Big D."

"A reference to whatever they're smuggling." Big D sounded like drugs, but the whole need for secrecy along a mountain pass and trail made him think of something larger. "I want you to interface with Logan's computer and find out more."

"Already done." Corelli permitted himself a grin. "Logan has been corresponding with other survivalist groups, similar to the Sons of Freedom."

"Meaning insignificant."

"Correct. These are small enclaves in remote areas of Texas, Arizona and Montana. None of them pop up on FBI surveillance records, but taken all together they form a network. My best guess is that they're smuggling illegal weaponry and drugs."

"Information that needs to be reported."

"Yes, sir," Corelli said.

An organized network of survivalists involved in smuggling was something the FBI—and several other government agencies—would be interested in. But Burke's main concern was Nicole's safety. "When the time is right, we'll pass this information along. For now. Our focus is the kidnap victim."

"Understood." Corelli looked toward a flashing light on

his phone bank. "That's another call from Logan. Should I tell Carolyn or let it go to voice mail?"

"I'll take it," Burke said. He held the receiver to his ear and identified himself. "Special Agent J. D. Burke."

"I want Carolyn," Logan said.

I'll bet you do. "You can talk to me."

There was a moment of silence while Logan considered.

Burke had nothing to say to this ass. Logan had probably kidnapped Nicole. He'd definitely terrorized Sunny and threatened Carolyn. If he acted on that threat, if he so much as touched one hair on her head, Burke would rain terror on this self-important survivalist.

But that wasn't how he'd been taught as a negotiator. His job was to get Logan talking. He forced a conversational tone. "Let's talk, Logan. Why did you call?"

"I know you have Sunny at the ranch. I want her back."

Burke couldn't really use Sunny as a bargaining chip; there was no way he'd return the new mother and her baby to the SOF compound. But Burke did have something to offer. Logan was expecting a big shipment, and he wouldn't want the FBI around for that delivery.

"Here's the deal, Logan. My only concern is Nicole Carlisle's safety. If you help me find her, I'll pack up and go, taking the choppers and the searchers with me. You'll be left in peace."

"I want Sunny back."

Burke's jaw tightened. "She's not here."

"You're lying."

"Tell me about Nicole."

"Go to hell, Burke. I'm not scared of you or any of your fed buddies. And you can tell Carolyn that, too. Tell her that I'm holding her personally responsible for Sunny. She knows better than to cross me."

"Leave her out of this. You're talking to me now."

"Then let the consequences rest on your head."

"What consequences?"

"I will have my revenge."

He hung up before Burke could tell him what real revenge looked like. He pried his tense fingers from the telephone receiver and turned to Corelli. "When is the Big D supposed to happen?"

"Monday night."

The same night that the ransom was supposed to be delivered. A plan began to form in Burke's mind.

Chapter Sixteen

The next morning, Carolyn wakened to the full light of morning glaring around the edges of the closed shades in her bedroom. She glanced at the digital clock on her bedside table. Ten thirty-seven? She seldom slept this late.

The need to get moving warred with a contented lassitude—the aftermath of last night's incredible passion in the office. *How did I get into my bed?* She looked under the comforter and saw that she was wearing a pair of sweatpants and a T-shirt. *I don't remember getting dressed.*

But she did recall—in spectacular detail—making love to Special Agent J. D. Burke. A happy little sigh escaped her lips as she snuggled deeper under the comforter. A quiver rippled through her, a reminder of Burke's touch. She licked her lips, imagining that she could still taste him. Behind closed eyes, she saw his muscular chest and arms. His powerful body…

The door to her bedroom crashed open. Dylan charged toward her bed and shook her. "Carolyn, get up."

In an instant, she went from sweet reverie to full alert. "What is it?"

"Proof of life. We got a videotape. You need to see this."

She lunged from the bed and grabbed her plaid flannel

bathrobe from the hook in the closet. Barefoot, she followed him down the stairs.

In the living room, she saw Corelli hooking up a dusty, old VCR player to the flat-screen television. In a crisp voice, he informed them that nobody used equipment like this anymore. Later, he'd transfer the images to a DVD. But they shouldn't hope for crystal-clear definition.

"Why not?" Polly demanded as she peeked over his shoulder.

"Twenty-first-century technology doesn't do me any good when the kidnapper is using stuff that's decades old. First, a Polaroid photograph. Then a pay phone. Now this."

Lucas was also in the room. And Special Agent Smith who, she assumed, had taken over the search coordination efforts since Silverman was at the hospital with Sunny.

Her gaze went to Burke. A forest-green turtleneck outlined his broad shoulders. Though his brown hair was mussed, he looked awake and supremely competent. His dark eyes met hers in brief acknowledgment. There was no time to indulge in morning-after conversation or sweet, sexy whispers. There could only be a glance between them.

Corelli pushed the play button and stepped away from the screen.

When Nicole's face appeared, Dylan shuddered.

"It's Sunday morning," Nicole said.

Behind her was a faded yellow sheet that looked like it had been tacked to a wall. The image showed only her head and shoulders. She reached up and tucked her blond hair behind her ear. "Don't worry about me," she said. "I'm fine. I have plenty to eat and drink, and I'm being well cared for."

Her blue eyes seemed calm and untroubled. Considering what she'd been through, she looked good.

"I've been asked to remind you about the ransom. One million dollars in cash. That's a lot of money, isn't it?" She drew her fingers across her lips. "If you follow instructions, everything will turn out okay. See you soon."

The screen went blank.

Burke moved in front of the screen. "First impressions?"

In a choked voice, Dylan spoke, "I've never seen that blouse before."

"Are you sure?" Carolyn asked. "I didn't think you paid much attention to clothes."

"I know what she had on yesterday. I'll never forget."

Polly said, "I think Dylan's right about the blouse. I've done my share of laundry here and Nicole doesn't have anything with flowers. I'm not so sure about the beige cardigan."

"First impressions," Burke repeated. "Carolyn?"

She forced her drowsy mind to focus. "It didn't sound like she was reading from a script. She was conversational, but distant. Like she was using her bedside manner."

"Explain," Burke said.

"I've gone with Nicole a couple of times when she's treating a sick animal. When she chats with the owner, she uses that tone."

"Right," Dylan said. "It's her 'Don't Panic' voice. She's trying to tell us to stay calm. Damn it, she always puts other people first."

"Lucas," Burke said, "what's your impression?"

"Didn't look like she'd been hurt none."

Carolyn studied the old, bowlegged cowboy. He sat on the edge of the sofa, leaning forward. His hair looked like it hadn't been washed recently, and his stubble was a couple of days old. More than anyone else in the room, he showed signs of falling apart. She wanted to believe it was because he was concerned about Nicole. But if he was the traitor, he'd feel guilty. Remorse would gnaw at his gut.

"Okay, Smith," Burke said. "Give us a profiler's opinion."

As Agent Smith stepped in front of the screen, Carolyn realized how short he was, probably only five feet seven inches, with square shoulders and a thick torso. His blond hair was cut short, military-style, and it made his head seem square.

"It's all good," he said. "As Lucas pointed out, she doesn't appear to be injured. Or drugged. The tone that Carolyn referred to as bedside manner might not only be for our benefit. She could have established a rapport with the kidnappers. That's positive."

"Why?" Dylan asked.

"In captivity, a hostage undergoes feelings of panic, fear and rage," he lectured. "Nicole appears to be suppressing those primal reactions. Instead, she's cooperating, forcing the kidnappers to see her as an individual, convincing them that she's on their side. In that circumstance, they're far less likely to hurt her."

As Burke paced across the floor, Carolyn couldn't help admiring the way he moved. Smooth, long strides. He said, "We're going to play this tape several times. I want you to look for any clue to her whereabouts. Nicole might be giving us some kind of signal."

"Like what?" Polly asked.

"A facial expression. The way she blinks. The way she phrases her words."

As she watched, again and again, Carolyn's anger returned. She wished she could jump inside the picture and drag Nicole home.

In the Polaroid, Nicole had put them on the right track with hand signals indicating the Circle M. This time, she seemed to be doing the same thing.

She had gestured twice. Once to tuck her hair behind her ear, forming a circle. Then she stroked her finger along the line of her mouth. Actually, three fingers. A sideways *M*.

Nicole's message was the same: Circle M.

Carolyn looked toward Lucas. If he was in communication with the SOF, she didn't want to say anything in front of him. He might report back and get Nicole in trouble. Why was Burke allowing Lucas to stay in the room?

"I'm drawing a blank," Polly said. "Anybody need coffee?"

Carolyn raised her hand. "I do."

Coffee and some kind of breakfast sounded heavenly. She followed Polly into the kitchen and poured herself a mug. "Thanks for moving up to the house, Polly. Did you sleep well?"

"I did, thank you. My husband could hardly close his eyes. He's so excited about being in the middle of all this. Not that he's happy about the kidnapping."

"Of course not." Carolyn understood that Polly's husband and his illness took precedence over anything else. "How long have you and Juan been married?"

"Almost twenty years. Second marriage for both of us." She grinned. "And the second time's the charm."

They had a good marriage, and Carolyn wondered what went into that kind of relationship. Was it something she could learn? "How did you know you and Juan were in love? Was it fast as lightning?"

"More like a slow, gathering storm. We were friends for months before anything happened. But as soon as he kissed me, I knew he was the man I'd spend the rest of my life with."

"All it took was one kiss?"

Polly raised an eyebrow. "You're asking a lot of questions, Carolyn. This wouldn't have anything to do with that good-looking FBI agent, would it?"

She wasn't ready to talk about Burke, not even to Polly.

Carolyn sipped her coffee. "Where do you think Nicole got that blouse?"

"Not sure, but I was glad to see her in clean clothes." Polly opened the fridge and took out an orange. "You didn't answer my question about Burke."

"I guess I didn't."

"The way you were brought up, surrounded by cowboys and having to be as tough as they are, you need a man who's as strong-willed and stubborn as you. Burke would be a good match for you."

"That's your opinion," Carolyn said.

"Mark my words. You're not going to end up with some fancy-pants, city-boy lawyer."

Burke strode into the kitchen and they both went silent. He was definitely not a fancy-pants. The opposite, in fact. Totally rugged, he exploded with masculine energy.

"Get dressed, Carolyn. We're going for a ride on the Indian Trail."

"Give me fifteen minutes."

He checked his wristwatch, a habit that she'd come to realize was his way of maintaining control. "Ten," he said.

"Twelve," she countered.

"Meet me in the barn."

BURKE STOOD IN THE BARN doorway and tapped the face of his wristwatch. Twelve minutes had passed. He hadn't really expected Carolyn to get ready so quickly, and he was surprised to see her stride from the house wearing her boots, hat and a canvas jacket. From this distance, her expression was unreadable, but her confidence showed in every swaggering step she took.

Stopping in front of him, she planted her fists on her hips. "Fast enough for you?"

"You're a speed demon." He wanted to tell her that she was the sexiest demon he'd ever seen. Naturally beautiful. No need for makeup. Her black lashes and arched brows highlighted her transparent green eyes.

Carolyn took an energy bar from her jacket pocket and tore off the wrapping. "Mind telling me why I'm here?"

"I need your help to find the cave Sunny mentioned."

"Ah, yes. Her supposedly romantic hideaway near Cathedral Rocks." She raised the bar to her mouth. "I don't know the exact location, but I can take you to the rocks. Why are we going there?"

"It occurred to me that a secluded hideout might be the place where Nicole is being held, being guarded by Butch Thurgood and Richter. I was wrong about that."

"How do you know?"

"This morning, at first light, I sent the chopper team to investigate. They located the cave. No one was there."

"Then, why are we—"

"Closer inspection," he said. He nodded to two uniformed men who were already on horseback, waiting outside the corral. "These deputies are going to run some forensic tests. We might find evidence that Nicole was at the cave."

The search team in the chopper had also made another discovery. Hovering near the pine trees where Sunny met up with them last night, they spotted a grave-sized mound of earth. Tonight, under cover of darkness, he'd take a team to excavate.

Past experience taught him that the body would be buried at least two-and-a-half feet deep with rocks on top. Otherwise, the coyotes would have dug up the corpse of Barbara Ayers. A check of the FBI database showed that she and her sister, Lisa, were listed as missing persons. The sisters had disappeared over a year ago.

Carolyn chomped on the energy bar. "If we head out on the road, we'll hook up with the Indian Trail. It's easy to follow."

"I don't want to go that way," he said. "The SOF could be watching the ranch, and I don't want them to know what we're doing."

"Good point. We can go west, then south over the ridge. That way, we'll stay on Carlisle land for most of the ride."

"I knew you'd have an answer." He turned on his heel and went into the barn where their horses were saddled and ready. After Logan's threat of revenge, he hadn't really wanted Carolyn to leave the house. But he needed her help. "GPS isn't much good in unmarked mountain terrain."

She went directly to Elvis and stroked his nose. "We're going for a ride, pal. What do you think about that?"

Elvis bobbed his head. Burke had never seen a horse with so much personality. The bay with a white blaze on his forehead was one of a kind. Like his owner.

He went to a wood bench and picked up a Kevlar vest. "You need to wear this, Carolyn."

A frown pulled at the corner of her soft pink lips. "Why?"

"Because we need to take the SOF seriously." He lowered his voice, though no one else was in the barn. "Corelli accessed Logan's computer and he's been listening to the bug. Logan didn't see us make the rescue, but he assumes you're somehow responsible. He thinks you influenced Sunny."

"Of course he'd blame me. The wicked city woman."

"Put on the vest, Carolyn." He paused, then added the magic word. "Please."

She took the vest from him. "I don't see you wearing any kind of protection."

"Logan's ticked off at you, not me." She seemed to have that effect on people. "But I suppose you're right. I'll stop at the van and pick up my own vest."

"I don't want anything bad to happen to you."

"I'll be okay," he said. "Logan might have shot up my vehicle, but he's not dumb enough to injure a fed."

"Don't underestimate Sam Logan," she said. "He's a lot dumber than you think."

Chapter Seventeen

In spite of the uncomfortable bulletproof vest under her jacket, Carolyn was glad to take an active part in the investigation. Astride Elvis, she rode with Burke and the two deputies from the sheriff's department. They headed west toward the burned-out structure of the old stable. The acrid stench of charred wood hung like a poisonous cloud in the crisp air.

This was the first time she'd seen the destruction up close, and she reined Elvis in to take a closer look. The one-story structure had been reduced to a grotesque skeleton with only parts of walls still standing and rubble where there had once been neat stalls. A scorched backhoe—an expensive piece of equipment—huddled at the far edge of the stable like the remains of a prehistoric beast.

The fire had been her motivation for coming home, and the sight troubled her. Was Lucas responsible for this needless destruction? He'd admitted to being first on the scene. He was the one who called in the alarm. But she couldn't imagine him doing this, risking the livestock, risking a wildfire that could have spread across the grassland. They could have lost acres and acres. Lucas wouldn't want that; he loved this ranch. Or did he?

She didn't trust her own judgment anymore, not after

seeing that list of enemies that Burke and his agents had compiled. Half the county seemed to hate the Carlisles.

Burke reined his big bay horse up beside her. She tore her gaze away from the ruins. Watching Burke was a welcome distraction. Despite the fact that he wore a Chicago Cubs cap instead of a Stetson, he looked comfortable in the saddle. Those summers he'd spent with his grandparents in rural Wisconsin had served him well. "You don't ride too badly," she said, "for a farmer."

"Once you learn how, you never forget."

But there seemed to be something else he'd entirely forgotten. He'd made no mention of their lovemaking. But then again, she hadn't said anything, either. *Should I tell him that he's the best lover I've ever known? That last night was spectacular?*

Though tempted to gush, she decided to play it cool. When she was younger, she'd had her share of meaningless sex and knew how it was supposed to work: no flowers, no phone calls in the morning, no sweet talk.

But last night was different. The depth of their passion wasn't what she expected from a one-night stand. Making love with Burke left her craving more. She didn't want last night to be the first and only time.

I should tell him. Instead, she nudged Elvis with her knees and moved forward. Skirting the edge of the forest, they came into sight of one of the main feeding pastures, about four miles from the ranch house. Contained by a barbed wire fence, over three hundred head of Black Angus milled from water troughs to feeding on the hay spread on the ground.

This was usually the last stop for these cattle before being herded to the slaughterhouse in Delta. Unlike non-organic ranches that crammed the cattle into feed lots and stuffed them with corn to fatten them up, this wide valley offered plenty of room to move around and graze.

Burke rode beside her. He pointed to a fat boulder near the south side of the field. "Interesting rock formation."

"*La Rana*," she said. "The frog. When I was a girl, I thought *La Rana* watched over the cattle at night and croaked really loud to chase away predators."

"A protector frog. Nice."

She regarded the herd with pride. "They're beautiful, aren't they?"

"Not the word that springs to mind when I think of a nine-hundred-pound steer."

"Don't you dare say fat." She bristled. "These guys are so healthy."

"When I think of beauty," he said, "I think of you."

Taken aback, she met his gaze. His dark brown eyes warmed her, melting her attempt to be cool. Without saying another word, he seemed to be telling her that last night had meant something more to him, too.

But they were busy people with full, active lives and tons of responsibility. She couldn't possibly think of settling down. Still, the idea of sharing her hectic life with Burke held a certain appeal. She imagined coming home after work and finding him waiting with a glass of Chardonnay. What would it be like to go on an actual date? Or to make love in an actual bed?

He urged his horse forward, leaving her gaping behind him. She took a moment to tamp down her fantasies, then tapped her heel against Elvis's flank. Her big brown horse happily sped up, bringing her even with Burke.

"About last night," she said, "I want you to know—"

"Not now," he interrupted.

His abrupt manner shouldn't have surprised her. By now she knew that Burke was a man whose action agenda easily outweighed his sensitivity. "Burke, I have something to say."

"So do I." The heat from his gaze poured over her like hot

fudge on a sundae. "There's a hell of a lot to say, but now isn't the time. We need to keep focused on the kidnapping."

"Fine," she responded with as much gumption as she could dredge up while her insides liquefied into a gooey mass of desire. "Here's a point of focus. Why did you leave Lucas in the room when you played the tape of Nicole?"

"You think he's the traitor?"

She hadn't clearly stated her suspicion. Even now she was hesitant to accuse. "It's possible."

"You didn't want to say anything in front of him," Burke said. "That's why you didn't mention Nicole's hand gestures. She made another Circle M."

"Pointing at Logan. Again."

"I agree that Logan is probably our culprit," Burke said, "but there's something bothering me. We got ransom calls from two different kidnappers with requests for two different amounts. I have a nasty feeling that Butch and Richter might have taken Nicole and split off from the SOF to make their own big score."

"Any evidence?" she asked.

"Nothing. Corelli has been listening to the bug I placed in Logan's office nonstop. He hasn't mentioned Nicole once."

At this point, the trail went uphill through thick forest and rocky terrain. They went single file with Carolyn in the lead. She hadn't been in this backcountry for years, and the land had changed, as it always did. Rock formations stayed pretty much the same, but the forest was always different. During the last few years, they'd lost a lot of trees to pine beetles. Whole hillsides had to be clear-cut. Later, they'd be replanted.

She picked her route carefully, relying on an internal compass. Figuring out directions had always been easy for her. Her father once said that he could drop her in the middle of a forest at midnight and she'd find her way home by morning.

Even with the sun almost directly overhead, she sensed that they were moving south and west.

If only life could be so easily navigated.

She paused at a high point on a ridge and waited for Burke and the deputies to ride up beside her. She pointed. "Over there. Do you see the sunlight hitting that jagged formation? Cathedral Rocks. That's where we're headed."

"Nice work," one of the deputies commented. "If I'd been leading the way, we would've been lost."

"When we get closer," Burke said, "it wouldn't hurt to be extra alert."

The two men nodded. One of them pulled his rifle from a scabbard attached to his saddle.

For the second time in as many days, Carolyn was on a mission with Burke where she was the only person without firepower. *Next time, I'll be armed.*

"You boys go first," Burke said. "I'll hang back with Carolyn."

As the deputies went around them, Carolyn gave a sharp tug on her horse's reins to hold him back. Elvis didn't like being in the rear.

The deputies in their brown uniform jackets rode carefully down a steep incline while Burke watched. Sitting straight in his saddle, he seemed suddenly alert. "This isn't your property anymore."

"It's National Forest."

He gave a nod. "You go first."

At the bottom of the craggy slope, they merged with the Indian Trail that led through the mountains. A dried-up creek bed sat on their left. On their right was a hillside of loose gravel. Compared to the narrow path they'd taken over the ridge, the Indian Trail was like a super highway with plenty of room to ride side by side.

"I can see why they'd use this route for smuggling," Burke said. "You could almost drive a truck through here."

"Not in the higher elevations. It's rugged. Crossing the pass isn't for sissies."

"When do you usually get snow around here?"

Supposedly, they couldn't mention last night because they needed to keep focus. But he was talking about the weather. The weather? She shot a ferocious glare in his direction and reined Elvis to a halt. "I refuse to go through a snowfall report. We need to talk about last night. About us."

"Not now." His gaze rested on her for a moment, then slid away. He was scanning the hillsides.

"What are you looking for?"

"Trouble," he said.

"Search no more. I'm sitting right here beside you. And I have a truckload of trouble to unload on your head." She paused for breath. "In the first place, I don't want you to think that I'm the kind of woman who tumbles into bed at a moment's notice."

"Why would I think that?"

She didn't stop to explain that she'd known him for only a day before they were making love on the floor in her brother's office. "Secondly, I don't expect any sort of commitment. I'm not looking to get married or anything."

"Carolyn, I don't—"

"Furthermore," she said, "last night was amazing. We have some kind of connection. I can't explain it."

"Then don't." He maneuvered his horse beside her and held out his hand. "Lean over here and kiss me."

"As if that will make everything all right?"

"You know it will."

She reached toward his hand. Before she could grasp it, he turned his head sharply. "Carolyn, get down."

She heard the gunfire. Then a thud.

She was hit.

Her breath was gone. It felt like all the air had been squeezed out of her lungs. *Breathe, damn it.* She gulped frantically but couldn't get air. She was losing consciousness. She slumped. Her feet came out of the stirrups. Falling, falling…

Burke was there. He caught her before she hit the ground. Ducking behind Elvis, he cradled her against him.

A throbbing pain spread from her chest to every part of her body. She'd been shot. If she hadn't been wearing the bulletproof vest, she'd be dead.

She sucked down a gasp of air, then another. Her arms and legs regained strength, but she wasn't able to stand on her own.

Burke yelled to the deputies. "Sniper. In the trees. Straight ahead."

Dazed, she leaned against him as he used his cell phone to summon the chopper. Using Elvis as a shield, he dragged her to the edge of the trail. Behind a boulder, they found shelter.

Her pain began to subside. Pressed against the rock, she looked up at him.

He had saved her life.

Chapter Eighteen

Burke held Carolyn close, protecting her with his body in case there was another shooter behind them. He pulled off his Cubs cap and rose up to look over the flat boulder where they were hiding. In his right hand, he held his gun, ready to return fire. He couldn't attack. There was no effective way to aim at the sniper perched on the hillside and keep Carolyn safe at the same time.

He knew where the shooter was. At the moment he'd been leaning toward Carolyn for a kiss, he'd caught a glimpse in his peripheral vision: the sharp reflection of sunlight on a rifle scope. But he'd been too late to do anything more than shout a warning.

Farther up the trail, the deputies returned fire. He hoped they could keep the sniper pinned down until the chopper arrived.

Carolyn moved in his arms. "Where's Elvis? And your horse?"

Burke looked over his shoulder. Both horses were gone. He didn't see the mounts the deputies had been riding. "They took off. They're safe."

"Let me up, Burke. I'm okay. I just had the wind knocked out of me."

He held her even tighter. Their Kevlar vests bumped against each other. "The chopper's going to be here in a minute."

"I can handle this. I'm okay."

He looked down into her anxious face. "Lie still and let me keep you safe. You don't have to prove anything to me."

Her green eyes flashed. "You're right. The only person I have to prove anything to…is me. I never thought of it that way before, but it's true."

He wasn't sure what she was talking about, but he was glad to hear her speaking. When she toppled from her horse and he thought she'd been seriously wounded, his world stopped. She'd almost gotten killed, and it was his fault. "I never should have put you in danger."

"You saved my life," she said. "If I hadn't been wearing this vest, I'd be dead."

"I shouldn't have brought you here."

After last night, when she'd been so effective in rescuing Sunny, he'd made the mistake of thinking that she was as experienced as Smith or Silverman. Using her as a guide through the mountains broke FBI protocol. She was a civilian, someone who shouldn't be placed in the line of fire.

She wriggled her arm free and touched the place on the vest where she'd been hit. "I was shot. I'm going to have a giant bruise. Otherwise, I'm fine. It's kind of amazing really."

"You're amazing," he said.

An exchange of gunfire between the deputies and the sniper distracted him. He peeked over the edge of the boulder they were hiding behind. The two deputies seemed to be doing a good job.

"Logan must really hate me," she said. "Do you think he's the sniper?"

"Is he a good shot?"

"Not really. He probably sent one of his men to do his dirty work."

He lay back down beside her, aware of the possibility that another of Logan's men had moved into position behind them. At any given moment, Burke could be shot in the back, and he didn't want to die—didn't want to go until he told her. "About last night…"

"Now you're ready to talk?"

"Here's how I feel. You said you wanted me to know you're not a bimbo who sleeps around. The thought never entered my mind. You're a smart, principled woman. Different from anyone—male or female—that I've ever known. Maybe that's why I'm drawn to you. I can't figure you out. You challenge me in a good way. And I want to be with you. You can call that a bond or kismet or fate. I don't know what it is. I'm not one for analyzing. I just know it's there. It's real."

A tear slipped down her cheek.

Gently, he wiped it away. "You said you weren't ready to get married. You're probably right about that. It might be too soon. But I want you to know that I'm not afraid of commitment."

"I'm not afraid, either," she said.

Pressed against the boulder, they held each other. Her legs twined with his. In the midst of danger, he felt at peace. He'd rather be here with Carolyn than anywhere else.

He heard the *thunk-thunk* of the helicopter rotors and looked up.

The chopper couldn't land in this canyon, but the hovering bird made an effective predator as it swooped down. There was more gunfire. More shouts from the deputies. A bullhorn voice from the chopper shouted an order to put down the weapon and raise both hands.

Carolyn looked up at him. "What's happening?"

"We're being rescued."

He rose to a crouch and peeked over the boulder.

The deputies were waving their arms. Coming toward Burke and Carolyn, they called out, "They got him."

Burke stood. On the far hillside, he saw a man standing with his arms raised over his head. Even at this distance, he knew it wasn't Logan; he wasn't blond.

One man from the chopper aimed a rifle at their quarry. Another descended on a rope to make the arrest. Impressive work.

Carolyn stood and leaned against his chest.

They were safe. For now.

TWO HOURS LATER, Carolyn had been evacuated from the Indian Trail. Elvis and all the other horses were safely tucked away in the stable. She'd been checked by a medic who told her that she was okay, apart from a bad bruise above her right breast. The medic gave her pain meds and suggested she go back to bed. Though she'd taken his advice, she couldn't sleep. Her mind whirled, remembering what had happened and trying to imagine what would come next.

She couldn't stop thinking about Burke. Instead of wondering whether or not he felt anything for her, she accepted him at his word. They had something special. And it might lead to a commitment between them. Joyful warmth flowed through her veins and she immediately felt guilty.

Nicole was still in danger. Jesse Longbridge was still unconscious in the hospital. The Carlisle Ranch was under siege. Not to mention the fact that Logan wanted her dead. In the middle of this disaster, how could she be happy?

She threw off the covers, climbed out of bed and got dressed. The pain medications were making her dizzy, and her bruise still throbbed, but she had to do something. It wasn't in her nature to lie back and let someone else take responsibility.

Completely dressed except for her boots, she heard a tap on her door. "Come in. I'm decent."

Burke stepped through her bedroom door and closed it behind him. His smile sparked those irrelevant happy feelings that she'd almost squelched.

"Too bad you're decent," he said. "I was hoping for a sexy lace negligee."

"Not at the ranch." She couldn't help smiling back. "All my classy nightwear is at my condo in Denver."

"Can't wait to see it."

He lived in Denver, too. That was his full-time residence when he wasn't on assignment. "What part of town do you live in?"

"I've got a duplex in Capitol Hill. You?"

"A condo. Twelfth floor. Downtown."

They lived less than five miles apart. They probably went to the same restaurants, shopped at the same stores, walked past each other on the street. But they had to come all the way to Carlisle Ranch to meet.

He sat on a burgundy upholstered chair beside her trophy case. "I wanted to give you an update."

She'd been thinking about something far more sensual, but Burke had gone into his get-things-done mode. Instead of stretching out on the bed, she perched on a chair opposite him and shoved her feet into her boots. "I'm ready."

"The sniper's name is Wesley Tindall. He's former military—and that's where he learned to shoot. We're holding him in FBI custody."

She touched the bruise below her shoulder. "Was he the guy who shot out the window of your van?"

"Don't know. He's not talking. Hasn't said anything about Nicole, either."

"So, basically, he's not much use."

"Except that he won't be riding with Logan when they go to pick up their big shipment. He's down a man. And that's good news for us."

"Why?"

"On Monday night, when Logan and his men go to pick up the shipment, they'll leave the Circle M with fewer guards than usual. That's when we'll make our move. We'll go in, get the women and children out. And search for Nicole."

She liked the way that sounded. If Sunny was any indication, there would be plenty of other women who were ready to leave the SOF. "I want to be a part of that action."

"No."

"But some of the women know me. I can talk to them."

"This isn't up for negotiation." He stood. "I almost lost you today. I won't put you in danger again."

She rose from her chair to face him. "That's my choice."

"I'm in charge here, Carolyn. It's my job."

But she didn't want to sit on the sidelines. "I'll be careful."

"We were careful today," he reminded her. "We went the long way around to avoid being seen."

Which brought up a question she hadn't considered before. "Why was Tindall there?"

"It wasn't an ambush," Burke said. "If Logan had been planning to trap us, there would have been more men. I think Tindall was posted as a lookout on the Indian Trail. It was our bad luck to run into him."

"Why did he shoot?"

"My guess? Logan has put out a bounty on you. He wants revenge. That's a damn good reason why you're not going to be involved in any more action."

"You make a good argument," she conceded. "But I still think I could—"

"No." He closed the distance between them in three quick strides. Reaching out, he caressed her shoulder. His hand came to rest behind her neck, and he held her so she couldn't look away from him. "Today, when I thought I'd lost you, my heart broke. If anything happened to you, I couldn't live with myself."

His tone struck a chord within her. "If I'm not there at your side," she said, "who's going to protect you?"

"I'll manage."

He kissed her hard, silencing her objections. Her body fit perfectly with his. Every contour matched. In his arms, she felt soft and feminine.

Just as quickly as he'd kissed her, he stepped back. "I wasn't planning to do that."

"I don't mind." She rested the flat of her palm against his solid, muscular chest. "Not a bit."

He caught her hand, brushed his lips against her knuckles. "There's more."

"I'm listening." She flopped on the bed, wishing that she was wearing a sexy negligee instead of jeans and boots.

"The sheriff's deputies finally got to do a forensic workup inside the cave. They found some fibers that look like they'd purposely been pulled from a sweater. The color matches the sweater Nicole was wearing when she was kidnapped."

"She was at the cave," Carolyn said. "Leaving us another clue."

"Here's the timeline I've got figured out," he said. "Nicole was grabbed at the creek by two guys associated with the SOF. They took her to the Circle M. Logan must have realized that there was a search underway."

"Right," she said, "my brother and his posse going door-to-door and asking questions."

"They had to get her out of there. Logan's men—Butch Thurgood and Pete Richter—took her to the cave, planning to wait until the search died down. The next day or late that night, he knew the FBI was involved. There'd be choppers and surveillance. The cave wasn't safe."

"So he had her brought back to the SOF compound," she said. "That's why Nicole keeps giving us Circle M clues."

Though he nodded, he didn't look convinced. It seemed like a lot of shuffling around. "Another alternative is that Butch and Richter took off with her. That would explain the second ransom call. They're trying to work their own angle."

She frowned. "If Nicole isn't at the Circle M, why would she give these clues and why *wouldn't* Logan let us search?"

"Because the place is loaded with illegal weapons and drugs. He can't allow an FBI search."

Carolyn wasn't sure if she preferred thinking of Nicole being with Logan or with his men. From what Sunny had told them, Pete Richter was mean.

"Tonight," Burke said, "we're going to excavate the grave site Sunny told us about. Chopper surveillance found a mound of earth near the pines."

This time, Carolyn didn't ask if she could come along. Digging up the remains of Barbara Ayers wasn't a mission she wanted to be part of. "Be careful, Burke."

Chapter Nineteen

The wind blew colder tonight. Heavy clouds scrolled across the face of the moon. Burke moved into position at the open field across from the pine trees where they'd met Sunny. He had a small army—Agent Smith and four other men called in for tactical support. Fully equipped, they were dressed like a SWAT team with weapons, full body armor and infrared goggles.

Their goal was to excavate Barbara Ayers's grave and recover her body. Her remains would be transported to the FBI medical examiner's office in Denver where a top-notch forensic team would read the evidence left behind in death— evidence that would lay the murder of this young, pregnant woman at the doorstep of Sam Logan and the SOF.

Furthermore, tonight was a practice run for tomorrow. Burke's men had studied the maps of the compound, but there was nothing like firsthand experience to get the lay of the land.

Tomorrow, while most of the SOF men were gone— dealing with their shipment on the Indian Trail—Burke and his force would penetrate the compound and extract the fourteen women and children. When these hostages were safe, he'd search for Nicole.

That rescue—less than twenty-four hours from right now—would take place at the same time Logan's men were meeting their contacts on the Indian Trail. At that location, he expected immediate surrender to a far superior force. There was nothing like a half dozen armed FBI agents and a chopper bearing down like a fierce, prehistoric beast to make a guy throw down his gun and beg for mercy.

At his signal, his men moved across the open field. The heat-sensing camera showed no guards in this area outside the barbed wire surrounding the compound.

They found the mound of earth that had been spotted by the chopper easily. Burke and Smith stood watch while the others dug. In less than five minutes, they had uncovered the remains of a small woman wrapped in a sheet.

They zipped her into a body bag, and spent another five minutes replacing the dirt.

They retreated across the field to the waiting vans.

The operation went off without a single hitch. Apparently, Logan had more to worry about than guarding the grave of a woman who had been under his care.

CAROLYN PACED IN HER BEDROOM, waiting for Burke to return. It was only ten o'clock but felt much later. After being cooped up in the house all afternoon, she yearned for action. But she had promised not to take any risks, which included standing at her bedroom window with the light behind her back, going onto the well-lit porch or—Heaven forbid!—going to the barn for a chat with Elvis.

She touched the injury on her chest as a reminder that she was a target. Her bruise had turned a dark, aching purple and her arm was sore, but otherwise she was fine.

Her pacing stopped in front of the trophy case, filled with dozens of blue ribbons and gold statuettes that she'd started collecting when she was eight. Life had been simple then. All she had to do was go to school, finish her chores and ride.

Perhaps it was childish to keep the glass-and-wood trophy case in her room, but her father had built it with his own hands and presented it to her on her sixteenth birthday. He'd told her that she was a winner, and she'd worked her hardest to prove him right. She hadn't displayed any of her second- or third-place awards because she needed to be number one—to make her father proud. *The ultimate daddy's girl. But what choice did I have after Mom left?*

Carolyn realized that she still hadn't told her mother about the kidnapping. She needed to do that, but ten o'clock in Colorado was midnight in New York. Too late to call?

But this was important—one of the few times in her life when she needed her mother's advice. Not only about the kidnapping. She wanted to talk about Burke. Her feelings for him were a jagged chart of highs and lows. The way he needed to always be in charge—their constant competition—irked her. But when he touched her, she soared to a high that was unlike anything she'd felt before. Was it love?

She needed her mother, and she needed to make that very private call on a phone that wasn't tied to the system being monitored by Corelli.

Leaving her bedroom, she went downstairs. In the dining room, Corelli—who never seemed to sleep—was still monitoring his computers. Dylan had zonked out in the easy chair. She didn't want to wake her brother by talking to Corelli. Nor did she want Dylan to know that she was calling Mom.

Instead, she went through the kitchen and out the back door where she sat on the step. With the Longbridge Security men and other patrolling cowboys around, she felt safe.

The night chill soothed her. Finally, the weather was beginning to feel more like December. She zipped up her sweatshirt. When this ordeal was over, she'd need a vacation. Maybe she should spend Christmas in New York with Mom. All the decorated store windows were spectacular, and she'd love to see the giant tree in Rockefeller Center. Maybe Burke would come with her. They could get a room in a plush hotel, eat fabulous sushi or take in a play. Would he like theater? He'd been a cop in Chicago. He must be okay with big cities.

She spotted someone heading toward the house. Even in the dim light of the cloud-covered moon, she recognized the bowlegged gait of Lucas Mann.

She waved to him, and he ambled toward her.

"It's late," she said. "What are you doing awake?"

"Can't sleep. That's one of them things about being an old codger. You get up during the night."

She didn't want to think he was sleepless because he was haunted by guilt or that he was awake because he was spying for Logan. "Do you ever think about retirement? Buying a little spread of your own?"

"Matter of fact, I do. A quiet spot with a couple of horses."

Had Logan bribed him? Offered him enough cash to make his dream come true? "We'd hate to lose you."

"A man gets old." His eyes were shaded and unreadable under his cowboy hat. "You know how people talk about a slippery slope? How you take one wrong step and the whole mountain slides out from under you?"

What wrong step had he taken? "Is there something you need to tell me?"

With a gloved hand, he patted her shoulder. "Don't you worry none. Nicole's coming back. Then everything's going to get back to normal."

"I hope so."

He touched the brim of his hat and walked away. She cared about this old cowboy. He was like part of the family.

But if he'd been involved in Nicole's kidnapping, in any way, she could never forgive him.

Before she could make her call, she heard vans pulling up at the front of the house. Burke was back. She rushed inside just as he came through the front door. In his full body armor, he was as impressive as an ancient warrior.

"It's done," he said.

"You found the body?"

He gave a somber nod.

In the back of her mind, she'd been hoping that the grave would be empty. Now there was evidence. One of the men in the SOF was a killer. That didn't bode well for Nicole.

She watched and listened while Burke debriefed Corelli and Dylan. At the same time, he peeled off his armor and returned to the shape of a mere mortal—a shape she found incredibly attractive.

They moved on to discuss other plans. Tomorrow night was when everything was going down. In less than twenty-four hours, the ransom was due. And the SOF would be accepting their big delivery.

Neither Carolyn nor Dylan would participate in the hostage rescue. Their job was to stay here by the phone, waiting for the kidnappers to call.

The tactical support team circled the table. None of these men asked for her opinion, much less her approval of their plan. She'd become a tiny, insignificant speck of female energy, silently worrying that someone would be hurt, fearing for the safety of Nicole and the other SOF women. She remembered Lisa Ayers's sad eyes. How would that delicate, waiflike creature deal with all of these rescuers? And what about Nicole, being held against her will? Carolyn wished with all her heart that there was another way to deal with the situation, but she knew Logan would never negotiate.

She stepped away from the table. "Good night, boys. I'm going to bed."

"That's the right idea," Burke said. "We need to be rested. It's all going down tomorrow night."

A deep rumble of masculine voices echoed his words. These were men at the edge of battle, fierce and determined. Unstoppable.

She'd barely gotten into her bedroom when Burke slipped through the door. He caught hold of her hand and yanked her into his arms. His lips were hot. Her body responded to his urgent need as she kissed him back and drew his tongue into her mouth. His hands slid under her sweatshirt. His touch against her bare skin set off a chain reaction of desire.

And yet she pulled away from him. "Wait a minute."

"Am I being too rough? Did I hurt your bruise?"

"I'm not in pain," she assured him. "I just wanted to have a say in what happens next."

He reached up and ran his fingers through her unbound hair. "Soft as silk," he murmured.

She'd had time today for washing and conditioning, even though it was difficult with her aching left arm.

"Burke," she snapped. "Pay attention."

"I'm listening."

All she wanted was to be heard. "Your tactical support team is even more overpowering than a roomful of cowboys."

"Adrenaline," he said. "Our mission went off with precision. It's a satisfying feeling, even though we were dealing with the tragedy of a murder."

"I felt invisible, and I hate that. It's not normal for me. I'm accustomed to being in charge."

"I'll make you a deal, Carolyn. In this room, you're the boss. I'll do anything you want."

His pseudonegotiation made her smile. "What if I tell you to hop on one leg and squawk like a chicken?"

"That's a little kinky." He leaned close and nipped at her earlobe. "But I'll do it. Whatever turns you on."

Her need for control was overwhelmed by a more powerful desire. She placed her cell phone on the bedside table. The call to her mom would have to wait.

"I want you in my bed. All night."

"Yes, ma'am."

THE NEXT MORNING started much like the day before, except with fewer doubts. Carolyn glowed with a pleasant certainty. Burke was the best, most skillful lover she'd ever known. His passion took her to sensual places she'd never been before.

For the moment, she didn't mind not being the boss. She'd gotten out of bed, dressed and readied herself for the big day when the ransom would be paid and Nicole returned.

In the kitchen, she was sipping Polly's excellent coffee and had almost finished a plate of scrambled eggs and toast when Dylan joined her.

"We got another tape," he said.

"Where did it come from?"

"Just like yesterday, it was hanging on a fence post near the road. Whoever is dropping these tapes off is doing it before dawn and disappearing. Corelli says there's no point in checking satellite surveillance. The mountains and trees make it impossible to identify the guy."

Taking her coffee, she followed him into the living room where Burke stood by the television. The sight of his big, muscular body gave her a warm feeling of possessiveness. *My man. He's my man.* And she wouldn't trade him in for a multimillion-dollar distribution contract.

Corelli pushed a button, and Nicole's image appeared on the

television screen. She was wearing a different blouse—cotton with blue flowers. The same faded sheet hung behind her.

"Monday morning," she said. "It's getting close to Christmas. I miss doing the decorating."

As she reached up and pushed her hair off her face, Carolyn noticed two things. This gesture wasn't any sort of clue. And Nicole was wearing her wedding band on the wrong hand. This wasn't a trick of videotape reversal. Carolyn knew the ring was on Nicole's right hand because she wore her wristwatch on her right wrist.

"Anyway," Nicole said, "I want to say that I'm sorry. I'm sorry for everything that's happened. Still, there might be a silver lining. I'm always an optimist. Right, Dylan? Maybe this is all for the best."

When the screen went blank, Carolyn felt an ominous chill. There was something very different about Nicole. She looked the same as yesterday—clean and healthy. But her attitude had changed. And why change her wedding ring to her right hand? It was almost like she didn't want to be married anymore.

"All for the best," Carolyn repeated Nicole's words. "What does that mean?"

Dylan's face was pale. His hands drew into fists. "She's an optimist. Always thinks things are going to be great, even when the odds are against it."

Was he talking about Nicole's desire to have a baby? The struggle they'd gone through trying to get pregnant? "What does that mean to you?"

"You know me, sis. I always look for problems, trying to anticipate what might go wrong."

"It sounds like Nicole is telling you to have hope. Tonight, we'll pay the ransom. She'll be back here where she belongs, hanging Christmas decorations and wrapping presents."

"Maybe," he conceded. "But we still haven't gotten a call

from the kidnappers telling us where to deliver the ransom. We still don't know where and how Nicole will be released. I see the glass as half-empty."

A lot could go wrong. They all knew it.

The trick was to make it through today into tonight. The long hours stretched in front of her like an eternity.

Carolyn went into the dining room and grabbed a cell phone that wasn't connected to anything else. She pressed in a number that she knew by heart.

When the phone was answered, Carolyn spoke four words that she'd never said before: "Mom? I need you."

Chapter Twenty

Burke hardly recognized Corelli without his tie and suit jacket. Wearing a bulletproof vest and a heavy jacket to ward off the night chill, the computer expert had positioned himself behind a bank of computer screens inside an FBI van. His job for the assault on the SOF compound would be communications.

Burke squatted beside him, cramped by the small space inside the van. "You know, Corelli, I'm still not sure you should leave the ranch house."

"I trained Dylan on how to work the phones. He's a smart guy. He can handle it." For proof, Corelli touched a button on one of the monitors. "Dylan? How's everything at the house?"

"Quiet." The answer came through, loud and clear.

"Is Carolyn there?" Burke asked.

"Hi, Burke. What's up?"

The sound of her voice made him want to turn around and go back to the ranch. He didn't like leaving her and Dylan there with only the cowboys and Sheriff Trainer for protection.

"We're waiting," he said. "It sounds like Logan and his boys are planning their meet on the Indian Trail any minute."

At this time of year, sundown came early. Right now, it was almost dark.

"We're waiting, too," she said. "For the ransom delivery call. Corelli is going to keep us posted, right?"

"Right," Burke said. "The same goes for you and Dylan. Let us know about any calls."

"Burke." She spoke his name softly. "Be careful. Please."

"Back at you."

He didn't repeat his warning that neither she nor her brother should leave the ranch house to deliver the ransom until he'd returned. He'd said those words so many times today that they should be permanently etched on that highly intelligent brain of hers.

She knew the risks. More importantly, she understood that a coordinated ransom delivery had a far greater likelihood of success than a half-baked effort from her and her brother.

Bottom line, he hoped the ransom would never need to be paid. Once his force got inside the SOF compound and searched, he hoped to find Nicole. At this point, that hope was paper-thin. Though Nicole had twice signaled them that she was at the Circle M and Burke was relatively sure that Logan made the second ransom call to Carolyn's phone, the kidnapping hadn't been mentioned on the bug in Logan's trailer office or in any e-mail correspondence.

"They're on the move," Corelli said.

Earlier today, three heat-sensing cameras had been placed at strategic locations to monitor activity inside the compound. One focused on the front gate. Another showed the western route that Burke and his men would use to enter the Circle M. A far-range scope showed the compound buildings, including Logan's trailer and the bunkhouse where the women and children spent most of their time.

Like the bugs and computers, these cameras showed no clue about Nicole's whereabouts. She might be mingled with the other women. *Or she might be somewhere else entirely.*

"Two trucks," Corelli said. "Driving toward the front gate."

The greatest threat to their rescue operation came from Logan's surveillance cameras. Very likely, he'd leave a man behind to monitor those cameras, which would show the approach of Burke and the seven men working with him.

The first order of business—Burke's job—was to pin down the man in the trailer so he couldn't interfere with the hostage rescue.

"Three men in each truck," Corelli said.

Burke did the math. Logan had told him there were thirteen men, counting himself. Tindall the sniper was already in custody. That made twelve.

In his surveillance, Corelli had only seen ten. Either Logan had a couple of defections or the notorious twosome of Thurgood and Richter weren't on the compound. They could be somewhere else, holding Nicole.

Even though storming the SOF compound might not bring Nicole back, there were other reasons to close Logan down: the murder of Barbara Ayers and the smuggling network.

Burke returned his focus to the screens in front of Corelli. There were thirteen men less Tindall, Thurgood, Richter and the six men in the trucks. "Only four men left at the Circle M," Burke said.

"Two at the gate. Two in the trailer, monitoring their surveillance cameras." Corelli gave a short laugh. "They're watching us watch them."

"Not for long."

Burke climbed out of the van and stretched. Even in body armor, he knew that he wasn't invincible, but he liked his odds for getting through this operation without injury. He had seven men in body armor to deal with four cowboys.

He activated the microphone that allowed him to communicate with the rest of his team. "Let's do it."

WITH SHERIFF TRAINER and two deputies keeping watch on the porch, Carolyn was alone with her brother in the dining room. He'd taken Corelli's position behind the computer monitors.

After all the activity of the past few days, it seemed strangely quiet. She drummed her fingers on the tabletop. Might as well tell Dylan now and get it over with. "I talked to Mom."

"Why?"

"Because this is a time when we need to reach out to family. She'll be here tomorrow around noon."

His forehead puckered as he frowned. Dylan had a lot more issues with their mother than she did. "I can't believe she agreed to come back to the ranch. When she left us, she couldn't get away from here fast enough."

"She came back for your wedding," Carolyn reminded him.

"And she gave us a very nice gift. And Nicole wrote her a very nice thank-you card. That's that."

She didn't mention her opinion that their father hadn't been the easiest man in the world to live with. The portrait of their father, Sterling Carlisle, as a rough and rugged rancher who was building an empire and not paying much attention to his family might also apply to Dylan.

In the videotape, Nicole had been wearing her wedding ring on the wrong hand. That worried Carolyn. She feared that the problems between Dylan and his wife ran deeper than a single issue, and she hated to see their family history repeat in another broken marriage.

Were the Carlisles incapable of handling long-term relationships? She rose from the table and paced. She and Burke weren't at the point where they were planning beyond tomorrow, but making a commitment didn't scare her. And Burke was, as he'd said himself, afraid of nothing.

Suddenly, Dylan scrambled with the phones. "It's the kidnapper. I recognize the phone number."

"I'll take the call," she said. "You record it and start the trace."

He nodded.

Carolyn tried not to show fear. "This is Carolyn."

"It's time," said the whispery voice on speakerphone. "Bring the ransom to *La Rana*."

Her instructions were to keep him talking. "That's a big pasture. I'm not exactly sure where you want me to put it."

"On the rocks. Go. Now."

"It's going to take a while to get saddled up and—"

"He hung up," Dylan said.

Burke's warning echoed in her head. He'd told them not to leave the house until he got back.

"Damn it," Dylan said. "He's calling back."

He put the call through. This time the voice was Nicole's. "Dylan, are you there?"

"Yes," he said. "Where are you?"

"Meet me at the creek in half an hour. After the ransom is dropped off."

"Are you all right?"

"Just be there."

The phone went dead.

AS SOON AS BURKE AND SMITH were on Circle M land and within range of the surveillance cameras, they started running. A full-out sprint in body armor while carrying a heavy-duty repeating rifle wasn't easy, but his adrenaline surged. Burke was flying.

He went first, since he'd actually been inside the compound and knew the layout of the buildings. The barn was in sight. He ran toward the trailer. His plan was to keep the men inside pinned down, unable to interfere in the rescue of the women and children.

Through his headset, he heard Corelli's voice. "Keep going. They're moving inside. Haven't left the trailer yet."

Burke and Smith split up. Smith ducked behind a Jeep parked to the left of the trailer door. Burke ran to the left side. He called out, "FBI. Throw down your weapons. Come out with your hands up."

The response was a blast of bullets fired through the door. If Burke had been dumb enough to stand there, he would have been mowed down.

Both he and Smith let loose with a barrage of gunfire. As agreed, they aimed low, almost into the dirt. Burke didn't want casualties. He circled the trailer, staying away from the windows.

From the bunkhouse, he heard shouts of protest.

The corresponding voices of his men, heard through his headset, were polite. They explained that they were there to protect the women and children, to remove them from a dangerous situation.

In just a few minutes, the head of the rescue team reported, "We're leaving with the hostages. Three men are escorting them. Two more are headed back toward the guys at the front gate."

The plan seemed to be operating smoothly, and that concerned Burke. After years in law enforcement, he knew that nothing was easy.

He spotted a woman running toward the trailer. One who had broken away from the others?

She screamed, "Logan, look out! They're coming for you, Logan!"

A shot was fired. *From inside the trailer.*

The woman fell.

DYLAN REFUSED TO WAIT. Nicole's phone call had raised his level of anxiety to a fever pitch. "We're going to deliver that damn ransom. And we're going to do it right now."

"Use your head, Dylan. It's a trick. The kidnappers have to be watching the house. They know we're alone. If we wait until Burke gets back…"

"Nicole could be dead by then."

Carolyn begged him. "Please. Let's call Burke."

"That was my wife on the phone. She wouldn't lie to me."

She might not have a choice. The kidnappers could be standing over her with a gun. "I heard her."

"She said to meet her in half an hour. After we pay the ransom." He held Carolyn's shoulders and looked into her eyes. In his face, she saw the depth of his suffering. "Either you help me with this or I'll do it alone."

How could she refuse her brother? She'd promised her father that she'd protect him. And he had a point. If they didn't deliver the ransom, Nicole might pay the ultimate price.

"I'll ride with you," she said.

"Not enough time. *La Rana* and the creek are in opposite directions. We'll never make it to both in half an hour."

He was correct, and the timing was important. She drew the obvious conclusion. "There must be two of them. One to pick up the ransom. The other to hold Nicole."

"Butch Thurgood and Pete Richter." He stormed from the dining room and grabbed his jacket near the door. "Bastards."

"I'll drop the ransom at *La Rana*," she said. "You go and wait for Nicole."

"I'll grab a couple of horses from the men and bring them to the back door. Hurry."

"What are you going to tell the sheriff?"

"I'll figure it out." He wrapped his arms around her for a quick hug. "Thanks, sis. I love you."

"Love you, too. Be careful."

While he went to make explanations and find them a couple of mounts, she entered the office to retrieve the ransom from the safe.

Her fingers trembled as she spun the dial on the combination lock and took out the heavy backpack. This might be the biggest mistake she'd ever made. Remembering the fierce blast to her chest when she'd been shot, she wished that she had one of those uncomfortable bulletproof vests.

She put on her jacket and jammed her arms into the straps of the backpack. No time to waste.

Still, she returned to the computers in the dining room and activated the channel Dylan had used to communicate with Corelli. "I have a message for Burke."

"Carolyn?"

"I'm delivering the ransom now."

"Wait," Corelli said. "Don't make a move until—"

"Tell him *La Rana*."

She turned off the channel and ran for the door, trying to outrace her better judgment.

Chapter Twenty-One

Burke watched the woman writhing on the ground, holding her leg and crying. He couldn't leave her there, suffering. But he couldn't rescue her without stepping directly into the line of fire. The man inside that trailer had been cold-blooded enough to shoot someone who was trying to warn him.

It had to be Logan.

"Logan," Burke yelled. "This is your last chance to disarm and come out with your hands up."

"Then what? Prison?" It was Logan, all right. "Get off my land, fed."

Burke would have preferred waiting until his teams had the women and children safely loaded into transport. He heard gunfire and shouting from the front gate where another confrontation was underway.

He spoke into his microphone, "Give me a report on the hostages."

"One woman ran off. We're almost to the vehicles with the others."

"Move fast," Burke said. He didn't know what else Logan might have up his sleeve.

Another voice came through the headset. "We're at the front gate. Both men have surrendered."

The only problem left was Logan, holed up in his trailer.

Burke wanted this over. He wanted to get back to the ranch and to Carolyn. The thought of her spurred him on.

He stepped away from the trailer. From his belt, he unclipped a flashbang canister—similar to a grenade but without the lethal effects. This canister would make a big noise and a fierce burst of blinding white light before exuding a stinging burst of smoke. Should be enough to drive the rattlesnake from his hole.

Aiming high, Burke shot out a side window on the trailer and lobbed the canister inside.

He turned his head aside so he wouldn't be affected by the flash. The blast was deafening. Smoke poured through the broken window.

From inside the trailer came yelps of surprise.

Burke moved into position near the bullet-riddled trailer door. He saw Agent Smith emerge from his hiding place behind the vehicle and position himself in front of the injured woman so she wouldn't be caught in the crossfire. Smith would take care of her.

Logan flung open the door. His heavy-duty rifle was poised at his hip. Before he could spray bullets, Burke lunged. He tackled Logan, pinning him to the ground on his belly.

A second man came out of the trailer with his hands in the air. "Don't shoot."

The only one who hadn't given up was Logan. He struggled on the ground. The correct protocol would be to cuff him and proceed with standard interrogation, but Burke had a different idea. If Logan thought he had a chance, he'd spill more information.

Purposely, Burke gave him just enough room to scramble to his feet. Logan took off, running toward the barn.

Burke pursued. Though he could have easily overtaken Logan, he stayed one step behind. Just before Logan entered the barn, he grabbed his collar and spun him around. They were face-to-face.

"Where's Nicole?" Burke demanded.

Logan took a wild swing, and Burke allowed the other man's fist to make contact with the Kevlar vest. That had to hurt.

Logan yelled in pain. "Take off your armor. Fight me like a man."

"Give me a reason," Burke said. "Where's Nicole?"

"She was here. But not anymore."

Burke flipped off his helmet. "Your men abducted her by the creek. Right?"

"It was a joke. I was going to let her go."

The cold night air felt good on Burke's face. He was nearly as anxious to take off the protective gear as Logan was to have him do so. He yanked off the arm guards and tossed them aside.

Remembering his training as a negotiator, Burke offered a morsel of hope. "If you're not involved in the kidnapping, this might turn out okay for you."

Except for the murder of Barbara Ayers and the illegal smuggling. But Burke didn't mention those charges. Or the fact that he'd just seen Logan shoot that woman in the leg.

Burke said, "We could make a deal."

Though Logan's eyes were red and watery from the smoke, he brightened. Deal making was his thing.

"It's Butch Thurgood and Pete Richter," he said. "They've got her. They took Nicole to the cave and never came back."

Burke shed his Kevlar vest. His arms and upper body were free. "You asked for half a mil in ransom."

"But I didn't have Nicole. Like I said, just a joke."

"Not very funny."

Burke balanced his weight on the balls of his feet, ready to attack. He laid back and waited for Logan to make the first move. Which he did.

Logan took a jab toward Burke's chin. He missed.

Burke retaliated with a quick body shot—hard enough to double Logan over. "You're working with somebody inside the Carlisle Ranch. Who is it?"

Logan dragged himself upright. "I'm not going to prison, right?"

"Give me a name."

"Lucas Mann. I paid him to help us with the sabotage. He let us know when we could get inside the ranch and make trouble."

Burke feinted right. With his left hand he smacked Logan's left arm. "Lucas wouldn't set fire to the stable."

Logan drew himself together. His posture signaled that he was getting ready for a final assault. But Burke was already thinking three steps ahead. He knew Logan would go for the body, the biggest target. Burke shifted just enough to let Logan's blow crease the outer edge of his ribs.

This negotiation was almost over. Burke shot out with his right fist, shoving Logan's shoulder. "Did Lucas set fire to the barn?"

"He didn't know what we were planning, but he told us a good time to strike. Then the old fool raised the alarm."

Burke ducked another flailing blow and responded with a pop to Logan's face, hard enough to break his handsome nose.

"Where's Nicole?"

"Don't know." Logan wailed. "You busted my nose."

Burke moved closer. "Last chance for you to get out of this. Where is she?"

"If I knew, I'd tell."

Burke believed him. Logan had been double-crossed by his own men. They had taken Nicole to make a big score for themselves. He spun Logan around and cuffed him. "Sam Logan, you're under arrest for the murder of Barbara Ayers. And for illegal smuggling."

Smith ran up beside him. "I have bad news, Burke."

"Now what?"

"Carolyn called Corelli. She's delivering the ransom. At *La Rana*."

Cold dread gripped his heart. There was no more time for strategy or tactics. Carolyn was in danger.

THE STRAP OF THE BACKPACK rubbed against the bruise where Carolyn had been shot. The pain reminded her that Logan wanted her dead. Even though she'd remembered to bring a gun this time, she didn't feel safe. His men had already tried to kill her once; she'd be crazy to ride into the center of the feeding pasture. Sitting erect in the saddle, she couldn't hide.

Throughout her ride from the house, she stayed low, leaning over her horse's neck. At the gate, she slipped to the ground and removed the heavy pack holding a million dollars.

Burke was going to be angry when he found out what she was doing. *Oh, Burke, I'm sorry. If I ever see you again, I'll make it up to you.*

On horseback, Carolyn could have easily maneuvered her way through the herd. But she assumed the kidnapper was close: she had to proceed on foot. She unlatched the gate and stepped inside the enclosure.

She couldn't turn back. Nicole's life was at stake.

Carolyn unlatched the gate and stepped inside. The musky scent from three hundred head of cattle didn't bother her; she'd grown up with that odor. Plenty of hay was strewn across the packed earth; she couldn't worry about where she was stepping or what she was stepping in. The dim moonlight shone on the fat rock formation that looked like a squatting frog. *La Rana.*

The herd seemed to sense that something was wrong. These were mature cattle, nine hundred pounds and up. Restlessly, they stamped their hooves and made nervous noises as if to warn each other of danger.

Using the cattle for cover, she crept closer to the rocks with the pack slung over her good right shoulder and her gun in hand. She didn't want to shoot; the noise could set off a stampede.

She heard a horseman approaching. He yelled, "Carolyn. Where the hell are you?"

Lucas. He'd almost admitted that he was the traitor. But was he the kidnapper? Was he here to collect the ransom?

She ducked down and said nothing.

"Damn it all," Lucas barked. "I'm on your side. I'm here to help you out."

Help me out of one million dollars? She didn't trust him. Not anymore.

He rode through the gate.

Though she tried to be invisible, he spotted her and approached. She dropped the ransom. Without hesitation, she aimed at the center of his chest. "I don't want to shoot you. Just take the money. And bring Nicole back to us."

"You got it wrong," he said. "When I hooked up with Logan, I thought I was just making some extra cash for letting him play harmless pranks. I didn't know—"

"Kidnapping isn't a prank. It's a federal offense."

"I'd never hurt Nicole. Don't you know that?"

She wanted to believe him. "How did you know to come here?"

"I followed you. When I saw you toting that backpack, I

guessed what was going on. That's the ransom, ain't it? What are you fixing to do with it?"

"The instruction was to leave it at *La Rana*."

"Hand it over to me. I'll do it for you."

Or he could ride off with the backpack. If Lucas wasn't the kidnapper, he could botch the ransom delivery. "If you really want to help me, back off."

"At least let me clear a path through these steers."

He rode past her, expertly using his horse to nudge the snorting, frightened cattle out of the way.

Carolyn saw her way clear to *La Rana*. She ran. Dropped the backpack. It was done. She'd fulfilled her part of the bargain.

Leaning against the rocks, she checked her wristwatch. Less than half an hour had passed since she and Dylan had taken the call from the kidnapper. Very soon, her brother would see his wife again. The nightmare would be over.

"This way," Lucas said.

Dodging a wild-eyed steer, she ran toward Lucas. He seemed to be helping her, forming a barrier between her and the other cattle. She was almost to the fence when she saw him turn in the saddle and glance over his shoulder toward *La Rana*.

"Look out," he yelled. He wheeled his horse around. His rifle was in hand.

Gunfire exploded.

Lucas was slammed out of the saddle.

The herd began to move, shuffling nervously. The gunshot had spooked them.

Carolyn peered through the darkness at the rock formation. The kidnapper was there, hiding like a coward. She raised her gun, ready to shoot if she saw the slightest movement. Firing her weapon while she stood in the midst of the herd was suicide; they'd stampede. But she had to face the son of a bitch—to shoot him before he shot her. Adrenaline pumped through her veins.

He'd have to show himself when he stepped out from behind the rocks to grab the ransom.

Behind her, she heard Lucas moan. *Help him? Or watch for the kidnapper?* Damn it, she couldn't let Lucas die. She lowered her gun and went toward the fallen man.

He was on his hands and knees beside his horse. He was bleeding heavily from a chest wound. "Save yourself."

"You're not dead yet."

Using every bit of her strength, she helped him onto his horse. They were near the fence. Not far from the gate.

Looking back toward *La Rana,* she saw a dark shadow against the rocks. *The kidnapper.* Before she could get her gun ready to shoot, he raised his rifle and fired several shots into the air.

The cattle reacted. Swept up in the rush of heavy flanks and shoulders, she was carried away from the fence, engulfed in the surging mass. She could only hope that Lucas's horse would make it to the gate. And that she would find her way clear.

Shouts filled the air. Peering over the backs of the cattle, she saw cowboys riding toward the field. She thought she recognized Burke's voice. He'd come for her.

The cattle jolted against each other. Three hundred of them in this field. There wasn't enough room for them to run full out, not unless they broke through the barbed wire. If they stampeded, she didn't have a chance.

She stumbled but didn't fall. Clinging to the side of a massive steer, she was carried forward by his momentum, almost losing her footing. Instead of escaping, she was pushed farther away from the barbed wire fence.

Desperately, she clung to the panicked steer. Another steer banged against her. If she didn't get out of here, she'd be crushed, pounded into the earth by the animals that were her livelihood.

Chapter Twenty-Two

Paying no attention to the warnings from cowboys who knew better, Burke rode through the gate into the mass of cattle. Being trampled was one hell of a way to die. He had to reach Carolyn.

He saw her. She clung desperately to a giant steer. He nudged his horse forward, glad that his mount was more experienced than he was.

Carolyn darted toward him. With one arm, he reached down and lifted her off the ground. She was in his arms, safely cradled against him.

In seconds, he was at the gate.

Outside the barbed wire fence, Burke held her close. He was still astride his horse so it wasn't the most comfortable position. But he didn't care. His arms clamped around her.

"Burke, you can put me down."

"Never."

The other cowboys who rode with him to *La Rana* were busy, getting the herd inside the fence under control and rescuing the man who'd been shot.

He kissed Carolyn's sweaty forehead. She didn't exactly smell like a rose garden, but he was happy to be near her, grateful that she was safe.

She turned her face up to look at him. Smears of grime

marred her pale cheeks and forehead. Her hat was gone. Her black hair tangled like a bird's nest. She'd never been so beautiful.

"I'm sorry," she said. "You told me not to leave the house without you."

"It doesn't matter who's right and who's wrong." He was in no mood for negotiating or competition. "You're safe. That's the important thing."

"We got a phone call from the kidnapper. And from Nicole. She told Dylan that—"

"Nicole? You're sure it was her?"

"Dylan recognized her voice, and he ought to know. She told him to meet her at the creek. She'd be there after the ransom was delivered here. So Dylan and I split up to handle both things. That must mean there are two kidnappers."

"Butch Thurgood and Pete Richter," he said. "Logan already ratted them out."

"Did you rescue the women and children at the compound?"

"Worked out as planned. Logan is in custody." He needed to step up and take charge of the operation again. "Before I get back to business, there's something I need to tell you."

A brave smile twitched her lips. "Do you mean I have your undivided attention? For the next two minutes?"

"Forever," he said. "You will always have my undivided attention. Carolyn, you're the center of my universe."

Her green eyes widened. "I am?"

"You look surprised."

"Oh, yeah. I definitely am. Stunned, even."

In a way, he was amazed, too. They'd only known each other for a couple of days, and he wasn't generally given to emotional outbursts. "I love you, Carolyn."

She wrapped her arms around his neck and kissed him hard. He loved her passion. Her strength. Her character.

She whispered, "I love you, too."

For a moment they stared into each other's eyes, basking in the strange glow of this shocking discovery. *They were in love, capital L-O-V-E.*

MacKenzie rode up beside them. His face was somber. "Lucas didn't make it."

"I'm sorry," Carolyn said in a measured tone. "He died trying to save my life."

If she didn't want to condemn him, Burke wouldn't refute her. Lucas had died and there was no reason to tarnish his good reputation. "Carolyn, where did you drop the ransom?"

"On the rocks."

He snapped off an order, "MacKenzie, go to those rocks in the center of the field. Look for a backpack."

"Backpack?"

"You heard him," Carolyn said. "A huge backpack full of money. A million dollars in cash."

The young man blinked. "Holy crap."

"Go," Burke ordered.

While he took out his cell phone, Carolyn repositioned herself so she was sitting in front of him on the saddle. He contacted Corelli and told him where Dylan was headed.

He hoped there would be a happy ending for all of them, that Dylan would ride back to the ranch with Nicole. He wrapped his arms around Carolyn's slender waist. "Do you want to ride back on your own horse?"

"Not really." She snuggled against him. "I used to be so concerned about appearances, worried that the ranch hands wouldn't respect me if I showed weakness or emotion."

"Unless they're blind and deaf, I'm pretty sure they know something's going on between us."

"Do you think so?"

He'd spent last night in her bed, and they hadn't exactly been silent. "They know."

As she rested against him, they watched the cowboys climbing over *La Rana,* searching every crevice. MacKenzie waved both arms. "It's not here."

The ransom was gone. Burke had expected as much. Butch and Richter had figured out a simple but clever drop point. All they had to do to create a diversion was fire a gun and get out of the way while the stampeding herd covered their escape. "What happened when Lucas was shot?"

"I had made the drop, and I was trying to get out of the field. He rode ahead of me, clearing a path. Then, he turned in the saddle and spotted something behind me."

"On *La Rana?*"

"Yes," she said. "Lucas didn't have time to pull his rifle before they opened fire. Lucas was the traitor."

"I know."

"But he admitted that he'd made a mistake." She exhaled a shuddering breath. "I want to remember the good things about him."

It was hard to believe Logan had no part in this operation, but he clearly hadn't expected the raid on the compound. Additionally, the FBI team with the chopper had taken the smugglers on the Indian Trail into custody. "When we get back to the ranch, it's going to be chaos. There will be hostages to process. And a mob of FBI to deal with."

"There's only one thing I'm worried about," she said.

"Me?" he asked hopefully.

She twisted her head to kiss his neck. "Do I need to worry about you?"

"Not really. I know where I stand."

"Where's that, Burke?"

"At your side. As long as you'll have me."

"That sounds good," she said. "But I wasn't really talking about you. I'm worried about what's happening between Dylan and Nicole. The problems between them run deep. What if she doesn't want to get back together with him?"

"That's her decision."

His job ended when Nicole was released.

AS BURKE HAD PREDICTED, the scene at the ranch house was crazy. Every light in the house was lit. Headlights from vans and trucks raced back and forth. There were terse conversations from cowboys and commandos alike.

Carolyn climbed down from the saddle and stood looking up at the man who had saved her life for the second time. The man she loved.

"Go ahead, Burke. I know you have a lot to do. I'm going to the corral to wait for Dylan."

He dismounted. "I'm staying with you."

It felt good to have him put her first. "Aren't there a lot of people you need to be ordering around?"

"They'll manage." He hooked his arm around her waist.

Together, they strolled toward the corral. The horse Burke had been riding trailed behind them. Though the night was far from silent, they seemed to be in their own little bubble of safety—a bubble that could be easily burst if Dylan didn't return to the ranch with his wife.

From across the moonlit field, she spotted her brother riding toward her. Alone.

Her heart skipped a beat. She couldn't be happy in her newfound love if Nicole was…

She ran to meet Dylan.

He dismounted slowly.

"I saw her," he said. "We talked."

"Is she all right?" Carolyn asked. "Where is she?"

"Not with me. Not anymore." He held out his open palm, showing her the wedding ring. "Nicole isn't coming back to me. She wants a divorce."

Carolyn took the ring and read the inscription: My horizon. *This couldn't be true.* "I don't believe—"

"Believe it," he said. "My horizon. My ass. The sun has set. She doesn't love me anymore."

There had been hints. When Carolyn first showed up at the ranch, Nicole hadn't wanted to talk. Not that they'd had many conversations lately. Carolyn had been too busy, hadn't expected to encounter a problem like this. A divorce.

"Your wife picked a hell of a way to break up with you," Burke said. "Was the kidnapping staged?"

"No."

She searched her brother's face for a clue. He wore a stern mask to hide his pain and humiliation. "I want some answers, Dylan. Why did she keep signaling us that she was at the Circle M?"

"We didn't talk about that. She told me that being kidnapped was a blessing in disguise. It gave her time to think."

"I want to talk to her." Carolyn needed to see for herself, wanted to hear the words from Nicole's lips.

"That's why she's not coming back to the ranch. Doesn't want to explain herself to anybody." He gestured to the ranch house where teams of FBI and cowboys hustled in and out. "It's over. All these damn people can go back to where they came from."

"Sorry," Burke said. "But that's not how this type of investigation works. I need to be sure the victim is all right."

"She's well." Dylan spat the words. "The only thing wrong is that…she's gone."

Carolyn pressed, "Tell me her exact words."

"None of your business. This is between me and my wife."
He straightened his shoulders. "My ex-wife."

"What about the ransom?" Burke asked.

"Money well spent," Dylan said, "if it means I'm done
with her. I'm calling off the investigation. Nicole isn't a missing person. Nobody was holding a gun to her head. She's
leaving of her own accord."

He turned his back and walked slowly toward the barn.
Though his posture was erect and stoic, Carolyn knew that he
was falling apart inside. And so was she. Her brief moment of
happiness seemed to be crumbling. "Do something, Burke."

"Legally, I can't track down a person who isn't missing."

"You've picked a fine time to play by the rules." Her hand
closed around the wedding band. "Can't you make Nicole
come back? Make her explain to me."

Her gaze searched his face, looking for a reason to hope
that this would turn out.

"I won't lie to you." His dark eyes shone in the night. He
kissed her forehead. "Dylan is satisfied that Nicole is well.
I don't have the authority to pursue further investigation."

"But I'm not satisfied." This wasn't the happy ending
she'd hoped for. "Dylan might be willing to write off a
million dollars, but I'm not. I want the ransom back."

"Good point."

Nicole had simple tastes. She wasn't the sort of woman
who needed a million dollars to start a new life. "I can't believe she took the money."

"That might have been the price the kidnappers required.
The price of her freedom."

"It's just not right."

"I won't leave you alone to handle this," he said. "The
kidnapping is over but I'm staying here. I won't abandon
you, Carolyn."

"Thank you." She clung to him, needing him more than ever. "You just keep saving my life, over and over."

"That's my job."

Never before did she have someone to lean on, someone to share the burden. And she was going to need his continued support, especially during the next few days. He was her rock, her strength, her one true love.

* * * * *

"Fate would have it, you'd be the robbery division's first female detective."

Sam flashed her a grin, clearly amused by the situation. "Think you're up to it, McIntyre?"

He was saying that to goad her, she thought. To make her stop focusing on the uncomfortable aspect of this situation and just view it as a challenge. Appreciating the intent, she had to give him his due. "You're not as dumb as you look, Wyatt."

The comment made him laugh. "Bet you say that to all the guys."

"Only the ones who deserve it."

"You know, McIntyre, this might be the beginning of a beautiful friendship."

"Too late for that. I already know you," she reminded him.

IN BED WITH
THE BADGE

BY

MARIE FERRARELLA

First published in Great Britain 2010
Harlequin Mills & Boon Limited,
Eton House, 18-24 Paradise Road, Richmond, Surrey TW9 1SR

© Marie Rydzynski-Ferrarella 2010

ISBN: 978 0 263 88263 6

46-1010

Harlequin Mills & Boon policy is to use papers that are natural, renewable and recyclable products and made from wood grown in sustainable forests. The logging and manufacturing processes conform to the legal environmental regulations of the country of origin.

Printed and bound in Spain
by Litografia Rosés S.A., Barcelona

USA TODAY bestselling and RITA® Award-winning author **Marie Ferrarella** has written almost two hundred novels, some under the name Marie Nicole. Her romances are beloved by fans worldwide. Visit her website at www.marieferrarella.com.

To
Sam Warren,
for lending me
his first name.
Hope you like this.

Chapter 1

"**I**'m worried about her, Brian." Lila Cavanaugh's eyes met her husband's in the long mirror that hung over the double, ice-blue-tiled sink in their bathroom. "She's never behaved like this before." They both hurried to get ready, to arrive at work early for completely different reasons.

Brian Cavanaugh, the Aurora Police Department's Chief of Detectives and, technically, Lila's superior, at least at the precinct, didn't have to ask his wife who *she* was, despite the fact that Lila's declaration had come out of the blue.

Lila referred to her younger daughter, Riley McIntyre.

Riley, like her three siblings as well as her mother, was a detective on the police force and ultimately under Brian Cavanaugh's command. Until a couple of months ago, the twenty-eight-year-old had been a happy-go-lucky, outgoing and upbeat young woman who greeted every morning with a grin and a wisecrack. Her deep blue eyes always sparkled. If Brian were to single out the stepchild with the most optimistic, positive view of life, it would have been Riley.

But the recent murder of her new partner, Detective Diego Sanchez, by the very serial killer that she and the rest of the homicide task force were pursuing at the time, had changed all that. Riley had become quiet, introspective and, at times, just plain unreachable.

It concerned him, as well.

In a way, she reminded him of his niece, Rayne, the youngest of his older brother, Andrew's, children. Right after her mother had disappeared and was presumed dead, Rayne began to act out, getting in trouble with the police despite the fact that Andrew was Aurora's Chief of Police at the time. Fortunately, Rayne had straightened out over time and made them all proud.

Granted, Riley wasn't acting out, but there was no denying that she was dealing with an excessive amount of emotional turmoil.

Was the change in her behavior permanent or temporary?

"She keeps saying she's all right, but I know she's not," Lila insisted. She gave up the pretense of applying her makeup and turned to face her husband. "I don't want her on the street like that, Brian. Being out there is hard enough when you're at the top of your game, let alone being off the way she seems to be these days." Lila hated asking for favors, even from her own husband, but this was for her daughter. "As her superior, can't you order her to take some time off until she's her old self again?"

Lila had long since accepted and made peace with the fact that her children had all followed her late husband and her into the police force. She did her best not to worry about them too much. But this new turn of events had thrown the balance off and she sincerely feared for Riley's well-being, not to mention her life.

"I could," Brian allowed slowly. His eyes met Lila's. "But I won't."

Disappointment sliced through her clear down to the bone. She had counted on his agreeing with her. "But Brian—"

"Lila, put yourself in Riley's place. When you were shot and almost died on me all those years ago, how did you feel, having all that time to think about what'd happened?" He deliberately made no reference to how he'd felt, watching her sink to the ground, or what had gone through his mind as his own hands tried to stop the bleeding, to desperately keep her life from flowing out of her body.

Her mouth turned grim. "Awful," Lila finally conceded.

And she had continued to feel that way long after she'd recuperated from her gunshot wound. Ben McIntyre, her first husband, had used the shooting to manipulate her. Jealous of what he thought was her relationship with Brian, her partner at the time, Ben had forced her to quit the force in order to become a full-time wife and mother. While she loved her children, she hated being away from the life that gave hers such meaning.

Giving up the force made her feel like only half a person.

"What I can do," Brian said, "is make Riley's status contingent on seeing the department's therapist."

"Hoolihan?" Even as she said the man's name, Lila shook her head. Her frown further underscored her disapproval.

Brian thought of himself as a fair man and he was always willing to listen to an opposing point of view. Turning around to face his wife, he leaned a hip against the sink and crossed his arms before his still rather buff chest.

"Okay, what's wrong with Hoolihan?" Brian asked.

After she'd been shot and before Ben had forced her to resign from the force, she'd seen the therapist on her own. She remembered it being a less-than-rewarding experience.

"Well, for one thing, I doubt if anyone but a robot could relate to the man." The session—and the man's cold, dead eyes—had left a bad taste in her mouth that existed to this day. "He's impersonal, removed and, frankly, the man gives me the creeps."

Brian thought it over for a moment. His own encounters with the therapist were limited to run-ins in the hall and an exchange of nods. He was in no position to champion the man.

"All right, we'll find someone else for Riley. That'll be your assignment," he said affectionately, punctuating the declaration with a quick kiss to her temple.

The corners of Lila's mouth lifted as she fisted one

hand at her hip. "And what'll you be doing while I'm searching for a sympathetic ear for Riley?"

"You mean what'll I be doing aside from the massive task of directing the detectives of all the departments?" he deadpanned. He thought of the reason he was going in so early. "I'll be making the final decision regarding finding our daughter a new partner."

Lila smiled. She liked his reference to Riley as "our daughter" despite the fact that their combined families consisted of eight adult children and he could have just as easily divided the two factions into "your kids" and "my kids." Instead, they became "ours." That was just the Cavanaugh way and it was only one of the many reasons why she loved this man so much.

"Do you have anyone in mind?" Lila asked, curious.

He looked back into the mirror to make sure he'd shaved evenly. "Yes, I have someone very definite in mind."

"Do I get a name, or do I have to guess?" she asked.

Brian looked away from the mirror. There was a glimmer in his eyes. "Depends on what you're willing to trade for the information," he teased.

Lila glanced at her watch. "We're both due at the precinct in half an hour," she pointed out.

Wide shoulders rose and fell in a pseudo-careless shrug. "Lots of things can be accomplished in a small amount of time, Mrs. Cavanaugh," he told her just as he began to skim his lips lightly along her neck.

He could make her heart race so easily, Lila thought.

She doubted if she would ever get used to this. Or take it for granted.

"So, we're skipping breakfast," she said with minor difficulty as he stole her breath away.

"Not always the most important meal of the day," he told her, slowly working his way around her throat. He lifted up her chin with the tip of his finger to expose more of the targeted area.

Lila gave up the pretense of leaving the house on time. She wove her arms around her husband's neck.

"Consider it skipped," she breathed, giving in to temptation.

"But I didn't put in for a transfer," Riley protested, stunned.

She was sitting in her stepfather's office. That morning she'd found a message on her desk saying that the Chief of Detectives wanted to see her. She'd come knowing that this had to be something official because if it was anything else, Brian would have picked up the telephone and called her at home to discuss it.

But she'd never expected to be hit with this.

"I know you didn't." Brian's voice was kind, but firm. "I decided to do it for you."

Riley had never been big on change, especially not now. "I've been assigned to Homicide ever since I made detective." A feeling of desperation began to sink hooks into her. She did her best to bank down the feeling. "Have I done something wrong? Because if I have, just tell me what it is and I'll—"

Brian cut her off. "No, nothing. You haven't done anything wrong, Riley," he emphasized. "You're an asset to the force and, most likely, this is only a temporary assignment. Robbery is currently shorthanded." He paused for a moment before adding, "And you need a change."

He saw her shoulders stiffen, as if his words had been a physical blow.

"I just need to get back in the saddle," Riley insisted.

"You never got out of the saddle, Riley," Brian contradicted. "You didn't take any time off after Sanchez was killed, even when I encouraged you. And I understand that. You're one of those people who needs to be busy in order to deal with something unpleasant that's bothering you." He smiled at her. "You're not all that different than I am in this respect," he acknowledged. Getting out of his chair and from behind his desk, he drew closer to her. "This isn't punishment, Riley. This is taking a breather, getting a change of pace—and doing me a favor," he added for good measure, hoping that would help her.

Riley took a breath. This was the man who had brightened her mother's world a thousandfold. The man who had always been more of a father to her and her brothers and sister than her own father had been. Brian was doing what he thought was best for her, but she didn't want to give up her routine, didn't want to be away from people she was accustomed to working with. This was *not* the time for her to build new relationships.

Still, when he put it like that, it was hard turning the Chief down—even though she knew what was really behind his so-called request. And "favors" had nothing to do with it.

Sighing, she realized she had no choice but to relent. Riley nodded. "All right, if it's really that important, I guess I can work in the robbery division—but just until you get someone else to fill the position."

"Thank you. I knew I could count on you," he told her. She noticed that he didn't agree with her about the temporariness of the situation. Instead, he seemed to be waiting a beat, then continued. "And there's something else."

She *knew* it. Riley looked at her stepfather warily. "What?"

"Nothing major," he assured her. "I want you to see a therapist."

Riley closed her eyes, searching for strength. "Oh, God, Chief, not Hoolihan."

"No," he agreed with a laugh, "not Hoolihan. Your mother already made that case for you," he explained when she eyed him curiously.

"Mother?" Riley repeated quietly.

So they were both conspiring against her, she thought, feeling more alone than ever. She loved them both, but didn't they understand that she'd deal with this on her own terms? In her own way? That it was just going to take her time to forget the image of Diego, lying in the alley, in a pool of his own blood, a stake driven through his heart like some character in a grade B horror movie?

This wasn't a head cold she was trying to get over

but a huge case of guilt. She should have been watching his back.

Brian nodded. "She made me see that talking to Hoolihan wasn't going to help. Your mother suggested that you find someone in private practice to help you deal with this."

Riley squared her shoulders in a defensive movement that, at one time or another, he'd seen his own four kids make. "But I am dealing with this."

Brian knew that he could successfully argue the case, but he merely said, "Humor me."

Riley sighed. She was stuck.

"How long do I have to find this 'shrink'?" She couldn't get herself to even say the word "therapist." Acknowledging the word would be like admitting that she needed help and she didn't. She just needed time, that was all.

"I would have preferred yesterday," Brian told her honestly, "but let's just say you need to find one by the end of the week."

She was definitely not looking forward to the search. "Yes, sir."

"Good, that's what I like to hear. Now, about your new partner—temporary partner," he threw in when he saw her grip the armrests and rise in her seat.

Sitting back down, Riley continued gripping the armrests as if ready to rip them out. "I don't need a partner," she protested with feeling. "I can work on my own."

"That's not how this operates, Riley, and you know it. The only time a detective goes solo is if his—or her—partner calls in sick for the day. We work in teams, Riley, we always have," he reminded her. "Homicide, Robbery, Vice, it doesn't matter what department, the procedure is the same."

Because he was a man she respected as well as loved, she decided to be honest with him, to bare her soul for the moment. "Chief, if something happens to my partner right now, I don't think I'm up to handling that."

"Which is why I said you need to see a therapist," Brian reminded her gently.

"Besides," a deep voice behind Riley said, "nothing's going to happen to me, although I'm touched that you're concerned."

Intent on making her point with the Chief, Riley hadn't heard anyone behind her. The voice, coming out of the blue the way it did, nearly made her jump. At the same time, she realized that it sounded vaguely familiar.

Riley twisted around in her chair just in time to see Detective Sam Wyatt stride in, then lean his long, muscular frame against the doorjamb. He'd filled out some since she'd last seen him.

"Morning, Chief," Sam said, nodding at Brian. "You sent for me?"

"Always know how to make an entrance, don't you, Detective Wyatt?" Brian said with a shake of his head. He gestured to the chair beside Riley. "Sit down," he instructed.

"Yes, sir." He deposited his body into the vacant chair, sparing Riley a nod. "And as for making an entrance, in this case, I had to, sir. I sneaked up on

McIntyre once and nearly wound up getting a .22 right to the chest." Sam flashed a wide, two-thousand-watt smile known to melt women at three hundred feet. "Still as fast on the draw as you were?" he asked Riley.

She wasn't the kind to boast, but something about his tone made her say, "Faster," without hesitation.

Not one to leave anything to chance, Brian made it a point to know as much as possible about the detectives under his command. He'd discovered a while back that Sam Wyatt and Riley had been friendly rivals coming up together at the academy. The thirty-two-year-old Wyatt was a bit of a charmer and there was no denying that he was flamboyant, but the man was still a fine detective and could be relied on to keep an eye on Riley until she was back in fighting form. To him, the two detectives made perfect partners—they would keep each other on their toes.

He'd gotten excellent feedback about Wyatt from Joe Barker, Wyatt's lieutenant and, as it happened, the detective's partner had just transferred back east to be near his ailing father. Wyatt needed a new partner.

And so did Riley.

"Well, since you two know each other, I'll leave it to you, Wyatt, to help McIntyre here get up to speed."

A sense of uneasiness wove its way through Riley. She really didn't want to switch departments right now. Ordinarily, she wasn't one to expect personal favors, but this one time, she fervently hoped that the chief's connection to both her mother and her would tip the scales in her favor.

Riley leaned forward in her chair. Blocking out Wyatt and focusing only on the chief, she asked, "Is this really necessary?"

"Yes, this is really necessary," Brian assured her.

Riley suppressed a sigh. There would be no winning today. "Yes, sir."

"All right, you're dismissed," he told them. Riley rose, as did Sam. She was about to leave the office when Brian said, "And Riley—"

She stopped and looked at her stepfather over her shoulder, hoping that he'd had second thoughts about this. "Yes, sir?"

"I want that name by the end of the week."

The therapist. In light of this new development, she'd almost forgotten about finding one for herself. There was no joy in Mudville tonight, she thought. "Yes, sir."

"What name?" Wyatt asked her as they walked out of the chief's office.

"Nothing that concerns you," she told him tersely.

Sam shrugged, taking her retort in stride. "Okay, but you'd better hustle."

Riley stopped walking and looked at her new, "temporary" partner. What was he talking about? "And why should I do that?"

"Because the end of the week's just three days away," he informed her simply, "and the chief likes things to reach his desk in the beginning of the day, not at the end of it."

Just who did Wyatt think he was, telling her things

about her own stepfather? Did he think she lived in a closet?

"You don't have to explain the chief to me," she retorted, annoyed, walking away from Sam.

"Right, he's your stepfather." He held his hands up as if surrendering. "I know, I know." Sam dropped his hands to his sides again as he increased his stride to keep up with her. Did she think this was a race? "I also know that him being your stepfather doesn't ultimately make any difference in the game plan. The chief's a fair man like that." The smile on his lips spread. "But there I go again, preaching to the choir. You'd already know that, too, wouldn't you?"

Give me strength, she prayed. "This arrangement is just temporary, you know."

"I know," he said cheerfully. "Until I get a better offer." Riley gave him a dirty glance. "Was I supposed to say until you get a better offer?" he asked innocently. And then he grinned again. "Sorry, didn't mean to hurt your feelings, McIntyre."

Reaching the elevator, she punched the up button. "I don't remember you being this annoying in the academy," she said.

Reaching over her, Sam pressed the down button. The look he gave her said that she'd made a mistake. Robbery was on the second floor. Homicide was located a floor above them. But she wasn't part of Homicide anymore. "Funny," he said, "I was just about to say the same about you."

Her temper flared. "Look—"

The elevator arrived. Stepping to the side to allow Riley to get on first, Sam followed and then pressed the button for the second floor.

"Hey, I get it. You feel like you've just had the rug pulled out from under you. Losing a partner can really do that to you," he agreed sympathetically. "But the only way you're going to land on your feet is to get over it and move on. I did," he told her. "Now stop feeling sorry for yourself and get on with your life—or the chief will leave you in Robbery—with me as your wet nurse."

Chapter 2

The fact that Wyatt could even *say* he thought of himself in those terms—as her *wet nurse*—made Riley's ordinarily subdued temper flare to dangerous new heights.

Since when did she need a babysitter, for pity's sake?

Was that what the chief thought, that she needed to be watched over? Worse, was that what her stepfather had intimated to Wyatt when he'd proposed the pairing to the smug, grinning hyena of a detective?

The idea sent a sick chill up and down her spine. She struggled not to shiver.

As for the other comparison he'd just made, well, Wyatt was way off base. That he even thought they were comparable showed just how little he understood. The man obviously had no instincts or feelings.

"Your partner transferred to another state," Riley told him through gritted teeth. "Mine was killed— murdered," she emphasized. "It's so far from being the same thing that it absolutely takes my breath away."

The thought of taking her breath away briefly flashed through Wyatt's mind. Not the way she implied, but the more standard, sensual way.

It was not without its appeal.

But Sam knew Riley McIntyre well enough to understand that it wasn't safe to tease her about that, at least, not right now. So instead, he took the easier route and just explained his reasoning.

"They're both gone."

"And you and mules both breathe, but that doesn't make you the same thing," she countered, then added a bit tartly, "despite the obvious resemblance."

If she expected him to take offense or announce that this partnership wasn't going to work, she was disappointed. Her words appeared to bounce right off him like rain off the freshly waxed hood of an automobile.

"Nice to know you're as sweet tempered as ever."

"Only with people who bring it out of me," she shot back, her mouth curving in a smile she definitely didn't feel.

The elevator stopped on the second floor and slowly opened its doors. Sam stepped out, then waited for her to do the same.

"Well, just a word to the wise—or in your case, wise ass," he said glibly. "Lt. Barker likes his detectives quiet—unless they're talking about an ongoing case."

She stopped walking and stared at him. "You're kidding, right?"

His face was deadly sober as he asked, "Do I look like I'm kidding?"

She couldn't tell if he was pulling her leg. She vaguely remembered that he had an outlandish sense of humor back in the day, but there was no glimmer of it right now. Or so it appeared.

"With you," she told him, "it was always hard to tell."

"Well, I'm not." He shoved his hands into his pockets as he resumed walking down the hall to the squad room. "Barker likes two things, hard workers and cases cleared. Personally," he confided, "I think Evans came up with that story about his ailing father because he couldn't take the lieutenant anymore."

"Evans," she repeated, rolling the last name over in her head. It wasn't really familiar. "That would be your partner?"

"Ex-partner," Wyatt corrected, then nodded. "Give the little lady a prize."

She stopped walking again. "Wyatt?"

Something in her tone told him to be on his guard. He had no idea what was coming. "Yeah?"

"You call me a 'little lady' again and an irreplaceable part of your anatomy will be handed to you so fast you won't know what hit you." She delivered her warning with an angelic smile.

"Yep," he murmured more to himself than to her, "every bit as charming now as you were back then."

Working with Riley McIntyre was going to be a challenge, he thought.

Once they arrived at the squad room, Sam pulled open the door for her, wondering as he did so if she would find the act of courtesy offensive on some militant-female level. But he wasn't about to make any apologies for the way he'd been raised.

"C'mon," he coaxed. "Might as well let Barker see what he's in for."

Bracing herself, Riley walked into the eerily quiet squad room.

The faces were different, the disorder was the same, she noted. Files haphazardly piled on desks and on top of computer towers. More than one stack threatened to fall at any second, waiting for the right passing vibration to send it cascading to the floor.

Organized chaos was the way she liked to think of it and she was as big an offender as anyone. Riley found she couldn't think clearly if the top of her desk was visible or her files were aligned neatly. When things were all spread out across her desk, her mind felt more opened, more prone to working fast.

Walking with Wyatt to the back of the room and Barker's office, Riley nodded at several familiar faces as she passed. The police community was a close-knit bunch and most detectives knew one another by sight, if not by reputation.

The latter was a communal one as far as she and her siblings went. At least, it had been, through no fault of their own. For a while there, all four of them were thought of as the offspring of an undercover agent gone bad.

But that was before Brian Cavanaugh had married her mother. Once vows were exchanged and it was clear that the Chief of Detectives considered Lila's children his own, the talk had abruptly stopped. Almost everyone liked the chief and those who didn't still respected and/or feared the man.

Chief of Detectives Brian Cavanaugh, younger brother of the former Chief of Police Andrew Cavanaugh, was known as a fair man who firmly believed in speaking softly and carrying a big stick. Not only carrying it but, on occasion, using that stick judiciously. The upshot of the situation was that no one wanted to get on the Chief of D's wrong side. Careers were known to have faded in that darkened area.

Seeing the way the detectives responded to his new partner, Sam commented, "I guess I won't have to introduce you to anyone."

"You can if you want to," she told him. "If it makes you feel useful, I wouldn't dream of depriving you."

Wyatt made an unintelligible noise she let pass rather than ask him to repeat himself. Instinctively, she knew it would be better all around that way.

Riley had never felt nervous meeting new people or even new superiors. But she felt something icy—a premonition?—slide down her spine as she looked through the glass wall that comprised Barker's office and saw the man sitting at his desk.

The word "trouble" ricocheted through her brain, refusing to fade away.

Sam knocked once then waited for the lieutenant to beckon him forward.

The latter, Riley noted, seemed oblivious to the knock. Either that, or he was deaf. If it was neither, then Barker was deliberately taking his time, keeping his eyes on the keyboard as he typed something. Finally, just as she was about to suggest to Wyatt that they come back later for an official introduction, Barker raised his intense dark brown eyes to silently regard the newest addition to his squad room.

An ex-marine, Lieutenant Joseph Barker looked every inch the part. From his close-cropped, salt-and-pepper hair, to his unsmiling demeanor, he was military through and through. She could almost feel the man's eyes wash over her, moving slowly as if he were conducting some kind of minute inventory.

"Take a seat, McIntyre," he finally said in a voice devoid of emotion. It certainly couldn't be termed as friendly. As Sam moved to join her, Barker stopped him before he could sit down in the second chair. "Not you, Wyatt. If I'd wanted you to sit, I would have said so, wouldn't I?"

The question was like a sharp poke in the ribs, meant to make the other detective retreat.

"Sorry, Lieutenant, don't know what came over me." The sarcastic response was delivered with an open, innocent smile.

Riley's respect for her new partner began to take form as she waited to see the lieutenant's reaction.

The look that Barker shot Wyatt was dark, bordering on black. Sam left without another word being exchanged between the two men.

Rather than say anything to Riley, the lieutenant resumed what he was working on.

Three more minutes passed before Barker looked up again.

Finally, Riley thought.

Hands loosely clasped in her lap, aware that on some level she represented her stepfather, Riley offered the man behind the desk an encouraging smile.

His first words to her were not what she would have expected.

"I heard you let your partner get killed."

Riley felt as if an arrow had been shot from a crossbow straight into her chest. Barker couldn't have said anything to make her feel worse if he'd deliberately tried. Maybe he had.

Squaring her shoulders, Riley lifted her chin and replied, "I wasn't with him at the time. Detective Sanchez went out on his own, without telling anyone."

Barker's eyes bored into her. As uncomfortable as it was, she refused to look away.

"He was your *partner,* McIntyre," the lieutenant emphasized. "You're always supposed to have your partner's back. Or didn't they teach you that at the academy?"

"They taught us that," she responded as politely as she could, then obviously surprised him by adding, "but they didn't say anything about having the ability to read minds."

His tone was dangerous. "I don't like flippant remarks, McIntyre."

She was in a no-win situation and she knew it. "It wasn't meant to be flippant, sir. I'm just stating my side."

"I'm not asking you to be a mind reader," Barker told her tersely. "It's called second-guessing and playing hunches," he informed her. "If you want to survive here, you're going to have to learn how to do that." His tone was close to belligerent as he asked, "Think you can manage that, McIntyre?"

God, but she wanted to defend herself, to make this man back off and put him in his place. But she knew she couldn't. So she did her best to sound subdued, as if his sarcasm didn't affect her.

"Yes, sir."

"Good," he bit off. "Then we'll get along. Keep your partner alive, McIntyre, and he'll do the same for you."

With that, the lieutenant went back to his work.

She sat, listening to the sound of keys being struck, for another three minutes. He behaved as if she wasn't even in the office. Was this some kind of an endurance test? Or a contest of wills? How much longer was she expected to sit here?

Finally, she couldn't take it any longer. "Will there be anything else, sir?"

Barker kept on typing, the sound of his keys echoing rhythmically. "If there is, McIntyre, you'll know it," he told her, never looking up.

Was he dismissing her? She realized that she was gripping the armrests. That was twice today. So far, this was not shaping up to be one of her better days. She bit back her temper.

"Then I can go?"

Two more keys were struck before Barker gave her an answer. "Please."

Riley left the office without another word.

This couldn't possibly be what her stepfather had had in mind for her, she thought, shutting the lieutenant's door behind her. It took maximum control not to slam it in her wake. She knew that Brian Cavanaugh liked his lieutenants to be in charge and authoritative, but Barker came across like a petulant dictator.

This was not going to go well, she reflected.

She supposed she could go to her stepfather and tell him what had just transpired, how Barker had all but ignored her and definitely treated her with a lack of respect. But that would be tantamount to whining and she absolutely refused to come across like some spoiled brat.

She'd always pulled her own weight. She was proud of that. Riley saw no reason to change now.

Somehow, she promised herself, she was going to get through this and show that pompous jerk of a lieutenant that she wasn't about to retreat like some overly indulged, know-nothing rookie.

Looking around the squad room, she spotted Wyatt sitting at a desk. More accurately, her new temporary partner was leaning back in his chair, rocking it in such a precarious manner that the chair appeared in danger of tilting backward and crashing to the floor.

Great, Wyatt still hadn't grown up yet.

Better and better.

Releasing a sigh, Riley quickly crossed over to her partner. The sooner she got to work, the sooner she could figure out her role here.

Nodding at her, Sam righted his chair. "How did it go?" he asked cheerfully.

"It didn't," she ground out.

Wyatt didn't bother trying to suppress the knowing grin that came to his lips. "A little conflict of personalities, perhaps?"

The man shot from being a possible ally to an antagonist in the space of a split second. "You think it's funny?" she demanded hotly.

Riley noticed that several of the people in the room were looking in their direction. She would have to work on lowering her voice.

"Yeah, I do," he replied. Before she could fashion a comeback, he added, "That gives us something in common. Actually," he went on, glancing around the area, "that gives you something in common with every man in this squad room."

Every man.

Until he'd slapped a singular gender to the occupants of the room, Riley hadn't consciously realized that she was the only female on the floor. Since each desk wasn't occupied, she just assumed that some of them belonged to women who were out in the field. Female detectives were a common occurrence where she came from. Her mother had been out in the field prior to being wounded. Her sister, Taylor, and the female Cavanaugh cousins who had come as part of the package deal when her mother married the chief, were all currently working in the field.

In fact, as far as she knew, there were only two Cavanaugh women, Patience and Janelle, who weren't part of the police department and even they were closely associated with it. Patience was a vet who took care of the K-9 squad and was married to a police officer and Janelle was an assistant district attorney. She too was married to a police detective.

Being the only woman in the room felt rather unusual to her.

After scanning the area, she looked at Sam again. "There're no women on the floor?"

"On the floor?" he echoed. "Yes. In the department?" which was what he figured she actually meant, "No. As fate would have it, you'd be robbery division's first female detective." He flashed her a grin, clearly amused by the situation. "Think you're up to it, McIntyre?"

He was saying that to goad her, she thought. To make her stop focusing on the uncomfortable aspect of this situation and just view it as a challenge. Appreciating the intent, she had to give him his due. "You're not as dumb as you look, Wyatt."

The comment made him laugh. "Bet you say that to all the guys."

"Only the ones who deserve it." She wanted to settle in, even if it was just for the time being. "Okay, where do I sit?"

His eyes met hers. "Any place you plant your butt,

McIntyre. I'd say 'pretty butt,' but then you'd probably have me hauled up to human resources on harassment charges."

Okay, he obviously needed to know some basic ground rules about her.

"I don't need anyone to fight my battles for me, Wyatt. If something you say bothers me—more than normal," she qualified, "I'll let you know. I won't resort to running off to a go-between."

She wasn't sure, but she thought she saw respect enter his eyes.

"Fair enough," Wyatt declared with a nod of his head before flashing that now famous grin. "You know, McIntyre, this might be the beginning of a beautiful friendship."

"Too late for that. I already know you," she reminded him.

The look in his eyes told her that she was a long way off from that.

"There's knowing a person to nod at and say hello to, and then there's working with him. That, Detective McIntyre, is a whole different ball game," Wyatt assured her.

He was right, she thought grudgingly. Right because it involved exactly what that pompous ass in the glass office had referred to just before she had left his office. She would have Wyatt's life in her hands and Wyatt would have hers. That made for a bond that wasn't usually formed between two average acquaintances.

"Her," Riley finally corrected him. "Working with *her*."

His next words surprised her. Mainly because she was aware of his reputation as a ladies' man.

"I'd rather not think of you as a girl, McIntyre. Or a woman," he added, anticipating that she was going to correct his age-related reference to her gender.

Her eyebrows drew together as she tried to fathom why Wyatt had said that. Moreover, how could he help but think of her in those terms? She *was* a woman. Or was this just a set up for some elaborate wisecrack on his part?

But she bit anyway. "What do you want to think of me as?"

"A slightly curvy guy will do." He spread his hands in a wide shrug. "If this is going to work between us, that's what you're going to have to be, McIntyre. A feminine-looking guy."

She sighed. "You're crazy, you know that, Wyatt?"

And, right now, she didn't exactly have high hopes that *any* of this was going to work. But this was what the chief wanted and she was not about to be the one rushing back to him, complaining. She refused to let a man she respected so highly think of her in an unflattering light.

About to remind Wyatt that he hadn't answered her as to where she was to sit, Riley decided to reword the question. "Where's my desk, Wyatt?"

He gestured to the one that was facing his. It looked just as cluttered as his own. As a matter of fact, on closer examination, it looked as if the folders on the desk had overflowed from his. She glanced at a couple of the ones on top.

"Whose files are these?" she asked Wyatt. The writing on top of the first folder looked vaguely like the writing on the notepad on Wyatt's desk.

"Mine," he told her, moving several of the folders back to his desk. "I kind of spread out after Evans left." He shrugged as he collected the rest and placed them on his desk. "You know how that is."

"No," she contradicted, "I don't."

Even though Sanchez's desk had faced hers like Wyatt's faced his old partner's, she had taken great pains to keep her things from inching onto Sanchez's desk, which she'd called "No Man's Land." After he had been murdered, she'd cleaned out the desk for the man's mother, placing everything into a box and bringing it to the woman's house herself. She recalled that the visit had ended with both of them in tears.

"Well, it's normal around here," Wyatt told her, adding in a knowing tone, "Trust me."

Trust me.

That summed up everything in two neat little words. In order for things to work—for *anything* to work— there had to be a certain amount of trust. But trust was exactly what was missing from her soul. She honestly didn't know if she could ever trust anyone outside the family again. Ever allow anyone to trust her again. Both ways, it was just too big a risk to take.

Chapter 3

It was officially Riley's first full day as part of the robbery division and her new partner was conspicuously absent from his desk.

At first, she thought he had just beaten her in and was engrossed in some task. She'd even envisioned him complaining to a sympathetic ear about this new partner who had been forced on him by the Chief of Ds.

But when the first hour dragged into the next with still no sign of Wyatt anywhere on the floor, Riley began to reexamine the situation.

Wyatt's computer wasn't on.

It had been on all day yesterday, even when they went to interview a pawnbroker on the other side of Aurora whose shop had been burglarized. Like everyone else, Wyatt turned his computer on in the morning and then left it that way all day. He'd even doubled back last night to turn off the machine before he left the squad room for the evening.

Was his being out some reflection on her? Maybe his silent way of protesting being forced to pair up with her?

Riley frowned. She had no answers and a ton of questions that began to multiply.

"McIntyre!"

Her head snapped up the second the lieutenant had barked out her name. The man stood in the doorway of his office, glaring her way. Riley was on her feet instantly, ready to be sent on police business or hurry to his office, whatever the martinet of a commanding officer dictated.

"Yes, sir?"

Barker appeared mildly pleased that she had whipped into shape so quickly. The next second the look was gone. A deep frown had taken over his craggy, hard-as-nails features as he asked, "Where's your partner?"

How was she supposed to know? she asked silently. She wasn't Wyatt's mother or his keeper.

Out loud, Riley said, "I don't know, Lieutenant. Didn't he call in?"

Barker watched her as if she lacked the intelligence of a single-celled amoeba.

"If Wyatt'd called in, I'd know where he was, wouldn't I?" Sarcasm dripped from every word. "You're on a new case as of right now, McIntyre. Find your partner and tell him to drag himself in here. This isn't a country club."

If it was, she'd be handing in her membership card right about now, Riley thought. "No, sir."

About to turn back to his desk, the lieutenant stopped and leveled a dark look at her over his shoulder. Even across the room, it appeared lethal in nature.

"'No, sir?'" Barker echoed, his thin eyebrows narrowing into a vee.

Riley immediately realized what Barker was thinking—and her mistake. She lost no time in clarifying her response.

"No, sir, this isn't a country club. Yes, sir, I'll track down Detective Wyatt."

Barker nodded, momentarily appeased. "See that you do, McIntyre," he ordered. "God save us from loose cannons and mavericks," he muttered under his breath, retreating again into his glass-walled office.

Riley's survival instinct warred with her desire to be a good detective, no matter what department she was assigned to. Good detective won out.

She crossed the room and knocked on the lieutenant's door, even though it was still open. "Um, sir?"

"What are you still doing here, McIntyre?" he demanded without looking up, some obvious sixth sense identifying her for him. "I gave you an assignment."

"Yes, sir, but this is about the assignment after this one." She saw that she had him confused. "The new one for Wyatt and me."

"Home invasion," he snapped out, then rattled off an address. It was in the better part of the city and not all that far from her own, she noted. "Details are similar to the case Wyatt worked on last month. The first is still an open case. I want it closed."

It wasn't a suggestion, but a direct order.

The administrative assistant on their floor gave Riley her partner's address and phone number, along with an unsolicited comment.

Virginia McKee, the perpetually perky assistant, wrote down the information in a bold hand and offered the slip of paper to Riley.

"Enjoy," Virginia told her with a wink that was anything but subtle.

Riley folded the paper, but kept it in her hand rather than tuck it into her pocket. "There's nothing to enjoy. The lieutenant's looking for him."

"You're wrong there," Virginia contradicted, a sly smile curving her lips.

If she was going to survive here for a while, Riley knew she had to make allies and come across as friendly even though right now, being friendly was her last desire. This had to be her stepfather's goal when he had transferred her here. The business of living and acclimating to a new situation put things into some kind of perspective and forced her to move forward.

"Oh?"

Virginia indicated the paper she'd just given her. "There's a *lot* to enjoy there."

Spoken like a woman who's been there, Riley thought. Apparently, Sam Wyatt was still just as much of a player as he'd ever been. She knew he'd been when they were in the academy together. As she recalled, if it had a pulse, the required body parts and a smile, Wyatt considered it fair game.

It was to Wyatt's credit that he wasn't pushy about it, but then, a guy with Sam Wyatt's face and build didn't have to be. Most of the time, what he needed was the proverbial stick in order to beat back the hordes of women.

Not her concern one way or another, Riley told herself.

Armed with the number of Wyatt's landline, Riley didn't bother going back to her desk to make the call. Instead, she walked out into the hallway, stopped in an alcove next to the women's restroom and called her missing partner on her cell phone.

The phone on the other end of the line rang five times. The sixth ring had the answering machine picking up. Riley frowned.

Was Wyatt playing hooky? When the beep sounded, she started talking.

"Wyatt, this is McIntyre. The lieutenant wants to know where you are. He wanted me to tell you that you'd better haul your tail in if you know what's good for y—" She stopped abruptly as she heard the phone being picked up. "Wyatt?"

"Yeah, look, I'm not coming in today. Tell Barker I'm taking a sick day."

He sounded pretty agitated. Big night gone bad? she wondered. "How sick are you?"

"I've never felt like this before in my life," was his vague response.

Riley hesitated for a moment, not completely convinced that he wasn't pulling her leg. But then, what if he really was sick? As far as she knew, he lived alone. Maybe he needed someone to pick up medication for him. As his partner, it fell to her.

"Flu?"

"No," he bit off.

It was the middle of October and the Santa Ana winds were kicking up, making half the population of California miserable by playing havoc with their allergies and sinuses. The partner she'd had before Sanchez was wedded to his box of tissues the entire time the winds blew. Maybe Wyatt had the same problem.

"Sinus infection?" she guessed.

"No."

This time, he sounded downright surly. Her patience was slipping away. "Then what've you got?"

There was a long pause on the other end of the line. She was about to ask if he was still there when she heard him say, "I've got a kid."

"You've got what?"

"A kid," he repeated, doing his best not to shout. "Look, I'll be in tomorrow."

The line went dead against her ear before she could press him any further.

Sam let the receiver fall into its cradle and looked at the perfect little bit of humanity sitting on his sofa, politely pretending to be absorbed in the educational programming he'd turned on for her.

Six years old, she seemed to have already mastered

everything the multicolored, furry, perky little creatures prancing across the screen could possibly teach her.

From the moment he'd hit puberty and discovered it exceedingly to his liking, Sam had never felt at a loss as to what to do in *any* given situation.

Except now.

What the hell was he going to do with her?

Nothing he'd gone through these last twenty years had prepared him for this. But "this" had definitely happened. And now it was up to him to deal with it responsibly.

Oh, damn.

Sam scrubbed his hand over his face, forcing himself to think. But rather than coming up with a game plan, all he could do was relive the morning's earthshaking events in his mind. It sounded like a dramatic assessment to anyone privy to what had transpired, but as far as he was concerned, it *was* dramatic.

He'd never been a father before.

He'd always thought that eventually he'd like to be one. But he'd just assumed that the timing would be of his own choosing and only after he'd married someone he felt completed his world. Currently, no candidates qualified for that position. But he'd obviously joined fatherhood without first acquiring the required wife.

What was he going to do?

When the doorbell rang this morning just as he'd finished getting ready for work, the thought that it was his new partner had flashed through his brain. Not that he was expecting her—or anyone—but if it was going to be someone, for some unknown reason, his money was on McIntyre.

He would have lost. Big time.

When he opened the door, there standing in his doorway was a woman he'd never seen before. She held the hand of an almost doll-like, perfect little girl. Petite, blond, blue-eyed, the girl already had the makings of a little princess. It vaguely registered that the little girl didn't look a thing like the dark-haired woman whose hand she was holding.

"I'm afraid you've got the wrong apartment," he'd said to the woman.

The woman appeared unwilling to leave. "Detective Wyatt?"

His "Yes?" had been wary. Life on the force had made him privy to the world's darker elements.

"Sam Wyatt?" the woman pressed.

"Yes." His eyes had narrowed as he'd studied the woman in his doorway. "Do I know you?" It was a gratuitous question because he prided himself on never forgetting a face.

"No. But you 'knew' Lisa's mother." She nodded toward the little girl. "In the biblical sense," she emphasized. "Andrea Coltrane."

He never forgot a name, either. When the woman mentioned Andrea, an image instantly materialized in his mind's eye. It was accompanied by half a dozen memories that spliced together in a quick mental slideshow.

Andrea, a cool, statuesque blonde, proved to be a red-hot lover. So hot that for a very short while, he'd contemplated entering into a long-term relationship with the upwardly mobile tax attorney, but he never got the chance.

Inexplicably, things suddenly cooled between them. Before he knew it, Andrea had disappeared from his life. He'd tried calling her a couple of times. The second time, he'd been informed by a metallic voice that the number he'd dialed was no longer in service. When he discovered that she'd moved as well, he figured he would take the hint.

It never occurred to him that Andrea had moved for any other reason than she'd wanted a change. During their time together, she'd insisted that she wanted no strings tying her down.

Glancing at the little girl, an uneasy feeling told him that he'd made the wrong assumption.

"Where is Andrea?" he asked the woman, his tone guarded.

Rather than answer, the woman handed him an eight-by-ten manila envelope and then, still holding the little girl by the hand, she walked into his apartment.

"I'm Carole Gilbert. I worked with Andrea for the last five years." She nodded at the envelope. "This'll explain everything."

Worked.

Sam'd had an uneasy feeling that there was a specific reason for the reference in the past tense, probably not because Andrea had moved on again.

Fingers poised over the envelope's clasp, he'd raised his eyes to look at Carole. "What am I going to find in here?"

"In a nutshell, 'Congratulations, Detective Wyatt,

you've just become a daddy.' She moved the little girl forward. "This is your daughter, Lisa. She's six." Carole bent down so that her face was close to the little girl's. "Say hello to your father, Lisa," Carole instructed gently.

Cornflower blue eyes widening ever so slightly, the little girl gave him a shy smile and in a voice that was soft and delicate as the first spring breeze, she said, "Hello."

Everything inside of Sam shouted *no!* even as he found himself looking down into *Andrea's* blue eyes. Lisa was Andrea's daughter, all right. A perfect miniature of her mother.

The word "perfect" really was not applicable here, he'd thought as he felt his stomach sinking past his knees.

Despite the fact that she appeared anxious to leave, Sam made the bearer of his unsettling news stay as he read, then reread the letter and the will enclosed. And then he fired questions at her as he tried to reconcile himself to this wildly abrupt turn of events.

Andrea, killed the week before by a drunk driver, had left very specific instructions as to whom was to take care of Lisa in the event of her untimely death. An only child whose parents were both deceased, Andrea had felt that Lisa needed to be raised by at least one parent and he, Sam, met that minimum requirement.

He stared at the birth date that Andrea had written down. Apparently Lisa was the direct result of the "wildly romantic" two months he and Andrea had spent together. When she'd discovered that she was pregnant, Andrea was determined to raise Lisa on her own and so she had disappeared.

"'Nothing against you, Sam,'" he read. "'But at the time, you didn't strike me as exactly father material. But since you're reading this, circumstances have obviously dictated otherwise. Lisa is a wonderful, intelligent little girl—with us as her parents, how could she not be?— who needs your love and support now. I wish I could be there to see it. Take good care of her. She is the precious gift that keeps on giving.'"

He'd folded the letter knowing, for the first time, exactly what a butterfly pinned and mounted on a display board felt like.

After answering more questions and giving him the key to Andrea's apartment where the rest of Lisa's belongings and other important documents were stored, Carole left. Due to coercion on his part, she'd given him a number where she could be reached. A work number, but at least it was something.

He wasn't good at talking to females under the age of twenty-one but he knew that, barring an eleventh-hour miracle of some sort, he would have to learn. And learn fast.

Sam couldn't shake the feeling that he was the child and she the adult. When he spoke to her, Lisa seemed to gently humor him, going along with his suggestion for breakfast—only eggs since he didn't think that a six-year-old drank coffee—and settling on the sofa to watch television when he turned on the set for her.

When Sam heard the doorbell ring again less than an hour after Carole's departure, hope suddenly sprang up in his chest. He thought—fervently prayed—that Carole had suddenly changed her mind about turning over the little girl to him and had, instead, decided that it would be best for all to take her in.

He lost no time hurrying to open the door.

Hope died a cruel, quick death, crashing to the ground like a falling comet.

"Oh, it's you." As an afterthought, he stepped to the side to allow Riley to enter.

But Riley remained where she was. He looked really shaken up, light years away from the smooth operator she had been with yesterday.

"You can cancel the marching brass band, Wyatt. Fanfare would only embarrass me," Riley quipped, then got down to why she was here. "Lieutenant Barker's fit to be tied."

His lieutenant's disposition was extremely low on Sam's list of concerns at the moment. But he needed to work, now more than ever. This little accident of nature would need to be fed and clothed. And sent off to college. If he was lucky, she'd turn out to be a genius, going through grades at an accelerated rate and displaying the kind of intellectual acumen that attracted scholarships.

He eyed Riley warily. So far his luck had been running rather poorly this morning. "What did you tell him?"

"That you were following up on a lead and I was meeting you at the possible suspect's house. He wants us to hand off that case to Rafferty and Kellogg," she said, mentioning two other robbery detectives. "Seems that another home invasion went down last night. They only got the 9-1-1 call an hour ago. Details of the invasion are similar to one that you were already handling. Then Barker grumbled something about loose cannons and mavericks and retreated into his lair. My guess is that he's been watching too many action movies."

Finished, she peered around her partner's arm into the apartment. Since Wyatt hadn't actually voiced an invitation, she decided to take matters into her own hands and crossed the threshold.

"What was all this about you coming down with a case of 'kid'?" she asked. "Is that short for something?"

"Yeah." Sam closed the door behind her and gestured for Riley to follow him to the living room. "It's short for 'big trouble.'"

About to ask him what he was babbling about, the next minute, she caught sight of the little blond girl on the sofa and had her answer.

Chapter 4

Standing just a few feet inside the apartment, Riley looked from the child seated on the sofa to Wyatt and then back again. Surprise mingled with disbelief. The little girl, who had a box and a couple of suitcases beside her, was the very last thing she'd expected to find in Wyatt's apartment.

She flashed a wide smile at the little girl. As an official Cavanaugh by marriage, Riley was now an aunt, by proxy, to a whole slew of children coming in all sizes, shapes and ages. Children represented innocence, a clean slate.

Everyone should remain a child for as long as possible, she thought, a wave of protectiveness washing over her.

Crossing into the living room, Riley was aware that Wyatt was behind her. "Hi," she said to the little girl. "I'm Riley. What's your name?"

"Lisa," came the prompt, polite response.

Riley looked back at Wyatt for some kind of enlightenment. "Your niece?" she guessed.

Rather than answer, Sam took her by the arm and led her to the kitchen.

But before he got there, Lisa raised her voice and called out after her, "I'm his daughter."

Riley froze just shy of the kitchen and looked up at her partner. "Did she just say…?"

There was no childlike lisp, no baby voice to misunderstand. Lisa's enunciation was perfect, the kind that belonged to precocious, budding geniuses poised to take the world by storm.

Sam nodded. "Yes."

Riley was sure she was still missing something. "She's your daughter," she said, leaving it as a statement.

This time the single world came out like an angry cannon shot. "Yes."

The police department had been growing in recent years, but they were still pretty much a tight community. There were fewer detectives than uniformed cops. Word got around. There was never even a hint that Wyatt was anything but an available stud. If a short person was in the wings, someone would have mentioned it in passing.

"Since when?" she said.

He glanced over her head toward the living room and the child with flawless posture. He used to curl up on the sofa when he watched TV at her age. With her hands folded in her lap and sitting ramrod straight, Lisa looked as if she was attending a meeting instead of watching television.

"Apparently since six years ago," he told Riley with a sigh.

Riley studied him for a moment. The detective seemed unsettled. They hadn't interacted very much in the last few years, but to her recollection, she'd never seen him rattled before.

"How long have you known?" she asked.

Sam looked at his watch. "Two hours, give or take a few minutes."

He wasn't volunteering anything, so she started piecing things together herself.

"This woman who obviously can keep a secret, she just left her daughter with you? Just like that?" Riley knew it happened but it was difficult to envision.

He had no idea why, but he suddenly felt defensive for Andrea. "She didn't have much choice, seeing as how she's—" His voice dropped before he said the last word. "—dead."

Thoroughly confused, Riley looked over her shoulder into the living room. "If her mother's dead, how did Lisa—"

Wyatt cut her off before she could finish. "Her friend brought Lisa over, along with a letter from Andrea and a copy of Andrea's will."

According to the document, his new daughter had a small trust fund set aside in her name. But she couldn't touch it until she turned eighteen. Twelve years from now, he thought.

The name meant nothing to Riley. "I take it Andrea was your—" She left the sentence unfinished, searching for the right word, hoping that Wyatt would supply it.

"Andrea wasn't anything of mine," he denied vehemently.

As far as he was concerned, until this morning, Andrea belonged to his past. Just one of the women he'd dated. Except now she wasn't. She was the mother of his child. The child that, less than three hours ago, he didn't even know he had.

"Well, she must have been 'something' of yours if that little girl in the next room really is your daughter." All sorts of thoughts rushed through her mind. She asked the first logical one that occurred to her. "Are you sure that she's yours?"

"If you mean did she come with DNA test results, then no. But there was no reason for Andrea to lie." Especially since the woman had never come to him with this news while she was alive and able to forge her own path. "Andrea is—was—a very independent woman." Even though she hadn't been part of his life for over six years, it was hard to think of the woman in the past tense. "This also explains a lot of things," he said more to himself than to Riley.

"Such as?" Riley coaxed, her curiosity jacked up to high.

For a second, he'd almost forgotten his partner was here.

"Why she disappeared so abruptly," he said. "One day she was there and we were talking about clearing out a drawer for her and giving her some space in my closet. The next," he snapped his fingers, "she was gone."

"Despite the enticing offer of a drawer and four hangers?" Riley marveled. "Woman didn't know when she had it good, huh?"

He looked at her, annoyed. "Sarcasm doesn't suit you."

"Funny, I always thought it did." Riley grew serious and asked, "Did you even try to find her after she disappeared?"

Ordinarily, he might not have. But then, no other woman had just vanished the way Andrea had. "Yes, I tried to find her."

"Obviously not hard enough." She saw that he took offense, so she told him why she felt that way. "You're a detective, Wyatt. Finding things—like people—is what you do. And yet, in this case, you didn't."

He blew out a frustrated breath. Maybe Riley was right. Maybe, deep down, he didn't want to find Andrea if she had thought so little of him to leave without a word. He wished now that he had pushed harder.

"Yeah, well, she moved, changed jobs, changed her phone number. For all I knew, she changed her name." He shrugged, trying to dismiss the incident. "I figured she got spooked."

This man couldn't have spooked a woman, she thought, dismissing his excuse. He was the kind of man that drew women.

"That's what you get for wearing your Godzilla suit when it's not even Halloween," she cracked.

"Spooked by the idea of commitment," he elaborated. He saw her opening her mouth, ready to argue the point. "You know, it's not just guys who have trouble wrapping their heads around making a commitment. Women have trouble with the concept, too."

Riley relented. She really couldn't argue with that. Her own sister, Taylor, was part of that group—until love ambushed her and tossed a tall, dark, handsome private investigator in her path. Now, she knew, Taylor couldn't begin to imagine life without J.C.

But rather than share this with Wyatt, she merely asked, "So you let her go?"

"I decided not to come on like a stalker," he corrected. "It was good while it lasted, but I assumed when she took off like that, whatever we had was over."

Riley glanced back at the little girl in the living room. Lisa was still sitting ramrod straight, watching television.

"Apparently not," Riley pointed out, then asked. "What's your next move?"

That was the sixty-four-million-dollar question. "Hell if I know."

Riley held up one finger. "Okay, first move. No more cursing."

"I wasn't cursing," Sam protested.

"Not by the standards we're used to," she allowed, "but 'hell' and 'damn' are curses of the venial variety." He looked unconvinced, so she explained further. "Think of it in the same terms as marijuana leading the user to cocaine. Both are illegal drugs, one just viewed as far more serious than the other. Next," she continued, now holding up a second finger, "you need to line up someone to stay with Lisa while you're working."

He hadn't even thought that far ahead yet. It was as if his brain was paralyzed, still trying to deal with this major curve. Now that he did think about it, it didn't help. There was no one to turn to.

"Everyone I know is at the precinct."

He'd never mentioned any relatives when they had attended the academy. Riley realized that she had no idea what his family dynamics were like. "No family to fall back on?"

He had family, or rather, a parent. His father, who lived in a retirement community. "In Arizona. Kind of a killer commute."

Riley stopped listening when he mentioned Arizona. "Let me see what I can do," she said, taking out her cell phone.

When she pressed a button on the keypad, he asked, "Who are you calling?"

Riley held up her hand, silently asking him to hold his thought until she got off the phone.

"Brenda? Hi, it's Riley. Look, I know that this is really short notice and I hate to impose on you, but my partner needs someone to watch his little girl—Six," she said in response to the question her stepbrother's wife asked her. "Her mother's dead and—" Again Riley paused, this time not for a question but to listen while Brenda expressed her sympathy for both her partner and his daughter. The next sentence had her smiling broadly. "Thanks, Brenda, you're a doll. We'll be over as soon as we can." With that, she slipped the cell phone closed again.

"Over where?" Wyatt pressed the second she ended the call.

"Brenda is one of the chief's daughters-in-law. She's married to Dax and she just said to bring Lisa over. Brenda works out of her house a lot so she can raise her own kids," Riley explained, then added, in case Wyatt needed further convincing, "She used to be a teacher. And she's great with kids. This way, you can appease the lieutenant and get back to work, and you get a little breathing space to calmly figure out how to proceed."

"Calmly," Sam echoed, shaking his head. His mouth curved in a smile he definitely didn't feel. "Too late. The ship has sailed on that one."

It might be better if he just took the day off after all. She took out her phone again. "Want me to call Brenda back and say you've changed your mind about bringing Lisa over?"

No, Riley was right. He should get back to work and he needed time to think. "What I really want is for you to turn the clock back six years and make sure you kick me in the pants when I suggest going to Malone's for a drink." Malone's was the bar where he had first met Andrea. She had been there with her friends, celebrating a major court-room win. She'd gone home with him that night.

Riley filled in the blanks herself, surmising that he had to be referring to approximately the time when Lisa had been conceived.

"Much as that's a very tempting offer, Wyatt, I first have

to point out that you mean seven years ago, not six. Nine months after conception, remember?" she prodded. "And second, magic and/or time travel are not part of my job description or, by any stretch of the imagination, my résumé."

Riley waited for her partner's response, but there was none. His eyes almost glazed over. She suspected that fatherhood bursting upon him like an exploding land mine was to blame.

She waved her hand in front of his eyes. "Earth to Wyatt, earth to Wyatt."

Catching her by the wrist, Sam pushed her hand back down. "What?"

"Do you or don't you want to take your daughter to Brenda's house?" she asked.

Sam supposed that solved the problem today but what about tomorrow? And all the tomorrows to come, what of them? He couldn't think about that now. They'd just have to work themselves out somehow. He had to believe that.

She was still watching him, waiting. "That would be good," he finally told her.

She crossed back into the living room. "Lisa, honey, your father and I are going to take you to this nice lady's house. Her name's Brenda. Brenda Cavanaugh."

Lisa slowly slid off the sofa, never taking her eyes from the man Carole had told her was her father. "To stay?" she asked hesitantly. "Don't you want me?"

Riley thought she saw the little girl's lower lip tremble as she asked the last question. Her heart twisted a little in sympathy.

"Of course he wants you," Riley said before Wyatt

had a chance to answer. "But he works, honey. As a police detective."

She turned toward Wyatt. "Isn't that right, Detective Wyatt?" she asked, keeping her voice purposely sweet.

He merely nodded, not unlike a man about to slip into shock.

"Wyatt, you okay?" she asked.

Sam waved off her concern. "I'll get the car started."

To her knowledge, his car didn't need to be warmed up but she didn't contradict him. Instead, she turned her attention to the little girl. She did her best to sound cheerful and reassuring. "Need help packing something to take with you?"

Lisa eyed her uncertainly. "Then I am staying at this other person's house?"

Lisa's voice was soft and low, but it seemed to Riley to hum with intelligence.

"Just for a few hours. You'll be coming back here later today. Tonight at the latest," Riley augmented. As detectives, they did have shifts, but their hours could still be rather erratic. If that home invasion had been reported last night, she had no doubt that both Wyatt and she would have gotten calls in the middle of the night to come to the scene of the crime.

She saw the solemn look on Lisa's face. Tears began to fill the little girl's eyes. Was she afraid? "What's the matter?"

Lisa swallowed before answering. "That's what Mama said before she left me. She didn't come back."

Riley bent down to embrace Lisa. She felt the little

girl stiffen at first, then melt into her arms. Poor thing just wants to be loved, she thought.

"Honey, your mama was in a car accident." As she spoke, Riley stroked Lisa's hair soothingly. "She wanted nothing more than to come back to you, but well, it didn't turn out that way."

Lisa raised her head to look up at her. "You'll come back?"

Riley rose to her feet. "We'll come back," she promised. She crossed her heart before she took the little girl's hand in hers.

Lisa asked her the same question again just before she and Wyatt left.

Wyatt was ahead of her, obviously anxious to get going. He said a quick goodbye to Lisa. She looked so lost, standing there so forlornly, that Riley bent down and hugged her. That was when Lisa asked her again. "You'll come back?"

"Your dad'll come back, honey," she promised, thinking that Lisa meant her question for Wyatt. "I guarantee it."

"No, you," Lisa corrected urgently. "You'll come back?"

Riley exchanged looks with Wyatt, caught off guard by Lisa's question. This wasn't the time for a philo-sophical debate as to her place in the scheme of things—or rather her lack of a place.

Instead, she rose to her feet and promised, "I'll come back. We both will."

Only then did Lisa's anxious expression begin to relax. "Okay."

Brenda moved forward, slipping her arm around the girl's shoulders. "C'mon, Lisa, let me introduce you to my kids."

Lisa allowed herself to be led away, although she kept looking over her shoulder at them until Wyatt closed the front door, effectively separating them from his daughter's view.

He blew out a breath as if he'd been holding it the entire time they'd been at Brenda's house. "Looks like she's already bonded with you."

Was that relief she saw in his eyes? "If her mother never married, Lisa's probably more comfortable around women."

"Great," he murmured under his breath.

"You'll rise to the challenge," she assured him. "Granted Lisa's a bit younger than you're used to, but once you turn on that charm, I'm sure you'll have her eating out of your hand." Her attempt to tease him out of his solemnity failed. She dropped her kidding tone. "What's the matter?"

He paused by his car. "I don't think I can be a father, McIntyre," he told her.

"You're perfectly normal. I'd say probably ninety-five percent of all fathers say that at the beginning."

"Yeah, but they all get nine months to get used to the idea. I didn't even get nine seconds. One minute I'm a bachelor. The next, I'm a family man," he complained, shaking his head.

Riley gave him a knowing look. "As I remember it, you were always a quick study. You'll get the hang of this in no time."

For the first time since she'd sat in front of him at the academy, Wyatt didn't look his usual confident self. Instead, he appeared worried.

As he opened the door to his vehicle, he paused. "I've never said this before," he started to confess, then stopped.

"Go ahead," she coaxed.

It took him a couple more seconds to frame his admission. "I've never said this before," he began again. "But I'm going to need help." And then, after taking a breath, he came to the crux of his request. "In short, McIntyre, I'm going to need you."

Chapter 5

For just a split second, when Sam said he needed her, a whole different meaning to his words flashed through her mind. A meaning that had nothing to do with the present set of circumstances her partner was facing.

Riley pushed that, and the unsettling, restless curiosity away. "Need me to what?" she heard herself asking.

"Help me with Lisa."

What else could he have meant, idiot? she silently demanded. Out loud Riley tried to sound casual as she said, "I thought I was already helping. I'm the one who got you a babysitter for the day." And, if necessary, a more long-term arrangement could be made with Brenda for Lisa's after-school care.

School.

Sam said his daughter was six. That meant she belonged in school. Another onslaught of questions rushed at her, temporarily squeezing out the feeling she'd just experienced.

Sam nodded. For a moment, he forgot about getting into his car and driving to the scene of the home invasion. He needed to air this out, get it said and at least temporarily straight in his mind. "And I appreciate it in case I forgot to mention it—"

"You did."

He suppressed an impatient sigh, knowing he didn't want to do or say anything that would alienate this woman right now. He *did* need her. Besides, she was his partner.

"But this isn't some two-hour movie where everything gets neatly wrapped up and uplifting music plays as the credits begin to roll. This is real life, McIntyre." He didn't add that it was *his* life and he had no idea how he'd found himself in this predicament. He'd always been so careful. But nothing—including birth control obviously—was foolproof. "And there's an ocean of tomorrows to face."

It occurred to her that there might be a very simple solution to his problem, at least for the time being. "Well, 'Daddy,' don't you have a current girlfriend you can turn to?" Someone eager to cull his favor by pitching in to care for his daughter would be really handy right about now.

But Sam shook his head. "Not at the moment. I seem to be in between shallow relationships."

Her mouth curved. "Glad you said it and not me."

The way he saw it, it had been a preemptive strike. "Figured you would." He looked at her hopefully. "How about it, McIntyre?" he pressed. "Can you run interference for me?"

She knew he wanted her to take over. Maybe volunteer to take his daughter to her extended family and have one or more of them become responsible for Lisa. *Ain't gonna happen, Wyatt,* she thought.

"No, but I can show up temporarily in the evening and lend you a hand if you like. You're going to have to be there, too," she specified. "In order to get used to each other, you and Lisa will have to actually *be* with each other."

Sam sighed and dragged a hand through his hair. The incredibly dry air sucked the moisture out of everything. He could feel static electricity crackling just above his scalp.

McIntyre was making sense, he knew that. But for the first time in his life, he felt unequal to the challenge that faced him. What did he know about raising a little girl? Or even interacting with one? He hadn't a clue.

But McIntyre did. He watched her as would a desperate man searching for a lifeline. "You've got a big family, right, McIntyre?"

"I do now," she qualified. Before the wedding, there had only been her brothers and her sister. Now, of course, besides the huge entourage she'd gained, there were also her siblings' better-halves to take into account. The size of her family had grown astronomically in a very short time. "Why? Are you thinking of trying to sneak Lisa in, hoping everyone just thinks she's part of the under-five-foot group?"

"Not exactly, but close," he admitted.

Riley shook her head. "Desperate doesn't look good on you," she told him, then smiled. "Don't worry, it'll be all right." A note of kindness entered her voice as she added, "And you'll have backup."

He would have preferred just handing off Lisa. Not because he was indifferent, or because having Lisa around would cramp his style—cute kids were known to attract women, not repel them—but because he didn't think it was fair to the little girl. She deserved to be raised by someone who knew what he was doing, not a father who would be stumbling around in the dark.

"Right," he muttered. He told himself to focus on work. "Okay, let's just table this for now. We need to get to this house before Barker has us shot." He opened the door on the driver's side.

After getting in, Riley found herself coaxing a reluctant seat belt to extend. On the way to Brenda's, she'd sat in the back with Lisa to make the girl not feel any more isolated than she probably already did. Riding shotgun in this case had its disadvantage.

"Want to sit in the back?" he proposed as he started the car.

"No," she bit off. She wasn't about to be defeated by a safety device.

It took her two hard tugs to properly extend the belt to the length where she could secure it around herself.

Holding onto it tightly, she slipped the metal tongue into its slot. That out of the way, Riley glanced at Wyatt.

He really did have one heck of a profile. No wonder he had to all but beat women off with a stick. The man was just too good-looking for his own good.

Or hers.

The thought surprised her. Riley searched for a safe topic, something to redirect her mind onto more neutral territory. She decided to ask about her new boss even though she could have just as easily asked one of her siblings, or her mother.

"How long has Barker been in charge of the department?"

Sam made a sharp right at the next light. The freeway he needed was just a block away. "For as long as I've been there."

That meant at least for the last five years. "Tell me, has he always had the personality of a piranha, or is that something new?"

Sam laughed, then felt duty bound to defend the man, at least a little. "Oh, he's a decent enough person—on his good days."

Neither yesterday nor today came under that heading. "These good days, do they happen with any kind of reliable frequency?" she asked. "Or are they like *Brigadoon*? Making an appearance once every hundred years?"

The reference she'd made meant nothing to him. He had no idea what or who Brigadoon was, but he let it go. "His wife left him a couple of years ago. It really tore him up."

"And he's been taking it out on everyone ever since?" she guessed.

Just making the light, Sam guided his vehicle onto the freeway. With rush hour over, traffic was flying this time of the morning.

"Something like that." He needed to focus on something other than his present situation. Maybe if he didn't think about it, a solution would eventually occur to him. "Did the lieutenant give you any details about this new case?"

Before leaving to find him, she'd gone back to her new superior to ask for any more information. The man had seemed annoyed and then tolerant. He'd spared her a few crumbs. She was glad now she'd asked. Though they knew each other, she and Wyatt had never worked a case together. She didn't want him thinking that he'd been harnessed with an idiot, there only because of her connections.

"Barker said the MO was like the home invasion you were already working on. No sign of a break-in, family bound in duct tape and held prisoner while two men dressed in black, wearing ski masks, systematically robbed the place. And when they were finished, they chloroformed the people so that they would be long gone before either of the victims could get loose and call the police."

Accelerating to pass a truck and take the off-ramp, Sam nodded. "Does sound like the other home invasion," he observed.

The bit about the chloroform had been left out of the

description they had released to the public. That was inside information only the victims and the thieves knew about.

"How far along are you on that case?" she asked.

He'd reached a dead end, which was why the lieutenant had assigned him to the case he'd just taken back today. "Would you like that in inches or centimeters?"

"That far, huh?"

Frustrated, he said, "Yeah, but now that you're here, we'll just whip right through the case and find the bad guys."

She silently counted to ten then said in a calm, neutral voice, "I don't think that sarcasm is the best way to go if you want my help."

Taking the off-ramp, Wyatt followed the winding path and found himself stuck at a red light. "You won't help me work the home invasion cases if your feelings are hurt?"

"I was talking about you needing my help with Lisa after we're off the clock."

He'd actually forgotten this newest development in his life for a second.

"Oh, right." He blew out a breath. "McIntyre, if I can't remember from one minute to the next that I'm supposed to be a father, how am I going to be one 24/7?"

She put herself in his place. This must have knocked him for a loop.

"First of all, you're new at it. Give yourself time to get used to the situation. Second, you're not 'supposed to be' a father. You *are* a father whether you like it or not. Your little 'play' time created a human being. Since you were the guy involved, that makes you the father.

The sooner you get used to it, Wyatt, the faster things'll start falling into place for you."

"What if I don't?" he asked.

He'd lost her. "Don't what?"

"Don't get used to it?" He paused for a second, then said what was really on his mind. "What if I don't want to be the dad?"

She tried to shift her body toward him but the seat belt held her tightly in place. "Are you talking about walking away?"

"I can do that?" he asked. Then, before she could form an answer that didn't have a slew of less-than-flattering names attached to it, Wyatt shot down his own question with a resigned sigh. "I can't do that. It's not her fault that she's here."

"I'd take the word 'fault' out of the conversation if I were you," she strongly advised. "Using it might undermine Lisa's worth in her own eyes if she happens to overhear you. As a matter of fact, I wouldn't go there at all."

"There?" he echoed, puzzled.

"The past," she explained. "How Lisa came to be, all that stuff. Get a paternity test if you want to. Then, if she turns out to be yours, accept the fact and go from there."

He didn't need a paternity test. As he'd told McIntyre earlier, there was no reason for Andrea to lie and the little girl's age gibed with when they were together. Lisa was his. He glanced at his partner. "You charge by the hour for this golden advice?"

He hid vulnerability behind sarcasm. She could identify with that. Her answer was as flippant as his question. "Since you're my partner, the first hundred hours are free."

Sam didn't completely suppress his groan as he contemplated hearing McIntyre's voice go on and on for the next one hundred hours. "I'd better start keeping track then."

The corners of her mouth curved. "I'll let you know when your time is up," she promised.

He felt like a man whose time was up already. But he couldn't think about that now, couldn't contemplate all the problems that lay ahead. He had a home invasion to investigate and—hopefully—solve.

Sam turned his vehicle onto the street where the invasion had taken place. "We're here," he announced.

"I never would have guessed," she cracked.

The breathtaking estate-sized house had a squad car parked in the middle of the driveway, forcing them to park at the curb. A crowd of curious people was being physically held back by several strategically positioned sawhorses. And even if none of that was there, the bright yellow crime scene tape across the front of the building would have been a dead giveaway.

Getting out of the car, Sam shook his head. "You'd think people living in this neighborhood would have a better security system in place."

She saw it differently. "On the contrary, people living here think they're safe *because* of the neighborhood. They plunk down money that once would have been

enough to buy them their own small European princi-
pality and they think that's enough to keep the bad guys
out, not realizing that the bad guys assume that the rich
are a bunch of wimps who won't offer any resistance if
confronted."

"I suppose that makes sense—in a perverse sort of
way," he allowed.

"Thank you." She took his comment as a compliment
and flashed him a smile before making her way toward
the front door. A stern-faced policeman stood before it
like a muscular roadblock. He made no attempt to move
out of her way. Riley held up her ID and her badge for
the officer to examine.

The stone face softened and took on mobility as the
officer looked from her wallet to her face.

"New on the job?" he asked, interest entering his
dark brown eyes.

"Just to the department," she corrected. "First full day."

"She's with me," Sam informed the beat policeman,
coming up behind her.

Recognition was immediate. "Oh, sorry, Detective
Wyatt. But you can't be too careful," he confided. "I
just had a reporter try to get inside by claiming he was
a relative."

"What gave him away?" Riley asked, curious.

A dimple appeared on his right cheek as he smiled.
"Got the victims' last name wrong," he told her, happy
to share the story.

"Keep up the good work," she said to the patrolman
as she followed Wyatt into the house.

Wyatt glanced at her over his shoulder. "What was that all about?"

"Just building goodwill," Riley told him. "I promised myself that if I ever made detective, I wouldn't forget where I came from and I wouldn't act cocky about my shield. We're all supposed to be on the same team, right?"

Was she for real? He thought he recalled her being more driven at the academy. "If you dip your finger into a cup of black coffee, does it become sickeningly sweet?"

She'd already made up her mind that he wasn't going to get under her skin no matter what he said. "I don't know. I'll have to try it someday. In the meantime, there's nothing wrong with wanting to get along with people."

"Didn't say that there was. I just like keeping the nausea level down." From the expression on her face, McIntyre wasn't listening to him anymore. Instead, her eyes were sweeping the area. The spiral staircase alone, leaving the entranceway on two sides rather than just the standard one, would have filled up over half his apartment. "What?" he prodded. This couldn't have been her first time in a house worth multiple millions.

She peered past the splendor, taking in, instead, the chaos. "This place looks like it was hit by a hurricane."

"It was. Two of them, actually," he said, referring to the fact that the victims had reported waking up to not one robber but two. "Thieves don't usually have to worry about being invited back. That frees them up to make as big a mess as they want while looking for things that make their risk-taking worthwhile."

She nodded, knowing that in this case, she was the

novice and he the experienced one. That meant she would have to follow his lead and, most likely, take orders from him—at least for the time being.

"How do you want to do this?" she asked.

He raised an eyebrow at the question. "Solving the case comes to mind."

"I mean, do you want to take the husband or the wife?"

Amused, knowing what she was after, he decided to yank her chain just a little. "They're being given away?"

"To question." She enunciated each syllable clearly, holding her exasperation in check.

"Why don't we make it a joint effort?" he suggested, his tone marginally patronizing. "That way, they won't feel as if they were being interrogated."

"I had no intentions of conducting an interrogation," she informed him. "I just thought we could compare stories after we finished, see if there're any inconsistencies. If we keep them together, they could keep each other in check."

He studied her for a long moment. What was going on in her head? he wondered. Despite his baiting her, he was aware that she was sharp. Had something occurred to her that he'd missed?

"You're assuming they have something to hide?" he asked.

"Not exactly, but maybe the wife wanted to get away from the husband and this so-called robbery could be a way of funding her escape. Or maybe she found out he was having an affair and she wanted to get even with him by scaring him. Then again, he might have wanted—

what?" she finally asked, unable to handle the way Wyatt looked at her any longer. She got the feeling that she provided him with his morning's entertainment.

"Homicide has certainly left its mark on you, hasn't it?"

"Being a good cop has left its mark on me," she informed him. "No stone unturned," she elaborated.

He rolled her suggestion over in his head. "Okay, have it your way. I'll take the husband, you take the wife—unless you'd rather have it the other way around. You get the guy and I take the woman."

"No, the first way's fine," she said. "Mrs. Wilson will probably feel better talking to a woman about what happened than someone who looks like he'd just finished a photo shoot for *GQ*."

"I could rub a little dirt on my sleeve if you think that'll make me look more capable."

"Now who's being sarcastic?" she asked.

He held up his hand. "That would be me. C'mon, we'll get this over with and let these people rest."

"You really think they can sleep after what happened?" she asked.

This morning's events had really shaken him up, Sam thought, annoyed with himself. He wasn't thinking clearly. "I guess not," he grudgingly admitted.

Directed by another officer on the scene, they walked into the living room where they found the couple, still in their nightclothes and frightened, like two people who had been through a nightmare. They sat on an expensive-looking, oversized yellow leather sofa, apparently unwilling or unable to move. Trapped in their own world, they seemed oblivious to all the crime scene investigators and police personnel moving about the area.

At least there was no need for a medical examiner, Riley thought with relief.

"Mr. and Mrs. Wilson?" Wyatt addressed the tense couple respectfully. Two sets of frightened brown eyes turned toward him. "I'm Detective Wyatt and this is my partner, Detective McIntyre. We'll be taking your statements."

"We already gave statements," Mr. Wilson protested, a mixture of weariness and indignation in his voice.

"We know," Riley told them sympathetically, moving in front of Wyatt. Her eyes were on the husband the entire time. It didn't take a psychiatrist to know he felt emasculated by what had happened. "You're tired and angry and you just want to forget the whole thing ever happened. But it would really be very helpful if you both went over the events again. Maybe this time you might remember something that hadn't occurred to you when you gave your statement earlier."

The couple exchanged glances as if that helped them to decide their next course of action. And then the husband inclined his head, still not a hundred percent sold yet. "Well, if you think it'll help—"

"We do," Riley was quick to assure him.

Robert Wilson blew out a long breath. "I guess we can go through it one more time," he said with resignation.

"We appreciate your cooperation," Wyatt told him, feeling as if his words were coming after the fact. This new partner of his, he thought, was a regular little ball of fire.

Chapter 6

At the last moment, because the woman looked so shaken, Riley decided not to separate the couple as initially planned. When Wyatt began to ask the husband to come with him, she laid a hand on her partner's arm and minutely shook her head.

Confused, Wyatt took his cue, wondering if changing her mind was a common thing with her.

Still scowling, whether at them or the situation was unclear, Robert Wilson began talking, telling them the way the robbery went down.

"They came in while we were asleep—"

Unable to contain her nervous energy, his wife broke into the narrative with her own reaction to the events. "I thought I heard a noise. When I opened my eyes, they were standing over us. On either side of the bed," she added breathlessly. She covered the lower part of her face with trembling hands. She gave the impression that she was trying to smother a scream. "It was awful."

"How many of them were there again?" Sam asked, looking at Mrs. Wilson now.

"Two." Shirley Wilson blurted out the word as if she couldn't keep it in her mouth a second longer.

"Two that we saw," her husband corrected, giving her a condescending look. Shirley Wilson's eyes widened with fear.

Sam's attention shifted back to Wilson. "Do you think there were more?"

Wilson appeared to lose all semblance of patience. "How should I know?" he snapped.

"No, there were only two," Shirley told them. "I'm sure of it."

"Right. The expert," Wilson grumbled darkly.

"What happened next?" Riley asked, trying to get the couple focused on the details of what had transpired during the robbery instead of arguing with each other.

It was obvious to her that Wilson and his wife were both scared in their own fashion. In addition, she was sure Robert Wilson felt more than a little humiliated because he couldn't protect either his home or his wife. That had to shake a man up, mess with his self-image.

"They dragged us out of bed, tied us up," Wilson recited through clenched teeth, obviously resenting having to go through this again. "Then they put duct tape across our mouths—"

Shirley grabbed onto Riley's wrist, pulling the detective's attention toward her. "I thought I was going to suffocate," the woman cried in a whimpering, shaky voice.

"But you didn't, did you?" her husband pointed out tersely, glaring at her. It wasn't clear if he resented her interruption, or the fact that she was bringing further attention to the fact that he'd been helpless to come to her aid.

"No." His wife stared down at the floor. Not, Riley thought, unlike a dog that had been beaten. Her own resentment immediately shot up. She was about to say something to the man when Wyatt spoke.

"Mr. Wilson, we realize that you've been through a lot, but so has your wife. There's no need to keep snapping at her," Sam told him. His voice was calm, but an underlying strength resonated in his words. "Now both of you take a deep breath and let's go on."

"Can I get you some water?" Riley asked the woman. Clasping her hands together in her lap, Shirley shook her head. Riley shifted her eyes toward the woman's husband. "You?" she asked more formally.

"I'd like a scotch," Wilson responded, frustrated. A huge sigh escaped his lips. "No, I'm okay," he amended.

"What happened next?" Sam coaxed.

Wilson seemed to brace himself. "They made us sit in chairs and tied us to them. Then they emptied our house."

"How long were they here?" Riley asked.

Wilson shrugged. There seemed to be no way to gauge time. "Maybe an hour at the most."

"It felt like forever," Shirley chimed in over his voice.

"And when they were finished, they put rags over our faces." Hysteria reentered her voice as she said, "I thought they were going to kill us—"

"They used chloroform," Wilson interrupted, talking over his wife. The disdain in his voice was impossible to miss. "Knocked us out so that we couldn't try to stop them."

"Like that could ever happen," Shirley murmured under her breath. It was still loud enough for all of them to hear.

Rising in his seat, Wilson looked as if he was about to argue with his wife again. Sam put his hand firmly on the man's shoulder, pressing him back down onto the sofa.

"You can tell it all to the marriage counselor later," Sam told him sternly. "Right now, we need a detailed list of everything that's missing."

"I don't know everything that's missing," Wilson snapped. "This is a big house, Officer—"

"Detective," Riley corrected before Sam had a chance to.

"Whatever," Wilson huffed out, dismissing the difference in title at the same time. "I just know they took most of my wife's jewelry." That brought up another bone of contention as he glared at her. "I *told* you to leave it in the safety deposit box at the bank."

"Then I'd have to go to the bank whenever I wanted to wear something," Shirley complained. By the sound of her voice, this wasn't a new argument. She turned to look at Riley, seeking an ally. "What's the point of having jewelry if you can't wear it?"

"Well, you certainly can't wear it now, can you?"

Wilson jeered. "Because *they've* got it," he emphasized heatedly.

This all had such a familiar ring to it, Riley thought, although her mother had never defended herself. For the sake of her children and hoping to cut the scene short, her mother had always let her father unload on her.

Riley hated the sound of an argument. "And the longer you bicker," she said, addressing them both, "the less of a chance we have of recovering anything."

"Who are you kidding?" Wilson demanded, turning on her. "You're both just going through the motions, covering your tails as it were. We're never going to see any of what those two made off with and you know it."

Sam answered before she could. "That's certainly true if you waste time arguing and don't cooperate," Sam told him coldly. Wilson shut his mouth. "Now is there anything else you remember?"

When Shirley looked at them blankly, Riley elaborated. "Did either of them have any kind of an accent? Or did either one of them slip up and call the other by a name?"

"They were just 'Smith' and 'Jones,'" Shirley told them.

"Those are aliases," Wilson shouted at her in disgust. Shirley looked at Riley, silently appealing to her to help.

Riley shook her head at Wilson. There was a smattering of sympathy in her expression. "Most likely," she agreed. "Can you remember anything else? Anything at all?"

Clearly frustrated as well as contrite, Shirley shook her head. Then suddenly, the light seemed to dawn in her eyes. "Wait a minute," she said excitedly. "Garlic." Looking from one to the other, she told them, "I remember garlic."

"Garlic?" Sam repeated uncertainly. He exchanged glances with his partner.

"What the hell are you babbling about now, woman?" Wilson demanded angrily.

This time Riley clamped her hand on the man's arm. "Mr. Wilson, don't have me ask you again to refrain from belittling your wife." She struggled to keep her voice level. "You've both been through an awful ordeal and you came out of it alive. That doesn't always happen with victims of a robbery," she emphasized. Turning toward the man's wife, Riley said, "Now, you were saying, Mrs. Wilson?"

"One of them smelled of garlic," she told Riley, then specified, "The one who tied me up. He seemed like the younger one."

"Because his ski mask wasn't as old as the other guy's?" Wilson asked, mocking his wife's assumption.

"Because his voice sounded younger," she answered him defiantly with a toss of her head.

Good for you, lady, Riley thought, keeping her expression deliberately blank.

"Anything else?" Sam coaxed, looking from one to the other. "Either of you?"

Not to be left out, Wilson repeated what had already been assessed. "They were thin, tall. And they seemed to know their way around."

That led them to one possibility. "Have you had any workmen in the house in the last six months?" Sam asked.

It was obvious that Wilson started to say no, then changed his mind as he remembered. "We had our bathrooms remodeled." The moment the words were out of his mouth, Wilson began to breathe more heavily, a bull pawing the ground, working himself up to attack. "Do you think someone from the crew could have—"

"We're just covering all bases," Riley interrupted him. "If you could give us the names of the people or the name of the company you hired to handle the remodeling, that would be a good start."

"Sure, right away. I've got the file in my office," Wilson said. "Lousy bastards," he cursed as he led the way down the hall.

"We're not saying they did it," Sam emphasized. Wilson didn't seem to accept anything unless he was shouted at. "But there was no sign of forced entry so unless you let them in yourselves or left a window on the ground floor opened …"

He let his voice trail off, waiting for a contradiction—or an admission of negligence. Some people still left their doors unlocked.

"Everything was closed tighter than a drum," Wilson assured them.

Reaching his office, he walked in. The condition of the room was like all the others. It had been summarily tossed in the search for valuables. Grumbling about what he wanted to do to the robbers if he ever got his hands on them, Wilson went to his desk and opened one of the drawers. It took him several minutes to find the file he was looking for.

"Here," he said, handing the file to Sam.

It was a rather thick file, Sam noted. He didn't feel like having to root around through the victim's personal papers.

"Just a business card'll do," Sam told him, handing the file back to Wilson.

Muttering under his breath, a man on his last nerve, Wilson rummaged through the file.

In the interim, Riley started to hand Shirley Wilson her card, only to stop and realize her business cards still had her old number from the homicide division. She would have to get new ones, she thought. Frustrated, she turned toward Wyatt.

"You have a card, Wyatt?" she asked, holding out her hand.

He paused to take one out of his wallet and gave it to her. She in turn handed the card to Mrs. Wilson. "If you think of anything, anything at all," she underscored, "please give us a call. Day or night." She pointed to the last line on the card. "That's my partner's number."

"Don't you have a number?" Shirley asked. She looked sheepishly at Sam, then said, "I'd rather, you know, talk to you if there's anything that comes up."

"Dial that number and ask for me," Riley told her. "My partner will transfer the call," she assured her, then added, "I don't have my cards yet."

"Oh." Shirley cast a quick, covert side glance at her husband who rifled through the file and had reached the end of his patience. "I know how that is," she said in a lowered voice.

Riley wasn't sure exactly what the woman was driving at, but she thought it best not to ask.

"Here," Wilson announced, thrusting a silver-faced business card at Wyatt. "Here's their card."

Sam glanced at it before slipping it into his pocket. "Thanks," he said. "We'll return this to you."

"Just get our things back," Wilson growled.

They remained a few more minutes, examining other rooms and trying not to get in the way of several crime scene investigators who were still there, cataloguing evidence.

When they finally left, Riley saw Sam shaking his head as they walked to his car.

"What?" she pressed. There was no way she wanted him to keep quiet when it came to the robbery. This was *their* case, not just his case. If she was going to be his partner, then she needed to know what was going on in his head.

But when he spoke, it had nothing to do with the case. "There's just another example of why I'm not married," he told her.

It had gotten pretty intense in there, but nothing she hadn't witnessed before. She'd lost count how many times she'd offered up thanks that her mother had wound up with Brian Cavanaugh and not, instead, a victim of domestic violence the way she'd been heading years ago. Granted she was a policewoman, trained to defend herself, but her father was a cop and ultimately, it came down to him being stronger.

"Not every couple bickers like that," she told Wyatt as they reached his vehicle.

"I dunno." Things, he reasoned, had a way of deteriorating and familiarity often bred contempt, not contentment. "I bet when they first got married, those two probably thought that the sun rose and set around each other."

"At least Wilson was pretty certain it did that around him," Riley couldn't help interjecting. She got into the car. When Wyatt sat behind the steering wheel, she continued. "People don't change *that* much," she maintained. "Cute little traits become annoying habits, but other than that …" Her voice trailed off and then she shrugged, thinking of what she'd just witnessed. "A jerk by any other name is still a jerk."

Sam laughed as he started up his car. "I take it you're referring to Mr. Wilson."

"He was the only jerk in the room."

He hadn't liked Wilson either, but he cut the man a little slack because of circumstances. "He'd just gotten his house robbed and had his manhood handed to him. It had to have stung his ego."

"Still no reason to take it out on his wife."

Pressing down on the accelerator, Sam made it through a yellow light. "No argument."

Riley sank into her seat, glaring straight ahead, memories crowding in her brain. She struggled to shut them out.

"My dad was like that," she said without any preamble as they flew through another yellow light. She felt Sam looking at her, but she kept her eyes front. "Always finding a reason to pick a fight." Like someone waking up from a trance, her words played themselves back to her and she glanced in Wyatt's direction, not knowing what to expect. She couldn't read his expression. He was someone she wouldn't have invited to a poker game. "We didn't have this conversation," she told him tersely.

He could respect privacy, even if it aroused his curiosity.

"What conversation?" Sam asked innocently.

They understood each other. Sort of. She nodded her head and looked straight ahead again. "Good."

"Anything else you need to say that you want to issue a disclaimer for afterward?" he asked.

"No." Shifting in her seat, the seat belt biting into her shoulder, she looked at Wyatt and said, "but I do have a question."

This time, he had to stop. There wasn't enough time to race through the amber light. He pressed down on the brake and then met her gaze.

"Shoot."

"Is this robbery really like the other case you have? I haven't had a chance to look at the file yet and thought you could give me a thumbnail sketch."

He nodded. He had no problem with that. He wasn't one of those people who felt everyone had to plow their own row. Sharing often sped things along.

"No forced entry. People are in the house, asleep," he recited. There had been four people in the house rather than just a married couple, but the basic facts were the same. "The robbers tie them up, then use chloroform on them so that they can escape without worrying about the police being summoned immediately. The garlic, though, is new," he allowed, shifting his foot back onto the accelerator.

She nodded. "You might consider going back to the first victims and asking about that detail."

"Why?" He saw no reason for something so trivial. "The robber probably ate something for dinner that had garlic in it. Even if he does that on a regular basis, it's not exactly something we can use."

"No, but what if it isn't because of something he eats?" she suggested. She saw she had his attention and went on. "Maybe when he sweats, he smells like garlic. I knew a kid in elementary school who was like that," she told him. It had been years since she'd thought of Joel Mayfield. "The kids made fun of him all the time. The sad thing was, the more fun they made of him, the worse it got."

He'd never been one to be singled out and picked on, nor had he ever picked on anyone, not even to be part of a group. Ever for the underdog, he hated people who did that.

"What happened to him?" he asked.

She thought a minute, then remembered. "His parents moved when he was ten." After that, she never heard about him again. No one she knew even wanted to stay in touch with Joel. "By now, he's either some wealthy millionaire, obsessively working his way into a fortune to show up all those kids who tormented him. Or he's a serial killer."

He nodded, understanding her reasoning. It was always people on the fringe of society that surprised the rest of the people. "For everyone's sake, I hope it's the former."

"Yeah." And then, remembering, Riley glanced at her watch. She took out her cell phone.

"Who are you calling?" he asked, making a right at the end of the next block.

She didn't answer him. The phone on the other end of the line was already ringing. "Hi, it's just me, Riley. I'm calling to check how everything's going. Uh-huh. Terrific. You know where to find me if you need to. Thanks. 'Bye." Closing the cell phone, she leaned slightly to the left to tuck it back into her pocket. She looked at him and smiled. "By the way, your daughter's doing fine."

His daughter.

God, he'd forgotten about her again. How long was it going to take for him to get used to the idea of having a child? Of being a parent? He had no answer for that.

"My daughter," he said out loud. "Do you have any idea how odd that sounds?"

"Probably as odd as having a dad seems to her," she speculated. "The only difference is Lisa will probably adjust to the concept very quickly. The same can't be said for you."

He spared her a glance, then took another right. He didn't like being typecast this way, even if there was more than a grain of truth in what she said.

"Just what makes you so certain you know me so well?" After all, they hadn't really seen each other since the academy.

"I don't," she admitted. "It's just a calculated guess on my part because you're a grown-up compared to her not being one. Kids are the resilient ones in this setup." She scanned the area. This didn't look familiar to her. "We on our way back to the precinct?"

"Nope."

Was he going to make her drag it out of him? "Then where?"

Obviously, the answer was yes. "Since you think you know me so well, you tell me."

She shook her head. She didn't like games. "You're losing the points you just gained."

"And what points would those be?"

"The points you got for sticking up for Mrs. Wilson when her husband started coming down on her."

That was business as usual for him. Realizing that the SUV in front of him was stalled, he swerved around it at the last minute.

"The woman had just been through a lot and she didn't need him needling her on top of it." He slanted a glance in her direction. "And that got me points?"

"Yeah, but don't let it go to your head," she warned. "And by the way, we're going to see the construction guy from the business card, right?"

He laughed. "Give the little lady a prize."

"I warned you about that 'little lady' stuff," she reminded him. "Okay, you're officially back to zero."

Sam laughed. He had to admit he was getting a kick out of this exchange. "Didn't take me long, did it?"

"No," she agreed, "it didn't."

And then, because she couldn't help herself, she laughed, as well. Maybe this being partnered with Wyatt wasn't going to be so bad after all.

At least not in the short run.

Chapter 7

The trip to C&R Construction turned out to be an exercise in futility. It was located clear across town in a tiny, broom-closet-sized suite that was part of a labyrinth-like, single-story industrial development.

The man who owned the company—and both of the initials, it turned out—had what he claimed was an airtight alibi for the time of the robbery. He'd been busy cheating on his wife with his mistress, a woman he'd been seeing for the last ten months. Since he spent the better part of half an hour trying to convince them jointly and then separately to make use of his professional skills, this little nugget of information took almost an hour and the threat of going to the precinct for interrogation before Calvin Richmond finally surrendered the alibi, along with his mistress's name, number and address.

"It's not that we don't believe you," Sam said, pocketing Richmond's note, "but we need to verify everything. You know how it is." His smile never wavered as he went on to ask, "What about your men?"

Richmond blinked, his dark eyebrows drawing together in consternation. "What men?"

"The ones who work for you," he replied patiently.

Richmond blew out a short breath. "Hell if I know," he grumbled.

"Where are they?" Sam asked, enunciating each word deliberately.

"Again, hell if I know," Richmond repeated, this time more defiantly.

It wasn't hard for Riley to read between the lines. "You use illegals, don't you?"

"I spread opportunity around," Richmond countered, daring her to prove anything.

"And these 'spreadees,' they have names?" Riley prodded.

Richmond raised and lowered his sloping shoulders. "They're all just willing hands to me."

Wyatt exchanged looks with her. "In other words, they're gone?" he asked.

Richmond allowed a note of exasperation to enter his voice, as if he was the victim here. "In any words, they're gone. Haven't you heard?" he asked, copping an attitude. "The economy's in a slump. People don't care about getting things upgraded if they're worried about making mortgage payments." His frustration slipped out. "Everyone's tightening their belts. What I do is considered nonessential." Holding up his thumb and forefinger, he created a tiny space between the two. "Right now, I'm this far away from declaring bankruptcy."

All the more reason to think that the man was behind the home invasions. "You sound like a desperate man," Riley observed, her eyes never leaving his.

Richmond opened his mouth to make a retort, then closed it abruptly.

Fear mingled with self-righteous indignation in his voice. "Hey, I know where you're going with this. Well, you're wrong," he declared. "I might be desperate, but not enough to break into anyone's house. That's illegal."

Wyatt moved to Richmond's other side. He and Riley now bracketed the man. "So is having people without green cards or social security numbers working for you."

"Yeah," Richmond reluctantly admitted, his small brown eyes shifting back and forth between the two detectives bedeviling him, "but I draw the line against *real* illegal stuff."

They weren't going to get any further here today, Wyatt thought. Two steps had him at the door. "We'll check out your alibi," he promised the construction company owner.

Riley lingered at the man's desk for a moment longer. "And don't try calling your girlfriend to make sure she backs you up. If you do, I promise you, we'll know," she warned ominously.

They walked out of the claustrophobic suite with Richmond, no doubt, nervously staring after them.

Wyatt waited until they were across the parking lot before saying, "Anyone ever tell you that you've got a way of unsettling a guy?"

Riley allowed a self-satisfied grin to curve her mouth. "Might have come up once or twice," she allowed, waiting for Wyatt to unlock the vehicle's doors.

Then they drove to see Richmond's girlfriend.

Thirty minutes later, after talking with Elaine Starling, a woman whose voice sounded as if she had a daily diet of helium, they got back into Wyatt's car. Elaine had verified Richmond's alibi. Of course, Riley speculated, since both robbers had been dressed in black from head to toe, the woman could have actually been Richmond's accomplice. And even if he was innocent, that still didn't rule out the men he'd had working for him on the Wilsons' bathrooms.

For now, they weren't going to get any further. Sitting back in her seat, Riley waited for her partner to start up the car again, but he paused.

When she looked at him quizzically, he said, "We're off the clock."

She glanced at her watch. "So we are."

Tired, frustrated, Wyatt rotated his shoulders. It didn't lessen the stranglehold tension had on them. "You want to go to Malone's for a drink?"

Malone's was the favorite gathering place for the Aurora detectives. At this point, it was almost a family place, except just a bit edgier.

"I'd like that," she admitted. "But you've got a kid

to pick up." She saw by the expression that entered Wyatt's eyes that she'd nudged his memory again. "You forgot again, didn't you?"

There was no point in denying it. He blew out an annoyed breath. "That's three times today. I really suck at this parenting thing, don't I?"

Was he expecting sympathy or agreement? She couldn't tell. She could only say what was on her mind. "It's just the first day, Wyatt. Cut yourself a little slack. You'll get better at it," she assured him with conviction. "Drop me off at the precinct so I can get my car," she requested. "I'll do the paperwork for today and you can go pick up your daughter."

"Aren't you coming, too?" he asked in a voice that wasn't nearly as authoritative as it had been when they were questioning Richmond.

"You don't need me to pick up your daughter. Brenda knows what you look like."

"I wasn't thinking of Brenda." He wanted her for backup. The way he saw it, this was not unlike a dangerous confrontation that could go either way.

She looked at him, surprised. "You're scared, aren't you?"

He could have bluffed, pretended that he didn't know what she was talking about. But Sam didn't see the point in pretending. "Petrified."

"She's only a little girl," Riley reminded him, her voice softening as sympathy wove through her. She remembered him asking her for help even as they left Lisa with Brenda this morning. The look on his face made her laugh. "Maybe I should rent *Sorrowful Jones* for you," she suggested whimsically.

Sam started the car and didn't have a clue what she was talking about. "What?"

"It's an old Bob Hope movie my mom and I used to watch," she told him, then went on to give him a synopsis of the simplistic plot. "A gambler leaves his little girl with a bookie as a marker in lieu of payment, promising to return right away. But something happens and he doesn't come back for her. Sorrowful is a stingy bachelor who hasn't dealt with anyone under the age of eighteen for years. He's left to figure out how to take care of the little girl until her father comes again."

He stared at her as if she'd just lost her mind. "You're kidding me."

Riley moved her head back and forth, her straight blond hair swinging softly to underscore the movement. "Things were a lot simpler back in the early fifties. Or maybe the movie took place in the forties," she told him. "I just remember there was a happy ending."

Then this was actually a movie? Someone had actually watched this? Had she? "Where do you get this stuff?"

"I told you, my mom turned me on to the classic movie channel. I like the movie," she answered with a trace of defensiveness. Straightening, she looked at Wyatt, and her defensiveness melted. "You'll be fine," she assured him.

"I'll be better if you come with me," he emphasized. "Lisa likes you. She'd feel less alienated if you're there, too."

That was when she remembered that she'd promised Lisa to come back. It wasn't in her to refuse a child. "You're playing dirty," she accused.

"No argument," he admitted freely, speeding up a little as the traffic opened up. "I'm playing any way I can to get you to say yes."

Riley was glad that there was no one to overhear them right now because, taken out of context, it could be misconstrued as a very loaded statement. This was how rumors got started.

"Okay," she relented, "but you do the report tomorrow."

"Done."

"We still need to stop at the precinct," she went on, "so I can pick up my own car." A skeptical look came over his face. She read it correctly. "Don't trust me?" She didn't bother waiting for him to answer. "Somebody actually take off on you?"

He thought of Andrea. And of his mother. "Yeah." The single word was expelled as if it had been clogging his lungs, keeping him from breathing.

Riley stared at him. She found that almost impossible to believe. She could see him walking away from a relationship, or what appeared to be the start of a relationship. She couldn't see a woman suddenly declaring that she was leaving him. Moreover, she couldn't even see a woman quietly slipping away. The man was mind-stoppingly handsome. But then, by his admission, Lisa's mother had left him. "Who?" she prodded.

Wyatt's face darkened. "That's not up for discussion."

Ordinarily, she retreated, letting people have their secrets. But in a way, this involved her. She needed to know. "It is now. Who walked out on you?" When he said nothing, she asked. "Lisa's mother?"

He stared straight ahead at the road, driving. "I already told you about that."

Riley studied his rigid profile. "But that's not who you were thinking of, was it?"

She was like a bulldog with a bone. Or a pit bull. "Ever think of using your powers for good instead of evil, McIntyre?"

"All the time," she deadpanned, then quipped, "Evil's more fun." For now, she let him keep his secret. "Okay, we're wasting time. Let's table this for now. But in case you think you're off the hook here, you're not," she assured him. "You owe me an answer." There was no room for argument in her voice.

All Sam really cared about was that she backed off. Since she had, he could pretend to go along with what she was saying. "Okay."

"And I'm going to collect." Riley sighed. "I'm serious, Wyatt."

Sam slanted a look in her direction. "It never occurred to me that you weren't."

"You know you need to take at least part of tomorrow off, don't you?" she asked just as they were approaching the precinct.

"Why?"

For an intelligent man, he was a babe in the woods when it came to his responsibilities toward his daughter.

"Because Lisa belongs in school and you need to enroll her. The sooner the better."

His only response was to groan.

"She was an absolute dream," Brenda told them less than half an hour later when they came to pick up the little girl. "Unlike my own children," she added, giving the two in question as stern a look as she could. They appeared properly subdued, an act that would likely last ten minutes. "Any time you need someone to look after her," she told Sam, "just give me a call."

"How do you feel about a permanent assignment?" Riley asked. "After school each day."

Brenda responded exactly the way Riley thought she would. "Sure, no problem. What elementary school does she attend?"

Sam was about to say that he needed to enroll the little girl when Lisa spoke up without warning. "St. Theresa's."

All three of the adults exchanged glances. "I can look it up," Riley volunteered, addressing Wyatt.

The next moment, the need for that was negated as Lisa rattled off the address. It turned out to be a local one, less than two miles away from where Sam lived. Which meant that the daughter he didn't know about had been close all this time. It was a small, small world, he concluded.

Riley ran her hand along Lisa's hair. "At least there won't be a problem with enrolling her quickly somewhere," she pointed out. "One problem down."

"And a thousand to go," Sam murmured under his breath.

To his surprise, Lisa turned around and looked up at him. "There aren't a thousand problems," she said with conviction.

Riley slipped her arm around the little girl's shoulders. "You're absolutely right. Your dad just likes to exaggerate sometimes. It helps him focus."

"What's he focusing on?"

"On what's important." Riley looked up at Wyatt. "Isn't that right, 'Dad'?" she asked pointedly, her expression telling him that she expected him to agree.

Feeling somewhat overwhelmed, Sam lost track of what she was talking about. He figured it was safe if he just shrugged his shoulders and went along with it.

"If you say so, it must be true." Before leaving, he stopped to say one last thing to Riley's stepsister-in-law. "Thanks a lot for taking Lisa on such short notice." He took out his wallet. Opening it, he drew out all the bills he had. "Look, I'm really, *really* new at this kind of thing, so I have no idea. What's the going rate for watching kids?"

Brenda shook her head, pushing his hand back toward him. "Put your money away, Detective. We'll talk about this some other time," she promised. And then she winked just before shutting the door.

The response surprised him a little. He tucked the bills into his wallet, then put the wallet into his back pocket.

"Your stepsister-in-law just winked at me," he told Riley as he quickly lengthened his stride to catch up. They reached the curb where both their vehicles were parked.

"That's just Brenda's way of saying she likes you."
It had taken her a little getting used to, but Riley kept
that to herself. She unlocked the door on the driver's side
of her car, then tossed her purse onto the passenger seat.
"She's one in a million."

Lisa moved closer to her. "May I go with you?" she
asked suddenly.

Was that relief Riley saw in Wyatt's eyes? He was
probably not looking forward to sharing the ride home
with the little girl. Conversations with a six-year-old
were probably unfamiliar to him, she guessed. Still, he
had to learn. He was the only parent Lisa had left.

"Don't you want to ride with your dad?" Riley asked
as tactfully as she could.

Lisa didn't take the hint. Like most children her age,
Wyatt's daughter was the personification of honesty.
"No, I want to ride with you," she quietly insisted.

Well, at least she doesn't throw tantrums, Riley thought.

She looked over the little girl's head at Wyatt, but the
latter seemed relieved. And Lisa gazed up at her with
pleading eyes.

Riley caved. "Fine with me."

That was all that Lisa needed to hear. Like a bullet,
the little girl raced to the passenger side of the vehicle,
pulling at the door handle.

Riley hit the lock release on the driver's armrest. The
other locks instantly popped up in unison.

"You have to ride in the back, honey," Riley told her
kindly, then turned toward her partner. She'd forgotten
about this earlier when they were coming here. "Doesn't

she have a car seat?" Lisa might be six, but she was petite and definitely under the weight cutoff point.

Wyatt started to say he didn't know, but Lisa cut in. "I do. It's at home." Lisa looked sad. "Car seats are for babies."

"And petite little girls. Trust me, you'll like that description some day," Riley said with a wink of her own. And then she replayed what Lisa had said. "Honey, if the car seat was in your mother's car, I'm afraid it's gone." The car had been totaled. "We'll have to get you another one."

Again Lisa shook her head. "Mama had another one for me. It was in the spare bedroom. In my home," she emphasized. "I've got more things there, too. Aunt Carole didn't bring everything with her when she brought me." A small, shaky sigh separated her sentences. "She just wanted me to start getting used to you," she explained, looking at Wyatt.

"I'm going to go see 'Aunt Carole' about getting a key to your mom's apartment so I can get the rest of your things," he promised.

No sooner were the words out of his mouth than Lisa dug into the tiny purse she had been carrying around and held up a key.

"Is this okay?" she asked innocently.

He took the key from her. "Is that a key to your apartment?" he asked the little girl in disbelief.

"Yes. That's why I gave it to you," she answered as if she didn't understand what the problem was.

He remembered being a lot older before his father

trusted him with a key to the house. "Aren't you a little young to have your own key?"

"No," she replied authoritatively.

Riley did her best to hide her amusement. "Guess we can't argue with that," she commented. For all they knew, the landlord was trying to rent out the apartment already. "Why don't you go over there and see about getting Lisa her things? And while you're doing that, I'll take Lisa over to your place." She looked at the little girl. "How do you feel about pizza for dinner?"

"No pepperoni," Lisa responded. "I'm not supposed to have meat."

"A miniature vegetarian," she marveled. "Okay, no pepperoni on your side," she compromised.

Wyatt struggled against feeling constricted. His first reaction to McIntyre's offer was relief. But that was wrong. This wasn't her problem, it was his and he had to face up to it sooner or later.

"You don't mind?" he asked.

"If I minded," Riley pointed out, "I wouldn't have suggested it. I don't do martyr well," she assured him, then put out her hand. "Now give me the keys to your apartment so I can get in. My B&E techniques are a little rusty."

Sam took his apartment key off his key chain and handed it to her. "I owe you."

Riley grinned and he caught himself thinking that she had the ability to light up an area with her smile. "Yeah, you do," she told him.

The next minute, she got into her car and drove off.

Chapter 8

It took Sam almost two hours before he finally returned to his own apartment.

He had trouble deciding exactly what to take and what to leave behind. He had no idea what little girls considered necessary. The two suitcases she'd brought with her had more than an adequate supply of clothing in them. But even he knew that little girls—even precocious ones—didn't live by simply clothes alone. So when he came across a somewhat misshapen teddy bear under the bed, he picked up the stuffed animal and dusted it off, tucking the toy into Lisa's car seat, which was one of the things he intended to take with him.

Sam didn't go into the apartment, or through its rooms, alone. The woman from the complex's rental office was just shutting down for the night when she saw him unlocking Andrea's door. Since she didn't recognize him and knew the circumstances surrounding her late tenant, as well as being incredibly curious, the matronly woman took it upon herself to investigate.

Accosting him as he went through the door, Mavis Patterson swiftly went from suspicious to sympathetic the moment she discovered that he was taking Lisa in and was there to pick up more of her things.

A widow for more than ten years, the heavyset woman insisted on helping him with his mission. She even brought several boxes from the rental office to help him pack up and volunteered to help carry the things he was taking to his car.

With an air of someone who had done this before, she supervised his selection.

"I like to think of everyone here as family," Mrs. Patterson told him as she trailed behind him when he made the final trip from the apartment to the car. "Some family members you can do without," she admitted, "but Andrea, she was really something else again. Always had a good word for everyone—when she stopped to talk," Mavis qualified. "Busy as all get-out most of the time." And then she switched gears as she continued her summation. "Sure was proud of that little girl of hers. Smartest thing I've ever seen. Smarter than a lot of the people living here," Mavis confided, lowering her voice.

"You need anything, you let me know," she instructed solemnly. "And not just until the end of the month, neither. Lease is up then," she informed him, "but I'm not." She patted his hand as he placed the last box into his trunk. Sam firmly shut the trunk. "Tell Lisa that Mrs. Patterson says hi."

"I'll be sure to do that," Wyatt promised.

Mrs. Patterson stood to the side as he pulled out of the covered parking slot, then watched as he drove away. She waved until he disappeared from view.

Guiding the vehicle out the apartment complex, Sam wondered if he could do anything to stall his arrival home a little longer.

The next moment, he grew annoyed with himself. Since when had he become a coward? Hell, he'd faced down armed felons. Why did the thought of coming home to his daughter suddenly send these chills shimmying up and down his spine?

His daughter.

That still didn't sound right to him. Wrapping his head around the concept of having and being responsible for a child would take him some time. A hell of a lot of time.

He glanced at his watch as he drove. Damn, Riley wasn't going to be happy about him being away for so long. Not that he blamed her.

Just what he needed. Two females to face, not just one.

He supposed it could have been worse. There could have been three of them.

It only occurred to Sam after he'd walked up to the front door of his ground floor apartment and slipped his hand into his pocket that he couldn't open the door. He had no key.

With a suppressed sigh, he realized that he had to knock on his own door in order to get in. So much for just quietly slipping inside.

He knocked. Several minutes went by. It didn't sound as if anyone stirred inside. Certainly no one was opening the door. Had Riley gone out with Lisa?

All kinds of alternate scenarios began to suggest themselves. Was this what parenthood was like? Half-formed fears chasing through his brain? He couldn't say he much cared for it.

Sam raised his hand, about to knock again, when the door finally opened.

Riley flashed him a somewhat weary smile. "I thought maybe you'd lost your way," she commented, opening the door wider to allow him to walk in.

"I had trouble deciding what she was going to need," he muttered, setting down the box he was carrying on the sofa.

Turning around to continue with his explanation, Sam faced the kitchen and saw the table. A pizza box, its bottom heavily leached with olive oil, took up nearly half of it. There was more than half a pie left. But it was the not-quite-fading aroma of the pizza that got to him, teasing awake his salivary glands.

"Did you get the car seat?" Riley was asking.

"Yes. I've got it in the car." He snapped out the answer, then told himself he had no right to lose his temper with her. Riley was doing him a favor, not the other way around. "I almost forgot it," he admitted. "Just as I was about to go into Andrea's apartment, the landlady came to check me out, probably to make sure I wasn't trying to break into the empty apartment." And then he sighed. "Once she heard that I was Lisa's father, she just wouldn't stop talking."

The corners of Riley's mouth curved in amusement. "So you're late because you couldn't decide what to bring back with you and because the landlady talked too much."

"Something like that," he mumbled.

"And being nervous about hanging around Lisa had nothing to do with dragging your feet getting back here?" Riley questioned.

He bristled at her implication—even if it was true. "What are you, trying out for the department's shrink now?"

"This whole thing has hit you right between the eyes. It's okay to be nervous. That's why I volunteered to stay with her."

He looked around. "Where is Lisa, by the way?"

"In the guest room," she replied. "Asleep." She didn't add that it took her making up two stories for the little girl before Lisa nodded off and finally fell asleep. "Poor thing's exhausted by her ordeal."

"That makes two of us," Sam admitted under his breath. Shoving his hands into his pockets, he began to move restlessly about the living room. He felt as if his back was against the wall and he didn't like it. "What am I going to do with her?" he asked helplessly, keeping his voice down as he turned to his partner.

"Love her," Riley answered very simply. "She is yours, you know. Can't go wrong when you give a kid love," she assured him, then added, "My brothers, sister and I had a very rocky childhood. But throughout it all, we knew our mother loved us with all her heart." Their father loved them in his own way, but it wasn't nearly enough to make up for the way he behaved both toward them and their mother. "In the end, that love saw us through an awful lot. It really helped smooth out some of the very rough patches we went through. Love is a very powerful, necessary emotion."

He supposed she had a point. Sam sighed. "She say anything about me?" The question was hesitantly framed. He wasn't sure if he wanted an answer.

She nodded. "She talked about you a little."

Curiosity got the better of him. "What did she say?"

Her eyes smiled first, creating a warm glow about her and, strangely enough, within him.

"Lisa said she thought you were very good-looking and that she could see why her mother 'fell' for you, I believe were the words she used." Riley laughed. "This kid of yours is pretty precocious. She's going to keep you on your toes," Riley predicted.

He didn't want a kid who kept him on his toes, who provided him with a mental challenge everywhere he turned. "That's what the cases I work on are for," he told Riley. "When I come home, all I want is to kick back and relax."

"Little kids can do that, too," Riley assured him, adding, "She's not going to require being mentally stimulated 24/7."

He had his doubts. Feeling like a man trying to cross

quicksand, he dragged his hand through his hair. "I'm going to suck at this."

"Give yourself a little credit, Wyatt. Every new dad thinks he's going to be a complete disaster when he starts out. This is all new for you." Hadn't they already been through this? She supposed that Wyatt just needed to hear it again. And maybe again after that, until it finally sank in. "You'll get used to it."

He had sincere doubts about that. Just because they had the equipment to make one, not everyone—male *or* female—was cut out to be a parent. "I don't even remember *being* a kid, much less how to treat one or relate to her."

"Practice makes perfect," Riley told him cheerfully. "Besides, this one is more adult than some of the people I know. That should make it easier for you than if you were dealing with a run-of-the-mill little kid." Not that she thought he'd have one of those. Riley patted him on the shoulder. "This time next year, you'll deny ever having this conversation and showing me your vulnerable side." She saw the uncertain expression in his eyes and grinned. "Trust me, I know. I grew up with two minimacho men. News flash," she added in a stage whisper. "There's nothing wrong with being vulnerable."

Sam still shook his head. "Not a condition I choose to be in."

"It's not always that easy, Wyatt. Sometimes, circumstances dictate otherwise," she said, thinking of how she had felt looking at her former partner's lifeless body.

It was then that she realized she hadn't thought about

Diego once this whole day, not since she came to pick up Wyatt and discovered what was keeping him from the precinct.

The realization made her feel both guilty for not thinking about him and, at the same time, hopeful. Maybe she was finally over the worst of it. Maybe, with luck, she would work her way back from the all-consuming darkness.

Without the benefit of the shrink Brian wanted her to see, she realized happily. First chance she got, she would talk to Brian and appeal his decision about her seeking therapy. She was beginning to see the light at the end of the tunnel without it.

Taking a deep, fortifying breath, she looked at her partner and asked, "Hungry?"

The question caught him off guard and he had to think about it for a second. That was when he became aware of the gnawing sensation in the pit of his stomach.

"Yeah," he told her, slowly coming around. "Yeah, I guess I am."

"Good, then have at it," she encouraged, gesturing toward the remainder of the pizza. "That's why I ordered an extra large one."

First things first. Before sitting down, he dug into his pocket for his wallet. "What do I owe you?" he asked.

"Not a thing—at least monetarily," she said, amusement dancing in her eyes. When he still took out some bills, she waved them away. "Don't worry, I can afford to spring for a pizza. Besides, you don't have to be gallant about it. This isn't exactly a date."

"A date?" he echoed.

The moment the word was out, something distant and vague inside his head began to entertain the notion. When they were attending the academy together, he and Riley had gone out a number of times, but there had always been other rookies around. It had never been a one-on-one scenario.

"Yeah, a date." Her amusement increased. The thought of dating her had obviously thrown him. "If we ever are, then I'll let you pay," she promised.

He merely nodded, struggling to place everything, including the myriad sensations swirling around inside him, into proper perspective. His thoughts, mostly unfocused, couldn't stop racing through his head. "Look, about tomorrow—"

"You take Lisa to school, introduce yourself as her dad to her teacher. Go through the motions of being normal—if you can. I'll cover for you with Barker, though I'm not looking forward to that," she had to admit.

She couldn't decide whether Barker was a good guy who just liked to growl, or an idiot who threw his weight around. But she supposed it was still early in the game for final opinions.

"We can trade," Wyatt offered, picking up a slice of pizza and putting it on a paper plate. "You take Lisa to school tomorrow and I'll cover for you with the lieutenant."

She shook her head. "Not going to happen. You need to build a relationship with your daughter and I need to show Barker that he doesn't scare me." Hopefully, the lieutenant respected people who didn't cave and wouldn't view them as a threat to his authority.

"He'll be sorry to hear that," Sam said with a quiet laugh. "He likes putting the fear of God into all his people."

"God, maybe," she allowed. "Him? No," she said as she watched Sam take a healthy bite of the pizza. "By the way, I looked through every cupboard, but all I found were paper plates."

He took another bite before answering. "That's because that's what I have. This way, when I'm finished, I can just throw them out. I'm not a big fan of having the dishes pile up in the sink."

"Then don't let them pile up in the sink," she told him simply. "You need plates, Wyatt. You have a daughter, you need plates." Since he eyed her skeptically, Riley added, "Kids need a sense of stability."

He wouldn't argue with that, just with her reasoning, which seemed a little off to him. "And having plates'll do this?"

"For openers," she said confidently. "Paper plates are transient, real plates aren't. They say 'we're staying put.'" She smiled at him. "I'll give you more tips as we go along."

Granted, she was a female, but that didn't immediately make her more qualified than he was at this. "You have any kids?"

"No." She knew where this was headed—or thought she did. "I've never been married."

"You don't need to be married to have a kid," he reminded her. "I seem to be living proof of that. But if you don't have any, what makes you think you're such an expert?"

She didn't know if he was challenging her, or just curious. The man was probably very stressed out by this sudden turn of events in his life so she gave him the benefit of the doubt.

"Easy." She smiled at him broadly. "I'm just good at everything."

"Right. I should have known." He knew her well enough to sense she was kidding. "Hey, McIntyre," he called after her as she walked into the living room and picked up her purse from the sofa.

On her way to the front door, she stopped and looked at him over her shoulder. "Yeah?"

Pushing his chair away from the table, Sam got up and crossed to her. "Thanks," he told her sincerely. "For everything."

She raised and lowered her shoulders in a careless gesture. There was no need to thank her, although she had to admit the fact that he did pleased her. "That's what partners are for."

An impulse suddenly flashed through him, so quickly and sharply that it stunned Sam. She was standing only a breath away from him. Maybe it was gratitude, or maybe it was a sudden need, but he wanted to kiss her.

Common sense prevailed and restrained him. "See you tomorrow."

Riley had absolutely no idea why there was this sudden rise of temperature within her body, why the space between them seemed to shrink without either one of them making a move. She needed fresh air, she decided.

Now.

"Tomorrow," Riley echoed. Still facing him, she reached behind her and pulled the door open. The next second, she'd made her retreat. It couldn't honestly be called anything else.

He thought the noise was coming from outside.

A moment ago he'd been asleep, but the sound had spliced through the darkness in his bedroom, rousing him even as it teased his brain for identification.

What *was* that?

Propping himself up on his elbows, Sam cocked his head and listened intensely. His apartment wasn't located that far from the communal pool. It seemed like someone was always throwing a party in that general vicinity. Parties that lasted well into the night and occasionally growing progressively louder by the hour. These hot October nights had everyone wanting to cool off in the pool.

But this didn't sound like some sort of a party noise. This sounded more like someone crying. A *young* someone.

And the sound wasn't coming from outside. It was coming from inside his apartment.

Sam bolted upright.

Lisa.

He was on his feet, heading toward her bedroom before his brain properly kicked in. Before his desire to maintain distance could keep him in his room, hoping to wait her out.

His inclination was to throw open the door, but he didn't want to frighten her, so he knocked. But there was no response, even when he gently rapped on the door again. He could hear her crying.

"The hell with this," he muttered under his breath. Turning the doorknob, he eased open the guest room door.

Lisa was there, a blond, wraithlike figure lost in a double bed.

Self-preservation had him momentarily entertaining the idea of quietly backtracking out and returning to his room. The next second, Sam kicked the notion to the curb and walked into the room.

"Lisa?"

There was no response. Her heart-wrenching sobbing continued. He couldn't just leave her like this.

If you woke up a kid in the middle of a nightmare, did it have any kind of repercussions? The magnitude of the things he didn't know when it came to kids was damn near overwhelming, he thought.

Taking a breath, Sam repeated her name. When Lisa still didn't respond, he bent over the bed and lightly shook her by the shoulder. "Lisa?"

Her eyes flew open.

Startled, confused, and almost immediately embarrassed, Lisa turned her face into her pillow, struggling to stop the sobs that had besieged her. Her body shook from the effort to silence herself.

Sam sat down on the edge of the bed. "Shh," he

soothed. "It's going to be okay." He said the words to
reassure himself as well as her. As gently as if he were
trying to capture a snowflake in his hand, he gathered
the little girl into his arms.

Frightened and still very embarrassed, Lisa attempted
to resist for a moment. But the sadness was just too
much for her and she gave in, melting into his embrace.

"I miss Mama," she sobbed against his shoulder.

Instinctively, he began to rock with her. "I know,
honey," he said softly. "I know. But it's going to be
all right."

Although, for the life of him, he didn't see how at
the moment.

She clung to him and he let her. It was the least he
could do.

And the most.

Sam held his daughter for a long time. Until she
finally fell asleep in his arms.

Then he held her a little longer.

Chapter 9

Pulling into the driveway of the modest two-story home she owned—the house that actually owned her—Riley turned off the ignition and just sat there for a moment, trying to summon a temporary wave of strength in order to get out of the vehicle.

Beyond bone-tired, she felt as if she'd crammed a full two days into one. She took in a deep breath and blew it out again. There were only two options open to her. She would either have to learn to do with less sleep—or find a way to become twins. Too much went on in each day for her to handle everything.

Because her garage was chock full of things she'd been promising herself to sort through—another chore waiting to be tackled, she thought, less than enthused—Riley had to park her car in the driveway the last few months.

The second she got out of the vehicle, she felt him watching her. Despite the hour, she knew he was out there, waiting for her. It had become a given.

Waving her hand above her head in a general greeting, she called out, "Hi, Howard."

The front door of the house next to hers opened. Or rather, it opened wider. He'd been posted there, his door ajar, for a while now, impatiently awaiting her arrival. Howard Gray, a retired, slightly overweight mechanical engineer in his early seventies stepped out onto his porch.

He smiled in response to her greeting. He hadn't always smiled. But growing close to Riley had coaxed it out of him.

"Getting in kind of late, aren't you, Riley?" he asked.

Still tired, she decided to talk to him for a moment and crossed from her driveway to his, moving around the plum tree that separated their properties.

"Howard, what did I tell you about waiting up for me?" she asked, not bothering to hide the affection in her voice.

Howard Gray had been her neighbor ever since she'd moved in three years ago. Somewhat standoffish in the beginning, the man had eventually warmed up to her. So much so that one evening, during a display of fireworks during the Memorial Day weekend, he had told her about his son.

Egan Gray had been one of the widower's two sons, a police officer with the Aurora Police Department just like she was at the time she'd moved in. The only difference was that Egan had been gunned down when he came to the aid of a convenience store clerk who was being robbed. Egan had been off duty at the time. Struggling to come to terms with the tragedy, Howard tried to bury his sorrow and lose himself in the various collections he'd amassed. Consequently, his five-bedroom house was filled to bursting with books, magazines and long-playing record albums he'd been collecting for more years than she'd been alive—but it was all to no avail. The hurt inside him continued to grow and fester—until Riley had moved in next door. After finding out about the old man's loss, Riley took it upon herself to get Howard to come around a little. In effect, she'd adopted him, making him the grandfather she'd never known. And whenever Andrew Cavanaugh threw a party, she made it a point to invite Howard.

At first Howard would drag his feet, coming up with excuse after excuse, none of which she accepted. With time, she wore him down completely and he began to attend willingly, looking forward to the gatherings.

In addition, the former engineer had also appointed himself her guardian angel, watching over her whenever he could. In a way, she kept him linked to Egan. And it was she who'd encouraged him to mend fences with his estranged son, Ethan. The latter lived back east but flew out to visit now twice a year.

"I forget," he deadpanned in response to her question. "A man my age, you can't expect me to remember everything now, can you?"

"A man your age," Riley echoed with a dismissive

laugh. "Howard, you are one of the youngest men that I know."

He chuckled. "Does your mother know you're flirting with a man three times your age?" he asked and she could have sworn she saw a twinkle in his eye, thanks to the porch being so well lit. "All right," he announced, "now that I know you're safe, I can go to bed."

"You should have gone to bed earlier," she told him. "Staying up, waiting for me to come home, isn't good for your health, Howard."

He paused in his doorway and gave her an enigmatic smile. "On the contrary, Riley, it's very good for my health."

She knew what he was saying. Everyone needed to be connected to someone. And he was connected to her. In an odd way, it gave him a reason to get up in the morning.

Riley smiled at him. "Good night, Howard."

"Good night, Riley," he replied, then closed his door.

She waited where she was until she heard him flip his lock into place, then withdrew. By the time she was on her own front step, Riley saw the lights on Howard's first floor go out. The rest of Howard's house went dark as she let herself into her house.

And another day draws to a close, she thought as another wave of weariness swept over her.

"Heads up, you've got a third one."

A little more than two weeks had passed since her stepfather had transferred her to the robbery division. She, along with Wyatt, had caught the second of the

home invasion cases on her first full day there. Consequently, she didn't have to ask what the lieutenant was
talking about as she looked over her shoulder to find him
planted directly behind her. Riley could feel the hairs
on the back of her neck standing up—and not in a good
way. She pushed away from her desk and turned around.

Questions regarding this news bulletin began to pop up,
then multiply in her head, but she knew better than to ask
them. That was for Wyatt to do since he was the primary
on the case and Barker, she'd quickly learned, was very
big on protocol and red tape. Red—if the ties he wore
every day were any indication—was his favorite color and
an affinity for red tape seemed to come naturally to him.

Wyatt's desk buttressed against hers so that he could
look up into the lieutenant's dark eyes. Wyatt's first
question was, "Same MO?"

"Yes, same MO. That's what makes it a third one,"
Barker replied, not sparing the sarcasm. He shifted his
stony gaze in Riley's direction. "Where are we on the
second one?"

We. As if the lieutenant had given them any input
beyond the first bit of information that had sent them to
the Wilsons. She had a feeling that he was the kind who
worked his people unsparingly, then took the credit for
their breakthroughs.

"'We' have questioned the Wilsons until they're sick
of the sight of us. We've run down everyone they've
spoken to in the last six months, including grocery clerks,"
she threw in, then concluded with disgust, "Nothing."

The answer obviously didn't please him. "Well, see

if you can come up with 'something' this time, McIntyre," the lieutenant said in a patronizing tone. He handed Wyatt the names and address of the home invaders' newest victims. "The mayor doesn't like unsolved crimes on the books."

"He's not the only one," she muttered under her breath as the lieutenant made his way back to his office.

Sam was already on his feet, slipping on his sports jacket. "Ready?" he asked.

"As I'll ever be," she responded, pushing back her chair a little farther. She grabbed her jacket and her shoulder bag, hurrying to catch up with him.

"Coming over tonight?" Sam asked her as they passed several detectives on their way out of the squad room.

One of them, Alex Sung, looked up. A twelve-year veteran of the division, there was mild surprise registered on his face as he looked from Wyatt to Riley and then back again.

"It's not what you think," Riley told the older man flippantly. "I'm helping him study for his citizenship test."

Sung's partner, Reed Allen, stared at Wyatt, confusion on his face. "You're not a citizen, Wyatt?" he asked uncertainly.

Wyatt blew out an annoyed breath. "Don't pay any attention to her," he advised. "Somewhere a village is looking for its idiot."

"Then we have somewhere to send your next job application," she countered cheerfully.

"Overdid that a little, don't you think?" Wyatt asked her when they were outside the squad room.

Her eyes widened in deliberate innocence. "Oh, you thought I was kidding?"

He laughed shortly, shaking his head.

Pressing for the elevator, Sam found that the car was already on their floor when the elevator opened its doors.

"With you," Sam said honestly, getting in, "I can never really tell."

She liked that. It meant she was keeping him on his toes. Off balance. That leveled the playing field for her. Because something about him definitely threw her off balance.

"To answer your question, yes, I can come over." The elevator closed its doors again. She pressed for the first floor. "Lisa asking for me?"

He nodded. "Every morning." While he was relieved to be sharing the responsibility, he had to admit that it did bother him a little that Lisa apparently preferred McIntyre to him.

"Eventually, you know, you're going to have to fly solo," she told him as the doors opened again. They got off and walked toward the front of the building. "Spend the morning *and* the evening with her without a go-between getting into the mix somewhere."

"I'll cross that bridge when I come to it," he replied vaguely. Reaching the front door, he opened it for her, then checked the address on the paper that Barker had given him. "Same part of town as the other two, except this one's a little closer to the center than the last one."

"Maybe the invaders are getting more democratic in their choice of victims," she cracked. Assuming that he would want to drive, she headed toward where he usually parked his vehicle.

"Sure would be nice to find that they had something more in common than just geography," Sam commented. He automatically slipped his hand into his pocket, feeling around for his car keys.

"We will," she promised.

Sam unlocked the door on her side. All the locks released at the same time. "I'm not as optimistic as you are," he told her, rounding the trunk and coming around to his side.

She got into the car. "I noticed. But we'll find it. Maybe even this time around," she added.

So far they'd established that the two couples didn't know each other and had nothing in common except for living in a house valued in the millions. Beyond that, there seemed to be no common denominator.

Early that morning, Riley had run down the list of information they'd compiled for what seemed like the umpteenth time. The first victims, Edith and Joel Marston, attended church services every Sunday, the Wilsons didn't. The Marstons had two children under the age of eighteen who went to private schools, the Wilsons were childless. The Marstons took three vacations a year. Mr. Wilson was a workaholic and he and his wife hadn't been away in close to three years. Mrs. Wilson went to the gym at least four times a week. The Marstons didn't have a gym membership.

And so it went. The two couples' paths didn't cross—

except that they had to, she thought as they drove to the home of the third victims. Someway, somehow, the paths *had* to cross.

The third home invasion victim was John Cahil, a divorced college professor and the father of two teenaged sons, neither of whom were with him at the time the invasion went down. His girlfriend of ten months wasn't as fortunate. After dining at their favorite restaurant, John Cahil and his girlfriend, Rhonda Williams, came back to his home, made love while inebriated and fell asleep in his California King-sized bed.

That was where they were, sound asleep in his bedroom, when the two black-clad robbers struck.

According to the information gathered by the first officer on the scene, the MO was identical to the other two robberies. With one slight difference. This time, one of the robbers, the smaller of the two, had lingered over Rhonda, who became hysterical. Despite being tied up, John had voiced his protest, calling the robber several unflattering names. He'd succeeded in diverting the threat away from Rhonda because the robber had beaten him for his stab at chivalry. His accomplice had been forced to pull him off the professor and angrily told him to remember what they had come for.

Other than that, everything went according to the old plan. The victims had been tied up, their mouths and limbs duct-taped and just before the ordeal was over, they were chloroformed.

When Riley and Wyatt arrived, the professor and his girlfriend were twelve hours into their ordeal. Other than the hours that she'd been unconscious, Rhonda looked as if she'd been crying for most of that time.

After introducing himself and Riley, and extending his sympathy and condolences for what they had been through, Sam asked them to please recount the events that occurred after the robbers had woken them up in the bedroom.

Outraged, the professor flatly refused to talk about it "again." "I've already told that officer everything that happened. You want to know, talk to him," Cahil snapped. Putting his arms around Rhonda, he tried to console her. She continued sobbing into the handkerchief he'd given her. By now, it was crumpled and soggy.

"Professor, we're hoping that you might remember something if you tell it again, something you forgot the first time around," Riley said, hoping to appeal to his softer side. "Even the smallest thing might help us finally get these people."

His gray eyes seemed to flash as he looked up at them. "I know the statistics for success in these things and they're dishearteningly low," he snapped at them. "I teach criminology, for God's sake." The statement was accompanied by self-depreciative laughter.

Riley exchanged looks with her partner. Had the experience of actually being the victim of a robbery made the professor go off the deep end?

"There's irony for you," Cahil announced bitterly,

still holding Rhonda. "The professor of criminology is a victim of a crime."

Sniffling, Rhonda gazed up at him. It was obvious that she was desperately trying to pull herself together— and move forward in a positive manner.

"John, calm down," Rhonda pleaded. She tried to soothe him by placing her hand on his arm, but he shook her off. Suddenly, their roles were reversed and it was she who was trying to comfort the professor.

From where Riley stood, the effort was doomed to failure.

"I don't *want* to calm down," he retorted with passion. "I want those two bastards dead and these two out of my house." The professor waved his hand at Riley and her partner, then glanced toward the bedroom. Commotion still came from within the room. "Along with all their unnecessary cronies."

"Those 'cronies' are very necessary, Professor," Wyatt assured him patiently. "I think you know that. And we'll be gone as soon as you give us your statement," he promised.

Tall, with gaunt features, the professor drew himself up and gave the impression of an annoyed creature of the night. "I was robbed, end of story."

"Oh, I think there's a little more to the story than that," Riley speculated, doing her best to sound sympathetic. She looked directly at the bruises on his face. "You did something to make at least one of them mad at you. What did you do?"

"Nothing." The single word effectively withdrew

him completely from the people who were in the room. Riley had a feeling the man was one hard-nosed educator. No curves when it came to grades in his class, she mused.

It was Rhonda who gave them their answer. "He stood up for me."

"Rhonda." There was a warning note in the professor's voice.

Well, at least he wasn't a man who liked to be in the center of things and draw attention to himself, Riley thought.

"Well, you did." Rhonda shifted and eyed the two detectives. "His own hands were tied up and everything, but Johnny still tried to get that awful creep to take his hands away from me."

"Very brave of you, Professor." Riley'd almost called him "Johnny" as well, but stopped herself just in time.

He shrugged off the compliment. "Yes, well, didn't get me very far, did it?" the professor grumbled.

Riley turned toward Wyatt. "May I see you for a second?" she asked.

Impatient, Wyatt excused himself from the two victims and stepped out of the room with Riley.

"What's up?" he asked. It wasn't customary to back away before an interview was over and as far as he was concerned, it wasn't over.

"Why don't you take the professor aside and question him by yourself? Without me or his girlfriend around," she suggested, keeping her voice low. "He might open up to another man." And then she smiled at him. "You know how fragile the male ego is."

"Not personally," he replied. "But that's not a bad idea, McIntyre," he said, nodding his head. "It's worth a try. Without him around, his girlfriend might feel more comfortable about telling you exactly what happened."

"Might," Riley agreed.

"Let's give it a shot," Sam said just before he crossed back into the living room.

New plan in place, they proceeded to divide and, with any luck, conquer.

Bringing the two victims together again, Riley and Sam were on the verge of wrapping up the interview when Rhonda commented to Cahil that Anna and Ellen would be in for a surprise tomorrow.

"Anna and Ellen?" Wyatt repeated. "Who are they and why are they going to be surprised?"

"Anna's my maid," Cahil answered. "Ellen's her daughter. They come in twice a week to clean my house. I don't see how that has anything to do with this." A private man, he resented having his life dissected this way. And then his eyes widened as he followed the train of thought he was sure was going through the detectives' minds. "It wasn't them," he said with feeling. "Weren't you listening? I said that those were men here last night, not women."

Sam made no comment on the professor's defense. Instead, he asked, "Do either Anna or Ellen have the key to your house?"

"Of course they have a key," was the exasperated answer. "How else are they going to get in here when I'm at the university? Through the chimney?"

"Works for Santa Claus," Riley quipped. It earned her a dark look from the professor.

Fear obviously trumped loyalty in Rhonda's eyes. Growing excited, she asked, "Do you think that was it? They gave the key to someone?"

"It's a possibility," Riley allowed. "We have to check it out. Until then," she continued as she looked at Cahil to emphasize her point, "they're innocent until proven otherwise. We'll need to get in contact with them."

Cahil grudgingly gave them Anna's phone number.

It was time to go. "Thank you, Professor Cahil, Ms. Williams," Sam said, calling an end to the interview. "We'll be getting back to you in the next few days," he promised.

With that, he placed his hand on the small of Riley's back, ushering her out of the room and toward the front door.

Behind them, they heard Professor Cahil snort. "I won't hold my breath."

There were days, Riley thought as she crossed the threshold, when protecting and serving turned out to be harder than others.

Chapter 10

Riley quickly discovered that, as in almost every department of the police force, man power in the robbery division was limited. She and Wyatt, along with the other detectives in Robbery, didn't lack for cases to work on. But due to the publicity that the home invasion cases had garnered and the fact that there were now three of them, they had gone to the top of the priority list.

Day in, day out, despite the fact that they sacrificed their lunchtimes and pored over the same evidence until they could re-create the reports from memory, the cases seemed to taunt them. They were still missing something.

Riley had a feeling that the solution was hiding in plain sight. She just couldn't grab onto it. Yet. It was only a matter of time before that one crucial piece of evidence would hit them. She just had to be patient.

"I must've been over all the details a hundred times," Sam complained, tossing down the folder he'd been looking through. With a deep, impatient sigh, he rocked back in his chair, staring at the bulletin board. Looking to find what he'd missed before.

Almost everything in the folders he'd put together matched, in some fashion, the abbreviated notes on the board they'd put up next to their desks.

But so far, there'd been no breakthroughs. The professor's cleaning ladies turned out to be just that: cleaning ladies. A background check on both women connected them to only one unsavory character. Anna's nephew, Jorge. But Jorge was currently doing time for almost beating someone to death who'd had the misfortune of looking at his wife. That ruled him out. In addition, a quick review of Jorge's history showed that he didn't have the kind of pull to get others to work for him and he definitely didn't have the smarts needed to run that kind of operation from his jail cell.

The other two families didn't employ any sort of cleaning service.

"You say something?" Riley asked, hearing Wyatt mutter something inaudible under his breath.

He glanced up at her. "Yeah. This running around in circles is getting to me."

That made two of them, she thought. "We need to unwind," she agreed. "Both of us," she emphasized with a sigh.

"Good luck with that." He looked accusingly at the piles on his desk, but he was too brain weary for the moment to pick up another folder.

It was Friday and it was late. He should be going home. But even that didn't mean he could unwind. Ever since Lisa had come into his life, he didn't even stop at Malone's. Alcohol might make his brain fuzzy just when he had to be sharp.

He closed his eyes for a moment. This parenting business weighed heavily on his shoulders.

"I'm surprised the lieutenant doesn't have us working overtime," he said. Whatever extra time he and McIntyre devoted to this was off the books and on their own time. "Barker did say that the mayor was really pressing to get these invasions cleared and off the books."

Riley didn't want to hear about official overtime. That meant having to put in a mandatory number of hours and this was already nagging her brain. "A tired mind doesn't operate at maximum efficiency," she pointed out.

He laughed shortly. "You thinking of having that embroidered on your towels, or just your T-shirt?" Wyatt asked.

"Just stating the obvious." Riley paused for a moment, looking at him, debating whether or not to say what had been buzzing around in her head for the last half hour.

The pensive expression on her face was not lost on him. Lately, he noted, especially when he was tired, he caught himself watching her more often than he should. Watching her and having thoughts that went beyond the realm of their professional partnership. Right now, he wished Evans was back—or that McIntyre wasn't so damn attractive.

"Something on your mind, McIntyre?" he asked.

Rather than say yes, she asked him a question of her own. "You like barbecued food?"

He stared at her. That wasn't what he'd expected her to ask. Actually, he wasn't really certain *what* he expected her to say. He'd just vaguely thought it would have to do with one of the cases. There were times when his partner's mind seemed to slip into an alternate universe.

"Well, do you?" she pressed when he didn't say anything.

"Yeah, I've been known to like barbecued food." Why was she asking him what he liked to eat? "McIntyre, are you asking me out on a date?" He splayed his hand against his chest, feigning surprise. "This is so sudden."

"It's not sudden, it's nonexistent," she informed him. "I'm just debating inviting you over to Andrew Cavanaugh's place tomorrow. You and Lisa," she added, realizing that she'd omitted that important piece of information. "By the way, Lisa's the only reason I'm even thinking about this invitation."

He thought of baiting her but was too tired to follow it through. "What's tomorrow?"

"Saturday," she answered glibly.

"I know it's Saturday." He tried not to sound exasperated. It wasn't Riley's fault he wasn't sleeping much at night, lying there listening for the sound of Lisa crying again. So far, except for that first night, the little girl hadn't. But that didn't mean she wouldn't again. If she did, he didn't want her to go uncomforted. "I mean why's the chief having a barbecue?"

"Because he can," she answered glibly, adding, "Because he likes to cook and because he *really* likes having family around to eat what he cooks. Technically, there's no occasion, but it's been so hot lately that he decided to take advantage of the weather."

He'd stopped listening at the end of the second sentence. "Only one problem with that. I'm not family," Sam pointed out in response to the eyebrow she lifted quizzically.

"You're a cop, that makes you family in the Chief's eyes. His mantra, not mine," she added in case Wyatt wanted to demur. "C'mon, what d'you say, Wyatt? There'll be great food, great conversation. Lisa can play with the gaggle of kids who'll be there and you'll get a chance to unwind."

He had to admit he was sorely tempted. Socializing had died by the wayside ever since he'd taken on the mantle of fatherhood. After hours, McIntyre was the only one he socialized with and both of them focused on Lisa.

"I've heard about these parties the Chief throws," he confessed. The food, he'd heard, was out of this world.

She laughed softly. "You'd have to live in another state in order not to hear about them. His hospitality— and culinary abilities—are famous." She looked at her partner. "So, how about it?"

He was already won over, but because it was Riley, he played it out a little longer. "I don't know. What time does it start?"

Riley grinned triumphantly. She knew she could wear him down. She wasn't about to explore why she felt this little thrill in the pit of her stomach.

"Starts at noon, goes on forever. Or at least until everyone's too tired to talk."

A whimsical smile played on his lips. "That include you?"

For a while there, because of what had happened to Sanchez, she hadn't been herself. But now Riley felt as if she was coming around again. Coming back from a dark mind-set she wouldn't have wished on anyone. The relief she experienced was incredible.

"Sometimes," she allowed.

"All right," he agreed, then qualified his reason for going. "I think you're right. Lisa might get a kick out of it."

"Of course I'm right," she said glibly. "I can swing by tomorrow, pick you up."

"Or you can just give me the address now."

Riley made no effort to reach for a piece of paper to write the address down. "That won't assure me that you'll come," she told Wyatt bluntly.

"Scout's honor carry any weight with you?" he asked archly.

"It would—if you'd been a Boy Scout," she told him with a knowing smile. "But you weren't."

"How would you know that?" Sam asked, then

realized the answer. "Have you been digging into my background, McIntyre?"

"Maybe a little," she admitted. There was no embarrassment, no apology in her voice.

Why would she go through the trouble? Was there something going on he wasn't aware of? An investigation came to mind, but there was no reason for one.

"But you know me," Sam protested.

She gave him what passed as a mysterious smile. "Does anyone really know anyone?"

The sigh that escaped was an impatient one. "Don't go all philosophical on me, McIntyre. Why were you digging into my background?"

"Because I don't like surprises. Because I wanted to know more about the man I'd been partnered with. Besides, it's not digging, it's just familiarizing myself with some background information."

Had she talked to someone, or just looked at his personnel file? In either case, he couldn't say he liked the invasion. "Asking me would have been simpler."

"Would you have answered?" she challenged.

"Maybe." His expression gave nothing away. "If you'd played your cards right," he added.

Yeah, right. "That's what I thought," she said out loud. "My way's better. Anyway, I wasn't going for any deep, dark secrets—"

"Good," he said, cutting her off. "Because I haven't got any."

Everyone had secrets, Riley thought. Some just had more or bigger ones than others. "—I just wanted to satisfy my curiosity," she concluded as if he hadn't interrupted her.

Riley leaned back in her chair, unconsciously rotating her shoulders to get rid of the cramp in her muscles. He looked up and saw her moving her head from left to right. It was a familiar movement that he'd seen boxers employ just before a bout was about to begin.

"Getting ready for a main event?" he asked her, amused.

"Just trying to get rid of this crick in my neck."

"That's what you get for hunching over your desk."

She hadn't noticed that Wyatt was observing her. Most of the time, she thought he was oblivious of her presence. "I didn't know posture counted in the robbery division."

"Everything counts in the robbery division," he said flippantly, getting up. He circled behind her.

She turned in her chair, trying to see where he was going. To her surprise, Wyatt righted her chair to keep her from facing him. "What are you doing?"

"Getting ready to strangle you and I'd rather do it from behind so those big blue eyes of yours don't get to me," he cracked as he put his hands on her shoulders. She jumped in response and he laughed. "Easy, McIntyre, I was only kidding about strangling you. I thought I'd try to help you work out those kinks." As he began to knead, he found that he had to use excessive pressure. "Damn, but you're tense," he commented, pressing harder. "This is what the Hulk must feel like after he goes green and winds up erupting out of his clothes."

Lovely, he was comparing her to a lumpy, angry

green comic book character. "Sure know how to turn a girl's head, don't you, Wyatt?"

"I don't think of you as a girl, McIntyre."

It was a lie, but a necessary one, he felt. Necessary because in reality he thought of her as a woman far too much for either of their good. Doing so interfered in so many different ways that it boggled the mind.

"Good to know," she murmured. She caught her breath, trying not to make any whimpering sounds. Wyatt was using way too much force kneading her shoulders, but she'd be damned if she'd give him the satisfaction of wincing. Instead, she tried to concentrate on something else. "You really think that I've got big blue eyes?"

Still working her shoulders, he leaned over and peered at her face. "Don't you?"

"Yes." She sat up a little straighter. The pain now shot to the top of her skull and the very roots of her hair. "But my other partners never noticed."

He sincerely doubted that. "Trust me, unless they needed a seeing eye dog to get around, they noticed."

Despite the fact that his rock-hard fingers created their own wave of pain with each pass of his hands, the stiffness in her shoulders seemed to abate somewhat. She felt almost human.

A sigh escaped her lips as she allowed herself to enjoy the sensation.

The moment was short-lived.

The phone on her desk rang. She glanced up at the clock on the wall. It was five-thirty. Thirty minutes past the end of their shift. If she picked up the phone and it turned out to be an official call, she might not go home for a while yet.

Wyatt withdrew his hands from her shoulders. "Are you going to answer that?" he asked.

"I was hoping to outlast it," she confessed with a sigh. Resigned, she picked up the receiver and put it to her ear. "McIntyre."

"Just me, honey. I tried calling your cell, but I think you let the battery wind down again. Anyway," the soft, familiar voice on the other end continued, "I'm calling to remind you about Andrew's barbecue. It's tomorrow."

She relaxed in her chair. No emergencies, no robbery to follow up on. "I was just talking about it."

"Oh?" Lila Cavanaugh made no attempt to hide her piqued interest. "To whom?"

"My partner, Mom." She watched as Wyatt went back to his desk and closed down his computer. "I invited him and his daughter. I didn't think Andrew would mind."

"Mind?" Lila echoed with a soft laugh. "You know Andrew, the more the merrier. So tell me, how's your partner adjusting to fatherhood?"

The question didn't surprise her. Even though she hadn't said a word about this new state of affairs that Wyatt found himself facing, she knew that word in her family traveled like the flames of a wildfire during the state's dry season. Brenda knew and that was enough. All for one and one for all wasn't just a slogan for a band of fictional Musketeers, it also seemed to be the Cavanaugh/McIntyre family's slogan, as well. What one knew, they all knew.

The price one paid for having them all there for you, she thought philosophically.

"Slowly, Mom, slowly." She tried to avoid looking at Wyatt, but it couldn't be helped. He had to know she was talking about him. "But he's getting there. Gotta go. See you tomorrow."

"I'm looking forward to it, honey," her mother said. "And Riley?"

She'd almost replaced the receiver when she heard her mother say her name. She snatched it up just before it connected with the cradle. "Yes?"

Her mother's warm voice embraced her. "I love you."

Riley knew her mother was still worried about her, worried that she wouldn't be able to pull out of the tailspin she'd found herself in right after Sanchez had been murdered. But, mercifully—maybe it was the work or maybe it was because she was helping out with Lisa—she seemed to be finally getting her act together.

"Me, too, Mom," she said quietly. With that, Riley hung up.

Sam waited until she replaced the receiver. "Everything okay on the home front?"

Nodding, she did her best to sound casual. "Just my mother, checking up on me."

"She have reason to worry?" he asked mildly, watching her face carefully.

"No."

The answer came out automatically, without thought so that she wouldn't be subjected to probing questions. But this time around, Riley realized there was more truth to it than just a few weeks ago. Progress. It felt good.

"But that doesn't stop her. Parents, according to my mother, worry about their kids for roughly the first hundred years. After that," she smiled, "they start to back off."

"That means you've got more than seventy years to go," he deadpanned.

Even if her life span and her mother's went that far, her mother would never completely stop worrying about them. It was an occupational hazard and the fact that all of them were on the police force didn't help matters.

"Something like that," she agreed.

"If that's what parenting's about, I'm glad I'm not like that," he told her.

There was humor in her eyes, as if telling him he would wind up eating his words. "Give yourself time. You will be. The best parents always worry, they just don't show it."

He made no comment. The thing of it was, he had this undercurrent of fear that Riley was right.

The next day, responding to the doorbell, Sam stared at the woman on his doorstep. Riley. He thought they'd settled this last night. Did she think he needed a keeper?

"You know, you didn't have to stop by. I told you that we were going to attend." He stood there looking at her, his body blocking the entrance to his apartment.

"Just wanted to be sure," she answered cheerfully. "Besides, I'm not going out of my way stopping here. I pass right by your complex when I go to Andrew's house." It wasn't entirely true, but close enough.

Riley shoved her hands into the back pockets of her denim shorts. Her very short denim shorts, Sam noted, his eyes sweeping over her. His partner wore a white halter top that emphasized her tan, but it was the shorts that really captured his attention as well as stimulated his imagination. He took slow inventory of her legs.

Who knew they were that long?

She could almost feel his eyes trailing along her body. Making her warmer. She did her best to sound blasé.

"Careful, Wyatt," she warned. "You're in danger of having your eyes fall out of your head."

"Your legs always been that long?" he asked, forcing his gaze back up to her face.

Riley looked down, pretending to take his question seriously. "Since the sixth grade. I was the tallest in my class until everyone else caught up. One of the guys used to call me Flamingo Legs."

His thoughts turned to Lisa. Someday, maybe soon, some little boy would be teasing her. How was she going to handle that? How was *he* going to handle that? He didn't want to be one of those overbearing fathers, but he knew he wouldn't like the idea of someone tormenting his daughter.

"Did it hurt?" he asked.

She grinned broadly. "No, but he did after I gave him a fat lip."

He laughed. She'd been tough even then, fighting her own battles. Maybe Lisa would be, too. "Why doesn't that surprise me?"

She couldn't pinpoint exactly why, but the sound of Wyatt's laughter shimmied up and down her spine, making her feel even warmer than the day warranted.

It also brought out his daughter from her room. Dressed in a red T-shirt and white shorts, Lisa came running up to her the moment she saw who it was.

"Riley, Riley, Sam and I are going to a barbecue," she announced.

Riley looked quizzically at Wyatt. Why was he still letting his daughter call him by his first name? "I know, honey. I invited you."

Lisa fairly danced from foot to foot. "You're going, too?" she squealed, then threw her small arms as far around Riley's hips as her arms could reach.

"You bet." Riley glanced toward her partner. "She still calls you Sam?" she asked, trying not to sound as if she had an opinion one way or the other.

Sam shrugged. "Easier to get used to than 'Dad,'" he told her.

"Same amount of letters," Riley pointed out.

"Yeah, well…" He let his voice trail off, then gazed down at his daughter. It wasn't a matter of letters, but of feelings. He'd been missing for the first years of her life. Getting used to being here with him was hard enough for her without thinking of him as her father. "C'mon, Lisa, let's get this show on the road."

He didn't have to tell her twice. Grabbing Riley's hand, Lisa fairly raced across the threshold, excitement apparently bubbling through her as she giggled.

Chapter 11

"Hear that?"

It was several hours later when Riley asked Sam the question.

When they'd arrived at Andrew's house, the barbecue was already in full swing and they were quickly embraced and then absorbed. Within minutes, Lisa had been "borrowed" from Sam. Clasping Brenda by the hand, the little girl was happily led away to join in a series of games that Brenda, Jared's wife, Maren, and Troy's wife, Delene, were overseeing, playing with the up and coming next generation of Cavanaughs. Lisa hadn't been back since.

In the interim, separately and together, Riley and Sam were drawn into one conversation after another.

The topics were varied, some serious, some humorous, but they were all spirited. Time, offset with an ever-changing array of snacks, appetizers and main meals, passed very quickly.

And now, the "official" barbecue foods—hot dogs, hamburgers and steaks—were being served. No one, even the most stuffed of them, could find it in their hearts to say no. It was all just too good. Sam had volunteered to get her serving and his, returning with both after ten minutes.

Sam handed his partner the plate Andrew had insisted on preparing for Riley himself.

"Hear what?" he asked, sitting down with his own plate on one of the dozens of folding chairs. It was nothing short of a balancing act, trying to keep everything on the extra-large paper plate rather than it come sliding onto his lap. Besides the hamburger, there were three kinds of salad, all vying for a limited amount of space. "With all this noise, it's hard to hear just one thing."

"*Listen,*" Riley underscored.

Humoring Riley, Sam cocked his head the way she was doing. He heard a lot of things, but nothing in particular. "So what am I listening for?" he asked.

Riley sighed. Men. "The sound of your daughter, laughing."

Sam straightened his head and looked at her. "You're kidding, right?" When she didn't say yes, he realized she was being serious. "You can actually hear that?" he marveled. "Lisa laughing?"

"Yes."

He listened again, then shook his head. Riley had to be pulling his leg. "There's got to be at least a dozen kids laughing, maybe more." Not to mention the countless high-pitched voices raised, competing with one another. "How can you possibly make her out?"

"I can," she insisted. "It's a matter of concentration. And attachment," she emphasized. "You're her dad, Wyatt, you are supposed to be able to tell the difference."

"Sorry," he quipped. "My 'dad' gene is a newly acquired one. It's going to take me some time to hone it properly."

Riley watched her partner for a long moment, gauging his tone. "You're making fun of me, aren't you, Wyatt?"

He pretended to be incredulous. "In a yard filled with your relatives, most of whom have access to guns?" He took a bite out of the hamburger. Damn if it wasn't heaven on a bun. How could a simple hamburger taste this good? "Wouldn't dream of it. I don't have a death wish," he assured her before he took another bite.

His comment made Riley look around for a second. As she did, she smiled to herself. She hadn't thought about it in those terms. But Wyatt was right. This *was* a yard full of her relatives.

Not blood relatives except for Taylor, Frank and Zack, and of course her mother, but one way or another, this really was her family now. And, no doubt, every last one of them would back her up whenever she needed it.

She hadn't realized how good that felt until this moment.

"You'd have to do something pretty terrible for them to shoot you," she quipped.

Swallowing another bite, Sam shook his head. "That's one envelope I have no desire in pushing."

"Oh? And what envelope would you like to push?"

Their eyes met and held for longer than she'd intended. Long enough to evoke that strange, funny shiver that danced along her spine these days whenever their hands accidentally brushed or she encountered him when she wasn't expecting to.

A strange, funny, *warm* shiver that spread out tributaries and left her stomach unsettled.

"I'll let you know when the time comes," he promised her quietly. So quietly that she had to look at his lips in order to have the words register completely.

"Oh. Okay." She went back to watching Lisa. Somehow, it seemed safer that way. And better for her digestion.

Watching Riley and her partner from across the yard, Lila smiled to herself.

A sense of relief intensified. The same relief that had begun when she first greeted Riley as she arrived with Sam and his daughter. Lila turned toward her husband, the man she could now freely admit she loved. The man who she'd loved in secret for so many years. Lila placed her hand on his arm.

"You did good, Brian," she praised in a soft, lowered voice.

"Of course I did," Brian replied, turning toward her.

Andrew had recruited him to bring another box of buns over to the grill, but that could wait. What his wife was saying intrigued him. "But just for edification purposes, is this in reference to anything specific or is this a general seal of approval?"

With a laugh, she shook her head. "Yes, it's specific. I'm talking about taking Riley out of Homicide and partnering her up with Sam Wyatt in Robbery. Look at her." Lila nodded in her daughter's direction. "She almost looks like her old self again." Lila turned toward Brian again and brushed a kiss against his cheek. "Thank you."

He took her hand and brought it to his lips, pressing a kiss against her knuckles. "No thanks necessary, milady. I'm always at the ready and at your service."

A little sigh of contentment escaped Lila's lips. After all these years, she was finally, blissfully, happy. And she owed it all to Brian.

"Nice to know," she murmured.

"I can show you just how ready I am once we get a chance to slip away and go home," he promised her with a wink.

"Brian," she laughed, glancing around to see if anyone had heard him. "You're the Chief of Detectives, don't let anyone overhear you."

"Why?" He grinned. "Where is it written that the Chief of Ds is supposed to be a robot? Or live by the letter of the law alone?" he challenged playfully. "Besides," he said, lowering his voice and whispering in her ear, "even a robot would find his mighty tin body getting overheated just by being so close to you."

She laughed again, shaking her head. It never oc-curred to her that she could be so happy. After what she'd gone through with her first husband, it was like living in a dream. One from which she hoped she'd never wake up.

"In my considered opinion, I'd say that Lisa is offi-cially worn out," Riley told her partner, inclining her head close to his so that Sam could hear her.

It was almost ten o'clock and Riley's description could have fit almost any one of them—except for Andrew who seemed to literally thrive on spending hours cooking for his family and friends.

When Sam looked at her, Riley indicated the sleeping child on her lap. A number of them had adjourned to the family room and she had commandeered the corner of one of the sofas for herself and Lisa. Lisa's head now rested against Riley's chest and the little girl was curled up into her. Somewhere in the last half hour, Sam's daughter had grown progressively more and more sub-dued, then, after protesting that she was wide awake, had fallen asleep.

"Here, I'll take her," he said, slipping his arms around his daughter and lifting her into his arms. "Never saw her fall asleep without a fight before," he commented with a touch of amusement.

Riley glanced at the few children still milling around. Most were asleep, like Lisa, resting securely in one of their parents' arms.

"This group'll do that to you, tire you out until there

isn't an ounce of energy left inside your body," she told him, a fond smile curving her mouth as she remembered. "My brothers, sister and I were exactly the same way."

Sam nodded. "I wouldn't know about things like that. I didn't have any siblings."

Riley thought of what her childhood would have been like without her siblings. Achingly lonely.

"I'm sorry."

Curiosity entered his eyes. "Why are you sorry?" He didn't see being an only child as missing out on anything. His mother had walked out on his father when Sam was young and *that* had hurt, but being an only child hadn't. "It's not like I didn't have enough to eat."

She saw it differently. "In a way, yes. You were deprived."

The shrug was careless in nature. "You don't miss what you don't have."

But Riley shook her head. "I don't think that's absolutely true."

The woman was something else, he thought, amused. "You'd argue with God, wouldn't you?"

The smile came into her eyes as she considered his question. "Depends on what point of view He was advancing."

Sam just laughed and shook his head. "Look, I hate to drag you away from this, but since you insisted on being my ride today—"

She was on her feet, ready to leave before he could finish his sentence.

"Don't say another word," she told him. "Of course

I'll take you and Sleeping Beauty here home." She looked around, trying to locate their hosts. "Just let me find either Andrew or Rose and make our goodbyes."

He had no intentions of leaving without doing the same. "You implying I'm not capable of saying my own goodbyes, McIntyre?"

She knew she had a tendency to take charge, especially when it came to the family. She would have to watch that, Riley told herself.

"Never even crossed my mind," she deadpanned, holding up her hand as if taking a solemn pledge.

With a chorus of goodbyes still ringing in her ears and a feeling of both contentment and unexpected anticipation, Riley drove her partner and his daughter the short distance home.

"You know," he pointed out again, "if you'd have let me drive to the barbecue in my own car, you could still be back there."

"Gaining more weight?" she speculated. "No, this is the right cutoff point," Riley assured him. "You were just my excuse for leaving before I put on another five pounds. In case you haven't noticed," she went on, squeaking through an amber light, "it's hard saying 'no' to Andrew, especially when the food he's trying to push on you tastes so good."

"I noticed."

I also noticed a lot of other things better left unsaid, he thought, covertly watching her profile as she spoke.

The close proximity had him entertaining thoughts that had no business coming up. He and McIntyre were partners. They worked together and needed clear heads and lives that weren't tangled up with one another's.

He knew all that, and yet…

Sam forced himself to concentrate on what she was saying.

"I'm surprised that Aurora doesn't have the fattest police force in the country. Thank God everyone in the family's so into physical fitness and working out." She made a mental note to get to the gym herself the first chance she got. She would need to add some reps to her workout. "Otherwise, we could probably just roll over the perps and squash them instead of taking them in."

The visual made him laugh. "Save the county a lot of money in court costs," he theorized.

Riley realized she was close to the apartment complex. That was fast. How was it that trips back from their destination always seemed so much quicker than the original trip there? She could have sworn that they'd gotten here in the blink of an eye.

"Please don't say that around Andrew," she begged. "The man will use it as an excuse to insist that we all eat more."

"My lips are sealed," he said as Riley guided the car into a spot in guest parking.

"Oh God, I hope not."

Did that just come out of her mouth? How the hell did she let that happen? Riley chastised herself. When in doubt, offer a diversion. She'd learned that, oddly enough, from her father.

"Um, let me help you with Lisa," she volunteered,

then quickly got out of the car before Sam had an opportunity to say anything.

Riley had the rear passenger door open and unstrapped Lisa from her seat before he could reach his daughter. Sam stepped back, watching her.

Acutely aware of him, Riley had no idea what was going on in Wyatt's head. Maybe it was better that way.

Very gently, she removed the sleeping girl from her car seat and scooped Lisa up. "Just unlock your front door," she requested.

Sam saw no reason to argue, or insist that he could take care of Lisa himself. Especially when he had a strong feeling that Riley, as usual, would win the argument.

Leading the way, he took out his key. "Why is it that when we were in the academy, I never noticed this 'take charge' personality of yours?"

They were friends back then, but for one reason or another, nothing more.

"Maybe because you were always surrounded by all those eager female rookies who were vying for your attention," she speculated.

Sam put his key in the lock, turning it. The time spent in the academy was all a blur, as if someone else had lived it. "I don't recall any eager rookies," he told her innocently.

Right, like she'd believe that. "Alzheimer's doesn't usually set in this early," she commented.

He held the door open for her. Riley walked into the apartment first. Behind her, Sam flipped the light switch, illuminating the area.

"Thanks," she murmured, cutting through the living room.

Making a left, she headed toward the former guest room, now Lisa's bedroom. The room had, in the last few weeks, undergone a major transformation. That was thanks in large part to the various things she had picked up for the little girl. Not to be left out, Brenda had donated a few things, as well. The anonymous feeling the room had had was gone. This was now definitely a room that belonged to a little girl.

Placing Lisa on the bed, Riley debated getting the sleeping child out of her clothes and into her pajamas. The next moment, she abandoned the idea. One night spent in her clothes wasn't going to hurt. If she started to change her, Lisa might wake up. Judging from how tense Sam seemed, he wouldn't exactly welcome an all-nighter.

Taking Lisa's shoes off, Riley threw the bedcover over the small body and let the little girl sleep.

Sam stood in the room, watching her and feeling a little useless—but not enough to take over. "Aren't you going to get her into her pajamas?" he asked, curious.

Riley shook her head, backing away from the canopied bed. Nice touch, she thought, admiring the frills that outlined the canopy.

"Lisa might wake up. It's not worth the trouble," she assured him. About to leave the room, Riley noticed that rather than turn them off, he lowered the overhead lights until they were very dim.

"Lisa's afraid of the dark," he explained.

She could certainly relate to that, she thought as she slipped out of the room. He eased the door closed behind him.

"So was I for the longest time."

She didn't add that right after Sanchez's murder, her fears had revisited her and she'd gone back to sleeping with the lights on. She'd continued doing that until sometime last week. The need to have every corner illuminated had passed, disappearing as mysteriously as it had come.

"I wasn't allowed to be afraid," Sam told her simply.

Riley stopped just short of the front door to turn around and look at him. "Wasn't 'allowed'?" she repeated in disbelief. What did permission have to do with it?

He didn't think of his father often. Unpleasant memories were best held at bay. He supposed that suddenly becoming one himself on such short notice had roused a great many incidents from his own childhood. He was determined to do the opposite of whatever had been done to him.

"My father told me leaving the light on in my room once I was in bed was a waste of electricity. He maintained that there was nothing in the dark that wasn't there in the light."

Thank God she'd had an understanding mother. "How did that work for you?"

One corner of his mouth lifted. "I spent ten years sleeping with my baseball bat."

Amusement entered Riley's eyes as she visualized him as a small boy in bed with his Louisville Slugger.

"Until you found that girls had more curves?" she guessed whimsically.

"And were a lot softer," he added, playing along. In truth, it had taken him some time to get over his need to protect himself.

She was on dangerous ground and she knew it. Taking a breath, Riley told herself it was time to go home. She took a step toward the door, moving backward.

"Well, hope you had a good time," she told him. Was that as inane as it sounded?

"We did," he assured her. "Thanks for inviting us." And then he hesitated.

Part of him would regret this, he thought. The other part would regret it if he didn't at least try.

"You know, you don't have to go just yet. Would you like something to drink?" he suggested.

"Why Detective Wyatt, are you trying to get me to take in spirits?" she teased. "If I do, I won't be able to drive home for several hours."

His smile was warm. Disarming. She felt herself sinking. "Maybe that's part of the idea."

Breathe, damn it, Riley, breathe. "And what's the rest of the idea?"

His eyes slid over her. She could almost feel their caress. "I thought that maybe that could work itself out slowly."

Why did she suddenly feel as if she was standing on the edge of a precipice? One that was utterly unstable and threatened to give way beneath her feet at any second?

"No previews?" she questioned. "I always love seeing coming attractions when I go to the movies."

"Previews you want, previews you'll get," he murmured softly. So softly that she inclined her head toward him in order to hear.

That was exactly when her lips were suddenly captured.

Chapter 12

Riley knew she should pull away.

Sooner or later, most likely sooner, there would be hell to pay for this huge transgression, this blurring of lines that separated her professional life from her private one.

But she didn't care.

Logic and common sense didn't stand a ghost of a chance in the face of the heat generated by the mere touch of his lips on hers. The heat that she now found consuming her body.

Giving in to the pleasure, Riley wrapped her arms around Sam's neck. As she did so, she curved her body into his. The fact that he wanted her, really wanted her, registered instantly. And just as instantly, it created a yearning within her.

The kind of yearning that she hadn't experienced in a very long time.

Maybe never.

His hands, which had initially framed her face when he first kissed her, now moved away, sliding along her sides. Encircling her body. Holding her closer than a heartbeat.

And all the while he deepened the kiss, silently making this moment an event to celebrate.

Riley desperately tried to hold up her part, kissing him back for all she was worth. Not just absorbing sensations but creating them, as well. Her pride demanded it.

She got caught in her own trap.

Riley's head was spinning. Badly.

She wanted to attribute it to something common, like the lack of oxygen, but she knew better. Ever since she was a little girl, she could hold her breath an inordinate amount of time. This kiss went far beyond that.

Before she was fully conscious of her actions, she found that her fingers worked away at the buttons on Sam's shirt, pushing them out of their holes, tugging out the ends of the shirt and swiftly moving it away from his chest.

As she slid the material from his shoulders, Sam caught her hands in his and forced himself to draw his head back. To draw his lips away from hers.

His eyes searched her face for his answer even as he asked, "Riley, are you sure?"

He'd called her Riley, which he'd never done before. This was the private woman, not the detective, he was addressing. The private woman who was being seduced, who was melting. And the private woman was oh so sure she wanted this, *needed* this no matter what tomorrow would demand as payment for her involvement.

"I'm sure," Riley whispered, her breath feathering along his mouth, along his skin.

Something flared in his eyes. Desire? Oh, God, she hoped so.

"Then far be it from me to say no," he breathed, trying to sound as if he was teasing her.

"It better be far," Riley warned.

The truth be known, she was ready to explode right here, right now. And would have if he had pulled away. To stop just as everything within her had been primed to continue.

She hadn't realized just how much she wanted Sam until he'd kissed her. Now, she was fairly certain that the world would come to an abrupt, jarring end if he just stopped, even if he was trying to be chivalrous.

Riley splayed her hands over his chest. Hard muscles seemed to ripple beneath her palms. She could feel her excitement literally multiplying with each moment that passed.

"I had no idea you were so ripped," she murmured, her eyes on his.

"Lots of things you have no idea about," Sam told her, his voice rumbling low.

Exciting her.

He was right. There was a great deal she didn't know about this man. But she knew she placed her life in his hands every day, trusting him to have her back. Trusting him to be there for her.

How much more was there?

Trust was the most important ingredient in their relationship. In *every* relationship. The rest was minor in comparison.

Except that right now, it didn't feel so minor, these things he was causing to happen inside her. His lips skimmed the sensitive skin just beneath her chin, just along her throat. The fire in her veins increased, raising to astonishing heights she wasn't sure she could properly control.

His shirt stripped from his body, Sam began to return the favor. His lips pressed against hers, he undid the ends of her halter. The double knot stubbornly resisted, then finally came undone.

The two sides of the halter hung about her, tempting him. He could feel his breath catch in his throat.

His mouth curving against hers, he coaxed the material away from her body and discovered that, just as he'd suspected, Riley hadn't worn a bra beneath the virgin white top.

With patient movements, he kneaded her skin, bringing his palms in closer with each agonizingly slow pass until he finally cupped her breasts.

When he heard her breath catch, felt the swell of her breasts beneath his hands, Sam was certain something had ignited inside his soul.

God, he wanted her.

But if this was going to go any further, it couldn't be

here, out in the open in the living room. They were completely exposed here. If Lisa suddenly woke up and came in search of him, there was nowhere to hide.

Rather than launch into any explanations, he scooped a surprised Riley up into his arms and moved across the room, heading toward his bedroom.

Her heart pounded harder. "How did you know?" she breathed.

He hadn't a clue what she was referring to. Was she talking about their kiss? About the fact that they were about to make love? Or was it something else? Riley was *not* a woman he could read like a book. He needed a translation.

"Know what?" he asked as he shouldered his door open, then closed it again, this time using his back.

She laced her arms around his neck. "That I've always had this Rhett Butler fantasy," she whispered, "about being carried off to a bedroom."

Sam knew he should capitalize on this stroke of blind luck, play it up to his advantage. Most men, he knew, would have done just that. But he wasn't most men. Besides, lies had a way of backfiring and he wanted to take no chances.

"I didn't," he told her. "The moment just called for it."

And that, in part, was true. Because if he had remained out there a moment longer, things like protecting his daughter from too much age-inappropriate education would have plummeted to the bottom of his list of things to do in the heat of his desire.

That meant, Riley thought as another surge of excitement shot through her, that Sam was a natural. He was a romantic without even having to think about it. And that was excellent. Because the last thing she wanted either one of them to do right now was think. This wasn't the time for it, for detailed thoughts to wedge their way into what was happening.

All she wanted was to savor these sensations rushing through her. Savor the feel of his hands on her skin, his mouth on hers, doing wonderful, clever things and making her feel like a Roman candle about to go off at any second, illuminating the darkness.

She felt the mattress against her back as he laid her down, felt the impression of his body against hers as he sank to join her. And she felt her breath all but vanishing as his mouth began to work its way along her torso.

While his lips fueled the fire within her, she could feel his fingers working away at the snap on her shorts. The material parted as he slid the zipper down. Ever so slowly, Sam moved the material along her hips. The slower he moved, the more excited she felt, her flesh burning for the caress of his.

She raised her hips, allowing him to rid her of the last of her clothing as he tugged away both her shorts and white thong.

A frenzy assaulted her. Opening the snap on his jeans, she began to tug them off, trying to sweep them away with just a few well-placed movements.

Riley felt her heart pounding harder and harder as she struggled to divest him of the jeans while he all but held her captive with his magical mouth.

She could feel the eruption gathering, growing in volume and force.

Threatening to go off suddenly.

When Sam pressed the heel of his hand against her core, she climaxed for the first time. That had never happened to her before, not from the mere touch of a man's hand.

The very sensation stole her breath away.

Arching so that she could feel his hand pressing harder against her, the desire for more filled her entire being. Raising her head, she caught his lips, pressing hers against them. A heated passion assaulted her in waves.

Their bodies mingled as their limbs tangled with one another and Riley moved on top of him. Their mouths slanted over and over again, unable to be satiated.

Demanding more.

Damn but this was different, Sam thought. He'd expected her to be hot, expected to enjoy her while creating a web of pleasure for her, but this went beyond anything he'd imagined. The intensity throbbing through his veins was something he'd never experienced before.

He could feel his pulse racing, his hunger increasing at a breathtaking rate, overpowering him and making it very, very difficult for him to hold himself in check as long as he had planned.

There were no plans anymore, no blueprints on how to proceed. They were caught up in the fire and had burned up.

He was being swept away by a woman he had seriously

underestimated. He had thought that making love with Riley would be a pleasant, pleasurable experience. This went so far beyond that that it couldn't even be measured.

He wanted to reach that final moment, to crest and feel the last, breathtaking surge sweeping through his body. And yet, he still wanted to hold onto the promise of all that was to come, to extend this experience for as long as he could.

This wasn't normal.

This wasn't like him.

What the hell was she doing to him?

Still struggling for control, Sam flipped so that he got Riley onto her back again. He saw the surprise in her eyes, the signs of mounting anticipation vibrating throughout her being. Pleased, he began to work his way down her slick, supple body. Nipping at the tempting curves, gliding his tongue along her heated flesh. Priming her with his warm breath that skimmed against her skin.

He heard Riley moan as his mouth teased the center of her passion.

Empowered, imprisoned, he began to use his tongue to flirt with, then press against, her moist, heaving and more-than-willing flesh.

Oh, God, she couldn't catch her breath. Sam had stolen it from her.

Feeling as if she was in the midst of an out-of-body experience, Riley raised her hips up higher, offering herself to him. Grasping a slice of paradise as the explosion racked her body. She didn't care about equality, about doing to him what he was doing to her. She just wanted this to go on and on.

And for a moment, it did.

Time seemed to stand still as the sensation swelled and continued.

And then she fell back, exhausted and spent beyond words. Or so she thought.

The next moment, Sam began to move his heated body along hers. Tantalizing her.

Her heart was already pounding hard enough to break through her rib cage. But when she felt him enter her, it sped up even more, beating double-time. The confinements of exhaustion fell away from her.

Riley wrapped her legs around his torso, the rhythm of her body echoing his as the pace heightened. Their movement became increasingly more frantic. She felt Sam wrap his arms about her, holding her to him as if he intended to absorb her wholly into himself.

That excited her. Everything *about* this man and the magic he wove excited her.

She held on tightly, desperate to keep pace, wanting to feel exactly what he felt at the final moment of impact.

And then it happened.

She reached the peak of the summit with him, felt the fireworks showering around her and prayed that somehow, it could go on forever. And even though it didn't, even though she could feel the euphoria recede, the sense of contentment that overshadowed the wonder remained with her for far longer than she'd anticipated.

Gladdening her heart.

As she caught her breath, Riley went on holding him to her. Went on savoring everything about the coupling that had taken her by such storm. Slowly, ever so slowly, her breathing evened out.

This had to be what a person felt like when they were struck by lightning, Sam thought, his body still tingling all over. He struggled to get some kind of a grip on himself.

He succeeded only moderately.

Afraid of crushing Riley, he slowly slid off, moving to her side. He was surprised when she turned her body into his. Surprised and pleased more than words could possibly express.

He smiled into her eyes as he closed his arms around her and held her to him.

"You're full of surprises, McIntyre," he said, whispering the words against her hair.

McIntyre.

Not "Riley" but "McIntyre." Was he trying to distance himself from what had just happened? Now that they had made love, did he want to reestablish the boundaries of their ongoing relationship? Did this make her sad, or provide her with the safety net she so badly needed?

Damn, but nothing made sense right now. She couldn't think, couldn't see her way clearly to any one sentiment yet.

"I like keeping you on your toes," she finally answered. She felt him laugh and the sound rumbled against her chest. She turned her head to look at him. "What?"

Amusement curved the corners of his mouth. "Let's just say it wasn't my toes that were being called into action."

She could almost feel his smile against her hair, against her forehead. "Sorry, anatomy wasn't my best subject in school."

He trailed his fingertips along her curves, stroking her ever so slowly. Excitement began to vibrate between them. "I would have never guessed. You seemed pretty knowledgeable to me."

"Smoke and mirrors," she quipped, though it was beginning to take considerable effort to remain focused on what he was saying.

"Felt a little more solid than smoke to me," he told her.

She raised her head to look at him. She'd always disliked women who insisted on having a relationship mapped out for them at every conceivable turn. But Sam *was* her partner and she was pretty sure that they had just violated at least several very basic ground rules.

"Is what just happened going to get in our way?" she asked.

He was quiet for a moment, as if considering what she'd just asked from all possible angles. "Well, that depends."

Her eyes never left his face. She'd looked at him countless times. So why did she suddenly feel this on-rush of heat, of excitement? How had the dynamics between them changed so much?

"On?" she asked.

Sam ran the back of his hand along her cheek. Wanting her. "On whether or not we stop to do this when we're supposed to be going after the bad guy."

"Seriously," Riley pressed.

Humor played along his mouth. "What makes you think I wasn't being serious?" Pulling her to him so that her body was suddenly on top of his, Sam stroked the sides of her torso. Watching in fascination as he saw desire flaring in her eyes. "I was deadly serious," he told her, raising his head to capture her lips again.

Instantly undone, she didn't press the subject again for a good long while. It amazed her that she could be so hungry so fast after feasting for so long.

But she was.

Chapter 13

It didn't take long.

Another home invasion occurred Wednesday, four days later. The invasion had all the earmarks of the other three cases. The thieves entered the house without having to resort to force despite the fact that, according to the frightened homeowners, every single window in the house was closed and locked, as were the front and back doors.

The inhabitants, this time a couple in their early seventies, had been in bed, asleep, like all the other victims. They'd been rousted, dragged from their bed, tied up and then chloroformed while their home was ransacked.

"There's got to be a common element here, there has to be. What is it that we're missing?" Riley demanded for the umpteenth time, pacing in front of the bulletin board where they had religiously tacked up all the available information on each invasion.

"A lot of sleep," Sam murmured. He sat at his desk, his chair turned around so that he faced the bulletin board. Nothing seemed to stand out to him either.

The tone of his voice wedged itself into her admittedly scattered thoughts. Riley turned looked at her partner.

Afraid that Saturday night would change things between them, she could have saved herself the trouble of worrying. The following Monday, when she came into work, Sam had behaved as if it was business as usual, making absolutely no mention of what had transpired between them. Taking her partner's cue, relieved and yet not so relieved, Riley had done the same. And continued to do so.

But occasionally, she'd catch Sam watching her, an unreadable expression on his face.

Or maybe that was just wishful thinking on her part— or her pride. After all, what woman wanted to believe that she was forgettable or could be so easily dismissed?

She hadn't exactly expected Sam to sweep her into his arms when she walked into the squad room, but a random private word or two, a secret, intimate glance, wouldn't have been entirely out of order. After all, she was fairly certain that the sheets on his bed had gotten really scorched Saturday night before she, exhausted, had elected to go home rather than come up with an excuse for Lisa in the morning as to why she was still there in the clothes she'd worn the day before.

"You losing sleep over this, Wyatt?" Riley asked archly.

"This among other things," he answered. And then he lowered his voice before continuing. "Lisa wants to know when you're coming over."

"Lisa," she repeated.

Was he being straightforward and just relaying his daughter's question, or was he using his daughter as a shill to cover up the fact that *he* wanted to know when she was coming over?

God, when did things suddenly become this complicated?

"Yeah, Lisa." His expression continued to be unreadable. "You remember, short little thing." He held his hand up approximately three and a half feet from the floor. "Talks like an old person even though she's only six." He paused, as if debating whether or not to say the next thing. "She wants to know if I did something to make you stop coming over. I told her I didn't think so, but she's not convinced." His eyes held hers, pregnant with things that weren't being said. "Did I?"

"No." She cleared her throat, wondering where this sudden case of nerves came from. Nerves neatly wrapped around a ray of sunshine. "Then I guess I'll have to come over." This time, she was the one looking into his eyes. "If Lisa wants to see me."

He glanced away, back at the bulletin board. Sam tilted his chair. "Yeah, she does."

"If you two are finished talking about your social agenda," Barker bit off, suddenly materializing behind them, "maybe one of you can tell me how the investigation's coming along?"

The lieutenant's dark brown eyes shifted from Sam to her.

That proved it, Riley thought. The man was the devil. "Which one?" she asked him politely.

"All of them," he growled.

Sam rose from his chair, moving so that his body was between Barker and Riley.

"The Hayworths kept to themselves for the most part," Sam told the lieutenant. "According to the descriptions they gave the first officer on the scene and then again to us, the two robbers were the same ones who robbed the other three houses. As far as McIntyre and I can see, this new couple has almost nothing in common with the other victims." Before Barker could comment, Sam enumerated. "They all drive different cars, have different careers—the Hayworths are retired," he inserted. "Move in different circles."

Barker was in no mood to play review. "Yeah, yeah, I've heard it all before and I don't want to hear it again," he snapped. "I also don't want to hear any more excuses. The next thing I want to hear is that you've cracked the case." His eyes swept over Sam and Riley, then took in the two detectives sitting closest to them, Sung and Allen. His manner was clear. As far as he was concerned, the whole department was responsible for this less-than-stellar performance. "Do I make myself clear?"

"Absolutely," Riley replied with the kind of cheerful enthusiasm she knew annoyed Barker and got under the man's skin.

The lieutenant's dark brown eyes grew even darker

as he narrowed them to focus only on her. "As long as we understand each other."

With that, the former marine turned on his well-worn heel and stalked back into his glass office. The blinds remained opened so that nothing would escape his attention.

"He makes Darth Vader come off like Pollyanna," Riley commented, keeping her voice low even though Barker had closed his door. She'd turned her back to the man's office. Barker was ornery enough to have learned how to read lips. "By the way, you didn't have to run interference for me," she told Sam. "I can take care of myself."

"Haven't the slightest idea what you're talking about, McIntyre," Sam said, his expression giving nothing away. He took his jacket off the back of his chair and threw it on. "C'mon, let's see if we can get the Hayworths to remember what they did in the last forty-eight hours." He saw the puzzled expression on her face and explained. "Maybe we'll get lucky and that'll give us the clue we need to solve this damn thing."

"I had no idea you were an optimist," she commented, grabbing her purse. She hurried after him.

Sam considered her remark as they walked out. "Must be the company I keep," he decided.

Riley smiled in response.

They tracked Professor Cahil to his office at the college.

"You again?" the professor groaned as he looked up to see who was coming into his office. Biting off an oath, Cahil set aside the less-than-engrossing term paper he was reading. "Aren't you people out of questions yet?" he asked, exasperated.

"Just a few more, Professor. It'll be painless and we'll be out of your hair before you know it," Riley promised.

The professor seemed less than convinced. "Not soon enough to suit me," he assured the two detectives. "Well, sit down." He gestured to the two chairs before his desk. "We might as well get this over with."

Sam waited for Riley to take a seat before he sat down in his. "Can you tell us what you did the two days before the robbers came into your house?"

Suspicion narrowed the professor's gaze. "Why?" he challenged.

This time Riley ran interference. "We're trying to see if you and the other victims might have all done the same thing."

Cahil had an air about him that said he didn't consider himself to be like anyone else. That would have been too common. "Like what?"

"That's just it," Sam interjected. "We don't know."

Contempt flared in the professor's expression. "There isn't a hell of a whole lot you people do know, is there?"

"We know uncooperative people when we talk to them," Riley said simply. She moved forward in her chair. "Now, you don't like being a victim, we get it. And I'm sorry if we're bothering you, Professor, but we're doing our best to recover your property. But to make any headway, we need your help. Yours and the other people who were robbed.

"We're working under the assumption that there's

some common thread, something that you all did, that pulls this together." Her tone was polite, but firm as she said, "Now if you could please just go over the two days before the robbery in as much detail as possible, we would greatly appreciate it." She looked at Cahil, waiting.

"Very well."

Sighing, the professor closed his eyes. To the best of his ability, he began to summon back the two days in question.

"You're pretty persuasive when you want to be," Sam commented as they left the professor's office less than twenty minutes later and walked through the visitor parking lot just beyond the criminology department's three-story building.

Riley grinned. "As the next to the youngest of four, I found being persuasive rather essential to my survival." She waited for Sam to unlock the doors, then got into the car. "Two down, two more to go."

"Can't say I'm feeling too hopeful," he admitted, putting the key into the ignition and turning it. The car started. "So far, beyond the essentials of eating and doing a few basic things involved with getting ready to face the day, the professor's two days don't sound as if they have anything in common with the Hayworths' two days."

"Keep the faith, Wyatt," she urged as they backtracked their way off the campus. "The day is still young."

He blew out a breath as he just missed a light that would have allowed him to get onto the main thoroughfare. Where was all this impatience coming from? "Yeah, but I feel like I'm getting older by the minute."

She smiled at him. "You'll feel young again once we make a breakthrough."

But they didn't and consequently, he didn't.

The case began to wear on Sam. Riley was right, they were missing something in plain sight and it frustrated the hell out of him.

Once they were finished taking information from the Marstons and the Wilsons, it was time to clock out for the day.

True to her word, Riley followed him to Brenda's house where they picked up Lisa. The little girl was nothing short of overjoyed when she saw Riley. The second she did, Lisa ran up to her and, standing on her toes, she wrapped her small arms around Riley. Lisa held on tightly and had to be coaxed to let go, which she did only after Riley promised to come over.

A warm feeling spread through Riley as she caught a glimpse of the three of them in Brenda's hall mirror when they were leaving the house.

They looked like a real family, she thought.

She'd never thought of herself in those terms before. Never really thought about being a wife *or* a mother. But now, there it suddenly was, front and center. And the idea had a charm and a pull that was very difficult to ignore.

Too bad, Riley thought as she adjusted the straps on Lisa's car seat, that it was never going to happen.

* * *

A pattern began to form. A pattern Riley knew she could easily get accustomed to and one that she was equally aware that she *shouldn't* allow.

It was happening anyway.

By day, she and Wyatt were professional partners, working feverishly to handle all the cases they caught while still seeking that one breakthrough. They needed to solve what had become a major obsession with the news media: the home invasion robberies.

And then, most nights, they were lovers, burning away the edges of the night until it was time for her to finally go back to her house.

Every time she did, she would find Howard waiting up for her like a doting grandfather, an indulgent, knowing expression on his face.

"So how's it going?" the retired engineer asked after another three weeks had passed.

"The case?" she responded.

He waved his hand at that. "I know you can't talk about an ongoing case—Egan taught me that," his voice swelling with pride the way it always did whenever he mentioned his late son. "And everything else I want to know about them is plastered all over the news anytime I want to catch up. No, I'm asking how's it going with you and that young man you've been keeping company with?"

Keeping company with. What a lovely, old-fashioned term for what she and Wyatt did together. Four weeks since the first time and the lovemaking was only getting better. Hotter. If it became any more so, she would need the fire department on standby.

"What makes you think I'm 'keeping company' with anyone?"

"You've got the same glow my Katie did when we were," and here he cleared his throat, whether because he needed to or by design wasn't evident, "keeping company. Is it that partner of yours?" he asked, then smiled. "It is, isn't it? Nice-looking boy," he said with a nod. "Hair's a little long for my taste, but he seems all right otherwise. He treating you well?" Howard asked.

"Howard, I think you've just exceeded your allotment of questions."

"Because if he isn't," Howard continued as she walked up her driveway toward her front door, "you just send him on to me and I'll set him straight."

It was hard not to laugh, given that the man had the body of a large Halloween skeleton, but she wouldn't have hurt Howard's feelings for the world. "Good night, Howard," she called out.

"Good night, Riley. Sleep tight."

Sleep fast, she corrected silently, because there weren't all that many hours left until daylight and her shift arrived.

But as well intentioned as Howard's concern was, it stirred up some questions that hovered in the back of her mind, questions she would have rather put off. Questions she knew she had to face eventually.

This "thing" with her and Wyatt wasn't a fling anymore, or just a flirtation that had temporarily deepened and she knew it. It had become so much more. She was attached to Lisa and, what was worse, she realized she was falling in love with Wyatt.

What falling? she silently jeered as she got ready for work the following day. She'd already fallen for the man, hook, line and sinker. For better or for worse, she was there, treading through No Man's Land, most likely alone because even as she felt the words "I love you" bubbling up in her throat, threatening to come spilling out of her mouth, she was almost certain those same words would not be echoed back to her.

Except maybe out of a sense of guilt.

No, Wyatt wasn't the type to do anything because he felt guilty. There wasn't even a token "I love you" in her future and she knew it.

Riley sighed. She needed to put a stop to this romance, to back away before she couldn't. But even as she gave herself the pep talk, she knew it would be more than difficult to end things between them. Still, she knew she had to make a concerted effort.

So much easier said than done.

Even as she tried, she found herself blocked at every turn. Each time she wanted to offer an excuse, to say no, that she couldn't go with him to pick up Lisa, the words never emerged.

Instead, she said, "Sure," and went along, basking in the bright light she saw in Lisa's eyes every time the little girl saw her.

After that, staying for dinner was a given. Besides,

there were cooking lessons involved. She wasn't even sure how it started, but somehow she gave Lisa simple cooking lessons and the two of them would prepare dinner together.

That had to stop, too.

Soon.

This time, on the trip home, Lisa was fairly bursting with news, but she kept it in until they walked into the apartment.

"Tonight," Lisa declared the moment the door was closed, "you don't have to cook, Riley. We're having pizza. My treat," she declared proudly, beaming.

"How is this going to be your treat?" Riley asked, looking toward Wyatt. But he indicated that his lips were sealed.

"I get an allowance," Lisa informed her with a little toss of her head. "Daddy gives me money and I saved it up, so this is my treat," she repeated, her eyes dancing with glee.

Riley exchanged looks with Sam. Lisa had just called him Daddy. Not Sam, but Daddy. Was this the first time? One glance at the surprised expression on his face gave her the answer. She had intended to begin the weaning process tonight, begging off from dinner and then, within a few days, from the ritual of picking Lisa up at Brenda's. But how could she say no after this? Lisa had just called Wyatt something other than his given name and offered to pay for the dinner with her own money. Turning the little girl down would be heartbreaking. For both of them.

So she said yes and she stayed.

But Riley promised herself that the moment the little girl was tucked into bed, she was going home. Tonight, there would be no lovemaking, no getting lost in Sam's arms. Tonight was going to be the beginning of the rest of her life. Without Sam.

Much as she didn't want to, Riley knew she had to take a stand somewhere. And this was somewhere.

Bedtime came all too quickly. She followed the ritual, getting Lisa ready for bed, then reading to her. She'd stumbled a few times. The lump in her throat kept getting in the way. But finally, Lisa drifted off to sleep.

The moment she did, Riley crept out of Lisa's room. She made her way to the living room. Expecting to see Sam, she was relieved when she didn't. Grabbing her purse, she quickly made her way to the front door.

"Where are you going?"

She froze when she heard his voice behind her. Without turning around, she answered, "I've got to go home."

Walking around to face her, Sam took the purse from her hand. That smile that always burrowed into the pit of her stomach, creating a squadron of butterflies, was on his lips. "No, you don't."

Telling herself to be strong, Riley reclaimed her purse, pulling it out of his hand. "Yes, I do," she insisted.

The teasing expression on his face faded. Concern entered his eyes as he searched her face. "Something wrong?"

"No. Yes." Damn, why did he always make her feel so tongue-tied? No one else ever did.

A hint of steely amusement curved his lips. "I didn't realize I asked a multiple-choice question."

"You didn't." Sighing, she tried again. "Look, this has been great—"

Has been. As in the past. Something *was* wrong. Sam braced himself. "But?"

Taking another breath didn't help. The ache she felt kept growing. "But it has to stop."

He wanted to grab hold of her shoulders and shake some sense into her head. It took extreme restraint just to stand there and ask, "Why?"

Such a simple word, so fraught with intense repercussions. "Because it's not going anywhere."

Was she pressing him for a commitment? Or trying to find a way out? Or was she just testing him? "Why does it have to 'go' somewhere? Why can't it just be?" he asked. "Sometimes things just have to remain the way they are in order to go forward later."

"Later" was a vague word that kept company with "never." This had to stop now, before the disappointment got too big for her to handle.

"Maybe," she allowed, letting him think she might agree with him. "But right now, I need to sort things out, think them through."

He would never force her to do anything she didn't want to do, be anywhere she didn't want to be. But letting her walk away, even for an evening, wasn't easy. "All right," he finally said. "If that's what you want."

No, that wasn't what she wanted. She wanted him. And Lisa. She knew that wasn't going to happen, not in the way she needed it to. Squaring her shoulders, she murmured, "I'll see you tomorrow."

As she put her hand on the doorknob, he asked, "No goodbye kiss?"

She looked at him over her shoulder, still holding onto the doorknob, as if that could somehow ground her. "If I kiss you goodbye, I won't leave."

"Sure you will." Sam turned her around and drew her into his arms. "You're stronger than that."

But she wasn't.

Chapter 14

Sam Wyatt was a dirty fighter. There was no other way to view what had happened but that, Riley thought several hours later when she finally got into her car and drove home. Once Wyatt kissed her, it was all over.

She and Sam made love. But even though every fiber of her being wanted to remain, locked tightly in his arms, she forced herself to leave after only a heavenly two hours had gone by. The earliest she'd left his apartment since they had begun sleeping together—or not sleeping together as the case was.

She should have been stronger than that, Riley upbraided herself. She *used* to be stronger than that. What was wrong with her?

Tomorrow, Riley solemnly swore. Tomorrow she

was going to be stronger. Tomorrow she'd leave right after Lisa went to bed, no wavering, no second thoughts, no side glances at Wyatt that only undermined her resolve. She'd make Wyatt read the bedtime story to his daughter instead of her and then slip out while he was busy.

It sounded like a plan.

Well, she tried to console herself, at least Howard would get to bed earlier tonight. Howard. Funny how her eccentric neighbor had taken her under his wing like that, appointing himself her guardian angel. Lately it seemed like most of their exchanges took place just before she walked into her house.

She would invite him next time the chief held another party at his place. With work—and Sam—taking up so much of her time, she'd gotten out of the habit of extending invitations to the older man. She needed to remedy that, remembering how difficult it had been the first time around. Riley turned off the main drag and into her development. For the most part, despite his apparent adoption of her, the retired engineer liked to keep to himself. In the three years she'd lived next door to him, she'd only seen one visitor enter the house and that had been his other son, Ethan, visiting from back east.

As she approached Howard's house, she saw that, as usual, he'd left his porch light on. Riley smiled. A beacon on the runway to guide her home, she mused.

She began to slow down to almost a crawl, giving Howard a chance to get up from the window seat where he had kept vigil lately and open the front door.

But the front door didn't move.

Odd. Howard never failed to come out, even that time he was fighting a cold. It was as if all the pieces of his world weren't in place until he bid her good-night and saw her go into her own place.

Pulling up into her driveway, Riley turned off her ignition and waited a moment before getting out. There was still no movement at the other house.

Maybe Howard had finally decided she was a big girl, Riley thought with a smile. Or gotten what his son had called his obsessive-compulsive disorder under control. Whatever the reason, it didn't look as if she'd be saying good-night to him tonight.

Key in hand, Riley was about to insert it into her door when she sighed, pocketed the key and doubled back down the front path. Moving around the plum tree that separated their two properties, she walked up to Howard's porch.

Something wasn't right, she could feel it. Howard wouldn't just leave the porch light on and go to bed. It wasn't like him. Though leaving an outside light on was considered a deterrent against amateur burglars, she knew that Howard stubbornly considered it a flagrant waste of electricity and money.

When ringing the doorbell twice got no response, Riley knocked on the man's door. Hard. Head cocked, she listened intently for the familiar shuffling sound that meant he was approaching.

Nothing.

"Howard?" she called out, knocking again. Her uneasiness growing, Riley tried the doorknob. It gave under her hand.

Howard *never* left his door unlocked.

Training had Riley pulling out her service weapon and taking off the safety.

"Howard?" she called again, slowly pushing open the door. Light not just from the porch but from the city street light that was situated directly behind Howard's mailbox illuminated the dark living room. It took her a moment to focus.

Riley's heart slammed into her chest the second she saw the slumped figure on the floor. Howard was tied to a dining room chair and the chair was over on its side. Howard's mouth, arms and legs were bound tightly with duct tape.

The home invaders had been here, right here, on her home territory!

Riley felt sick to the bottom of her stomach and incredibly violated.

Her first impulse was to untie Howard, to remain with him and assure herself that he was all right. But the cop in her knew that she needed to clear the area first because if the robbers were still here, it could go badly for her, not to mention Howard.

They didn't kill their victims, she silently insisted, trying to comfort herself as she began to sweep through the rooms. Moving as quickly as she could and exercising just the barest minimum of caution, Riley swiftly swept through the rooms as best she could. It was harder than she'd expected.

Howard had done some really heavy-duty collecting since he'd last had her over, she noted. Books of all kinds, magazines, record albums were piled from floor to ceiling in several of the rooms, challenging anyone to get through or even access certain areas. The man was a serious pack rat—and she prayed that he would be able to spend a great many more years feeding his compulsion.

Done, Riley hurried back to her neighbor, pausing only in the kitchen to get a pair of scissors out of his utility drawer.

That, too, proved to be a challenge. All sorts of things were jammed into the drawer, as well as all the other drawers. Howard had never come across anything he wanted to throw out.

Finally finding the scissors, Riley rushed back into the living room. Dropping to her knees, she carefully began to cut apart the duct tape wound around him as tightly as a cocoon.

She was only halfway through when Howard groaned, sounding like a man struggling to wake up from a bad dream. There was the distinct odor of chloroform about him.

The irony of the situation was appalling to Riley. There she and Wyatt were, methodically trying to track down the home invaders and meanwhile, the larcenous duo had struck right under her nose. The worse part of it was that it had happened while she and Wyatt were busy making love.

But if she'd come home earlier, the invaders might not have struck yet and she'd have gone to bed, she realized. She wouldn't have known anything was wrong until the following night. She hardly even saw Howard before she left in the morning.

Something about the scenario didn't feel right, but she wasn't sure what it was.

Removing the last of the tape, she sat back on her heels, waiting for Howard to come around. His breathing was normal, and when she pressed her fingers to his throat, she found that his heart rate was only slightly elevated. At least the bastards hadn't given him a heart attack.

She placed a call to the firehouse located three miles from her development. After identifying herself and giving her shield number, she asked the person on the other end of the line to send a couple of paramedics over. She wanted them to check out Howard just in case.

And then she called Wyatt.

"You're sure they were the same ones?" Sam asked half an hour later. He'd just left Lisa, along with his apologies, at Brenda and Dax's house. The couple had assured him that there was nothing to apologize for, they understood the erratic life police detectives were forced to lead. Now that he was here, Sam could hardly believe what Riley was telling him.

The paramedics had arrived five minutes after she'd placed her call to them and, despite Howard's protests, had checked out the man from top to bottom. Except for the bump on his head, sustained when the chair was knocked over, the only thing that was wounded was Howard's pride.

"I should have been able to fight them off," he complained to Riley as the paramedics withdrew. "I placed second in my weight class at the gym."

Riley had heard the story more than once. "No disrespect intended, Howard," she said softly, gently rubbing her hand along his back, trying to soothe away his agitation, "but you did tell me that was almost fifty years ago."

And then it suddenly hit her. Riley realized what had been bothering her since she'd come on the scene to find him unconscious and bound to the chair. "Wait a minute, were you in bed?"

"No." He tried to rise to his feet from the sofa but his legs were a little wobbly. He sank back down again just as Wyatt and Riley reached out to catch him. "I was waiting up for you. Like always."

Wyatt looked to Riley for elaboration.

"Howard likes to make sure I get home in one piece," she told him. "He's my self-appointed guardian angel. Long story," she added before turning her attention back to her neighbor. "But if you weren't in bed—why would they have come in? They *always* come in when their victims are in bed."

"Did you have the lights on in the house?" Sam asked the man.

"No, why waste it?" Howard asked defensively. "It's not like I'm reading."

It still didn't make any sense to Riley. "But they would have seen you—and you would have seen them if you were by the window."

His cheeks turned a slight shade of pink. "I had to go to the bathroom," Howard mumbled. "They jumped me right when I came out," he accused, then shook his head. "I dunno who was more surprised, them or me. It looked like they were on their way to the staircase when I opened the bathroom door. Next thing I knew, the tall one was grabbing my arms, pinning them behind my back and the little guy started punching me. Dunno what *they* were afraid of since I couldn't use my hands."

She winced as she envisioned the scene. She could almost feel the blows, but this wasn't the time to be emotional. She had to be a detective first, not Howard's friend. This could be the break they'd been looking for. "Howard, this is very important, did you recognize either of them?"

"How could I?" he protested. "They were dressed in black with ski masks on."

She shook her head. "No, I mean was there something familiar about the way they moved, the way they talked? Was there anything unique to set them apart in your mind? A smell, perhaps. Did either of them call the other by a name?"

At each suggestion, Howard shook his head. Until she mentioned smell. "The little guy smelled like garlic," he told her. "And …"

That was what one of the other couples had said, she thought, suddenly excited. "And?" she coaxed.

"The tall, skinny one kept dropping his Gs. He sounded a little like that valet."

Sam and Riley exchanged glances. "What valet?" Sam asked.

"That one at that place—" Howard looked frustrated as he tried to summon the right words.

"Which one at what place, Howard?" Riley pressed gently.

Howard closed his eyes for a moment, regrouping.

All around them were members of the crime scene investigation unit, methodically going about their business, trying to piece together physical evidence. Riley heard one of the men complaining to the woman in charge that he'd almost gotten attacked by a tall stack of books. The stack, one of dozens, that had dislodged when he'd opened the door leading into the room.

"Ethan was here last week," Howard told her.

"I remember."

"Ethan?" Sam looked from Howard to her. "Who's Ethan?"

"His son," Riley said, not taking her eyes off Howard. "Go on."

"Ethan's a doctor," Howard tagged on. "He insisted on taking me to this fancy restaurant." He snorted his disapproval. "I used to get weekly paychecks that were smaller than what these people charged for a meal, but Ethan insisted we go there, said he was paying. So I said I'd drive."

That meant that they had driven to the restaurant in Howard's secondhand Mercedes. He babied that car, kept it in prime condition. Sundays would find him polishing and waxing the vehicle until it was almost blinding to look at.

Alarms went off in Riley's head.

One slanted glance toward Wyatt told her they were having a mutual epiphany.

"And you left your keys with the valet," Wyatt said out loud.

Obviously confused, Howard looked from Riley to her partner. "How else was he going to park my car?"

"Is your house key on the same key chain as your car key?" Riley asked him, doing her best not to raise her voice or allow the building excitement she felt to surface.

Again, Howard seemed puzzled. "I've only got the two keys," he told her. "Why should I keep them on separate key chains? It's easier to lose one of them that way," he pointed out.

Everything fell into place.

Oh, God, could it really be as simple as that? The valets had access to the keys and to the client's address because registrations were required to be kept in the glove compartment of each car on the road. All the valet needed to do was to copy down the address and make an impression of the house key. When his shift was over, he could take the impression to a locksmith who might be bribed to look the other way and have made a key.

Or who knows, maybe the valet could make the keys himself, Riley speculated. Once the valet made a copy of the key, he and his partner could drive to the address, case out the house and its surrounding neighborhood with a minimum of danger to see if a break-in would be profitable.

Wyatt knew what Riley was thinking. But he had a basic problem with the theory. "If the thieves have a copy of the key, why wouldn't they just break into the house during the day when everyone's gone?"

It was the simplest way to go, but simple didn't always mean best. "Because there's always a chance that someone might be in the house," she guessed. "Doing it at night fairly assures them that everyone's asleep so they can get the upper hand. Besides, I don't think it's just about the robbery."

"Then what?" Wyatt wanted to know.

"I think it's a power trip. The people they rob have things, can afford to go to fancy restaurants, are most likely better off than our thieves. To them, it's 'anything you've got, I can take away,' that sort of thing."

Riley turned to look at her neighbor. Saying her theory out loud had gelled it for her. She threw her arms around him and hugged Howard as gently as she could, trying not to let her enthusiasm get the better of her.

"Oh, Howard, I think you just might have solved the crime for us."

Howard looked almost bashful. "Glad I wasn't banged around for nothing," he mumbled.

Riley laughed and pressed a kiss to the large bare expanse just above his forehead.

"I'm just glad you're all right. I'll be right back," she promised, getting up. Moving to the far end of the living room, she took out her cell phone.

Wyatt followed her. "Who are you calling?"

About to press a number on the cell's keypad, she stopped for a second. "I'm going to see if our other victims ever went to The Crown Jewels Restaurant."

He glanced at his watch. It was now close to eleven o'clock. "Isn't it a little late to be calling?" he pointed out.

"Justice never sleeps." Riley pressed a single button and the phone on the other end of the line began to ring.

"You've got them on speed dial?" he asked.

"Sure. Just until the cases are solved. Why, don't you?" she asked.

But before Wyatt could answer, she held up her finger, asking for silence. She heard someone come on the line.

"Four out of five is a pretty good track record," Riley declared some twenty minutes later. She, Wyatt and Howard had adjourned to the kitchen to keep out of the crime scene investigators' way as she made the rest of her calls. "Everyone but the Marstons remember going to The Crown Jewels Restaurant some time before they were robbed."

"I'm sure they enjoyed going down memory lane with you at almost midnight," Sam commented.

"I doubt if any of them are heavy sleepers anymore," she answered. "And maybe they'll sleep better once we get the bad guys."

"But *are* they the bad guys if the Marstons never went to The Crown Jewels?" Sam asked. "Their home invasion was exactly like the others and we'd need a hundred percent match in order to establish—" Sam didn't get a chance to finish.

Riley's cell phone rang.

Flipping it open again, she put it against her ear. "McIntyre. Yes. What? Oh. Okay." Sam saw a radiant smile blooming on her lips. "Well, thank you for calling back, Mr. Marston. Yes, yes, that was extremely helpful. And yes, I would ground him if I were you. Uh-huh. I promise I'll let you know the second we find out. Goodbye."

"What's extremely helpful and who are you grounding?" Sam asked the second she flipped the cell phone closed again.

"You look like the cat that ate the canary," Howard observed, curiosity getting the better of him, as well.

Excitement vibrated in Riley's voice as she filled in Sam and Howard about the home invaders' other victim. "Mr. and Mrs. Marston didn't go to The Crown Jewels Restaurant, but it seems that their son took his dad's credit card and his girl there. Junior overheard the conversation and just confessed."

Howard shook his head. "Teenagers. Absolutely no respect for money these days."

"Not to mention that if he hadn't taken his girl there, his parents wouldn't have been targeted by the home invaders. He's probably going to be grounded until he collects social security," she commented just before clapping her hands together. "Okay, now we're batting a thousand. What do you say you and I have a late lunch at The Crown Jewels tomorrow? We'll use my car."

It seemed like the way to go. Except for one thing. "Why your car?" Sam asked.

"Elementary, my dear Watson. Your registration will tell them that you live in an apartment. These people only rob houses."

He conceded the point, but there was a larger one to consider. "This is a long shot, you know. There's no guarantee that they'll take the bait. I mean, they have to park hundreds of cars during the week."

"That's why I'm going to ask to borrow that rock that the chief gave Rose for their last anniversary. That, and a few other 'trinkets' from the family should do it. If I sparkle enough," she looked at Sam and batted her eyelashes, "I'm sure I'll move right up to the top of their list."

It crossed Sam's mind that Riley sparkled enough without any jewelry, but, since they weren't alone, he decided to keep that to himself.

Chapter 15

"I know you want to keep your neighbor out of this if possible, but I think we should bring those valets in for questioning. This plan of yours just isn't working," Sam told Riley.

He was sitting in his car, parked down the block and across the street from her house and talking to her via his cell phone. His muscles felt cramped and he was going just a little stir crazy.

As she sat in the dark in her living room, Riley hoped that the sight of her house locked down for the night would give the home invaders the go-ahead signal. So far, nothing had happened.

Though she didn't want to, she was beginning to agree with her partner. She and Wyatt had been at this for almost two straight weeks now with no success. Night after night went by and still no sign of the home invaders.

She'd thought for certain that flashing her borrowed jewelry would be a definite come-on to the robbers. That and the fact that when the valet had brought back her car, she'd loudly refused, as they'd previously agreed, to allow Wyatt to give the man a generous tip.

"You don't need to give him that big tip," she'd admonished. "For heaven's sake, it's not like he had to fight off some roving gang of bikers to bring the car to us. He just drove the thing around the corner. Honestly, Sam, you're just too generous for your own good."

If looks could kill, Riley would have been dead on the spot. The glare the valet had given her would have cut her to ribbons.

Maybe it had been the wrong valet. But he'd been tall and thin and looked exactly as Howard had described him. Besides, the valet dropped his Gs, just the way Howard had remembered.

Riley sighed into her phone. "You're probably right. This is getting us nowhere." For all she knew, they were still at square one, except she had a gut feeling that she was right: valets operating at The Crown Jewels Restaurant were behind the robberies. Nothing else made sense to her. "Go home to Lisa."

"Will do. Good night, partner," Sam said, flipping his phone closed.

He tossed the phone onto the seat next to him. The seat Riley ordinarily occupied. This surveillance cut into not just the time he spent with his daughter, but the time he spent with Riley, as well. They hadn't gotten together intimately since this surveillance began and he missed her. Missed being with her. Missed the scent of her skin, the feel of her body against his. He missed the sound of her breath growing erratic as they came together, pleasuring one another.

He'd never felt this way about a woman before, not to this extent and not for this long. He'd certainly never caught himself longing for a woman the way he longed for Riley.

This was all new to him and confusing as hell.

Or maybe not so confusing, just scary, he amended, because, like it or not, he felt vulnerable.

Sam glanced at his watch. He knew Riley was right, he should be getting home. For the last few days, Riley's mother had volunteered to stay with the little girl so that Lisa could sleep in her own bed and not have her routine constantly disrupted.

Six months ago if anyone would have told him that the Chief of Detectives' wife would be babysitting for his daughter and that he would be physically—and emotionally—involved with the chief's stepdaughter, he would have laughed until gasping for breath. He'd had no daughter and he just wasn't the lasting kind. Women came and went in his life like the seasons back east, one fading away just as another came along.

What a difference half a year made, he mused.

Maybe he'd wait just a little longer, Sam decided. He didn't want to leave too early, just in case…

Forty-five minutes later, tired, Sam called it a night.

There was no point in doing this, he thought. The robbers weren't coming. He needed to go before he was too exhausted to drive and fell asleep at the wheel.

Putting his key into the ignition, he turned it on. The car quietly came to life. Going up the next driveway, he turned his car around and began to drive down the street that eventually led out of the development.

It was late and hardly any vehicles were on the road. Anyone with an ounce of sense was home. Where he needed to be.

Even though it hardly felt like home without Riley there.

Don't start in, just get home, Sam silently lectured himself.

Coming to the edge of the development, he passed a car heading in. Sam pressed his lips together to stifle a yawn. Damn, but he was tired.

Riley bolted upright.

Was that a noise, or just an overly realistic dream spilling out into her awakened state?

She listened intently, trying to decide.

Leaving her living room, at the last minute she'd left a pile of books right by the front door—just in case. If someone came in, they'd knock the books over when they opened the door.

That was what she'd heard, the books being knocked over. She was sure of it.

Her heart pounding, Riley grabbed the telephone receiver to call for backup.

There was no dial tone.

The line was dead.

And she'd left her cell phone downstairs.

Thank God she hadn't put her service revolver away in its usual place, she thought. Instead, she'd brought it to her bedroom and placed it on the nightstand. She put her hand on it now for reassurance.

Slipping quickly out of bed, she made to the doorway as quietly as possible. Holding her breath, she crept to the hallway.

Someone from the left grabbed her by the waist, pulling her so hard, he all but knocked the air out of her. The gun was wrenched out of her hand.

And then there was this awful pain in the back of her head. He'd hit her with something hard.

Riley struggled to keep from fading into the darkness that grabbed her. Instead of fighting back, she pretended to be limp, hoping that the home invader would drop his guard.

Whoever had hit her was carrying her down the stairs. And then she felt herself being roughly deposited onto a chair. It was now or never. She knew what came next. Duct taping her to the chair. The second she made contact with the seat, she leaped up, grappling with her assailant.

She'd caught him off guard. But not his partner. Behind her Riley heard a gun being cocked.

"I wouldn't do that if I were you, bitch," a raspy voice warned.

"Good advice. I suggest you follow it."

A split second earlier, the unlocked door had slammed against the opposite wall. Riley whirled around and saw that Sam had his gun out and pointed toward the robber with the gun on her.

Some kind of inner instinct had her envisioning the next move. The shorter of the two men spun around, his gun still in hand, except that this time, the weapon was pointed toward Sam.

His eyes looked crazy enough for him to use it.

With a guttural scream, Riley launched herself at the man with the gun, grabbing his arm and trying to point it up in the air. The distinct odor of garlic assaulted her nose. The gun discharged, the bullet going wild and hitting the overhead chandelier just as the sound of sirens filled the air.

Backup, she thought, a tidal wave of relief washing over her. Sam had called for backup. God love 'im.

"I give up, man, I give up!" the taller of the two cried, raising his hands in the air. They were trembling. "I don't have a gun. The gun's Jason's. It's not mine."

"You don't have the guts to even hold a gun," the one called Jason retorted in disgust, taunting his partner. "You'd be nowhere without me."

"And now you'll be in jail because of him," Sam chimed in sarcastically.

Quickly stuffing Jason's weapon into his belt, he handcuffed the man and turned toward Riley. He was about to ask her where her handcuffs were when he saw her pallor.

Pointing his gun at both the men, he glanced at her again, concerned. "Are you all right?"

"Just fine," she answered before she sank to her knees and everything went black.

Her eyelids felt as if they were being weighed down by anvils as she struggled to lift them and open her eyes.

It took her several tries before she succeeded. As she fought, she heard voices, felt the presence of bodies moving around her, surrounding her.

What was going on?

Oh, right, the invasion.

Two men in black, they'd broken into her house. One of them had grabbed her and hit her from behind.

Sam.

Sam!

That was when Riley finally opened her eyes. The first face she saw was Sam's.

"You're all right." She thought she shouted the words, but all she heard was a raspy whisper.

It was her own.

"Don't talk," Sam cautioned. He had his hands on her shoulders, restraining her as she tried to get up. "We're going to take you to the hospital."

There was a gurney beside the sofa. When had she laid down on the sofa? A gurney meant paramedics and an ambulance. Where had that come from? More importantly, why was it here? Her mother would have heart failure if she heard that an ambulance had been summoned for her.

"No, no hospital. I'm fine," she insisted. "Really."

The words carried no weight for Sam. "That's what you said before you passed out."

"I didn't pass out," she protested with as much indignation as she could muster under the circumstances.

"Okay," Sam allowed tersely. "You took a short nap. Either way, you sank to the floor and there's a nasty bump on the back of your head along with a nastier gash. You're bleeding. I want that gash looked at," he told her sternly.

"So look at it." She tried to raise her head to allow him to do just that, but the room began to spin. She fell back against the sofa again.

He saw the split second of weakness. "Damn it, woman, you're going to the hospital and that's that. I've had enough of a scare tonight. Do I make myself clear?" he demanded.

Riley stared at him as she tried to focus on what was going on. "The robbers?"

He assumed she was asking about the fact that the two were no longer in the room. "On their way to the precinct."

A lot of police personnel crowded into the room and most likely, beyond. Crime scene investigators? When had they gotten here? "How long was I out?"

"Too long," was all that Sam would tell her.

In reality, he'd spent a harrowing, endless fifteen minutes staring at her unconscious face, terrified and wondering if she would come to or wind up in a coma.

"You're not supposed to be here," she realized. When had he come back? And why? "You went home."

Sam shrugged, as if his appearance on the scene was of no great consequence. "I hung around for another forty-five minutes or so, thinking they might show up late. I was on my way out of your development when I passed a car with two guys sitting in the front. They looked like they had on black pullovers. It's too hot for black pullovers," he pointed out. "So I doubled back— just in case my hunch was right. And it was."

Riley began to nod, then stopped. The waves of pain crowding into her head made the motion impossible to complete.

"Good thing you did. I was already in bed, asleep. They caught me off guard."

Sam glanced toward the pile of books scattered on the floor near the door. "I'm guessing not entirely." He laughed, nodding toward the books. "First-class security alarm you have there."

"But it did the trick," she pointed out. "When they hit the books, the sound of them falling woke me up."

He should have stuck around, Sam admonished himself silently. If he had, they would have never gotten to her, never roughed her up. "Good thing."

She took a deep breath, letting it go again. It was over. They'd gotten the home invaders and she was incredibly relieved.

"You'd better go home to Lisa. I can handle the paperwork," she added in case that was on his mind.

Sam looked at her as if she was crazy. "You're not handling anything. What you're doing is going to the ER to get a once-over."

Riley huffed impatiently. "Wyatt, I already said that I'm—"

"Don't care what you said. I'm primary on this," he reminded her, "and what I say goes. Besides, I called your mother to tell her that we caught the robbers—"

Riley looked at him, horrified. "You didn't tell her I was hurt, did you?"

Wyatt made no attempt to hem and haw. "Your mother asked for details and I had to tell her. She's sending the chief to the hospital to see you so you'd better make an appearance there."

Riley closed her eyes, sighing. "I hate you," she said with no feeling.

"Yeah, I hate you, too," he told her with a grin. "Now get on the damn gurney before these paramedics grow old."

With another plaintive sigh—and help from Sam—Riley grudgingly got off the sofa and onto the gurney.

"I told you I was all right." A note of triumph registered in her voice as she turned toward Sam after receiving her discharge papers at the hospital some four hours later.

The woman was incorrigible. "They had to stitch up the gash in back of your head. Fifteen stitches is not 'all right,'" Sam pointed out, helping her off the hospital bed. He pulled back the curtain for her.

Her shrug was dismissive. "I had worse when Frank tackled me for taunting him when I was ten," she informed him.

Tonight was an education. If she'd ever doubted it,

she now had undeniable proof that word spread fast in the Cavanaugh network. She and Wyatt had barely gotten there when the first wave appeared. For a while, the hospital turned into a hotbed of activity as her siblings, stepbrothers, mother and stepfather came to the hospital to see how she was doing. It wasn't long before the rest of them turned up, as well. Only Zack's wife didn't come, but she had been pressed into service to remain with a sleeping Lisa so that Lila could come and see for herself that her youngest daughter was really all right the way she claimed.

"A hospital is a hell of a place to hold a family reunion," Riley had quipped at the height of the Cavanaugh influx. She felt absolutely awful about being the cause of concern for her mother and all the others who had abandoned their beds to come to the hospital in the middle of the night.

Satisfied that only "Riley's hard head," as Frank put it, was involved and that she would be all right, it had still taken a while for everyone to finally leave the premises.

"So how's your head?" Sam asked as he took her arm.

Riley hated to admit that she felt wobbly at first. But with each step, she became a little more sure-footed, a little stronger.

"Fine. Really," she underscored, knowing the last time she'd said that, it hadn't been true. But the bleeding had stopped and the wound sewn up, so by tomorrow, it would be business as usual. Except for maybe a headache.

Instead of going outside, Sam sat her down in the outer waiting area. For the time being, it was empty, but that was subject to change. "Clear enough to understand things?"

Why were they sitting here? She wanted to go home and put all this behind her. But she wasn't up to struggling with him, so she stayed where she was and humored him. "As long as you don't lapse into a foreign language, yes."

"Now that the cases are solved, I'm thinking of taking a couple of weeks off to spend some quality time with Lisa."

Why did he feel he had to sit her down to tell her this? "Good idea," she agreed. "I highly approve." But as she began to get up, he surprised her by gently pushing her back down.

"I'm not finished yet," he told her. "What do you think of taking some time off yourself—to spend with us?" Sam added when she made no response at first.

It took her only a second to roll the suggestion over in her head. Riley smiled. "I think that I'd like that."

Still, he made no attempt to get up.

"You know," Sam continued, "I'm really glad this is finally over—in large part thanks to you—and we can go back to the way things were."

He was buttering her up and it was working, she thought, suppressing a smile. "And what things are those?"

"Having you in my bed." Sam took a breath before continuing, taking her hands into his. "I'd never thought I'd hear myself saying this—hell, I never thought I'd catch myself feeling this way—but I've missed you, Riley. Missed being with you."

She felt herself melting. Still she wasn't sure where he was going with this. She only knew where she wished he'd go. "We were together every day."

"Not the way I wanted to be." Again, he paused and took a deep breath, as if that helped him get the rest of it out. He'd never been nervous around a woman before and it wasn't a feeling he welcomed. But this woman mattered more than any other ever had. "I love you, Riley."

She blinked. "Maybe my head isn't as fine as I thought," she confessed, her heart suddenly tap dancing in her chest. "I could have sworn I just heard you say you loved me."

"You did. I do." He watched the way surprise bloomed in her eyes. That made two of them. He never thought he would ever say those words to a woman. Love was something that happened to other men, not him. "I've suspected it for a while but wouldn't let myself think about it until tonight. Tonight, when I came in and that bastard had his gun on you, I thought I'd lost you. It was like having my gut ripped out with a jagged piece of glass."

Now there was an image to win over a woman's heart. "Very poetic," she said wryly.

"You want poetic?" he asked, then nodded. "I can try that. Might not be for a while, but I can try." His eyes held hers. "If you marry me."

She felt as if someone had just jumped on her stomach, making all the air come rushing out. "Did you just ask me to—"

"I did." He sat there, waiting for her answer.

He was serious, she thought. Actually serious. A myriad of fireflies suddenly materialized inside of her, filling her with light. She smiled at him. "You do drive a hard bargain, Wyatt, but I guess it'll be worth the trade."

"So is that a yes?"

An impish smile curved the corners of her mouth. "You need it spelled out?"

"Yes. Definitely. In big block letters."

She'd hire a skywriter if necessary. "All right. Yes, I'll marry you."

"Is that because you love me?"

Now there was a dumb question, she thought. "No, it's because I like doing penance. Yes, it's because I love you, idiot."

He finally rose, bringing her up with him. "Try it again without the idiot part."

Riley laughed as she entwined her arms around his neck. Her head didn't hurt anymore. Nothing hurt when there was this euphoria taking hold.

"Maybe later." She raised her lips to his. "Got something more important to do right now."

They both did.

* * * * *

Mills & Boon® Intrigue
brings you a sneak preview of …

Cassie Miles's Bodyguard Under the Mistletoe

Young widow Fiona only had one thing on her
Christmas list: keeping her daughter safe. So when a
body was discovered on her property, Fiona jumped
at bodyguard Jesse's offer to stay for the holidays.
He had a stoic face, but honest, caring eyes. And no
matter how she ached to feel his toned and chiseled
arms around her, she needed the protection that
only a man like Jesse could provide.

Don't miss this thrilling new story available
next month from Mills & Boon® Intrigue.

He wasn't dead yet.

The darkness behind his eyelids thinned. Sensation prickled the hairs on his arm. Inside his head, he heard the beat of his heart—as loud and steady as the Ghost Dance drum. That sacred rhythm called him back to life.

His ears picked up other sounds. The *beep-beep-beep* of a monitor. The shuffle of quiet footsteps. The creaking of a chair. A cough. Someone else was in the room with him.

The drumming accelerated.

His eyelids opened—just a slit. Sunlight through the window blinds reflected off the white sheet that covered his prone body. Hospital equipment surrounded the bed. Oxygen. An IV drip on a metal pole. A heart monitor that beeped. Faster. Faster. Faster.

"Jesse?" A deep voice called to him. "Jesse, are you awake?"

Jesse Longbridge tried to move, tried to respond. Pain radiated from his left shoulder. He remembered being shot, falling from his saddle to the cold earth and lying there, helpless. He remembered a gush of blood. He remembered…

"Come on, Jesse. Open your eyes."

He recognized the voice of Bill Wentworth. A friend. A coworker. *Good old Wentworth.* He'd been a paramedic in Iraq, but that wasn't the main reason Jesse had hired him. This lean, mean former marine—like Jesse himself—always got the job done.

They had a mission, he and Wentworth. No time to waste. They needed to get into the field, needed to protect...

Jesse bolted upright on the bed and gripped Wentworth's arm. "Is she safe?"

"You're awake." Wentworth grinned without showing his teeth. "It's about time."

One of the monitor wires detached, and the beeping became a high-pitched whine. "Is Nicole safe?"

"She's all right. Arrests have been made."

Wentworth was one of Jesse's best employees—a credit to Longbridge Security, an outstanding bodyguard. But he wasn't much of a liar.

The pain in his shoulder spiked again, threatening to drag Jesse back into peaceful unconsciousness. He licked his lips. His mouth was parched. He needed water. More than that, he needed the truth. He knew that Nicole had been kidnapped. He'd seen it happen. He'd been shot trying to protect her.

He tightened his grip on Wentworth's arm. "Has Nicole Carlisle been safely returned to her husband?"

"No."

Dylan Carlisle had hired Longbridge Security to protect his family and to keep his cattle ranch safe. If his wife was missing, they'd failed. Jesse had failed.

He released Wentworth. Using his right hand, he detached the nasal cannula that had been feeding oxygen to his lungs. Rubbing the bridge of his nose, he felt the bump where it had been broken a long time ago in a school-yard fight. He hadn't given up then. Wouldn't give up now. "I'm out of here."

Two nurses rushed into the room. While one of them turned off the screeching monitor, the other shoved Wentworth aside and stood by the bed. "You're wide-awake. That's wonderful."

"Ready to leave," Jesse said.

"Oh, I don't think so. You've been pretty much unconscious for three days and—"

"What's the date?"

"It's Tuesday morning. December ninth," she said.

Nicole had been kidnapped on the prior Friday, near dusk. "Was I in a coma?"

"After surgery, your brain activity stabilized. You've been consistently responsive to external stimuli."

"I'll say," Wentworth muttered. "When a lab tech tried to draw blood, you woke up long enough to grab him by the throat and shove him down on his butt."

"I didn't hurt him, did I?"

"He's fine," the nurse said, "but you're not his favorite patient."

He didn't belong in a hospital. Three days was long enough for recuperation. "I want my clothes."

The nurse scowled. "I know you're in pain."

Nothing he couldn't handle. "Are you going to take these needles out of my arms or should I pull them myself?"

She glanced toward Wentworth. "Is he always this difficult?"

"Always."

FIONA GRANT PLACED a polished, rectangular oak box on her kitchen table and lifted the lid. Inside, nestled in red velvet, was a pearl-handled, antique Colt .45 revolver.

In her husband's will, he'd left this heirloom to Jesse Longbridge, and Fiona didn't begrudge his legacy. She'd tried to arrange a meeting with Jesse to present this gift, but their schedules had gotten in the way. After her husband's death, she hadn't been efficient in handling the myriad details, and she hoped Jesse would understand. She was eternally grateful to the bodyguard who had saved her husband's life. Because of Jesse's quick actions, she'd gained a few more precious years with her darling Wyatt before he died from a heart attack at age forty-eight.

People always said she was too young to be a widow. Not even thirty when Wyatt died. Now thirty-two. Too young? As if there was an acceptable age for widowhood? As if her daughter—now four years old—would have been better off losing her dad when she was ten? Or fifteen? Or twenty?

Age made no difference. Fiona hadn't been bothered by the age disparity between Wyatt and herself when they married. All she knew was that she had loved her husband with all her heart. And so she was thankful to Jesse Longbridge. She fully intended to hand over the gun to him when he got out of the hospital. In the meantime, she didn't think he'd mind if she used it.

Her fingertips tentatively touched the cold metal barrel and recoiled. She didn't like guns, but owning one was prudent—almost mandatory for ranchers in western Colorado. Not that Fiona considered herself a rancher. Her hundred-acre property was tiny compared to the neighboring Carlisle empire that had over two thousand head of Black Angus. She had no livestock, even though her daughter, Abby, kept telling her that she really, really, really wanted a pony.

Fiona frowned at the gun. *Who am I kidding? I'm not someone who can handle a Colt .45.* She turned, paced and paused. Stared through the window above the sink. The view of distant snow-covered peaks, pine forests and the faded yellow grasses of winter pastures failed to calm her jangled nerves.

For the past three days, a terrible kidnapping drama had been playing out at the Carlisle Ranch. Their usually pastoral valley had been invaded by posses, FBI agents, search helicopters and bloodhounds that sniffed their way right up to her front doorstep.

Last night, people were taken into custody. The danger should have been over. But just after two o'clock last night, Fiona had heard voices outside her house. She hadn't been able to tell how close they were and hadn't seen the men. But they were loud and angry, then suddenly silent.

The quiet that followed their argument had frightened her more than the shouts. What if they came to her door? Could she stop them if they tried to break in? The sheriff was twenty miles away. If she'd called the Carlisle Ranch, someone would come running. But would they arrive in time?

The truth had dawned with awful clarity. She and Abby had no one to protect them. Their safety was her responsibility.

Hence, the gun.

Returning to the kitchen table, she stared at it. She never expected to be alone, never expected to be living in this rustic log house on a full-time basis. This was a vacation home—a place where she and Abby and Wyatt spent time in the summer so her husband could unwind from his high-stress job as Denver's district attorney.

Water under the bridge. She was here now. This was her home, and she needed to be able to defend it.

INTRIGUE...

& INTRIGUE...

2-IN-1 ANTHOLOGY

BODYGUARD UNDER THE MISTLETOE
by Cassie Miles

When Jesse became worried for Fiona's safety following a dramatic kidnapping, he moved in with her. Yet as he searches for the culprits, he starts to fall in love...

CAVANAUGH JUDGEMENT
by Marie Ferrarella

Judge Blake doesn't need a bodyguard after being threatened, especially not a young, attractive woman! But he can't deny Greer's bravery or the chemistry between them.

...

SINGLE TITLE

BIG SKY DYNASTY
by BJ Daniels

Dalton thought his past was dead and forgotten. But it's back and threatening Georgia, the woman he's falling in love with. Can he save her from his past mistakes?

On sale from 5th November 2010
Don't miss out!

2 FREE BOOKS
AND A SURPRISE GIFT

We would like to take this opportunity to thank you for reading this Mills & Boon® book by offering you the chance to take TWO more specially selected books from the Intrigue series absolutely FREE! We're also making this offer to introduce you to the benefits of the Mills & Boon® Book Club™—

- **FREE home delivery**
- **FREE gifts and competitions**
- **FREE monthly Newsletter**
- **Exclusive Mills & Boon Book Club offers**
- **Books available before they're in the shops**

Accepting these FREE books and gift places you under no obligation to buy, you may cancel at any time, even after receiving your free books. Simply complete your details below and return the entire page to the address below. You don't even need a stamp!

YES Please send me 2 free Intrigue books and a surprise gift. I understand that unless you hear from me, I will receive 5 superb new stories every month, including two 2-in-1 books priced at £5.30 each and a single book priced at £3.30, postage and packing free. I am under no obligation to purchase any books and may cancel my subscription at any time. The free books and gift will be mine to keep in any case.

Ms/Mrs/Miss/Mr _____ Initials _____

Surname _____

Address _____

_____

_____ Postcode _____

E-mail _____

Send this whole page to: Mills & Boon Book Club, Free Book Offer, FREEPOST NAT 10298, Richmond, TW9 1BR